Printed in the United States of America.

First printing, 2016

ISBN 978-0-9973240-0-6

Tsuga's Legacy Publishing Company
PO Box 488
Cuero, TX 77954

I0523282

Acknowledgements

I would like to take a moment to thank all of those who have been such a tremendous help with this book. First, the ladies that helped start this all, either with help creating this world or by the contribution of ideas or the basis of characters: Aubrey Newson and Lee Fuchs. Second, all of those who have read, edited, and listened to me prattle on about this project for the past decade: Haylie, Rosalie, Shane, and Jake. Thirdly, my sweetheart Travis, who has been unbelievably supportive and has even provided the artwork and illustrations for this work. Fourth, to all of those who helped with the final editing stages and offered advice and guidance through this whole process of publishing. Fifth, the wonderfully supportive friends, family, and extended family whose show of faith in the form of financial support helped to finally get this project in the hands of the public. And lastly, to my parents and teachers, without whose support and input none of this would have been possible. Thank you all, and I hope you enjoy!

Tsuga

Volume One of *The Loss of Magic*

Maghren Islis
Teeth of the Wilm
Fardu
Devali
Gilead
Dubai Plains
Sennor
Desert
N

Part One: Born in Blood

As a babe just torn from its mother's womb –
As a girl newly open to a suitor's charms –
As a wife spending the first night in her husband's arms –
As a new mother, sweating in the birthing room –
So we are, all of us, born in blood.

"That's good, Tsu; head up, heels down. Don't let her get away with that! There you are; keep her going nice and easy, now."

The voice of the man speaking was friendly and warm as his brown eyes followed the little girl jouncing about on her pony. It was a perfect day to be outdoors: the sun was shining, and a light breeze tickled the branches of the trees into a gentle laughter. The grass in the fields had faded to a golden brown this time of year, but the air did not yet hold the bite of winter's chill.

Eyes dancing, the little girl – no older than four, certainly – reined her pony in a wide circle, keeping the wheat-colored mare to a brisk trot. The pony tried to stop and snatch a mouthful of the dying grass every few steps, but each time the lanky child would haul on the reins and give the animal a good kick to keep her moving.

When several rounds had been completed with the pony doing no more than looking at the grass with longing, Tsuga drew the little mare to a walk, and then a stop. She sat there, hands resting in the butter-colored mare's mane, and beamed over at the man. He nodded.

"That's enough for today. Let's get Butterball back in the stables. Then we can see about –"

"Lunch!" The little girl broke in with her piping voice as she swung herself out of the saddle, keeping a grip on the pony's reins as she dismounted. The man laughed and tucked his daughter – for she could be no other, sharing his slender build, brown eyes and hair as she did – under his arm.

"Yes, lunch."

The two began walking, making their way to the barn just visible through the tree line. It made a pretty picture of peace, with the animals outside and the people bustling about on their daily business. It was a scene Tsuga would hold dear to her heart in the years to come.

"Happy birthday, Tsuga."

The small girl was sitting at a table in the mess hall with her mouse-brown hair pulled back from her face with a leather thong. At the familiar voice, she looked up and scowled.

"Hello, Elbon." Her voice held the same disgusted sneer as his. It irked the young noble boy no end that Tsuga's father was so honored by his own, the Lord over this small holding. No doubt it rankled even more that his father always had a smile or kind word for the daughter of his healer, while scarcely giving his own son the time of day.

"Didja hear the news?" His eyes, a brown dark as pitch and the only remarkable thing about him, held a malicious gleam that chilled Tsuga to her five-year-old core.

"What news?" It was a small victory that her voice held steady, though the sense of dread seemed to be stretching its fingers around her throat and squeezing.

Elbon's eyes darted to the door and he sneered again. "You'll see." He laughed – not a cheerful sound – and scurried off. Tsuga started to pursue him, but a hand closed on her shoulder before she could stand. She turned, expecting to see her Da, but it was Elbon's father whose hand rested so heavily there.

As the Lord's favored healer, her father often traveled with the war band. They had ridden to stop a border raid a few days prior. Lord Gregory had led them, and so it stood to reason that if he was back, then surely her father must be, too. She looked around eagerly, seeking the tell-tale green clothing that marked a man of his status.

"Tsuga, I have some bad news."

Her face fell, and as he tried to explain the ways of war to her, she felt the world narrowing, spinning, and then expanding wildly as the news hit home. She didn't even hear the rest of what the man was telling her, but she knew without a doubt that Elbon had known even before she did. Her father, the most important figure in her young life, was gone forever.

Happy birthday, indeed.

She struck again, and then a third time, and a fourth, pushing her advantage with fierce, determined strokes – left shoulder, right hip, torso, head. Okay, so one couldn't gain an advantage over a wooden practice dummy, but she could pretend, couldn't she?

This was the only solace she had any more. Since her father's death nearly eight years ago, she had changed considerably. No longer did smiles come so easily to her face, nor did she laugh as freely as she once had. His absence haunted her constantly, and as she had become more sullen and withdrawn, her friends had begun to drift away one by one.

She didn't care. Probably, it was fright as much as anything else. Her training in weaponry had begun at age six, a year after her father's death, and she had delved into it relentlessly. It kept her mind off of her sudden loss. Although Elbon's father had taken her in as one of his own and doted on her as he would a favorite daughter, there was simply no replacing her Da. When she worked herself to exhaustion, reality seemed a little less terrifying.

Sweat beaded on her forehead and dripped down her back, making slightly cleaner tracks on her mud- and grime-smeared face as she pummeled her "opponent." Her wooden sword did very little real damage, but it felt good to hit something. Finally, fatigue got the better of her and her foot slipped. She blinked in surprise when she suddenly found herself sprawled on the ground. She lay there a moment as she gasped in air. Her mind drifted for a bit, and she didn't move as she watched the clouds' slow progress across the sky.

"Taking a break, I see."

Tsuga started guiltily and quickly scrambled to find her sword and stand to face the wry smile of the grizzled veteran. The Weaponsmaster was not a cruel man, and in fact the old soldier was the closest thing Tsuga had to a friend. She started to stammer out an apology as she wiped the sweat from her brow, but he waved her off. He came closer and took the sword from her loose grasp and replaced it with a quarterstaff. Tsuga hefted it, only then remembering their appointment. She'd been training in every weapon she could get her hands on, but the staff was her newest and also, therefore, her weakest.

Her friend did not wait for her to brace herself, but advanced quickly, striking for her head without a sound aside from the scuffling of his foot on the ground. Tsuga managed to block him – barely – and thus the lesson began.

For more than a month now Tsuga had had the feeling that something was coming, a feeling of dread which made the days pass in a blur of anxiety. She feared something truly horrible waited for her just around the bend; it was, after all, time for her birthday once again (her thirteenth), and as the day also marked the anniversary of her Da's death, it was seldom cause for celebration. She felt his loss most keenly on this day, and what should have been a cheerful event served only to highlight just how alone she truly was.

A feast was held that evening in her honor, and Tsuga managed to sit and smile through it despite having been stuffed into a dress – yellow, so that it made her face look quite green – and had her hair curled and fluffed. She felt rather like one of those useless, fluffy dogs that the noble ladies favored: with no purpose save to look pretty (in her opinion, most of these pets looked positively ridiculous).

At last, as the festivities began to devolve into drinking and revelry, she was able to slip out and make her way through the gardens to enjoy the quiet, cooler air outside and try to block out the noise of the rowdy young lordlings still in the hall. The night had been spent forcing smiles and courteously conversing with the eligible men to whom she was presented.

She was of a marriageable age now, and her first bleeding had already come and gone. It was time for a husband to be found for her, though she doubted that anyone would be seeking her for a bride when she had no parents to give a dowry.

It was probably for the best; the thought of having to be someone's wife and have nothing to do in life save look pretty and serve as a brood mare positively sickened her.

She paused beside a bush that, in summer, had been covered with beautiful, fragrant roses. Now, with autumn well underway, the petals were falling from the last stubborn bloom and the gardeners had begun to prune back in preparation for the new growth that the far-off spring would bring. There was a soft rustle of cloth behind her, and she spun quickly as she cursed herself for letting her guard down. It was difficult to make out more than the black outline of the intruder, but as he stepped closer, she recognized the way he moved – one advantage of sparring most every person who could hold a weapon throughout the entire holding.

"Elbon." Her voice was cold; she felt her stomach roil in disgust, but she held her ground. He sneered, his teeth a brief flash of white in the dark, and moved forward. Instinctively, Tsuga stepped back, but he reached out to grasp her wrist in a painful grip.

Why am I allowing this? It would be so easy for her to free herself, but she couldn't seem to move. She struggled fiercely with the strange lethargy that gripped her mind – tried to scream at the top of her lungs, to pull away – but her body leaned against his and her voice remained still.

"You think you're something, don't you?"

He reeked of ale; she could smell it on his person, and when he spoke the stench of it on his breath made her retch. Or at least, it should have; even as her stomach clenched, she felt her lips twist into a smile, seemingly of their own accord.

"Soooo special." His words were slurred, and he blinked a little too carefully in the dim light of the stars overhead. "Everybody loves little Tsuga. 'Such a blessing,' they say. 'A real prodigy.' The best they've ever seen with a weapon. But you can't fight back now, can you? Can you?"

Her teeth rattled when he shook her for emphasis, but she could still feel the inane smile stretching the muscles of her face. Elbon pressed closer, and though her mind struggled against the invisible grip on her voice and limbs – on any freedom she could hope for – her body didn't even resist as he kissed her sloppily. For the sake of her sanity, her terrified mind retreated to hide in a small corner and try to ignore the proceedings. Somewhere in that small, frightened self, she realized that she was being controlled by magic, but it scarcely mattered: there was nothing she could do about it.

Tsuga lay on the ground, unmoving. He'd kept his hold on her mind long enough to make her put her clothes back on, shredded though they were. It was an odd show of decency that seemed out of place after what he'd done to her. Then he had left, stumbling back into the night. Now she lay still, feeling broken, battered, and worthless. And filthy. She wanted desperately to wash, but she hadn't the will to move.

The people in the hall were still merrymaking, none of them even thinking to wonder where she'd gone. She could hear their laughter, painfully close by. Still too far away for anyone to have helped her. Not a one of them cared what might have happened to her after she had left their company – her Da had been the only one to ever care enough to look after her. Well, Lord Gregory did seem to like her, but she wondered now if his kindness wasn't merely out of pity for her situation rather than any true fondness.

She kept her sword and its matching dagger on her person at all times – even when they were juxtaposed with a trumped up costume, as they were now – as well as a handful of other small weapons. They had been gifts for her birthday over the years, with the exception of her Da's sword and knife, which she'd inherited as his only worldly wealth after his death. They hadn't helped her tonight, though – not against a dark magic that controlled her mind and body.

Now, she reached down to the sword belt around her waist and drew the shorter weapon kept there. She held it above her head, watching the way it caught the moon's light and seemed to spark with a life of its own. Finally, she managed to push herself to a sitting position. She ran her fingers along the blade's edge, staring absently at the line of blood it drew.

Maybe it would be better to just end it. No one's going to notice. Who cares about the bastard orphan of a dead healer?

The dagger was razor sharp (she always kept it that way), so it was only a matter of propping it up, the hilt clutched between her bloodied thighs and the point reaching for the stars. She placed her arms on either side of the blade, and then paused to take a deep, steadying breath. She closed her eyes, and then thrust downward with all her might as she pressed her forearms against the edge to reap the full effect.

When Tsuga regained consciousness, she experienced a moment of disorientation. Her first thought was that she was dead, but the lead weight pressing her down seemed to indicate otherwise.

She struggled to open her eyes, but even when she managed to, she still could not see. Wherever she was, it was pitch black. She tried to sit up, but when she put weight on her hands she felt a flash of white-hot pain and collapsed with a cry of agony against

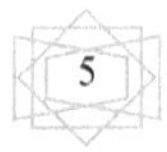

the pillows. As the pain cleared her thoughts, she was able to recognize the feel of her own bed, but she still wasn't quite clear on what had happened. Her memory of the night (how long had she been unconscious? An hour? A week?) seemed hazed, as though she were trying to gaze out through a filthy window into the night.

With an effort, she lifted her arms and pulled them closer to her face. They felt oddly bulky, and as she dropped them back to her side, she realized that they were heavily bandaged from wrist to elbow.

She didn't feel sleepy, so she fought against the covers briefly before she managed to kick them off. There was nowhere to go, however – even if she had any energy left to stand (which she didn't), she wouldn't have been able to see where she was going. Exasperated, she resigned herself to her relative imprisonment and settled back against her pillow, staring up into the darkness.

"I don't know why. I found her in the gardens with her forearms slashed almost to the bone. She was bleeding dry. I did what I could to save her, but my talents are limited. She may not pull through."

Tsuga seemed to be floating in space. She wasn't sure how much time had passed since they had poured the foul-tasting brew down her throat, but now her mind seemed to be expanding infinitely, awareness returning as sensation flooded her. Pain shot up her arms every time she tried to move her hands; it warred with a desperate hunger that spoke of the days she'd gone without solid food. When at last she managed to open her eyes, she closed them again immediately as the intensity of the light renewed her headache. Determined to get a handle on her situation and more prepared this time, she opened them once more and squinted against the brightness.

She was still in her room, but she could hear people moving around. It was hard to make out any real shapes as her eyes watered in reaction to the light. The man's voice she'd heard before went on, describing what he'd done and her chances of survival. As he numbered the stitches he'd put in each wrist, Tsuga felt herself shudder; she must have managed to hurt herself pretty badly, though not enough to kill herself as she had planned. An attempt at speech turned into a moan as her left hand spasmed, and this gained the attention of the other man in the room. His face swam into view, and Tsuga had the time to recognize Lord Gregory, Elbon's father, before his face disappeared.

"She's awake, Healer." This brought forth an exclamation of surprise from the as-yet unseen healer, and he bustled over. He seemed vaguely familiar: a face she had seen in passing, but no one she had spoken to before.

"How do you feel?" She managed a grunt. Her tongue felt swollen to twice its proper size. "Thirsty?" She grunted again and tried to sit up. This time, she didn't even get her arms under herself before she was pushed back firmly. When a cup was pressed to her lips she took a sip, but the medicinal taste made her cough.

"Are you trying to kill me?" she croaked after the spasm had passed. The healer's face reappeared, this time marred by a scowl.

"I could ask you much the same question, child. Such an injury as yours could hardly be called accidental. What were you thinking?"

The Lord's voice intruded a bit more gently, though it was obvious he, too, was upset. "Did something happen? What's wrong, Tsu?"

She looked at them in confusion. What *had* happened? She recalled thinking that no one cared about her, that she was a burden on the world. She even remembered drawing her blade and making the cut that should have been fatal. The rest of the night, including the minutes before the suicide attempt, was a blur.

"I . . . don't know." The healer's frown deepened, but before he could voice another accusation, she managed to speak again. "Could I have some food?"

A few weeks had passed, and though Tsuga still felt weak, she was growing restless. She was allowed to walk now, but everyone watched her closely, as they might a woman at the edge of a cliff who was convinced she could fly. They treated her as though with kid gloves, and a quick search through her room had revealed that they had taken her every weapon. They no longer trusted her.

Well, no matter. She had been thinking since she had regained enough energy to follow a train of thought, dwelling on the revelation that had gotten her into this predicament to begin with: she was a burden. An orphan. An outcast. Everyone thought they had to take care of her, that she was not able to contribute anything worthwhile. A few days ago, she had reached a decision. It was time to leave.

Once she was able to walk again, she had begun working to regain her strength. And it was time. She was too weak to carry much, so her pack was light, mostly consisting of tools she'd need to catch food. The only things left to do were those she dreaded most. She *had* to have weapons, after all, and a horse for at least the first leg of her journey. It pained her to have to steal these things from the man who had shown her so much kindness, but she was out of options.

Darkness was just beginning to fall. Under the cover of the lengthening shadows she managed to slip into the stables unseen. It took every bit of strength she had just to saddle one of the horses for travel. Somehow, she'd chosen the tallest horse the Lord had to his name, and the mundane task she'd done thousands of times so drained her that she had to sit on a bale of hay, panting, for several tense minutes. Finally, still drenched with sweat and tired beyond measure, Tsuga managed to stand, double-check the horse's tack, and then unclip the beast from the ties and lead it outside.

Luckily the armory was not a far walk from the stables; as often as she was forced to pause to catch her breath, any further distance would have been impossible to breech. She took yet another brief rest while she leaned against the wall near the entrance to the indoor practice arena, then pushed away from the support, hobbled the horse, and walked inside.

The armory was usually guarded at night, but Tsuga hadn't any spare energy to ponder why she had not yet been seen. The inside of the building was so dark that she may as well have blindfolded herself, but she had spent so many hours within these walls that she could have navigated the large open room confidently in her sleep.

It seemed to take years for her to reach the door to the Weaponsmaster's office; each step took such an effort on her part that she was forced to pause every two or three strides to rest, lest she collapse to the ground in a wave of dizziness. At last the door swung inward and Tsuga stumbled inside. As she remembered, there was a lamp and flint just to the right of the door. Several minutes later, her hands shaking with exhaustion, the wick caught a tiny spark that bloomed slowly into a healthy flame. She trimmed the wick as best she could and then turned, brandishing the lamp as she might a weapon against the darkness.

The room was, as always, tidy and sparsely furnished. Because of this, it was easy to spy the neat, careful row of her beloved weapons leaned against the wall beside the desk. As she fastened them in their proper, familiar places and ran her fingers lovingly along the well-worn leather hilts, she counted them.

Her sword belt settled comfortably around her hips, the long-absent weights of her sword and dagger on opposite sides offering warmth and support. Two smaller knives were slipped into each of her boots, and the arm sheathes for her throwing knives fastened with long-practiced ease, their daggers sliding into place with the soft hiss of leather on iron. The dagger she wore tucked beneath her shirt settled easily into the small of her back, and the smaller one around her neck was a comfortable weight alongside her coin purse with its meager supply of money.

She also selected a small hunting bow and quiver of arrows, which she knew she would need. Finally, she felt whole – naked and defenseless no longer. Despite its added weight, the cool metal seemed to have boosted her energy level considerably, because after she blew out the lamp and returned it to its proper place, she made it back to her horse with fewer halts than on her trip inside.

Mounting the animal was an ordeal that nearly bested her. The beast was huge, taller and broader than anything she had ever known the Lord to own for himself. She vaguely remembered something about a "demon horse" recently acquired that four grown men had difficulty controlling. Surely this was not the same beast, for this mount stood patiently; each time Tsuga fell, the mare only turned her head to watch her antics with a placid stare.

Tsuga wondered if it was pity or exasperation she saw in the animal's gaze. She managed at last to clamber atop the beast, at which point she sat swaying for several minutes while the monster pitched and rolled beneath her. When things settled down, she was ashamed to realize *she* had been the one moving, rather than her mount.

Thankfully she was so at home in a saddle that she could ride half dead, and so it was with relative ease that she turned the horse in the proper direction and started it walking towards the gates. She did not look back, for in the dark, even if she had wanted to mourn the end of this chapter of her life, she would have been able to see nothing more than hulking shapes in the night.

She came to gradually, suffering a split second of disorientation at the hard, lumpy surface beneath her and the fuzzy warmth of a very large animal next to her. She opened her eyes and closed them again quickly against the harsh light of what must have been a midday sun. As her sluggish mind threw off the ties of sleep, memory began to return. When she opened her eyes a second time, she merely squinted against the glare and was able to sit up. The horse – a young, dark bay mare, she now saw – watched calmly from where she lay as Tsuga struggled to her feet.

When they had stopped before dawn, Tsuga had literally fallen asleep where she'd landed. She was somewhat surprised that she had managed to untack the horse before collapsing, but the lessons engrained in her since childhood (at least, those she had not conveniently forgotten to serve her own purposes, such as the lesson not to steal) had held firm.

She found it odd that the horse had chosen to lie next to her and keep her warm against the bitter chill of the fast-approaching winter. It wasn't unheard of, though, so she dismissed it from her mind and stumbled over to where she had left the tack the night before. There were enough rations in the saddle bags to last her a day or two, but after that she would have to fend for herself.

Perhaps this wasn't the best planning, she mused. Winter was coming, and neither game nor employment would be easy to find.

There was a bite in the air that made her shiver as she squatted near the horse and wolfed down a cold portion of the food she'd brought with her. As was to be expected, the bread was rock-hard; the meat had a tenderness along the lines of new leather. The small meal served only to whet her appetite, but she pushed aside the remaining rations in the hopes of avoiding the folly of finding herself with nothing to eat before she was able to take down any game.

Still disoriented, Tsuga stood and looked around in an effort to find her bearings. The walls of the keep, still visible to the east, sent a jolt of fear up her spine. Surely they had discovered her absence by now, and she was not so conceited as to think herself capable of eluding them in her present condition. Her tracks would be easy for even an infant to follow, and no doubt a search party was mere minutes away.

If anyone even cares enough to look for me.

Drawing energy from her fear, Tsuga hefted the saddle and turned to face the horse. The beast snorted in alarm and lurched to her feet. Tsuga sneezed when the horse shook dust from her shaggy coat. She managed to get the enormous animal saddled, even though she had to throw the tack above her head to do so. The horse was taller than her at its withers, and when she registered the quality of the animal her stomach began to churn. She must have stolen one of the lord's best warhorses, for surely a mount this fine could be nothing else. This thought brought her actions to a halt as she simply stood and stared, unwilling to accept what she had done.

The beast stood around seventeen hands in height, and her muscles bunched and rippled under her dark bay coat as she craned her proportionally short neck to watch Tsuga with wide-set brown eyes full of intelligence.

Well if you're going to steal, you might as well take something valuable.

Tsuga jumped. The voice had not been hers, and had seemed to come from everywhere and nowhere at once. She spun around quickly and backed up against the horse as she drew her sword against the unseen spy. The weight of the weapon seemed to have multiplied tenfold since the last time she'd wielded it; her weakened muscles shook from the effort of simply holding it in place. Still, she forced herself to keep it upright and ready to ward off any attack.

The horse snorted and turned its head to observe the young girl's antics with one large brown eye. It whickered – a sound Tsuga could have sworn was a laugh – and nudged her so firmly that she staggered a bit. The voice didn't come again, so after another long minute, Tsuga finished tacking the horse and mounted. Once more, the pair was on their way.

Traveling was *not* a fun experience. Though the night had been cool, the afternoon sun was so hot Tsuga felt as though she rode through a furnace. Even though the horse was doing all the work, she still sweated profusely in her perch atop the saddle. She was thirsty, but scarcely dared to drink for fear of diminishing her sparse water supply before they came across more potable water with which to fill her small skin.

Time passed at an indeterminable pace while she drifted in and out of consciousness. In her brief moments of coherence, she offered up prayers of thanks to the Goddess that she had managed thus far without falling from the saddle. When darkness fell at last, Tsuga knew that it was time to stop, despite the relief of the cooler air. The mare could not see in the dark, and she had been going all day without respite. She didn't seem fatigued in the least, but Tsuga didn't want to push her unnecessarily. Besides, as her stomach did not hesitate to remind her, it was past time to eat.

The girl stopped her mount (or rather, the horse stopped as Tsuga had the thought of calling a halt), and looked around for anything nearby they could use as a shelter. With a jolt, she realized that they had wandered onto the Bloody Plains – the battlefield that marked the ambiguous border between her native Sennor and Devali, the nation with which they were at war. The jolt of terror that shot down Tsuga's spine as this knowledge struck her made her limbs tingle and her heart race.

Her first instinct was to turn around and run her horse back to the safety of her native soil, but she fought the urge and held herself steady. At thirteen, her spirit guardian – the animal who held the other half of her soul and would thus make her feel complete for the first time in her life – had yet to find her. She was too weak to effectively hold her sword, and she looked like a boy – and one scarcely old enough to be away from home, at that.

Who was she kidding? Any Devalians would be too busy laughing at the pathetic image she presented to do anything about a lone Sennorran crossing their border. Besides, maybe she *belonged* in Devali. Most people were united with their guardians while they were still children, but hers had never come. She had spent her entire life in a fortified holding so near the border that it could barely even be considered part of Sennor, and her father had frequently made excursions into their neighboring land. For all she knew, she *was* Devalian.

Exhausted and dizzy from so many conflicting thoughts, Tsuga gave up on seeking shelter and simply slid to the ground. She paused long enough to take a few steadying breaths and brace herself, then removed the saddle and bridle from the horse. As she turned to sling the headstall over the back of the saddle, there was a dizzying moment of disorientation where Tsuga seemed to be looking through the eyes of some other (not human) being. She saw not only herself, but also the stretch of prairie grass on the other side of the horse. The girl swayed and the bridle slipped from her numbed fingers as she collapsed to the ground.

When she regained consciousness, the first things to register were the smell of sweaty horse and the warmth of grass-scented breath across her skin. She had fallen in an awkward position, with one leg twisted beneath her and the bit of the bridle digging painfully into her side. The mare was snuffling around her, and when Tsuga sat up it whickered and nudged her gently. The girl grinned and shoved the blocky head aside, amused at such behavior from a horse so obviously bred to be a killer.

She rose to her feet with an effort and began setting up a make-shift camp. A fire was out of the question with so much dry grass just waiting for a spark of ignition, so once again she ate cold trail rations and curled up to sleep.

The similarities in the two countrysides were shocking, for although the terrain was a bit rockier, the land a tad less forgiving, and the people spoke with slightly foreign accents, the sights, sounds, and smells throughout Devali were all so utterly similar to those she was used to that Tsuga found herself feeling safe as she had not since her Da's death.

Months on the road may have strengthened her muscles, but her resolve was wearing thin. She missed the familiar faces of people who cared about her, the comfort of having a roof over her head and a soft pillow beneath it, and all of the other things she had always taken for granted. Now, as she wove through the throngs of people and led her horse along the busy streets of a Devalian marketplace, she found herself forgetting that she was not, in fact, in Sennor. Perhaps she really *did* belong here.

Then again, certain things in Devali were so different that she worried she would never grow used to them. Since the incident a few days after she'd crossed the border with the rabbit that had shape-shifted into a terrified little boy, she'd been afraid to kill any animal she saw, lest it be another such person. Suddenly, the scary bedtime stories of Devalians who could turn into terrifying beasts that ripped out your entrails with their horrible claws seemed a little less far-fetched.

When Tsuga had begun regaining her endurance and wits, things she had failed to notice before suddenly became painfully obvious. For example, the horse that she had stolen turned out to be scarcely more than a couple of years old – still a filly, and shockingly young to have already been as impeccably trained as she had proven to be. She handled and behaved so well that at times, Tsuga almost believed the horse able to read her mind.

She had also begun tracking the days. Once she was finally able to figure out exactly *when* it was, she realized she had missed her monthly bleeding. That was not so uncommon for her, but to have missed it three months in a row was cause for some alarm. Every time she considered such thoughts, she would pass a brief moment in which she would curse Elbon, experience a wave of dizziness, and then forget what she'd been doing a moment before.

Unable to pay for a room in even the cheapest inn, Tsuga had taken to sleeping outside the walls of town at night. There were a few houses in the area, but they were spaced so far apart that she could make a camp each night without being thought much of. Each day, she made the trip into town and looked for someone willing to hire a young girl (or a boy, as many people mistook her for a lad of about ten). She had taken to keeping her hair shorn just above her shoulders, as she'd noticed the guardsmen here did, and pulling it back from her face. It was the style worn by most of the boys her age she'd seen and brought her one step closer to blending in.

Unfortunately, with her skill set limited to playing soldier, she was left with absolutely no employment prospects, and so had been forced to start filching her meals from nearby farms – just enough to get by, and never enough from one place at a time to be truly missed. As a result, Tsuga was thinner even than usual, and though she could feel the life stirring within her, she certainly did not look pregnant. Even when she tried, she could not quite recall how this condition had come about.

Desperate to find work, Tsuga stopped nearly every prosperous-looking person she passed to beg for a job – any job – just so that she might have a meal to count on each day. Most merely scoffed at her and moved on. The few who did bother to listen or who seemed somewhat sympathetic turned her away when they discovered her limited knowledge.

Devali did not let children fight, and since this was the only thing she had any talent for aside from tending animals (and all of those positions were already filled), Tsuga was unable to lay claim to any marketable skills. At last, as night began to creep over the city, Tsuga turned to start the long trek back to the gates and a sparse meal stolen from one of the farms.

"Who's there?" Tsuga froze, feeling like a child who'd been caught with her finger in the pie, and prayed fervently that she wouldn't be seen.

"Hello?" It was a woman's voice, but this realization didn't slow her heartbeat in the least. She really had no desire to hurt anyone, but she couldn't afford to be caught.

She set down the handful of eggs she carried snug in one of her spare socks gingerly and eased her dagger from its sheath as she pulled her right sleeve down to keep it concealed. Around the corner of the barn came a woman who looked to be getting on in years. She had probably seen half of her allotted life already – if not more – if the gray sprinkled throughout her brown hair was a fair indication.

Wary, Tsuga crouched into a defensive position, left hand poised to grab the eggs, legs quivering with a readiness to run. The woman stopped well out of range and slowly moved to show that she carried no weapons. Still cautious, Tsuga remained where she was.

"Are you my little fox, then?" Tsuga blinked in confusion and shifted slightly, but remained silent. "Why, you're no more than a child!" The girl bristled at hearing this. She was tired of people thinking she was helpless just because she was skinny and female.

"I'm woman enough." The stranger nodded and smiled sympathetically.

"Indeed? Then I suppose I should turn you over to the law to be tried as such."

Tsuga winced. Why did she always have to open her big mouth? When she didn't answer, the stranger's expression softened.

"Do you have somewhere to sleep, child?" Having been put in her place before, Tsuga kept her retorts in check and managed to respond in a civil tone (or at least, what passed for civil coming from her).

"I have a fire and a bedroll a little ways from here." The woman shook her head.

"It's a wonder you've not caught your death of cold. I'll tell you what . . . why don't you go get your things, and you can sleep in the barn tonight. You can share my supper, and we can talk further in the morning." Not sure if she should trust the woman, Tsuga hesitated. In the end, hunger won out over fear, as it is wont to do with skittish animals.

"Alright."

Tsuga hadn't even thought about the horse when she'd made the decision to trust the stranger's offer of kindness. What was she to do with the mare? It was obviously too fine a mount for a runaway child, as the woman had apparently pegged her to be. Yet, at the same time, she couldn't just leave the animal to wander about on her own; she might be stolen by someone else.

If you trust her enough to go to all this trouble, why not trust that she'll understand about this, too?

The girl spun, looking for the source of the voice. Nothing greeted her save the rustle of leaves in the wind and the large brown eyes of the horse.

"I think I'm losing it." She shook her head and continued saddling the filly and cleaning up her campsite. "Now I know I am – I'm talking to myself!" Exasperated, she shook her head again in an effort to clear it and went on with her tasks.

As it turned out, the woman said nothing about the horse, but instead acted as though such a pairing was perfectly normal. Relieved not to have to answer any questions on the topic, Tsuga set up her sparse belongings in the loft of the stable before she followed the woman inside. Though she was still wary of such unexpected kindness, it wasn't long before she had let herself be lulled by the warmth.

The woman liked to talk, and as Tsuga tried to make herself useful over the next few days, she learned that the stranger's husband had been a farmer, and that though they had made little enough coin, they'd had a better life than many. They, at least, had always been able to eat three meals each day. Things were harder now that he was gone, but the woman still managed to keep her land and livestock.

Although Tsuga had been raised on an estate where such luxuries as a roof over your head and food in your belly were taken for granted, she found herself envying the widow after her months alone. The sting of jealousy grew as the woman began to speak of her daughter, bragging about how her only remaining kin attended the mage school at the palace.

The woman spoke so openly and lovingly of her family that Tsuga found herself fiercely missing her own home, and most especially the father she'd barely known and the mother she'd never met. Had her mother ever taken in a stranger she had no reason to help? She had no way of knowing. Before Tsuga realized what was happening, she had dissolved into tears. When the woman dropped her knife and left the vegetables she was cutting to wrap Tsuga in a warm bear hug, the last of her shaky resolve crumbled and she leaned against the woman for support as her body was wracked with sobs.

What she felt must have been the passage of days had in fact seen the span of less than an hour. When at last Tsuga heaved a sigh and pulled back, she wiped the tears from her face and sniffed loudly.

"I'm sorry. It's just . . .."
The woman shushed her and patted her shoulder firmly.

"Hush now. No need to explain. Come on, let's finish making dinner."
Tsuga nodded, and after a few moments she stood and resumed her task of peeling carrots for the stew. The conversation resumed shortly, but this time the woman focused on asking Tsuga questions.

"Where do you hail from, child? With that accent, you're hardly from around here, are you?" Tsuga shook her head.

"No, actually I grew up in –" she stopped just short of saying Sennor. "No, I'm not from around here." She hoped the woman would just let the subject drop, and breathed a sigh of relief when the conversation moved on.

"I assume you have a name, or is that a secret, too?" The woman was smiling in an obvious attempt to lighten Tsuga's mood, so the girl forced a laugh.

"Tsuga." The woman nodded thoughtfully.

"A lovely name. You know, the queen before the war – back when Sennor and Devali were one nation – had an older sister named Tsuga."

"Really?" Tsuga knew the woman was only trying to distract her from her troubles, but her curiosity was piqued despite her reservations.

"Indeed. Tsuga turned down the throne because she knew her sister would make a better queen. But she remained Sennorra's most trusted advisor. You know, if I remember correctly, she was also a Royal Mage. You do still have those in Sennor, don't you?"

"Oh, of course. Though the title is Queen's Mage, now. They live in the Castle with the –" she broke off, realizing her mistake too late. The woman offered a kindly smile.

"Don't fret, Tsuga. Not all Devalians loathe our neighbors. Now, where was I? Oh, yes. Tsuga was the Royal Mage. It's said she even had one of those spirit-things all Sennorrans have these days." Tsuga winced at the reference to something she didn't have, but the woman didn't seem to notice; she was too caught up in the recounting of her tale. "Only a very few people had them back then. It was supposed to be a jihai, one of those water-birds."

Tsuga nodded. "They're supposed to live around bodies of water," she said, "especially the ocean. They're supposedly the most beautiful of all mythical creatures, even more than their phoenix cousins."

The woman smiled again. "That's right. You certainly know your animals." Tsuga blushed and ducked her head, and then raised it again when she had a thought occur to her.

"You know my name, but you've not told me yours."

"Fair enough. My name is Tau. My husband isn't with us anymore, and my only child is in Capitol City, studying her magery."

Tsuga made an appreciative sound; the woman was obviously proud of this, as it was far from the first time the girl had been mentioned.

"So you're all alone here?" She frowned in concern at this, inexplicably worried for Tau's safety.

"Oh, well, it's not so bad. Having a mage for a daughter offers a good deal of protection, you know. And besides, now I've got you."

This blithe statement caused Tsuga to flinch and her hands to pause in their progress on the carrots as her mind froze in fear. This time, Tau noticed the reaction and looked up from her own preparations.

"Tsuga? Is something the matter?"
Somehow, the worry evident in Tau's voice penetrated the fog, and the young girl was able to shake herself into motion again. She tried her best to play off the thoughts racing through her mind as inconsequential so that the issue would be dropped.

"Oh, no. It's just that I didn't expect to be so welcomed in the country we're at war with. Especially when I was never this welcome back home. How many carrots do you need for this?"
Tau still was not working, but instead watched Tsuga carefully chop the carrots, as though she might be able to tell by the girl's methodical work what she was thinking.

"You've had a hard life, haven't you?"

Tsuga shrugged again, eyes still on the carrots even though her hands had stilled.

"I guess. I've been on my own for a while. I mean, I had a place to live and everything, but no family . . . .." She trailed off as a sense of alarm warned her away from . . . what? She'd left because she was a burden on the lord's kindness, hadn't she? So why did her mind refuse to let her dwell on that departure?

Tau was speaking, but Tsuga really hadn't caught any of it, and didn't bother trying to figure out what she had said. Instead, she simply tuned in now, just in time to catch the end of a sentence.

"...Their parents." Tsuga could only nod, as she had no idea how to respond to something she hadn't heard. In any case, talking about herself so much made her uncomfortable.

"So does your daughter ever come to visit, now that she has her studies?"

The woman still looked concerned, but allowed the change of subject without further comment.

"Oh, Ramira comes home on the holidays, but it's still not enough. I'm glad she's going to be a mage – it's about the best we could have hoped for – but it does get lonesome." Tsuga nodded absently. She understood loneliness all too well. Tau continued. "Will you be staying for a while, Tsuga?"

The girl frowned at this. She really hadn't given much thought to what she was going to do, and the proposal caught her off-guard. In an effort to stall for time to think, she gave the first excuse that came to mind. "I don't have any money. I can't pay you, or anything . . .."

Tau was already shaking her head before Tsuga could finish.

"Nonsense. Your company and the help around the house will be payment enough."

"Oh. Well . . .."

What was there to say in the face of such generosity? She would be foolish to refuse, but also foolish to think that such an offer came without another price. For now, though, it was the only offer of a roof and meal that she had, and her stomach certainly didn't seem inclined to let her pass it up so easily.

"Sure. I can stay for a while, I guess."

Tau didn't say anything in response to this; she merely flashed a delighted smile before she turned back to their dinner preparations.

Tsuga soon learned that the price of Tau's generosity was, much as she had expected, not as easily paid as the woman had implied. Tau was the only person in charge of several acres of land, a spread which was home to a flock of sheep, several goats, a handful of cattle, a mule, too many chickens to count, and one rather annoying rooster.

In addition to these animals, Tau also tended rows of vegetables and herbs. She was fully self-sufficient, and Tsuga was amazed at the amount of work it took to make everything run smoothly. Somehow the widow kept up with all of this in addition to the cooking, cleaning, and all the other menial tasks that went with such activities, such as chopping wood and making the occasional trip to town.

With a young, able-bodied worker on the premisis the load became lighter, but was still in no way easy. Tau left the majority of the physical tasks up to her guest and took the more tedious things upon herself.

Tsuga didn't mind this arrangement in the least; after seven years of weapons' training she was used to hard work, even if she was currently very out of shape. So-called "womanly" tasks, however, had always been beyond her patience; her stitches were uneven, her washing sub-par, and her cooking . . . well, at least she'd never killed anyone with a soup kettle.

As the weeks passed, her strength began to return. It was not long before Tsuga found that she actually looked forward to her back-breaking labor each day. With her daylight hours filled with chores, the girl was forced to restrict her weapons practices to the hours after Tau had gone to bed and there was nothing left to be done for the evening.

Tonight, because there was no light with the moon and stars hidden behind low-hanging clouds, she couldn't practice with her bow and arrow. She favored the sword over her smaller daggers, so she moved herself through the darkness in the forms she had practiced for years, using the familiar motion to calm her thoughts and forget, however briefly, her problems. It was not until the next morning, when Tau made mention of her nighttime activities over breakfast, that Tsuga realized the woman must have been watching her.

"You're good with that sword of yours."

Tsuga nodded slightly and ducked her head, muttering a thanks.

"Why do you practice at night?"

This simple question caused Tsuga's head to shoot up in surprise. Wasn't the reason obvious?

"I have work to do during the day."

Tau frowned at this, and Tsuga flinched away from the hurt in the woman's eyes.

"Tsu, I'm not a slave driver."

Tsuga firmly shoved aside the wave of grief that the nickname brought on (no one had called her that since her father's death all those years ago) and forced herself to ignore the pang. "If your swordsmanship is important to you, I'm not going to stop you from practicing any time you want."

The girl shook her head adamantly, eyes wide. "Oh, no, I'd never dream of leaving all that work to you!"

"Nonsense." Tau's voice was firmer now. "You will practice at least two hours every day, or you will leave."

An ultimatum was the last thing she'd expected, and Tsuga hesitated for a moment, unsure how to react. Tau's smile, though, was a kind one, and Tsuga realized that the woman merely wanted to be supportive.

"All right," she relented, returning the smile. "I'll practice."

A mother will often count the days until she can see her absent child again, and Tau was no exception. Less than a month after Tsuga's arrival at the small farm, the girl woke to find a flurry of activity in the kitchen. When she asked what was going on, Tau looked up without stopping and grinned. Her eyes danced in anticipation.

"It's Midwinter's Day tomorrow!"

Tsuga's blank look brought on a brief fit of laughter, and Tau actually paused in her task of scrubbing the floor to explain.

"It's a national holiday marking the mid-way point of the season. Devalians celebrate it as the day of hope that they will survive another winter. The mage school will be closed. Ramira's coming home to visit!"

Tsuga of course knew what the holiday was, but it hadn't dawned on her that the school, too, would close. She was nearly overwhelmed by a surge of nervousness at the prospect of meeting a mage, and some animalistic terror in her caused her to grasp at her side for the sword she'd left in her room.

Her room. She supposed that wasn't right. It would have been Ramira's room, before she'd gone off to school. No doubt the other girl would want it back when she came to visit. Tsuga turned and walked back across the little kitchen and dining area and stood for a moment in the doorway that she had come to think of as hers. It was foolish of her to have such possessiveness, being a guest and all, but there it was.

She was a tidy person, but the room still looked a great deal more lived-in than it had when she'd arrived. The wardrobes she'd left alone – they were still full of Ramira's things, a detail she should have registered sooner. Besides, the few changes of clothes she had (much mended by this time) she could keep in the packs she'd used while traveling.

Tsuga had never really contemplated it before, but as she looked now it was obvious that she didn't belong in this room. The décor was feminine: flowers and pastel colors, with all kinds of little things stashed about to maintain a perfumed smell.

Tsuga's belongings clashed horribly with Ramira's decorations; her packs were simple, plain, and quite well-worn. The few things that weren't stashed neatly in these leather saddle bags were things more typically found in a boy's room: a stone to sharpen her weapons, oil for polishing, and all of the trappings necessary to fletch arrows. She'd recently re-covered the hilt on her eating knife (it had been worn to the point of fraying), and little pieces of leather still littered the corner by the stool she'd been sitting on.

Though she tried to resist, she couldn't help but heave a little sigh. She had thought she'd come to think of Tau's house as home, but now it was obvious that something had held her back from truly settling in. Perhaps on some level, she'd always known she couldn't stay. As Tsuga moved into the room and began gathering her things, she had to stifle a pang of regret.

It was mid-afternoon before Ramira arrived. Tau was preparing a meal, and Tsuga stood outside grooming her horse; though it was stolen, she still thought of it as *hers*, a problem that seemed to be cropping up quite often of a sudden. Tsuga paused with the brush poised above her young mare's withers for a moment as she wondered at this strange trend. The horse turned and nudged her to remind the girl of the task at hand. Tsuga managed a weak laugh and shoved the horse's head aside to continue the grooming. It was as she led the horse back to its stall that a flicker of movement caught her eye.

She turned to get a better look and nearly yelped aloud at the sight of a young woman a few years her senior materializing out of nowhere. Once the apparition had become completely solid-looking, it tucked a stone worn about its neck beneath its mage's robes and seemed to focus on reality for the first time. It saw Tsuga at this point, and the girl was somewhat mollified to see the illusion look just as shocked to see her.

"Who are you?" Tsuga started in alarm as the illusion spoke (wraiths didn't talk, did they?) and took an involuntary step back when the figure moved forward. Her hand moved automatically to the hilt of her sword, though the good steel edge would be of little use against the spook.

"I'm Tsuga. Who're you?"

Blunt to be sure, but at least she'd managed not to ask the obvious question: *Are you a ghost?* The figure frowned and looked somewhat confused, but answered nonetheless.

"Ramira."

This was yet another unexpected development. Tsuga had been expecting the absent mage to come riding up on a fine white horse, or maybe in a carriage. She had *not* expected Tau's daughter to just . . . appear.

Awkward didn't even begin to describe the atmosphere as the two girls considered each other, but ultimately the tension was shattered by the horse, which chose that moment to blow a snort onto Tsuga, who adopted a look of mock irritation when she was sprayed with snot.

"You devil!"

Ramira laughed at this display, and Tsuga herself managed a weak smile. It was at this point that Tau looked out the window, presumably to check on Tsuga and see what had caused the exclamation. A shriek of delight startled both of the girls, and Tsuga quickly backed out of the way to avoid being plowed down as Tau raced over to embrace her daughter.

Suddenly feeling very uncomfortable at the sight of such a touching family moment, Tsuga mumbled something about chores and hurried off towards the barn with her horse. She wasn't sure what this twisting pain in her gut was, but she attributed it to the emotional sight outside. She couldn't recall such a tender moment with her own mother, and precious few with her Da before he'd died.

While she tried to work through the strange mix of emotions, Tsuga lingered over her chores in the barn until her stomach stopped its churning and she felt she might be able to keep lunch down.

When she finally entered the house, Tau was just beginning to dish out the meal. She looked up from her position by the fire at the sound of Tsuga's entrance and smiled warmly.

"Tsuga, I'd like you to meet my daughter Ramira." The girls both mumbled the obligatory polite greetings, and Tau went on. "Tsuga's staying here for a while, Ramira. Found the poor thing half-starved and almost dead, but she's been a huge help with everything."

Tau didn't mention where Tsuga had been sleeping, so the girl refrained from commenting on it. The woman was also kind enough not to tell the buxom, dark-haired mage any of the more private things that the two near-strangers had discussed. As her hostess approached the table with the food, Tsuga caught Ramira staring at her. When the other girl realized she'd been seen, she offered a smile.

"Sorry, I didn't mean to stare," she apologized. "It's just . . . you look so peculiar."

Tsuga frowned and shot Ramira a venomous glare. Sure, she wasn't the beautiful, shapely, feminine creature Ramira was, but she wouldn't go so far as to call herself peculiar, and therefore felt no one else had the right to do so, either. Ramira caught the look and flushed, quick to correct herself.

"No, no, not like that! I mean . . . well, how to put it?" Ramira hesitated a moment while Tsuga continued to glare, and then at last seemed to straighten out her thoughts. "Well, you know I'm a mage trainee, right?" She didn't wait for Tsuga's reluctant nod before going on. "Well, mages see things a little differently than everybody else. Everything has a different color to it, when a mage looks. It's the energy a particular person, animal, or object has; even rocks have it. Mum, for example, is kind of a neutral mix of colors – she's not any more magical than any other Devalian, but if a mage looks closely, they can see she's been touched by magic. Someone familiar with me might even be able to trace that magical signature back to me."

Tsuga's attention began to wander less than half way through this lecture, and in order to cover her disinterest she walked over to the bucket of clean water Tau kept in the kitchen, where she moistened a rag so that she could clean herself up. Ramira turned to follow the movement, still talking.

"I'd look like a very bright rainbow, some colors more brilliant or vivid than others, because as the next King's Mage I can access the energy of any of the elements, as well as some other stuff, like manipulating the energies of people and animals."

This caught Tsuga's attention, and she actually shuddered at the thought of anyone manipulating her. For some reason as she considered the notion a blinding headache caused her to stagger a bit and drop the rag she'd been using to dry her hands. Ramira, who was still watching her intently, stood and hurried to offer her support.

"What was that?" Tsuga shrugged her off and stepped away as the headache ebbed a bit.

"Nothing. Just a little headache." Ramira frowned.

"Maybe you should sit down while I finish."

Tsuga shook her head and remained standing, causing the mage – the next Queen's (no, this was Devali; they had a king here) Mage, she'd said, which reminded Tsuga of Tau's tale about Sennorra's sister – to shake her head in disapproval before resuming her explanation.

"Well, I was saying how some mages can use people's energy. Empaths, for example, can read the energy of someone and tell how they're feeling. They can also manipulate those energies to make a person feel a certain way. Anyone who's had that done to them will show it, the way your skin stains green after picking herbs, or orange after peeling carrots. To mage sight, a person who has been touched by magic will show a residual color for a certain length of time. The period varies depending on how much they were changed or manipulated; a more powerful use of magic or a more extreme manipulation will stay visible for longer, but the color eventually fades as the effects wear off."

Tsuga, still irritated by her show of weakness in front of Ramira, shook her head in exasperation.

"What does any of this have to do with me?"

Ramira smiled softly as she continued.

"Your color is so distorted that I can't tell what it's supposed to be. You're covered in a net of sickly-looking colors that don't really match any patterns an educated mage would produce, and they're all pulsing and moving like they're still active."

Tsuga didn't hear the majority of this explanation; as soon as the other girl had begun her declaration, she collapsed in a dead faint.

Tsuga woke in an unfamiliar bed. When she tried to move, firm hands held her in place. Alarmed, the girl began to thrash and instinctively reached to grasp for her sword.

"Be still. You've been very sick, so you're not going to be able to do much for a while. Lay back down."

The familiar voice finally penetrated the fog of delirium, and Tsuga sank back against her pillows as Tau released the pressure on her shoulders. When she tried to speak, her voice fled for a moment before she could master it.

"What happened? The last thing I remember is Ramira talking nonsense about my being colorful."

Tau smiled, but as the woman opened her mouth to answer a man in green robes came up to the bed.

"How are you feeling, Tsuga?"

The healer was a man shorter than she and more than twice her weight. He had a kindly look, but the very fact that this stranger knew her name set her teeth on edge.

"Okay, I guess. Confused. What happened?"

As she spoke, Tau stood and walked off. Tsuga was left alone with the stranger, who approached the stool Tau had just vacated and seated himself with a sigh. Tsuga cringed away from the look of pity on his face.

"You're not from Devali, are you Tsuga?" She blanched, and he smiled sympathetically. "It's okay, you're protected here. Healers are duty-bound to care for anyone who needs them, and in your case, I'd risk my own life to keep you safe."

This admission alarmed Tsuga further, and her mind raced to figure out what he meant.

"Why?"

"You know what a mindhealer is?" He waited for Tsuga's nod before continuing. "Well, that's what I am. Ramira and Tau brought you to me after you'd fainted, and it's a good thing they did."

A cold fist of dread tightened around Tsuga's heart, but she couldn't resist asking again, "Why?"

"You were almost dead within minutes of when you collapsed." Her heart began to hammer in alarm, her blood to pound in her ears, but the healer was still talking. "Do you remember why you came to Devali, Tsuga?"

"I was a burden on everyone, and had nowhere else to go." Even as she spoke the by-now-automatic response, she felt the words ring falsely. She paused for a moment, searching her memory, and then swayed as the recollection struck her full force.

"He raped me." Her voice was scarcely above a whisper, her eyes squeezed shut against the remembered horror. "He raped me, then made me kill myself. Only . . .." The pain was fresh, as though it had happened minutes ago, rather than months. In her mind, it had; she was only recalling this now.

"Only someone found you in time to save you. When he realized he couldn't just do away with you and knew himself unable to craft a strong enough manipulation on your mind, he made sure that if you ever came close to remembering what had happened, your body would shut down until you died."

Tsuga was nodding, unable to think enough to wonder how the healer knew all of this.

"And he made sure that I'd be far away when it happened, so that no one would ever trace it to him."

Over the next couple of days Tsuga recovered slowly. She slept much of the time and spent her few waking hours eating and rebuilding her strength. She saw her healer once or twice a day, mostly for a brief check of how she was feeling. On the third day he sat down beside her bed as she ate, and she could tell from the way he looked at her that he had something serious to discuss with her.

"Tsuga, how long ago was your birthday?"

Of course he knew that had been the day all of the trouble had started; she'd told him as much, in one of their long talks. What she couldn't figure out was what he was getting at.

"Well, it's more than a week after Midwinter now, so . . . almost four months ago. Why?" The healer didn't answer directly; he apparently harbored some hope that she might figure it out on her own.

"Other than the headaches, how have you been feeling recently?"

She set down the knife she'd been using to cut her apple (her favorite fruit, and a rare commodity this late in the year) and looked at the man, trying to see what he wanted her to.

"Fine. Strong, until last week."

"Hungrier than usual?"

"No."

"Emotional?"

"Well, I just found out someone raped me, then made me try to kill myself. I'd say I have a good reason to be a little mixed up, wouldn't you?"

The healer sighed and sat back, obviously looking for an easy way to say something he anticipated she would not like.

"When you were unconscious, we had a healer who is better than I at the more physical aspects present to make sure you didn't die on us." Tsuga nodded; he'd told her this already. "She told me that the healing was harder than it should have been. She couldn't figure out why at first, but she told me later that about half way through her work, she knew. She wasn't trying to save just your one spark of life, but three."

Tsuga looked at him in disbelief for a moment, then finally managed a strangled "Three?!"

"Of course, when I told her you were from Sennor, she was able to give a shape to the not-quite-animal life: your spirit guardian." Tsuga was shaking her head even before the healer had finished speaking.

"But I've never found my guardian. That can't be it." The man smiled.

"No, you didn't find her. She found you."

At her look of consternation, he smiled and moved her lunch aside.

"Come outside. You two have obviously not been properly introduced." Tsuga stood and trailed the healer out, but when he led her to her stolen horse she only laughed.

"Oh, that's not my guardian! I stole her the night I ran away."

You picked a horse without thinking. Do you honestly think you would have been able to take me if I hadn't let you? Your heart knew you needed me, even if your head didn't.

Tsuga yelped in alarm at the voice in her head – the one she'd formerly attributed to insanity – and for the first time truly *looked* at the horse. The bay looked like a young filly scarcely broken to a saddle, but Tsuga knew for a fact that she was impeccably trained to listen to her rider – so much so that she seemed a seasoned warhorse. She certainly looked as though she might become one in time; her broad forehead, wide-set brown eyes, and squareish nose screamed intelligence. When coupled with her powerful build and imposing height, it was obvious she'd been bred for war.

Are you going to gawk all day, or are you going to say something?

The horse's sarcasm startled Tsuga out of her paralysis, and the girl moved forward. The horse – no, her guardian was much more than a mere horse – shoved her nose into Tsuga's hands and snuffled curiously.

You didn't bring me an apple?

"Sorry, I didn't know I was coming out to meet you –" **Devilsbane**, the horse provided, and Tsuga smiled. "Well, you've certainly helped me face down my devils."

The healer chose this time to clear his throat, and Tsuga jumped again, face flushed. She couldn't remember the last time she'd managed to forget that someone else was present, and that she'd done so now was highly embarrassing.

"I forgot you were there. Sorry, it's just . . .." As she searched for the words to describe the flood of emotion she felt, her vision blurred and she had to blink away tears.

"Never mind that."

Once Tsuga had regained her composure (after several minutes of leaning against Devilsbane for support), something occurred to her.

"You said three sparks. Who's the third?"

The healer heaved a sigh of dismay, obviously not happy about having to impart this piece of information. He muttered something about good news, bad news, and then finally met her eye. He opened his mouth to speak, and – **You're pregnant.** Her dumbfounded expression must have been telling, because the healer deflated with a look of relief.

"She told you?" Tsuga swallowed convulsively and nodded, unable to speak. The healer glanced about, obviously at a loss as to what to do now. At last, he cleared his throat. "I'll be around, if you need me."

Tsuga still stood frozen, and after a moment the man walked off, glancing back once as though concerned about her. Tsuga didn't notice – she was still trying to absorb everything that had just happened. A mindhealer he might have been, but an empath he was not; obviously he was unprepared to deal with an emotional pregnant woman.

A few more moments passed without change, but when the guardian made as if to speak, Tsuga burst into sobs. She cursed vehemently between gulps of air. The horse moved forward to offer her comfort, but the girl was unable to control her tears for a long while.

"I hate this!"

Emotional outbursts such as this had grown increasingly common as the months passed during Tsuga's pregnancy.

"I hate not being able to *do* anything!"

It had been nearly three months since Tsuga's latest near-death experience, and as the size of her stomach grew, the number of things Tau still allowed her to do decreased. Now, heavy with a child that only reminded her of things best forgotten, the idle hours had begun to take their toll on her temper. The Devalian had restricted her to the tasks Tsuga most hated: those that required long hours of sitting and a good deal of attention to detail. Tsuga had never been fond of the womanly pastimes like sewing and embroidery, but now these were the things on which she spent most of her hours. It did not make her happy, as evidenced by her now-frequent rages.

Tau, luckily, had learned how to deal with these outbursts and knew not to take them personally. She simply let Tsuga complain while she listened quietly. When the fit subsided, she would pick up anything that had been thrown and calmly return it to its proper place.

Devilsbane was perhaps the thing that most unbalanced Tsuga. She was so used to being alone in her own mind that when the mare would break unexpectedly into her thoughts, it startled her so much that she would, often as not, suffer a fit of emotional tears. Now that she knew what the horse was, the young girl often spent hours with her guardian talking things over. Sometimes they simply sat together in companionable silence. This period of bonding for a Sennorran and her guardian typically took place in early childhood, but for whatever reasons, it had been delayed for this particular pair until now.

It never ceased to frustrate Tsuga that, with her stomach now too round to be accommodated by her saddle, the pair of them could not ride or train together properly. Still, Tsuga gradually grew closer to her guardian. More and more when she heard the voice in her head – at least, when it wasn't breaking into her private thoughts unexpectedly – she not only answered it, but cherished it as belonging to the other half of her soul. The horse proved entirely too much like her human counterpart in personality, though. For the first dozen or so times that Tsuga had fallen into one of her rages, the guardian's attempts at help had only made matters worse.

When Tsuga had banished the horse from her mind that first time (an ability she hadn't known existed until then), the animal had been so hurt that she, in turn, had refused to acknowledge Tsuga for days. Because of their bond, their moods fed off of each other to create a spiral of pain and resentment that was hard to break. The process of reaching this discovery had been a painful one, but now that the pair better understood their bond the going was a great deal easier. Except, of course, for Tsuga's unpredictable moods.

In the past, she had always coped with things by avoiding them (not coping at all, truly) and distracting herself from the issue however she possibly could. Unfortunately, with both Tau and Devilsbane constantly reminding her of her condition – and by association, her rape – she was unable to forget for more than a precious few moments what had happened. Unable to master her situation enough to gain control of her spiraling emotions, Tsuga's thoughts sped down the dark and treacherous turns of memory lane with increasing frequency.

She could pinpoint the exact moment her life had begun spiraling out of control. It had all started with her father's death. Had he still been alive, she never would have become so dependent on Lord Gregory. The noble never would have become so fond of her, Elbon would have had no reason to be so jealous of the love his father showed her, and she never would have been raped. And even if she *had* been, having a live and loving father might somehow have helped. He certainly would have seen the boy put to justice, at the very least.

Tsuga sighed and had to fight the urge to cry as she looked in frustration at the embroidery she had botched. The sudden mood swings were her new normal, but she was quite sick of them all the same. With a wet sniff, she set down her project and stood with some difficulty. She teetered a bit as she adjusted her balance for the extra weight she now carried, then walked over to Tau, who was busy sorting out the things she did and didn't trust to the needle of the young mother-to-be.

"I'm sorry, Tau." Tsuga embraced the woman (another thing that had become more complicated of late) and dabbed at her eyes. "I just . . . I can't control myself anymore."

Tau looked up into the girl's face with a knowing smile and shook her head.

"Don't worry about it, dear. Every woman has mood swings during pregnancy. But you're so young that you can't control them as well as someone older might be able to. None of this is your fault. None of it."

Tsuga smiled, though she felt her eyes fill with tears.

"I think I'll go outside for a while." Once free of the oppressive house, Tsuga made a beeline for the field that had become Devilsbane's favorite escape. Once the discovery had been made about the true nature of the horse it had seemed pointless to keep her locked in a stall, so now the guardian had free roam of the area. She'd chosen a small pasture that had been left fallow this planting season and claimed it as her own.

Luckily Devilsbane had sensed her human's approach and so met Tsuga half way across the stretch of unused land; even the short walk to the pasture had the girl panting and out of breath. It was quite amazing, really; Tsuga had spent nearly her entire life without a single friend, but with the appearance of her guardian she now had a steadfast companion of a kind she had never expected. When Devilsbane reached her, Tsuga wrapped her arms around the beast's thick neck and breathed in the comforting smell of horse and sun-baked grass. The pair stayed like this a while, until at length the girl drew back a bit.

"I'm so tired of this. I can't do anything useful, and I can't even keep my emotions in check. What's wrong with me?"

It's all part of being pregnant, Tsu. But don't worry – things will get better.

"How can you know that for sure?"

I guess I don't. But I have faith that the Goddess will bring us through this, and you will be stronger for it. You have to believe that, too.

"I try, but it's just so hard! When Da was killed, I tried to tell myself it was Auriga's will, and that helped some. When I was so close to Death's gate but came back, I honestly believed it would make me stronger. But having a kid? Another mouth to feed? Having to pay someone to watch it so I can earn the money to pay the nurse? How will that be anything but bad?"

Devilsbane snorted, and Tsuga got the distinct impression that the horse had sighed. **I don't know.** The guardian did not, of course, want to get in to the truth of the matter.

"Don't push yet – just breathe."

Tsuga bent over the birthing stool and did her best to follow Tau's calm instructions. It wasn't easy, though: the child was ready to come into the world, and the order to wait went against every instinct that told her to push NOW. But she waited.

"You're doing fine. Just keep breathing nice and easy."

Tsuga had known her time had come with the same instinct of any animal that birthed live young. The wetness staining her dress (for she'd been forced by her expanding stomach out of her breeches and into the looser garments as her time drew nigh) had not been the first sign of something amiss; it had only confirmed what the contractions had indicated.

She'd been in the stables with her guardian at the time, and had flat refused to be moved from the beast's side. Tau hadn't been thrilled to hear that Tsuga insisted on giving birth in the barn, but she had at last consented and brought the supplies from the house before helping Tsuga into a clean, empty stall and immediately adopting the role of midwife.

The two women had discussed this at length. Tsuga did not feel comfortable with a stranger being present at the birth. After much deliberation, Tau had agreed – with the condition that Ramira could be summoned at the first sign of trouble. It had taken weeks, but finally Tsuga yielded to the wisdom of the decision to keep a healer listening for their call in case anything should go wrong.

A sharp gasp escaped the young girl as she felt a pressure release, and then the words, "Okay, push," came as though spoken by the Goddess Herself.

The pain was intense. As the babe tore its way into the world, the barn became suddenly hot and stuffy. Tsuga coughed as the smoke filled her lungs – and where had that come from? The braziers for boiling water were outside, not in here – and with one final push, the child was out. Tsuga started to relax, but a scant few minutes later the afterbirth followed with a fresh jolt of pain, and the heat in the barn rose tangibly. Unable to force her young body to endure any more, Tsuga blacked out.

She woke to a rush of cool air on her skin and the sounds of panic. As she tried to sit up, a gentle hand restrained her. She could still smell smoke in the air, and the sounds of frenzied livestock told her it was not her imagination running wild. Tsuga didn't recognize the person with her, and though she mumbled something, Tsuga couldn't focus on the words before she lost consciousness once more.

The healer stood with a sigh when the young girl passed out again. It was probably best that she not be confronted with the entirety of the day's events until she had recovered. The babe was fine – a healthy little boy – but the birth had been quite hard on the mother. As she looked around the yard, the older woman took in the chaos the fire had caused. The animals were beginning to calm down now that the fire was out, but with nowhere to put them, havoc still reigned.

As was the custom in Devali, a council of mages constantly monitored the magic within their borders – an uncontrolled and untrained mage could be even more dangerous than an enemy's attack, after all. When the powerful burst of fire magic had exploded so near the border with Sennor, a group of mages had been immediately dispatched – two healers, a pyro, and a mindspeaker that specialized in animals. And, of course, the teleporter. Between them, they had quickly gotten the situation under control (more or less, anyway), but now the aged healer faced a dilemma.

Through sheer coincidence (or cruel irony), she had been summoned to help only to find that the cause of all the fuss was the very same Sennorran girl she'd saved some few months back.

Of course, she could not explain any of this to the other mages: they would insist on taking the child into custody. Yet, by the oath she had sworn to her country, the woman was duty-bound to report the girl. At the same time, the far more sacred (to her) oath of a healer to protect those who needed them compelled her to keep silent.

But someone had to know about the girl's abilities, not the least of which was the young mother herself. Certainly now that the child was unconscious there was no hope of being able to warn the girl of the danger she posed to herself and those around her.

With the report written and the situation under control, the other mages were prepared to leave. The healer joined them reluctantly and did her best to dodge their curiosity.

"So how'd she take the news?"

The question came from their fire mage, a young man with a foul temper and a lust for causing pain that frightened her. The healer shook her head.

"Not well. She's out cold again."

The pyro laughed while the animal mindspeaker shook her head.

"Poor kitten. She'll be coming to the College to train?"

The healer shrugged, wishing they'd leave off the questions already.

"She passed out before we got that far. Someone will have to take that up with her when she's in a less fragile state."

This brought a chorus of "mm hmms" and "oh of course," and at last the questions stopped as they all reached out to the teleporter in preparation for their departure.

When Tsuga next woke it was to a pounding headache, an empty stomach, and a squalling baby. It took a while for memory to return, but when it did she simply groaned and threw the covers over her head. She hoped the child died, just so the screaming might stop.

Tau sat with the young boy cradled in her arms. Both healers had assured her that, while not ideal, goats' milk would keep him alive until the mother had recovered enough to nurse him. The child had scarcely stopped screaming since his birth, and still refused the milk. Tau was at her wits' end.

Impatient for the young mother to recover and take responsibility for what was hers, Tau rose from her chair with the babe and ventured into the girl's room. For days the young woman had lain in bed like a corpse, unmoving save for the gentle rise and fall of her chest that signaled life. Now, however, the covers had been pulled up over her head, and as the babe renewed his cries, an irritable head poked out from under the covers.

"Can't you make it shut its trap?"

Tau's jaw dropped in shock and anger ignited in her eyes. "He's hungry."

Tsuga just snorted. "So am I, but I'm not screaming. Feed it."

Tau caught herself clenching her free hand into a fist in her irritation and forced herself to relax with an effort. The tightness was evident in her voice when she spoke.

"He needs his mother's milk. *Your* milk. *You* feed him." With that, she deposited the still-screaming baby into Tsuga's unwilling arms and left the room.

Tsuga stared at the demon seed, lost as to what to do. Finally, it occurred to her that there was nothing she *could* do to make the child stop its wailing. A mother should produce milk when she heard her child's cries, but Tsuga's body remained unresponsive no matter how loudly the thing shrieked. After going so long without nursing the child during her recovery, her body had assumed the boy dead. All motherly functions had, therefore, simply stopped.

Tsuga set the boy down on the bed and stared at him as she tried to ignore the painful pounding in her head. She waited a while for Tau to return and take it away, but when the widow didn't come, Tsuga at last gave up and lay back down. Head back on her pillow, she prayed to the Goddess to grant her oblivion.

Three days. Since she'd been awake, it had not stopped crying for three days. When Tau had at last come to take it away that first afternoon, Tsuga had explained her predicament. A nursemaid had been sent for but had not yet arrived, and Tsuga had not been able to even muster the energy to walk outside. Night was coming on now, and as Tsuga sat in a chair and stared at the screaming thing in Tau's arms, she felt herself reach a decision.

Devilsbane had been positively frantic ever since Tsuga's labor pains had begun. To have that kind of pain crippling someone with whom you were so closely bonded and be unable to do anything about it was maddening. And then the fire had started, and Tsuga had lost consciousness.

Devilsbane had been unable to eat or rest while her bonded lay in this purgatory, and the horse's health had begun to suffer. When Tsuga at last woke, the guardian flooded the girl's mind with relief and love – only to be promptly locked out. The ensuing panic very nearly resulted in a destroyed wall before the girl realized what was wrong and opened her mind again. Oh, sure, she'd explained things to the horse, but after that hasty conversation, Tsuga had withdrawn so deeply into herself that the girl may as well have shoved her guardian aside in rejection. That was certainly how it felt to Devilsane.

When Tsuga appeared outside for the first time three days later with a pack on her shoulders, Devilsbane was both relieved and frightened. It was the middle of the night, and this kind of appearance could only mean one thing: they were running again. Tsuga may have rejoined her guardian physically, but her mind was still far distant. Hurt and confused, Devilsbane went along with the escape, wondering all the while if this were really for the best.

Tsuga huddled in her blankets under the sparse protection of a dying oak, wondering sullenly why she had chosen to leave the shelter provided out of Tau's hospitality to brave the elements. She'd been on the road for months now. Her food had run out long ago, but that remembered incident with the boy-rabbit kept her from hunting. She had been forced once again to resort to stealing.

Luckily she had stumbled onto the trail of the Devalian army marching in full force a few weeks after her departure. With winter all but here, the captains were withdrawing their commands to various fortresses to rebuild their strength and lick their wounds. Tsuga fell into their wake and shadowed them closely; their presence enabled her to pilfer with much less fear of discovery; any small thefts she made would be blamed on the soldiers.

Her life had became a good deal easier then. Until the temperature dropped she had been able to, if not quite thrive, at least be more assured of her survival. But as they had marched north, the army had walked into the teeth of winter. Not only was it now increasingly cold at night when she tried to sleep, but the frigid days made it impossible for her to get warm. The weak light of the sun hid behind clouds as often as not, and when it did shine its pale face down on the world below it afforded no warmth at all.

Shelter was next to impossible to find. She had even seriously considered turning herself in to one of the patrols she so often had to dodge, simply because death would be less miserable. The only thing that kept her from doing so was the knowledge that torture was far more likely to precede her death. She didn't want to do that to Devilsbane. Novere in Sennor was typically chill and rainy, but snow this early in the year was unheard of in her home. Here, the loathesome stuff packed down under the feet of thousands of soldiers and churned into a frozen mud beneath the wheels of the wagons.

Good thing I cropped my hair again, she mused. The upkeep of long hair tried her patience, and living on the road wrought havoc on her unruly tresses. Such random thoughts often ran through her mind these days as she shivered in misery, straining for enough warmth to lull her into sleep. This night, she finally drifted off near dawn.

"Cap'n, scout report."

Seth looked up from the paperwork he was completing at the announcement and gestured for his man to enter. He preferred to take these reports personally, rather than reading a copy from a clerk. There were things a man could pick up in a face-to-face conversation that he just couldn't get from ink on paper.

"Is he still there?"

The scout nodded. The news of their stalker was by now known throughout the camp; the scouts had taken to considering the lad their responsibility and made it a point to check up on him each time they rode out. All wondered where he'd gotten the fine horse, and recently some betting on the answer had broken out. Most seemed to have their money riding on theft.

"Oh, aye, sir. Still there, though 'e looks right mis'rable this mornin'. Y'know, sir, winter's comin' on. 'E's not very equipped fer it. Couldn' we take 'im in?"

Seth laughed at hearing his own plans voiced by the young man and nodded.

"I've actually just sent word to the men who'll be in the group that rides out with me. We'll be confronting the lad this morning." The scout grinned.

"Sir, would it be poss'ble fer –"

"For you to come along?" Seth shook his head. "I'm afraid the members have already been selected. But don't worry, I'll be sure to help you all resolve your bets as soon as we return to camp." The scout laughed and finished his report. When he was done, Seth dismissed him.

Tsuga woke to the sensation of being watched, and though her thoughts were sluggish at first, once Devilsbane's alarm registered she came abruptly alert and leapt to her feet. Her brown eyes, the color of molding red clay, swept the ring of unfamiliar faces frantically as her mind immediately sought out Bane. The horse stood with teeth bared, doing her best to stay between the men and her bonded.

What's going on?

I'm not sure. The guardian switched her tail in annoyance. **They have horses in the trees. They just walked up, like they didn't think we were anything to worry about.**

Tsuga could hear the worry in Bane's mindvoice and silently cursed herself for leaving her sword safely packed away. She distinctly remembered thinking last night that she wasn't likely to need it. Now she regretted that decision.

Tsuga gathered her wits about her hastily and cleared her throat. When she spoke, she used the muddled border dialect that could place her in either country.

"Is there summut I done wrong?"

Seth fought the urge to laugh as the boy scrambled to his feet. The behavior of the horse, though rather peculiar, was not unheard of; a well-trained and truly loyal warhorse would do the same. The captain watched as the boy gathered his wits and formed a question, then stepped forward from amongst his men.

Tsuga's eyes focused immediately on the man who moved first. She assumed he must be the one in charge, and so she took stock of him hastily, eager to feel out just how much trouble she was in.

"Well, let's see . . .." The man's voice was deep and powerful, and if the knots of rank on his uniform were any indication, he was indeed a man of some authority. "You've been trailing us for a while now, stealing from the citizens so that we are blamed, and have driven my soldiers to distraction."

Tsuga had cringed as the man – a Captain, if her knowledge of Devalian ranking knots was accurate – began ticking off her sins, but the last comment was so odd that it caught her attention.

"Sir?"

She thought she caught a hint of a smile before the man continued.

"Tell me, son – did you really think you could hide from our scouts?"

Tsuga felt her face flush in embarrassment. She *had* thought she'd managed to stay hidden. The question bruised her ego, but she did her best to shrug it off. She had not caught the misreading of her gender, driven to distraction by the far more humiliating prospect that these men had been merely toying with her, but Devilsbane heard the mistake immediately.

Maybe it's best they keep thinking you're a lad, Tsu.

Over the past few months, the relationship between girl and guardian had more-or-less been restored. The crippling depression had lifted, and once it was gone Tsuga had returned to her old self. Now she considered Bane's advice while she tried not to betray the horse for what she was. If these soldiers thought for one second that she was some sort of Sennorran spy, they would not hesitate to take her into custody.

The boy didn't answer Seth's question. Of course, he didn't need to; the reddened face showed the truth plainly enough. From behind him, he heard one of his men mutter something about scaring the kid to death, and now that he looked again, the Captain could see the boy was positively terrified. No matter; he wouldn't drag this out much longer.

"Maybe you could help me settle a bet."

When the boy looked at him suspiciously, Seth moved towards the horse and extended a hand. The little filly (for she was surely no older than two or three years) squealed and snapped at him, and he withdrew with a chuckle.

"Where'd you get such a spunky mount?"

A few of his men laughed at that. Seth had made sure the soldiers he'd chosen for this outing were some of the biggest gossipers. Most of them also had money riding on one aspect of the kid's story or another. The bets would all be settled within minutes of their return to camp, and his men – hopefully – would be able to resume business as usual.

Tsuga looked askance at the captain. Was it possible he knew the truth? She didn't think so, but the man was hard to figure out. She couldn't be at all certain where this was going. After a few moments, she decided to go with a part-truth.

"She's mine." If she sounded a bit petulant, well, that couldn't be helped. "She was a gift, Cap'n." Several of the soldiers surrounding the pair groaned, and Tsuga looked at them in confusion. The captain didn't comment, but instead moved on to a different subject completely.

"You know, winter's nearly here." At Tsuga's forlorn face, he finally cracked a grin. "You as good with horses as you seem to be, judging by that one?" The change of topic was completely unexpected, and it took Tsuga a few moments to manage a response.

Finally, she came back with "Oh, yessir. An' I kin take care of armor 'n weapons 'n stuff, too." At the dubious look the captain gave her, Tsuga felt obliged to explain. "M' Da was a medic fer th' army. I got t' he'p th' injured men wi' their gear."

Something about the boy's story struck Seth as odd, but he didn't press. Instead, he reached out and clapped the kid on the shoulder. The boy was tense, and the captain did his best to put the lad more at ease.

"Well then, what say you help tend the army's mounts? We lost our last stable boy. The army doesn't pay much, but you'll have food and clothes and a way to stay warm this winter." The boy's expression turned wistful as he nodded, and Seth laughed.

"Well, come on, then. You'll need the grand tour before you can get to work, and you've got plenty to do."

Tsuga could scarcely believe her luck. Not only had she not been found out or taken prisoner, she'd been offered a job! Auriga was no doubt smiling on her, though the girl could scarcely fathom why.

It wasn't long before Tsuga had fallen into the routine of her duties. In fact, she had done so so easily that Seth no longer doubted her story. She knew she had been officially accepted when the men stopped testing her knowledge of horse care and weaponry and began seeking her honest opinion. She soon had countless friends among the pages, and the fighting men seemed to adopt her as a little brother. Tsuga could not remember ever having been so happy or accepted in her life. She only wished that it had not come at the price of so many lies.

As the company's unofficial little brother, she had gained the protectiveness of – it seemed – the whole of the Devalian army, though she knew in truth she traveled with only a fraction of the national force.

Various men in the group began taking her under their wings to teach her different things: the scouts began showing her how to track and move with stealth; the cavalry coached her on tricks on horseback that could save her life in a charge and helped her "train" Devilsbane to attack and defend; the archers taught her to make, string, and fire her own bow and arrows; the assassins showed her the use of daggers, throwing knives and poisons. Much of this she already knew, but she accepted instruction even in those things at which she most excelled readily because it seemed to make them happy to teach. Even the healers worked with her on the basics of tending the sick and wounded.

So many varieties of weapons were used in the Devalian army that she actually came across several she'd never even heard of. It seemed one man who favored each weapon had been elected to teach her its use and care. Soon she was improving her mastery of the staff, sword, and spear, as well as learning how to use the brutish war hammer and battle axe. The Devalian weapons were – for the most part – heavy and clumsy, designed to utilize more brute strength than cunning. The only exceptions to this rule seemed to be the assassins' tools and the most universal of weaponry, like the sword, spear, staff, and bow.

As in Sennor, there were several kinds of swords used in Devali, many of which she was already familiar with. There was a greatsword, with a blade as wide as Tsuga's arm and nearly of a height with her. This fell into the category of brutish weapons. However, there was also the shortsword, which was approximately the length of her arm and, though small, very sturdy. This was the weapon she'd learned at a young age, and her skill with it the first time surprised the grizzled man teaching her so much that he seemed at a loss and soon pitted her against several of the younger soldiers.

Her favorite, though, was the one her father had carried. It had come into her possession after his death, and here in Devali it was called a bastard. Its name was ironic, but the weapon was perfectly sized for her.

A bastard sword was about the length of a man's stride, placing it between a broadsword and a shortsword in size. The hilt had a grip just a little too short to hold both a man's hands comfortably, but it was lightweight enough to be wielded in one. The blade was about the width of her forearm (around three inches). All in all, the bastard was the perfect size and weight for her to wield effectively. She excelled most in the use of this weapon, both on foot and on horseback, due in no small part to her background in swordsmanship.

Her training, though, was not just physical. Seth somehow managed to turn the stable boy into a page at need, and so she was able to listen in on many of the meetings where plans, strategies, or supplies were discussed. He even found time, occasionally, to play games of logic and strategy with her. While dicing or playing cards with the common soldiers was entertaining, the war games against the captain schooled her in tactics and advance thinking in ways she'd never dreamed possible. She found the convoluted plots and manueverings to be fascinating.

The busy routine generated by such intensive training caused Tsuga's days to pass in a blur. She had no further time to regret leaving Tau and her son Trag, who she had named for her father (incidentally the same name she went by here in the army). At night she was so tired that she curled up in her bedroll out by the horses to fall asleep and did not wake until morning. Before long, Tsuga's muscles had reemerged and developed into hard, wiry masses. This, of course, only enhanced her boyish appearance.

A year passed almost without her realizing it. In fact, she'd have forgotten completely had Bane not made an off-handed comment the first day there was a chill in the air – or what she now thought of as one, though not so long ago she would have called the day bitterly cold.

Your birthday is next week.

This pronouncement came while Tsuga was leading a group of spare horses to drink from the river they'd camped by for the night, and it caused her to stumble. One of the soldiers cleaning his axe nearby saw her and laughed, calling out, "Careful, Little Brother! Wouldn't want to hurt ourselves, heyla?" Tsuga laughed and cursed him lightly, causing the soldier to roar with mirth, before she continued on her way.

Next week? But that means I've been with the army for nearly a year now! . . . And that Trag is over a year old. She could scarcely believe so much time had gone by.

Tsuga had told only one of her closest friends – a sixteen-year-old archer named Sen – about her upcoming birthday. He had apparently spread the word without her knowledge, because when the day dawned bright and crisp, the girl was woken quite rudely by several sets of hands. She was hefted onto someone's shoulders, sleeping roll and all, and paraded through the camp to cheers of "happy birthday!" and "shoulda told us!" She didn't recall any of the other pages receiving such fanfare on their birthdays, and indeed, as she was carried through camp she caught several of the boys glowering at her in jealousy.

Such worries were soon forgotten, however, as she was dropped unceremoniously on a bench before the fire, where her hands were promptly filled with food and drink. She was scarcely able to eat between claps on the back, exchanged jests, and roars of laughter. And then the question she'd been dreading came up.

"So, Little Brother, 'ow old're ya?" Tsuga chased her mouthful of meat with a swig of ale to buy herself time to think. She knew that she looked like a boy of twelve or thirteen, though today actually marked her fifteenth year. But what were the odds that these men would believe that? Ultimately, she opted for a joke.

"One."

The men roared with laughter, and after a moment another soldier asked, "An 'ow d'ya reckon that, Little Brother?" Tsuga grinned and winked at the inquirer.

"Well, Trag's fourteen, but I been answerin' t' 'Little Brother' fer nigh on a year now!"

This brought another collective roar of laughter from the men, peppered here and there with calls of "well put!" and "kid's got a sharp wit, 'e does!" And it wasn't too far from the truth. After all, fourteen was close to her age, and a good deal more believable than the truth, considering her disguised gender.

After she'd finished her breakfast, Tsuga looked up to see that the assassin that had been sharing his trade with her was standing between her and the fire, hands behind his back. When she looked to him questioningly, he began to speak.

"Well, Little Brother," he said in the oily hiss one might expect from a thief (which he had been, once) more than an assassin, "I been figurin' 's 'bout time yeh had summut to practice with yerself, rather'n' runnin' off wit' m' thin's all th' time. So . . . 'ere. 'Appy birthday, 'n all that."

As he finished speaking, he removed his hands from behind his back, revealing a plain but beautifully crafted pair of throwing knives, complete with the necessary arm sheathes to keep them concealed beneath her sleeves. Tsuga gasped in appreciation as she took them and shook her head in wonder.

"But Hari, I can't 'cept these!" *Especially since I already have a perfectly good set.* The oily little man just shook his head.

"Nonsense. They're yers. I ain't got no use fer 'em no more. Ain't used 'em in years, near fergot I had 'em." He winked at her. "Killed m' first guardsman wit' 'em when I was younger'n you."

Tsuga made the appropriate noises and he chuckled, moving back. She started to call out a thank you to him, but another soldier had already taken his place and begun speaking.

Tsuga had never received so many gifts in all her life. Even when her father had been alive, he'd tended to give her one big thing (a pony, a dagger, or a toy sword, for example). Never before had she felt so loved by so many people. The gift-giving took most of the morning, and by the end of it Tsuga could scarcely stand under the weight of such generosity.

Besides the throwing knives from Hari (which she was now wearing), there was: a long wooden staff painted and engraved in fantastical designs; a new pair of boots; a new cape; a new bow (not painted or engraved, but of a fine, springy wood the likes of which she'd never seen); a spear with a tip larger than her hand and barbed to inflict more damage on removal than insertion; a dagger smaller than her palm with a secret compartment for poison; a set of small reed pipes from Sen (who hated fighting and nurtured dreams of becoming a bard some day); and even a simple wooden chess set from Seth. One of the men had even somehow managed to get hold of her sword belt (which housed both her father's bastard sword and the matched dagger) and replaced the grips on both weapons with sharkskin, which offered an impeccable grip even when wet and would stay in good condition for years even with considerable abuse. Someone gave her a new belt to hold the newly-wrapped weapons, complete with a place to attach a quiver as well as a pouch to hold her bowstrings or coin.

Tsuga was completely overwhelmed by this show of affection, and she had to bite her cheek until she drew blood just so that she wouldn't tear up. When the last gift had been presented, Tsuga stood and looked around at all the smiling faces of her friends and cleared her throat. They all hushed expectantly.

"I jes' wanna thank ever'un fer th' best birthday I ever had. Us'ly, somebody dies or gets hurt or blows up. I cain't even 'member a time summut bad didn' happen. I guess what 'm getting' at is . . . thanks. Thanks fer givin' me a real birthday." There was a brief pause, and then the gathered men burst into spontaneous cheers.

Tsuga could feel herself choking up as the men all swarmed her and clapped her on the back in congratulations, and she bit into her other cheek, using the quick burst of pain to lessen her urge to cry.

By the end of the week, the army had reached and settled into their winter stronghold to wait out the cold months. The season came on sooner and lasted longer here in Devali than back home in Sennor (though since she'd grown up on the border herself, the change here in the southern reaches of the country wasn't too much more drastic than what she was used to). Sure enough, less than a week after their arrival the first snowstorm of the year hit and blanketed the entire countryside in snow as far as the eye could see. It seemed a particularly festive occasion, especially since Tsuga's workload had been cut nearly in half by the surplus of servants present in the winter fortress.

The over-abundance of fighting men left the soldiers (whose only duty now other than menial tasks was to guard the walls) rather bored. As a result, Tsuga's training intensified threefold; she was worked well past exhaustion each night. Consequently, she soon became so proficient with every weapon the men knew the use of that they began searching for ways to trip her up and keep her interested. Of course, her years of prior training facilitated her in thwarting most of their attempts to trick her, though she had to admit they came up with some very unique ideas.

After they tried setting her against opponents who were similarly armed, removing the padding and the safety of the practice blades and setting the rules of the sparring matches as first blood, they started having her fight men equipped with heavier weapons while she struggled to best them with something much smaller and lighter. They fought under the same rules, but when one afternoon Tsuga managed to nick the wrist of a man wielding a warhammer with her dagger, her mentors decided that this, too, had grown too easy for her. The roles were reversed, so that she was slowed by the bulk of a weapon too heavy for her while she faced off against someone armed with much lighter gear.

Eventually this, too, lost its ability to undermine her. Fighting against uneven odds came next, forcing her to learn to combat more than one opponent at a time. Next came fighting as part of a group, but when she had at last mastered this as well, all of her teachers seemed at a loss as to what to do next. Spring campaign was still a month away.

"Oh, 'e's ready, Cap'n. Best boy I ever seen wit' any weapon ye can throw at 'im, an' can fight wit' anythin' and win, even 'gainst unb'lievable odds." Seth frowned at the veteran standing before him. He paced across the room again to stand at the fire, staring into the flames.

"I can't in good conscience send the boy to war!" The other man cleared his throat loudly, and Seth looked up with a frown. "You have something you want to say, soldier?" The grizzled man smiled slightly.

"Well, wit' all due r'spec' Cap'n, 'ow old were yeh, when you kilt yer first bitch-lover?"

"Thirteen." At his man's look of triumph, Seth shook his head adamantly. "But that was different."

"Oh, aye. Yeh were 'alf trained 'n' stumbled inter a fight yeh weren' ready fer. An' Trag, well, 'e's been trained fer more'n a year by t' best fighters Ketral's got ter 'is name. 'E's ready, Cap'n. Admit it. Let th' boy fight."

"Cap'n?" Tsuga poked her head through the open doorway, checking to be sure she wasn't interrupting anything. The man waved her inside. "Yeh wanted t' speak t' me?"

She'd just come from the practice arena, where she'd been taking on two men armed with sword and shield, and so was drenched in sweat. She also sported a ragged new tear in the left shoulder of her stable boy's uniform, under which she could feel a colorful bruise blooming. She had various additional bruises on other parts of her body, concealed beneath her clothing. Tsuga wasn't sure why she'd been summoned, but the boy who'd come for her had been wide-eyed and skittish.

Since her skills with weaponry had first begun to outpace her fellow pages, she'd found that she no longer fit with them quite as well. Too old to be a page and too inexperienced to go to war, she felt as though she were trapped in some sort of limbo.

As she stood before him, the captain looked her up and down, a frown on his face, and Tsuga wondered what she'd done wrong.

"Trag, I've been getting reports from your teachers." She nodded – she'd know that already; it was to be expected, after all. "It seems they think you've learned everything they have to teach you."

The boy's eyes widened, and he shook his head frantically.

"Oh, nossir!" Seth quirked an eyebrow, and the boy fell silent.

"You're telling me you don't win the vast majority of your spars? That you haven't had to deal with overwhelming odds, and come out on top more often than not? You haven't noticed your teachers running out of new things to tell you?"

The boy ducked his head, confirming Seth's guesses.

"As I thought. In that case, Trag, you are officially discharged as page and stable boy for the Devalian army." The boy's head shot up, eyes widening in alarm.

"But sir, what'd I do?" Seth held up a hand, forestalling any further questions.

"Henceforth, you are Private Trag of the Eighth Calvary Division of the Devalian army."

Tsuga sat in stunned silence for several heartbeats, unable to think coherently, or even to breathe. After a few moments, she awoke from her stupor as the Captain held out a large package to her. She accepted it dumbly as he spoke.

"This is your pack. It contains three uniforms. One is to be kept immaculate and worn on special occasions only. The others are for daily wear. It also holds a bedroll and medicinal pack, as well as a few other things you'll find yourself needing on campaign."

Tsuga opened the pack as he spoke and took stock of the other items. There was a length of sturdy rope, tools for basic weapon care, and a plain but warm woolen cloak emblazoned with the crest of Devali. She closed the pack without looking further as the captain continued.

"You will report to Sergeant West after I dismiss you. He will give you your orders, and you will continue to report to him. As your commander, his orders are to over-rule all others, save only those of higher-ranking officers and, of course, the king."

Tsuga nodded her understanding, fully able to read between the lines. Seth was telling her she may well wish to balk at some of the orders. She knew what that would entail; the loyalty a soldier owed his superiors took precedence over personal preferences. As a militant healer, her father had died holding to that code of conduct. Her family honor demanded no less.

Ironic that you feel such a sense of duty to a nation that your homeland has been at war with for over a century.

Tsuga ducked her head in embarrassment at the truthfulness of Bane's comment and mumbled a quiet "Yessir. I un'erstan'."

Seth watched as the weight of adulthood settled on the boy's shoulders. Some carried the burden better than others, and the Captain was hoping Trag would be one of the strong ones.

"Yessir. I un'erstan'." The Captain nodded his approval with a slight sense of relief. The boy was a sharp one.

"Good man."

The kid looked up sharply, and Seth could still see the terrified little boy lurking behind his eyes. But the lad held steady and simply drew himself straighter. Seth watched as the enormity of the situation visibly settled over the boy. It was evident in the draining of blood from the lad's face, the way his hands clenched on the pack, and the sudden loss of the timidity with which the boy usually spoke and carried himself.

"You're dismissed. Report to your sergeant immediately."

The boy stood and saluted smartly before turning to march out the door. As he left, Seth's shoulders slumped and he swallowed hard around the cold lump of guilt that had risen in his throat. He could very well be sending the promising lad to an early grave. Sending a man to war was never an easy thing to do, and the necessarily rapid maturing of the young boy broke his heart.

Alone in his office, Seth picked up his little clay figurine of Ketral, the God of war, and ran his thumb along its length. His fist clenched briefly around the small model of the God, and then, angry at the injustice of it all, he hurled it against the wall and watched it shatter like glass into a million shards. Shaking, he dropped his head into his hands and tried to calm the angry beating of his heart.

Something changed that day. It seemed that in the eyes of her friends, she was no longer a little boy who needed to be taught or protected. She no longer had a protector and companion everywhere she went, and so for the first time since joining the army, she was jostled and more-or-less ignored by her comrades. She was one of them now, no longer someone who needed to be sheltered. At first the independence was terrifying, and for a few nights she woke in a cold sweat, afraid she might slip up if left to her own devices this way. As she became used to the notion however, it occurred to her that her relationships with the men who had become her family were not gone; they had simply changed.

Because she was no longer in training, her former teachers no longer drove her to exhaustion, and she had no more guaranteed sparring partners. She felt the lack of activity keenly, and after two days of mourning its loss she decided to take it upon herself to see to the furthering of her abilities.

Resolved, she went on the afternoon of the third day to the training yard. She left her weapons behind in the hopes that she would be better able to find someone willing to spar against her if she was unarmed.

As always, the yard bustled with activity. Men sparred against each other while the women and other camp followers stayed on the sidelines, cheering or gasping as their heroes scored a good hit or were scored against. Tsuga had avoided the women carefully during her time with the army out of fear that their better perception would see the end of her ruse. The most contact she'd had with them had been in passing; her cycles had eventually resumed after the birth of her son, but she had been careful to keep them hidden. She'd stolen the cloths necessary for her monthly bleed from the women's laundry baskets, and with the freedom granted her by being a mere servant, she had enough free time to take care of things without being constantly observed. The presence of the women here now made her uncomfortable, but she was determined to train nevertheless.

For the first time, she did not have an expectant mentor with an area cleared and waiting for her. As a result, she had no real space to practice. She knew from experience that waiting on the sidelines for one to open up would avail her nothing, so she let her eyes roam casually over those battling in the arena.

For soldiers stuck in a winter fortress, practice was a prime source of entertainment. Many men watched each pair of combatants, and money changed hands with a steady regularity at the end of each match. At last Tsuga's gaze settled on a young man around her own age fighting against a seasoned veteran who sent the kid sprawling again even as she made her decision. Several men laughed, and Tsuga joined them to lean across the wooden fence separating the spectators from the packed dirt of the practice arena and jeer.

"C'mon Tim, my Grandam moves faster'n you!"

Even from this distance, Tsuga could see the boy's face redden and his shoulders hunch. The veteran took advantage of the lad's distraction to flip him again. Tsuga made a point of laughing over-loud and turned to one of the chuckling soldiers at her side, speaking with more volume than was absolutely necessary to be heard over the general din.

"Kid's a bit pathetic, ain't 'e?"

The grizzled soldier turned to look her up and down, and then scoffed at her assessment.

"Aye, that 'e is, but yer a fine one t' be callin' anyone kid, ain'tcha squirt?"

Tsuga laughed at the jest, glad that she'd found someone willing to play along.

"Oh, I may be li'il, but I reckon I could take th' lad's staff away without bein' armed m'self. Maybe teach 'im a thin' or two while 'm at it, too."

The man to whom she'd been speaking laughed uproariously and turned to one of his friends, bringing the other man in on the banter.

"Ya 'ear that? Th' squirt says 'e kin fight!"

None of these men were familiar to her; they were from one of the other companies wintering at the fort.

By now Tim had quit his match and stood, face red, and glared at Tsuga. He'd been sparring with a staff, and now he brandished the weapon in what to Tsuga's trained eye was a clumsy manner. At last, after hearing her cohort's declaration, the boy broke and yelled a challenge at her across the yard.

"Well come on, then! You think you can disarm me barehanded, come and try!"

Tsuga could tell from the boy's accent that he was of noble blood. She'd have known it even if she hadn't heard the talk around camp. The older soldiers enjoyed taking the boy down a few pegs, and Tsuga was looking forward to a chance to take her own turn. Humiliating Timoranth was in many ways a rite of passage, a way of building camaraderie. For a girl whose entire world had been turned upside-down so recently, the opportunity to solidify her new status was one she couldn't pass up.

She turned to face Tim fully as the challenge was voiced and allowed herself a slow grin. She shrugged and ducked through the horizontal slats of the fence. As she strolled up to the boy, she adopted the casual swagger of someone who knew their own body and capabilities intimately and allowed herself a slow smile. Tim's face was flushed both from exertion and anger, and he was already filthy and bruised from his previous defeat. He was no longer thinking rationally, and so would be even less able to hold his own than usual.

Although Tsuga hadn't warmed up her muscles, she knew that she would have plenty of time to limber up as she toyed with the boy; his attacks would be clumsy and easy to dodge. Exactly what she'd been hoping for. As she came to a stop before him, Tsuga could hear bets being placed on the sidelines. One in particular caught her attention, and she turned to address the young soldier that had spoken.

"Oh c'mon, you aughta wager more'n a pint 'f ale on me winnin'! If I was you, I'd wager summut more 'long th' lines 'f a good 'orse!"

This brought laughter and cheers from the spectators, and just as Tsuga registered the sound of rustling cloth behind her, she heard one of the women gasp dramatically.

Tsuga ducked to her right and rolled, so that Tim's staff was left to blur through the air where her head had been moments before. She sprung to her feet and winked at the woman who had given her the warning before turning her attention to her opponent.

"Attackin' while m' back's turned? That be summut I'd 'spect from a S'norran whelp, not th' likes 'f good Devalian stock!"

Tim's face reddened further and he charged with a little roar to aim a swing at Tsuga's midsection. She knew that to earn the respect of her comrades, she would have to show not only bravado, but skill and wit as well. She was more than prepared to draw out the fight.

So, rather than diving under Tim's assault to counter with an attack of her own, Tsuga merely stepped aside and danced easily out of the boy's range. Her opponent's rage and frustration grew with each failed attack, and he became sloppier and less coordinated as time went on.

Eventually Tsuga grew bored with the game, and when Tim aimed a particularly clumsy attack at her head after some ten minutes of sparring, she stepped neatly under the boy's lunge, inside his defense, and swiftly buried her fist in his midsection so that Tim's momentum lent the blow additional force.

As she struck with her right hand, Tsuga reached up and grasped her opponent's staff with her left. She twisted harshly and thrust it with a rapid movement back toward Tim. Between his pain-loosed grip and the unexpected direction of the staff's movement, Tim was unable to keep his hold on the weapon. It slipped from his fingers and Tsuga grasped the length of wood in her own hands. She adjusted her hold instinctively so she could attack Tim with a rapid flurry of blows to the noble's head, shoulders, and legs.

Presently, Tsuga stopped and grounded Tim's staff with a flourish as she turned to face the audience, which by this time was laughing and clapping at the show. One man in the crowd shouted a wordless alarm, and Tsuga hesitated a moment, listening to her instincts to gague what to do before simply ducking where she stood to drop herself flat to the ground. As Tim's momentum sent him sprawling in the dirt in front of her, Tsuga caught the glint of sunlight on metal and felt her blood run cold. The boy had been seconds away from burying the long-bladed dagger in the soft spot at the base of her skull. While she'd been showboating, he had nearly killed her.

Tsuga learned two lessons that day that she would never forget: always watch your back, and the only trustworthy enemy is a dead one.

Spring in eastern Devali arrived suddenly and without warning. One night, the men guarding the fortress' walls stood shivering in their thick winter uniforms; the next morning, the snow began to melt. The abrupt change in seasons took Tsuga by surprise, but it seemed the rest of the army had been anticipating this sudden warming for weeks. At Mother Nature's signal, the men finished the few preparations that remained incomplete for the spring campaign with the ease of long practice and familiarity.

It seemed to the new private that these few days passed in a whirlwind of activity, where she was quite frequently in the way. Before she had even had time to consider the consequences of being a Sennorran woman who was an active part of the Devalian army (which she had somehow managed to avoid contemplating until now), the troops were leaving the close confines of their winter stronghold and taking to the muddy roads.

Traveling the Devalian roads in spring, as Tsuga soon found out, was miserable. She had wondered at first why the captain hadn't waited for the roads to dry after the spring thaw before he mobilized his troops. Now she understood. The bi-daily snows of the winter were gone, but to take their place came the unceasing rains of spring. The roads here, like those in Sennor, were made of hard-packed dirt, but with the added moisture of the heavy rains and the long-awaited thaw combined with the traffic of thousands of feet, the paths were churned to a soupy mess almost before the travel had even begun.

Seth assigned a different group to trail the wagons each day and help the drivers pull themselves out of the muck, repair broken wheels and axels, and to serve as a rear guard. This duty was miserable at any time of year; in the dry seasons of summer and fall, the unlucky soldiers assigned to the rear would be coated with dust and downwind of hundreds of filthy horses and men. As a century of cavalry soldiers, there were at least a hundred horses in use at any given time, and Tsuga knew from caring for them all for the better part of a year that there were far more than a mere hundred backup horses. Now, in the wet season, these unfortunate men waded through freshly-churned muck and tried to motivate tired and irritable animals to a task they thoroughly disliked.

All winter, Tsuga had looked forward to the spring campaign with nervous anticipation. When they'd first left the fortress, she had worried incessantly about the upcoming battles, trying to come to terms with what she faced as a Sennorran woman masquerading as a member of the Devalian army. Now, she realized the moral issues would not arise for some weeks yet. No sane commander would engage his troops in such conditions – not when just placing one foot in front of the other was a battle all its own. Until the rains stopped, no one would be fighting anything much other than illness and short tempers.

Tsuga had begun to doubt her memories of a time without the soupy mud of the road. Either those times were nothing more than a child's dream, or else the here and now was a waking nightmare she could not escape. The mud was *everywhere*. It found its way into her hair, under her clothes, and somehow even into her packs and all over everything that was not carefully stored in water- and weatherproof packaging. It didn't take her long to learn the method of packing the Devalians used in the wet season.

A layer of weatherproofing went on the sides as well as beneath and on top of everything else in the bags. The things that could stand a bit of mud or rain went on the bottom, top, and around the edges of the packs. Those delicate things that must be kept from the weather at all costs were tucked carefully within this protective cocoon, and another layer of weatherproofing was placed atop it all.

This unfavorable weather would have been miserable enough had she not had the added problem of keeping her secrets. In the beginning, she had been afforded at least some privacy as a stable boy, left to her own devices often enough that she could take care of business. For nearly six months after the birth of her bastard son, the bleeding hadn't been an issue at all. Now that it had become next to impossible to deal with this feminine difficulty in privacy, she began to long for those days.

The close confines of the winter fortress had made hiding her condition difficult, but she'd been able to manage. With the rigors of the road and the inclement weather, the hassle took on all new dimensions of misery. The rags had to be kept clean and dry – a daily battle. Second, because she was now considered a comrade, she was welcomed into the folds of the army and surrounded by a group of her fellows most everywhere she went. She couldn't even beg the excuse of needing to pee; she had never before realized that these men considered a call of nature to be a social affair.

As a result, keeping her monthly cycle – as well as her gender – hidden had suddenly become a good deal more difficult, and she was rapidly running out of excuses to steal a few private moments away from prying eyes.

When she overheard the camp women talking one evening about an herb that prevented the bleedings, she made it a point to acquire some.

Just when she began to think the monotony of the road coupled with the constant fear of discovery would drive her mad, the miserable weather broke. One day, while they were trudging through the mud, heads ducked against the endless rains, the water simply ceased to fall. All along the line, soldiers cast their eyes heavenward in disbelief and saw a break in the clouds and the first glimpse of blue sky any of them had spied in months. A ragged cheer went up, but Tsuga could find very little to be happy about. True, the onslaught from the skies had ceased, but the roads would take days or even weeks to dry completely, and in the meantime the men would continue to fight their way through the insufferable muck.

It did not immediately occur to Tsuga when the weather broke that the increased mobility meant the campaign would soon begin in earnest. In fact, she did not truly realize the implications of the onset of summer until Seth gathered his men one night to rally them for an upcoming battle – less than two days' march away, he said.

As the captain's words rang out through the camp, Tsuga felt herself go cold and break into a nervous sweat. All of the fears of fighting her countrymen rushed back to the fore of her thoughts, and as these worries chased themselves around her mind, Seth's speech continued on. She scarcely even registered what he said. As the men began to disperse, she was jostled out of her thoughts, knocked repeatedly out of the way by other soldiers. She did her best to shake herself out of the black mood and walked off with the others to find the dinner that no longer smelled as appealing as it had a moment before.

"Sen, I'm not sure I can do this!"

Tsuga sat in the tent she shared with her dearest friend in the company, laying bare her fears for tomorrow as best she could without touching on the secrets that still loomed like a stone wall between them.

"I've never killed anyone before. What if I can't do it? What if I freeze, an' they jus' run me through? What if –"

"What if you stop wondering 'what if' and look at what you *know*?" Sen interrupted her panicked musings with a sensible tone and held up his hands as he began ticking off his points. "You wouldn't freeze, first off. I've seen you fight, Trag. You don't hesitate, and you have an instinctive knowledge of how to keep your hide intact. Second, even if you're not experienced in battle, you've had the best training imaginable. You'll be able to hold your own as well as a lot of the grizzled old veterans."

Tsuga just shook her head. He hadn't addressed her biggest fear: her potential reaction to her first kill.

"An' murder, Sen? That gonna be easy for me, too?" Sen frowned and shook his head.

"No, it's not. And it's not ever going to be *easy*. If it ever gets to that point, you won't be human anymore."

Her friend's words struck deep, and she looked up in surprise at the catch in his voice. Sen's green eyes reflected a pain she could scarcely fathom, and in the dim light of their shared tent, she shuddered slightly.

"How d'you do it, then? How d'you go into battle, time after time, knowin' how hard it'll be?"

"I don't have a choice. I can sit here and try to tell you I want glory, or to fight for the love of my country, or any of the tripe they try and feed us, but the truth is that war isn't about any of that horse shit. At least, not for us. It may be that way for the Lords and Ladies, but not for their fighting men. We don't have any choice in where we go or who we fight. Our only choice is in choosing not to die easily.

"Out there on that battlefield tomorrow, you won't be fighting to defend the king's honor, or even for something as noble as to protect the women and children on the border from the ravages of the Sennorran barbarians. You'll be fighting to live, simple as that. To buy a few more days or weeks of your own life at the expense of the lives of men you're told are the enemy.

"Honestly, Trag? We're not in a war; we're in hell. We're forced to kill men no different than us in the hope that we'll be able to live with ourselves afterward. For the soldier, war's not about taking what's yours or seeking glory. War is about saving your own skin as best you can, and praying to Ketral that those you've sent to ride under the banner of the God will not seek you out first when they ride with Him to cleanse the world in blood and flame."

Tsuga watched her friend's face in silence. The pain she saw etched there gave her a glimpse into the boy's tortured soul. It hurt to see one so young already so haunted by his actions, and Tsuga had to swallow hard against the bile rising in her throat at the idea that after tomorrow, she would share in his pain.

"Why do you do it, Sen? Why not just resign, or desert? Or... something."

"Because this is all I know."

Tsuga shuddered, hearing in this simple statement a portent of the future. Disturbed by the turn of this conversation, Tsuga moved to lay down in her bedroll. Sen, sensing her need to mull this over, did the same. As Tsuga closed her eyes and strove for sleep, she was overcome with a wave of sorrow for the blood that would be shed in the morning.

Tsuga's dreams that night were haunted by wild imaginings of families dying because she had killed their provider. The thought of killing a Sennorran was awful not just for this reason – one which would be true for any fighting man – nor only because she would be facing her countrymen. Rather, she was sickened by the knowledge that every man she would kill the next day would be bonded to a guardian. She would be snuffing out the lives of not one soul at a time, but two.

Finally, after a particularly horrendous dream in which she killed her own father, Tsuga gave up on sleep. She had, out of necessity, managed to train herself not to scream when in the throes of a nightmare, and so when she woke sobbing in a cold sweat, Sen still slept fitfully, wrestling with his own demons as he tossed and turned. She shivered in the cool night air as she crawled quietly out of her blankets, careful not to further disturb her sleeping friend.

Tsuga retrieved her sword belt from beside her bedroll and quickly checked to be sure that her throwing knives were properly fixed in their arm sheathes before she made her way silently towards the tent flap. On her way out, she took her boots in hand so that she could don them in the damp darkness outside. Once finished, Tsuga paused long enough to buckle on her sword belt before she headed off towards the horse lines.

Devilsbane despised having to be hobbled and guarded like a mere horse, but since they were not in Sennor, the guardian had no choice but to comply, lest the two of them be found out. The Devalian military stuck rigidly to tradition and routine, and though this made her life quite complicated in many other ways, it was nonetheless the reason Tsuga was able to navigate confidently through the maze of dark tents now without error. The camp was erected the same way every evening, down to the very smallest detail.

As she neared the place where the horses were kept hobbled at night, a familiar equine whicker greeted her. She found her guardian amongst the common mounts and buried her head in the beast's neck so that she could breathe in the soothing scent of horse.

Bane, I don't know if I can do this. I can't kill these men!

The guardian snorted and craned her neck so that she could nuzzle her human's short-cropped hair comfortingly.

If you don't raise your sword in your own defense, they will kill you.

Tsuga drew a shuddering breath.

I know. But what if I didn't kill *them? What if I just injured them so they couldn't fight?*

There was a pause.

You can try . . ..

What's wrong?

It's just . . . don't try to spare them at the expense of your own life, okay?

Tsuga winced. *I wish I could see some other way out of this. Okay, I –*

"Hey, you there!"

Tsuga looked up at the summons and turned to find one of the guards striding towards her.

"Probl'm, Gabe?" The older man stopped and peered at her through the darkness.

"Oh, Trag, 's just you. Didn' reckernize ya there. Why ain't you asleep, lad?"

Tsuga tried not to wince at the question as she clutched her left hand more tightly around her guardian's neck where her mane had been sheared in the military fashion, trying to draw comfort and support into herself through this small contact.

"Excited, I guess."

Gabe was one of the most grizzled of the older veterans, and the one who'd taught her some of the more complicated maneuvers on horseback. At her statement, he nodded wisely and frowned.

"That's right, t'morruh's the first fer you, ain't it lad?" Tsuga nodded and tried to swallow around the sudden lump in her throat.

"Well, don't fret too much. You're gonna be fine. Try 'n' get some sleep while ya can."

The man turned to walk away, and after a moment of hesitation Tsuga called after him.

"Hey, Gabe? C'n I ask you a question?"

The soldier turned and chuckled slightly.

"Ya just did, lad. But sure, ask away."

"Does th' killin' ever get easier?"

Gabe frowned and turned fully so that he could look her up and down curiously. The old soldier seemed to consider his answer a moment before he finally spoke.

"The killin', no. But you learn 'fore long, you gotta strike first an' question the morality later. That's the only way t' stay alive. That answer your question, lad?"

Tsuga nodded absently, lost in thought as the soldier turned and left. Once she was sure he was gone, she again buried her head in Devilsbane's neck.

Then may Auriga forgive me for what I have to do.

The day of the battle dawned so unexpectedly warm that what little moisture was left in the road entered the air and made the atmosphere unbearably muggy. Tsuga rode in the middle of the ranks, lost in her own thoughts. She had considered, as she waited for the sun to rise above the horizon, arming herself with all of the weaponry she'd acquired over her time in the army. However, even a brief moment of thought brought her to the inevitable conclusion that the numerous blades and other weapons would be more cumbersome than helpful, and so she had left them packed on the carts where they stayed when she wasn't using them.

The only things she now carried, aside from the teardrop-shaped shield issued to every mounted soldier in the Devalian army, were the throwing knives in her arm sheathes, the dagger with the hidden poison that she kept in her boot, and the two weapons that stayed always on her sword belt: her father's sword and the long dagger that would be her only hope if she lost the longer blade. She was a fair archer on solid ground, but she was worse than hopeless trying to shoot from horseback – that was something at which she required a great deal more practice – so her bow and the quiver full of arrows rested with the remainder of her belongongs on one of the supply carts.

Now, as she rode beside men she worried she may never again see alive, Tsuga reached down with her free hand to grip the sword that was all she had left of her dead father. Although he'd been a healer sworn never to take the life of another man, he had also been a pragmatist who knew that a soldier did not always see the green a man wore when it was concealed by dirt and gore. Thus, this sword had only ever been used in self-defense, and had never drawn a man's life-blood. As she rode with the army on the way to the site of the planned ambush, Tsuga mourned the fact that she would not be able to say the same about the blade after today.

The wait seemed to stretch out endlessly. Tsuga sat astride Devilsbane, who stood still other than the occasional shifting of weight or swish of her tail to chase off a bug. The guardian seemed infinitely calmer than Tsuga felt as she shifted her position in the saddle frequently and repeatedly reached down to check that all of her gear was in place and confirm the tightness of Devilsbane's girth strap.

Seth had secreted his entire cavalry unit in the woods surrounding the bend in the road he'd chosen for this ambush. The mounted soldiers had been sent ahead, while the century of foot soldiers they'd been traveling with all spring had circled around to conceal themselves farther along.

Aside from the rather bedraggled-looking officers, only a handful of poorly-armed foot soldiers marched up the road. These select few were the best soldiers of the bunch, and so had the best odds of survival. Earlier in the morning, these men had taken great pleasure in "wounding" themselves, so that now this pathetic-looking band of men seemed to be the few lucky survivors of a skirmish that had not gone in their favor. To Tsuga's eye, untested though it was, the ambush had been planned quite well. Now, they had only to wait until this ragtag band of men met with the Sennorran army.

After what seemed an interminable wait, Tsuga spied a cloud of dust on the road coming from the east. Devilsbane swiveled her ears as the girl reached down to ease her sword in its sheath. Tsuga could hear her heart hammering as she forced aside the moral dilemma with which she'd been wrestling and prepared to fight for her life.

The enemy approached slowly, which lead her to believe the force to be immense. She began to worry about her odds of survival against such an awesome power, and her blood pounded painfully in her temples. From the west, the smaller band of Devalians finally started walking, shuffling along to ensure their meeting would occur at the chosen location.

In the years that would come, what happened next would always be a bit of a mystery. Tsuga remembered only that Seth, the captain, was shouting in alarm. She couldn't understand his words over the confusion. Tsuga had no choice but to be borne forward on the force of her comrades' momentum as the men surged forth from the wood, lest she be ground to dust beneath it. She drew her sword, ducked behind her shield, and let her mount charge into the fray.

She broke free into the road without warning and struck out at the man nearest her before she could think. The world seemed to slow to a crawl, and she saw a metallic glint in his hand as it raised in a futile effort to fend off her attack. She lopped off his head as easily as she might have shorn the tips from the wheatgrass that blew on the plains in the fall. Her fastidiously sharpened blade slid through the bones in his neck without hesitation and burst through the other side with a spray of blood that burned itself into her mind. The man's body hung in suspended animation for a few seconds before it crumpled in a heap to the ground.

While her blood pounded in her hears, Tsuga took a moment to look down at the dead man. An icy-hot stab of horror clenched the muscles of her stomach as realization dawned and the fever of battle leeched from her. The man was not the ferocious Sennorran warrior she'd anticipated. In fact, he wasn't even armed. He was dressed in peasant's clothes: the simple, rough woolen garments of the poor. The metallic glint she'd spied in his hand, which she had presumed to be a lethal weapon, was in fact nothing more than a small dagger commonly used for eating. Indeed, he held in his other hand a now-bloody and half-eaten meal that she could no longer identify.

As she took in this information, Tsuga felt the blood drain from her face. With the fierce intensity of her concentration broken, her surroundings began to register. She could hear the terrified bellowing of oxen; when she looked, she saw the wagons to which they'd been attached overturned, their contents (surely every possession this small group of travelers had owned) spilled out across the road, trampled beneath the feet of men and animals alike. Now the Captain's frenzied shouts began to register, and Tsuga felt the cold in the pit of her stomach spread to the rest of her body as she began to shake with the horror of what had just happened.

"Stand down! Ketral's big sweaty balls, men, stand down! *STOP!*"

A bit further up the road, other peasants had been slaughtered. With the assailants' weapons not slowed by armor, the wounds inflicted seemed unduly savage and gruesome. The gore had mixed with the dirt of the road, and the chaos of so many confused feet had churned the dirt into a bloody soup. This had not been the battle Tsuga had dreaded.

None of her friends lay writhing in agony. Instead, it had turned into a senseless slaughter. And to what ends? Innocent Sennorran citizens had been annihilated with a savage efficiency.

Their ambush had been spoiled; this bend in the road no longer served as a hidden glen in which to surprise the enemy. Tsuga shivered at the thought of the poor souls bound to this place for eternity, left to haunt travelers and bemoan their cruel fate.

She glanced to her right as Devilsbane sidestepped something on the ground and snorted like any jittery horse. What Tsuga saw turned her stomach. A little boy no older than five lay sprawled on the ground with the spear that had taken his life protruding from his stomach, the point slippery with gore. The child had never seen his death riding for him; he'd been stabbed through the back, oblivious to the horrors that were unfolding around him. Unable to restrain herself any longer, Tsuga all but fell from Devilsbane's saddle and landed on her knees in a puddle of blood. There, the fifteen-year-old girl joined with the most hardened veterans in the century of men and rid her stomach of its contents until there was nothing left. She had never, in all of her wildest, most horrific nightmares, expected her first kill to be such brutal murder.

The entire company was berated soundly for the fiasco. They had failed to use their own eyes, and did not heed orders given in the heat of battle. For the pride of the Devalian army, Seth said, it showed an appalling lack of discipline, and he was positively disgusted. Tsuga scarcely registered the Captain's tirade. She was present, but after this afternoon's events she existed in a fog of horror, utterly oblivious to everything around her.

Somehow she found her way back to the smallish tent she shared with Sen, but once inside she merely stood, staring down at her neatly-packed things. Devilsbane was in the care of the new stable boy, but Tsuga had no one to soothe her fears and tell her where to go or what to do. She had no idea how long she stood this way, but eventually the tent flap opened behind her and Sen entered.

"You should clean your blade."

Tsuga startled and turned to look at Sen, eyes vacant.

"What?" Sen stepped forward and let the flap close behind him.

"Your sword. You should clean the gore off."

Tsuga blinked in surprise and looked to where he was pointing. Somehow, despite all the confusion she had managed to hold on to her weapon. Now she could see that it was indeed coated in drying blood. In fact, she could see the farmer's blood staining her hand as well, now that she looked; there were drying splotches of it all across her uniform. The knees of her pants were irrevocably stained from where she'd knelt to vomit in the road. Tsuga shuddered and looked up at Sen, the look on her face one of horrified guilt.

"By the Bitch, Sen, what did we do?"

Sen had been considerably shaken by today's events, but at least he was still able to function. Trag, on the other hand, seemed utterly lost to the world. The boy hadn't even bothered to clean his sword, and Sen had never known him to neglect his weaponry. When the older soldier commented on this oversight, the younger boy merely looked at him with a glassy stare. The private watched as realization dawned on his friend's face, and he started to move forward to offer comfort when the boy spoke.

Trag's words stopped Sen where he stood, and the turn of phrase knocked the wind out of him as effectively as if the younger soldier had kicked him in the walnuts. Sen didn't even notice the sudden loss of Trag's accent, so shocked was he by the use of the Sennorran expletive.

"What?" Sen managed the strangled question, but Trag just looked at him blankly. "Ketral's balls, man, what did you just say?"

Sen watched as the confusion on the boy's face turned to terror, and felt bile rise as his fear was confirmed.

"Blood and war! Sen, you won't tell anyone, will you?"

Sen looked at the boy he'd grown so close to as horror twisted his guts. By all rights, he should kill the lad where he stood, no questions asked. A Sennorran in the midst of the Devalian army could be nothing but a spy, and as such deserved instant death. But Sen couldn't quite bring himself to draw his sword and lop off the traitor's head. He wanted to know for sure before he took such drastic measures.

"Tell anyone what?" It was possible, after all, that the boy was merely ignorant, and not a spy at all. Unlikely when one considered his uncanny skill with weaponry, but possible nonetheless.

Tsuga winced at the tone of Sen's voice. Said differently, the question might have assured her of the safety of her secret. However, the inflection the boy used was far from conspiratorial. She felt her heart sink, and briefly she considered trying to play off her lapse. She couldn't force herself to lie outright to her best friend, though. Not when she'd already been caught. She took a deep breath and tried to steel herself for what was to come.

"I'm not a spy, Sen. I just want to say that before anything else. I ran away from something in Sennor, something I don't ever want to go back to. I'm just trying to stay alive and forget all that, you know? I'd never dream of betraying a single one of you. You're the closest thing to family I've ever really known." She was babbling now, but once she'd started pouring out the fears she'd been harboring this past year, she couldn't make herself stop.

"For everyone to just take me in like this, no questions asked . . . I was amazed. I was never so accepted back home, even. This place, these people, it's all given me a reason to live, and I don't want to lose that. Even with the bad stuff like what happened today, I still wouldn't trade this for the world, and –"

Sen held up a hand to silence her, and she stopped abruptly and shifted nervously as she watched for his reaction. She could see the gears turning as he mulled over everything she'd just said, and she instinctively gripped her sword more firmly. If he decided to attack, she would have to kill him; if she left him merely wounded, he would raise an alarm. Only if she left him dead could she trust that her secret would stay such.

Sen tried to sort out the sudden torrent of words, but the ceaseless babble made doing so difficult. Finally, he held up a hand to ask for silence. When it came, he examined his friend's face. Something had changed drastically since last night. The little boy who'd asked for reassurance was gone, and in his place stood a man. Granted, Trag was an inexperienced and nervous warrior, but he was one, all the same. The fellow was cornered, and instead of fleeing or begging or dissolving into tears, as a boy might do, Trag stood his ground. Sen did not miss the subtle change in stance or the tightened grip on the sword.

He'd sparred Trag many times, and knew that though the other soldier was young and thin, Sen was no match for him. If the private tried to attack or call out, he would lose his life. Sen told himself this, more than his fondness for the Sennorran lad, was what stayed his hand. After a moment, he nodded sharply as he reached a decision.

"Clean your sword and get some sleep."

He spun on his heel and lifted the tent flap. Half-gone, he turned back to give Trag a half-hearted smile to pair with a macabre joke. "And mind your language."

Tsuga heaved a sigh of relief and sank to the ground as she watched the tent flaps close behind Sen. She shook uncontrollably – as much from what she'd almost done as from the discovery. To have come so close to killing a boy she considered a brother frightened her. Just last night she'd been unable to fathom killing a complete stranger, but today she'd been ready to slay her dearest friend just to prolong her own life. If someone were to come to her now with the same questions she'd grappled with the night before, she knew what she'd say. She'd tell them that war is an ugly thing that pits brother against brother and friend against friend. She'd say that if you want to live through one, you must turn your back on all such ties, and kill your own father as easily as you might slaughter a chicken for your dinner.

It was a disturbing philosophy and would be a hard discipline to hold to, but Tsuga knew she would forever live by it. She no longer had a choice. She mourned the loss of her innocence, but even more, she now worried for the safety of her friends. Sen had nearly lost his life tonight because he'd uncovered one of her secrets. What would become of her if she was faced with such a situation again? More importantly, what would happen to the person who put her in that situation?

With a sigh, Tsuga steeled herself and stood to carry her sword with her outside so that she could cleanse the stain of the farmer's blood. The gore could be removed from the iron, but she knew that she could never wash the memory of her first kill from her soul.

For a time, life around camp returned to normal. In the light of day, the men seemed to forget the horrific events easily enough as the bright sun of summer made the gloom of that early morning seem nothing more than a dream. Tsuga knew the truth, though. She was not the only one who woke in the night or sought solace in exhaustion. Once, she had roused in a cold sweat to find Sen sobbing and thrashing in his sleep. She had been merciful and woken him.

At first, Tsuga had feared Sen's loyalty to his country might win out over their friendship, but the boy had seemed to forget the incident entirely. She'd felt tense around him at first, but after a time she too was able to make believe that nothing had changed. While the sun shone, it was easy to forget past horrors and looming fears, but in the quiet darkness of night, they returned.

The lack of sleep made her paranoid, and she worried now even more than before that she would be found out, or that Sen would let something slip. Indeed, the tension among all of the men in the army was mounting, and it was not a surprise when it all came to a head. It started simply: one horse jostled another, and the offending mount was kicked. The riders began bickering, and then without warning swords were in hand.

Tsuga was farther back, and so she did not see or hear that first incident herself, but word of it passed through the ranks like wildfire through a dry forest. Within minutes, fighting had broken out all along the line. Tsuga looked about in dismay as men who were closer than brothers fought against each other for no better reason than that nerves had been strung too tight for too long.

As Tsuga lay in a semiconscious state, the words of the healer came distorted as though down a long tunnel.

"She's got fire in her blood. She can't control it yet, and that makes her dangerous to herself as much as to everyone around her. I have to leave, but you must tell her when she wakes. She must receive training."

The memory of the healer's voice faded, and Tsuga felt her world spin as she returned to the present. Her surroundings dipped violently, and she felt herself begin to fall.

Tsuga had an irritating habit of blocking out unpleasant memories, only to remember them at the most inopportune times. Now, as Devilsbane felt her bonded lose consciousness and slip from the saddle, she let out a terrified equine scream and took up a defensive position over the girl. She, too, had seen the flash of memory, and as chaos raged about her, she couldn't help feeling that this was only the beginning of a long and painful journey.

When Tsuga roused, it was with a pleasant sensation of warmth on her face. Eyes still closed, she smiled and moved closer to its source.

"Stop him! He's going to roll right into the fire!"

This yelp startled her into full wakefulness, and she sat up and opened her eyes. The light of the flames danced madly on the walls of the large healers' tent, and as memory flooded Tsuga, she whimpered and backed away from the heat hastily.

"Put it out!"

The healer looked at her in consternation, and she felt her panic rise. As it did the fire flared alarmingly, causing Tsuga to shrink back further. The healer cursed as a log popped and sent a coal to land on his robes, which promptly caught flame. He cursed again and quickly stamped out the burning green hem; the fire was promptly doused. The man with the charred robes took a moment to look Tsuga up and down, and then waved her away, turning back to the patient he'd been focusing on.

"Bloody boy fainted," he muttered as though to himself. "Get out of here," he said more loudly. "I've got too many men that need my ministrations to humor a little kid. Go on, boy, get out of here!"

After fleeing the medical tent, Tsuga quickly lost track of where she was going as she engrossed herself in fretting about this new discovery and how she was to keep *it* a secret, on top of everything else she already had to hide.

I don't think secret's such a good idea. Tsuga startled and looked around in surprise. Only then did she realize that her feet had taken her within sight of the horse lines. Desperate to confer with her guardian, Tsuga picked up her pace.

What do you mean? Of course I have to keep it a secret! If they know I'm a mage, they won't let me fight any more!

Oh, and what makes you think that? Who's to say they wouldn't see you as an even more formidable weapon?

By this time Tsuga had reached her guardian's side, and she took Bane's blocky head in her hands and stroked the mare's face absently as she stared into the wide-set brown eyes. The horse's small ears pricked forward as she *whuffed* a warm, oat-scented breath onto Tsuga's shirt.

Besides, I thought you hated war? Tsuga frowned in thought, and when her hand consequently paused for a moment, Devilsbane nudged her back into motion.

I do, but I can't exactly stop. How else am I supposed to make a living? Devilsbane didn't answer, and after a moment Tsuga mused, *More formidable, huh?*

"You what?"

Tsuga took a deep breath to help steel her nerves. She'd rehearsed this speech with Devilsbane, and then had presented it to Sen as well. He'd had much the same reaction to the news as the Captain was having now, but she had eventually won him over (though now he avoided her, acting much as he had when he'd first found out she was Sennorran). She only hoped she could convince Seth as well.

"I want t' train as a fire mage so I c'n better serve Devali." Seth shook his head.

"What makes you think you're a fire mage?"

This was a good sign. No outright refusal, no raging, and no attempts at exorcism. Yet. Tsuga suspected the only reason for this was that she had offered herself as a potential weapon. Luckily, Sen's disbelief had adequately prepared her for this question.

"I acciden'ly set a lady's barn on fire awhile back after she caught me stealin' eggs. Mages an' healers all came out t' investigate, an' they tol' me t' get m'self trained."

This story came all the more easily because it was true. She'd merely left out the intervening months. The captain's expression changed from dubious to thoughtful as she spoke.

"Well, we *do* have a journeyman fire mage that could start your training . . .."

Tsuga tried to hide her smile as she mentally congratulated herself on this victory.

Part Two: Forged in Flame

The forge
Purges flaws with immolating fire.
Only the purest ore survives the heat;
Stronger.
Better.
A weapon forged in flame.

"Focus on the flames. They do not move randomly, see? The wind blows them, they respond. They find new fuel, they leap higher. See?"

So far, Tsuga was not terribly impressed by her first lesson in fire. The mage – a man, of course – had begun by asking her to show what she knew. When that had been nothing, he'd seemed to be at a loss; she had then been instructed to sit here and watch a small campfire. In the hour that had passed, so far all he'd done was ask her if she could see any patterns in the flames. She still couldn't.   The tongues of fire seemed to move and dance randomly, with no visible motivation as far as she could tell.

"I see *nothing!*"

This outburst was punctuated by a pounding of her fist against her thigh, and the flames leapt higher as though to emphasize her anger. The man's eyes danced at this display.

"You don't see the fire move, but you control it. You are fueled by emotion. You must train differently than this."

Tsuga only vaguely heard him. She was too busy watching the fire as the flames surged and crackled. Distantly she heard the mage laugh, his dry voice not unlike the whispering heat of the fire.

"Again!"

Tsuga reached once more into the hidden wellspring of power within herself that she'd only just discovered. She formed the crackling, unruly energy into a sphere with her hands and hurled it with an overhand throwing motion. It exploded against the boulder they used as a target and left a charred place where it had made contact.

"Again!"

Tsuga staggered and shook her head against blurred vision as she blinked.

"I can't." Her voice was a hoarse croak, raspy from exposure to heat and smoke. Her instructor frowned.

"When the captain tells you 'save your friend's life,' will you tell him 'I'm tired,' or will you do it?"

Tsuga shook her head in an attempt to clear it. She knew he was right. She took a deep breath and drew herself up as she reached within and once more seized her magic. She formed the power into a ball and prepared to hurl it. As she concentrated, her vision narrowed until all she could see what the flaming sphere in her hands. And then, she could see nothing at all.

Tsuga woke to a cool rag on her face, and after a moment she shoved at the hand holding it weakly. She opened her eyes and tried to focus on the blurry view of reality.

"Just hold still. You came damn close to killing yourself back there."

Tsuga blinked a few times, which caused the colors to swim a bit, but still none converged to form a coherent image. The voice was not that of the mage who had been teaching her; it belonged to a female.

"I did?"

Her own words came out in a weak croak, and she suddenly realized she was very thirsty. "Water?" The colors moved and blurred again, and then an arm supported her shoulders as a cup was pressed against her lips.

"Drink slowly. And yes, you did nearly put yourself in the ground. That damn fire mage drove you too hard. It's not safe to use your magic when you're that drained! You were drawing out your vitality – your life energy. If you'd kept going, you'd be dead!" Tsuga shuddered.

"Is that why I got tired so fast?"

The healer was silent a moment before speaking.

"How fast?"

The girl considered for a bit as she tried to remember.

"Every time I did something, even something small, I felt like I'd been running for hours."

There was a string of curses from the green blur, and then the healer addressed her again.

"That thrice-blasted man's an idiot! Here, eat this." Tsuga felt something pressed into her hand. She must have looked dubious, because the healer went on to explain.

"Sweets help restore a mage's magic stores. It'll help get you back to normal."

Still not quite trusting that there wouldn't be a bitter medicinal taste, Tsuga took a small bite of the object, and then a larger one as her mouth was flooded with a pleasantly sweet flavor.

"He had you hurling fireballs without drawing on anything but your own reserves. That's why when you ran out, it was just second-nature for you to start drawing on your life force! Any idiot with half a brain knows you're supposed to draw on the energy of the world around you. Why didn't you use your focus stone?"

"My what?" The question was muffled somewhat by the mouthful of pastry Tsuga had spoken around.

"Your focus stone."

When Tsuga continued to look at her blankly, the woman shook her head in exasperation and went on. The colors were starting to converge a bit, though her vision was still blurry.

"It's a stone that a mage has a certain affinity to. You reach through it, and it softens your contact with the power, so that you can control and shape it." Tsuga was silent a moment as she absorbed this information. She used the time to lick the sticky glaze from her fingers, absently amazed at the speed with which she had devoured the sweet treat she'd been given.

"Could you show me?" There was a pause, and Tsuga had the distinct feeling the woman was watching her doubtfully. "I don't much trust the fire mage," she expounded, "especially now. And you sound like you know what you're talking about."

The healer hesitated a moment longer, and then consented.

"We'll start in the morning."

Tsuga had been dubious when the woman had first told her they would begin so soon. After all, this conversation had taken place late in the evening, and she was too weak even to stand after her ordeal. However, when she woke the next day she was inexplicably energetic in comparison to how she'd felt the night before. After a breakfast heavy on fruits, nuts, and cheeses – which was supposed to help restore her magical and physical energies both – she felt nearly like her old self.

Glad to see you're feeling well again.

Sorry. I didn't realize what I was doing.

Yeah, well . . . be careful next time. With our bond, you would have started drawing out my life next. Tsuga shuddered at the image that statement produced and blanched from guilt. Just as she was about to apologize in earnest, the healer appeared around the bend, a bright smile on her pale and freckled face.

Now that she could see clearly again, Tsuga took the opportunity to examine the woman. The healer was young – possibly only about five years older than Tsuga – and very attractive. She seemed to radiate an aura of confidence, from her long mane of fiery red hair down to the bottoms of her short legs. She was petite, but with her womanly figure and pale skin (a marvel in itself, after so long marching on the road and so much exposure to sun and wind), the men would find her more than attractive. Tsuga, however, would have been unlikely to garner so much as a second look if she'd been openly female.

She felt her spine stiffen as she drew herself up to her full height in an effort to seem less self-conscious.

As was to be expected, the redheaded woman wore healer's colors. The shade sharply contrasted with her hair and made her green eyes seem to sparkle like the depths of the sea. Tsuga found that she admired the unusual coloring, but she was jolted out of her assessment by the woman's greeting.

"Good morning! Are you ready?"

Tsuga nodded and shook off her reverie as she automatically checked to be sure all of her weaponry was still in place. For her, that was the largest part of being ready for anything.

"Good. Come on; we're going into town."

Tsuga shot her a puzzled look, and the healer laughed at her expression– a silvery, musical sound.

"We have to find your focus stone!"

The younger girl winced at this pronouncement, almost as though she could already feel the depletion of her small stash of coins. She was paid a small salary as a soldier – a pittance, really – and she had a few additional coppers from victories in cards and dice with the men, but she'd been saving these meager funds for a new pair of boots (hers were nearly worn through). She was loathe to spend her coin even on this necessity, and so the prospect of having to buy a trinket for herself was troublesome. The healer didn't seem to notice Tsuga's reaction, though; she had already walked to the far side of the healers' tent where Tsuga had spent the night.

"I'm Affaila, by the way. Never really got a chance to introduce myself last night."

Tsuga nodded and hurried to follow her. She quickly found it necessary to shorten her strides so that she would not outpace the shorter woman as Affaila ducked through the tent flap and into the bright sun outside.

"I'm Trag."

The older woman nodded and smiled. "I know. Now come on – we have to get to the market early if we want to have any luck!"

"How does this one feel?"

Affaila was watching her expectantly as Tsuga held a piece of rough purple topaz in her hand. The girl shook her head.

"Nope. I'm not feelin' any tingle."

The healer sighed and gave an apologetic smile to the merchant as the gem was returned and the pair moved on. The two had been looking through the various stones on display in the marketplace for several hours now with no luck.

As this most recent example was replaced and the girls turned to walk away, Tsuga caught sight of something out of the corner of her eye and turned to examine it more closely.

"What's this?"

She pointed to a green stone about the size of her pinky that was banded in patterns of lighter and darker green. It was gently pointed on the end that was visible, and the top was capped in copper, with a thin band of the metal spiraling around it lengthwise to form a cage. It sported a delicate copper chain; as her hand neared it, she felt a pins-and-needles sensation in her finger. The merchant gave her his gap-toothed smile.

"Ah, a magnificent piece. Malachite. Very powerful stone. It is said to help ward off bad dreams."

As he spoke, he took the piece in hand to show her. Tsuga started to reach for it, intrigued by the vibrations it sent up her arm as her fingers drew closer.

"May I?"

The man nodded and relinquished the pendant, though he watched her closely. Tsuga took it and held the stone up to the light to search for any flaws or weaknesses. Affaila had warned her that such imperfections may result in a stone that would shatter when used. Tsuga had no desire to experience the painful magical backlash the healer assured her such an event would cause. She handed the stone to the older mage so Affaila could look it over in turn.

"What do you think?"

The redhead took the malachite and turned it over in her hands thoughtfully.

"A pretty enough bauble, and it's well made. I'd offer three coppers for it."

A look of consternation stole over the merchant's face, and he shook his head adamantly.

"No, no! That is real copper in the chain and the cage! I will take no less than a silver piece for it."

Tsuga snorted and took the piece back from Affaila. She had to fight to hide her reaction to the stone as she took over the negotiations.

"Nonsense! Malachite is a cheap stone, and there's less than three copper coins' worth of metal in the whole thing! It's but a trinket, nothing more. Four coppers."

After several minutes of hard bargaining, Tsuga had managed to haggle the man down to just under half of his original price. The coins changed hands, and the two girls turned to walk out of town. Tsuga held the pendant before her to examine it. Affaila glanced over at her and smiled.

"A good choice, though unexpected. Malachite is most atuned to the earth-based magicks, so to have malachite as your stone means you have a soft spot for the defenseless. And they're very receptive to personalities with a strong sense of justice. It's a good omen."

Tsuga nodded and donned the pendant so that she could slip it beneath her tunic for safekeeping. She was careful to turn so that Affaila would not be able to see the brief show of flesh by which her gender might have been disclosed.

"And how is it for offensive magicks?"

Affaila looked at her askance and shrugged.

"I don't know; I've never actually known anyone that used it. I just know what they told me about it at the Mage College."

Tsuga dodged out of the way of a pair of children as they ran through the crowds and screamed with laughter. She shuddered at the sight, seeing instead of their happy faces the frozen visage of the young boy she'd seen murdered on the road.

"Will it really help with bad dreams?" she asked, hope that the healer would answer affirmatively plain in her voice. She would give most anything to be able to rest peacefully at night. She was sick to heart of waking in a cold sweat from nightmares of her past.

Affaila shrugged and looked at her new pupil from the corner of her eye. Something in Tsuga's voice or face must have caught her attention, because when she answered her voice was full of sympathy.

"That's just an old wives' tale, I'm afraid."

The younger girl sighed and shook her head ruefully as she tore her gaze away from the laughing children to look at her teacher.

"I was afraid of that."

"I don't understand."

Tsuga's inept attempts to learn magic had begun to frustrate her. She was used to weaponry, which came as naturally to her as swimming to a fish. Magic, however, seemed more akin to trying to teach that same fish to sprout wings and fly.

"How do you 'enter' the stone?"

Affaila sighed and shook her head. Tsuga could tell that the healer had begun to lose patience, too.

"I don't know how else to explain it. You feel the tingly sensation, right?" Tsuga nodded. "That means you should be able to use this particular stone with very little effort. You just focus on making the malachite a part of yourself. Once you can do that, you use the stone like a channel and pull the power through it."

Tsuga was shaking her head throughout this explanation, and when Affaila finished, she spoke.

"But you said earlier it was like a bucket. That you fill it, then you draw from it. How can it be like a bucket *and* a channel?"

Affaila frowned thoughtfully.

"Right now, if you were to make a fireball you'd be using your own energy. Without the stone, you can't access the power that's flowing around you in the world. The stone can act like a container to hold some of that power and store what you're not using, but you haven't filled it yet. So right now, it's like an empty bucket. Now, if you were trying to reach through it and draw power to use immediately, you'd need to use it like a channel. Does that make any more sense?"

"Not really." Tsuga shook her head. "I'm still not sure I understand how to actually *use* the stone."

Affaila sighed and ran a hand through her vibrant hair, obviously frazzled by this declaration.

"You know how to use mage sight –"

"No, I don't." Tsuga shook her head irritably. "I don't even know what it is."

The healer broke off in surprise, and only after several moments during which she cursed the fire mage again did she continue. She took a deep breath to steady herself and reached beneath her own robes to produce another stone.

She held the piece of amber in her hand and exposed it to the light. It was about half again as large as the stone Tsuga'd chosen. Affaila closed her fingers around it and shook her head.

"I should have known. If you could see, you'd know exactly what I'm talking about."

"Don't tell me you're going to start in on this, too!"

Affaila cocked an eyebrow and looked at her curiously. "Start in on what, Trag?"

"The fire mage kept telling me that I needed to see the flames. I could see them, but it didn't help anything!" Affaila laughed at this, and Tsuga scowled at her reaction. "What's so funny?"

"That imbecile didn't bother explaining anything to you, did he?" She didn't wait for Tsuga's confirmation before she continued. "He was talking about using mage sight. Once you learn how to see magic, it becomes infinitely easier to understand what's being asked of you. What you've done so far is like . . . like using a sword for the first time while blindfolded."

Tsuga winced; she'd had a good deal of experience wielding a sword while blindfolded. Affaila laughed at the reaction, but she sobered again after a moment and continued.

"That blasted man should have done this first, but obviously he's incompetent. Now, close your eyes."

Tsuga blinked in confusion. "How can I see with my eyes closed?"

Affaila frowned and adopted a stern tone of voice. "Do you want to go back to the teacher that almost killed you?" Tsuga shook her head quickly, and Affaila nodded sharply. "Then do it."

The healer waited until Tsuga had complied before continuing.

"Now, I'm going to access my magic. Try to see if you can sense anything. Just breathe deeply and try not to concentrate too hard. The sight is more of a state of mind than a skill. You have to be serene when you want to see. That's why mages try so hard to stay calm, and why one who loses his temper often loses his life. Being able to see the attacks aimed at you makes it much easier to counter them. Otherwise, it's like having that blindfold on and fighting someone fully sighted."

As she spoke, Affaila reached through her stone and drew on the pulsing energy around her so that she could begin to pull it through the amber and into herself. By now, she looked like a shining green beacon to her own sight. If Trag could access his ability, he would see much the same.

Affaila was about to ask if the boy had noticed anything yet when he gasped. She hurriedly spoke to steady him.

"Stay calm, or you'll lose it. Keep your breathing even." She waited until the boy's vitals slowed to normal (something her own particular magic allowed her to sense) before continuing. "Now, open your eyes." She heard the boy catch his breath and shook her head. "Breathe slowly. Steadily. Can you see me?" The boy nodded, but Affaila sought further confirmation. "What do you see?" The boy paused a moment, as though trying to find the right words, before he spoke.

"I see . . . it's hard to describe. The whole world is glowing, like little rivers of light running in and through everything. Even the air. It's not any color, but, it's every color, too. Then, I see some of the rivers diverted to flow into your stone. But no, that's not quite right either. It's more like you're tapping into a bunch of the little rivers and drawing out some of the light. Your threads are green, like . . . like your robes. The color of new leaves on those thorny trees that're so common out here. And you and your stone, you're both shining like tiny green suns."

Affaila broke into a wide grin. She knew which trees Trag was talking about – they were common in southern Devali and northern Sennor, especially around the Dubai Plains. The Devalians called them mesquite, and though they were painful to tangle with and more of a nuisance than they were worth, they were very hardy; they could survive long droughts and harsh winters. They were often used as fuel for cookfires by travelers, and gave a very pleasant flavor to anything roasted over their wood. She'd never noticed the similarity in color before, but now that Trag had pointed it out she could see just how accurate it was.

"Good! Do you see what I'm doing now? The green rivers you described are like extensions of my thoughts, and I'm using them to pull some of the power into myself."

The boy nodded, and Affaila allowed the magic she'd drawn into herself to drain back out. She didn't need the power now, and her stone already brimmed over with healing energies.

"Now you try."

Tsuga felt something click once she was able to see what Affaila had been trying to explain. Suddenly, all the metaphors made perfect sense. It was as if someone had tried to describe a horse to her without her ever having seen one before. It was impossible to get a good idea of how one of the beasts looked without ever laying eyes on one of them. Now, it was as though she had found one for the first time; suddenly she could see how each description was accurate and was able to piece them together into the whole that had until now been beyond her grasp. When Affaila released the power she'd held and told Tsuga to try, the girl drew herself up and prepared to copy what she'd just seen the healer do.

She tried to send her thoughts into and through her chunk of malachite, and was obliged to see weak, pale tendrils of orange thought snake forth from her. She concentrated on them, and they grew brighter and more defined with the attention. She could tell when she successfully connected to her stone even without looking; it was like a door unlocked, and suddenly she had access to an immense room that waited to be filled. She came through this vastness, and then watched as her thought tendrils reached out to the pulsing rivers of light.

"Trag, stop!"

Affaila let loose a string of curses as the boy sent out his consciousness to dip into a flow of power that ran wide and deep. She had always been told these powerful channels were dangerous and unruly, and could kill even an experienced Master, let alone someone who wasn't even as knowledgeable as an Apprentice.

Her warning was almost too late. The boy had just touched the flow of old magic, but had not yet begun to draw from it. Affaila's call broke the boy's concentration, and his threads snapped back to him with a backlash that Affaila knew from experience was very painful. Trag collapsed, but her healer's sense told her he was merely unconscious, not dead – which he would have been if he'd proceeded. Affaila sighed and crawled on her knees until she was at the boy's side, where she tried to wake him.

Tsuga woke just as Affaila landed a particularly enthusiastic slap in an attempt to bring her back to consciousness. The young girl yelped and tried to sit up, but firm hands pushed her back down.

"Take it slow. Magical backlash feels worse than you might think."

The girl groaned and reached a hand up to her forehead. She attempted to rub the pain out of her skull this way, but it didn't seem to be very effective.

"I feel like an army is marching on my head." Affaila laughed lightly and moved aside so she could help Tsuga sit up slowly.

"Sounds about right. Here; eat this and I'll explain what happened."

Tsuga accepted the food without reservation this time, knowing it would be sweet and tasty, rather than bitter or medicinal. It was a chewy candy that stuck to her teeth when she bit down, so she settled for sucking on it like a child on a sugartit instead.

"You were doing fine," Affaila began. "You accessed the stone well, and were doing great leading up to when you started trying to draw on the power. Want to tell me what you were thinking, trying to use the old magic like that?" Tsuga blinked, the reference lost on her. Affaila caught on to her confusion and smiled.

"Old magic moves differently than the newer magic you saw me using," she explained. "Old magic has been around since the beginning of time. The channels are deep from the power running the same course for millennia. The magic has had so long to build unchecked that now it's impossible for any human to use it. The only beings that can use the old magic safely are dragons, phoenix, jihai, and the other surviving ancient races. If you'd pulled on that channel successfully instead of barely touching it like you did, you'd be dead now."

Tsuga winced. This statement had come to crop up so frequently of late that it had become rather irritating. She couldn't even begin to count how many times she'd almost-died.

"Next time, be sure you draw on the smallest channels of newer magic, especially the first few times until you get the hang of it."

As she said this last, Affaila rose to her feet and helped Tsuga up.

"Come on. That's enough for today. Eat plenty of sweets and get some rest. We'll pick it up here tomorrow."

"Now that you know how to see magic and how to access your stone, this should go much easier."

Trag and Affaila walked together to the clearing in the tents that was always left in the camp. The Devalians always set out their tents in a precise layout that never varied – helpful for organization, but Affaila felt it begged exploitation. If an enemy knew where each officer slept, the location of the supplies, and where the horses were tethered, he could cause a lot of trouble with very little effort. It was no small wonder, then, that the Devalians kept such a strong guard on their camps.

This morning, she felt inexplicably chipper. She tossed her red hair over her shoulder as she sidestepped a pungent pile of horse shit and smiled brightly.

"Of course, drawing on the power will still tire you, but not nearly as fast as what you were trying to do before," she said, picking up where their former lesson had left off. "It takes a very small fraction of your own power stores to control the magic you'll be drawing from the world. You can't just hurl fireballs forever without getting tired. But now that you'll be able to draw on power outside yourself, you'll be fighting at much less of a disadvantage."

As she'd spoken, the pair had reached the place of their lesson. Affaila gestured for the boy to sit down as she sank to the ground herself.

"Now, you remember how to see? It should be easier this time, now that you know what you're looking for."

The boy nodded and after a few moments declared that he had it. Affaila smiled; this would indeed go a great deal smoother today.

"Good. Now, reach through your stone and try to draw some of the power through it and into yourself." She hesitated a moment, and then clarified, "Some of the *new* power, that is. Let's not try killing ourselves again today, hmm?"

Tsuga winced at the jibe about yesterday's incident, and in her moment of embarrassment she lost her mage sight. She cried out in dismay and tried hastily to regain it, but it slipped away, as impossible to hold on to as a breath of wind. Affaila watched her with a frown.

"Calm down. You can't achieve the sight if you're not serene."

Tsuga blew out a frustrated sigh and tried again, determined to master this skill. The healer shook her head firmly.

"Stop."

The commanding tone to the woman's voice caught Tsuga's attention, and she looked to the healer sheepishly. Affaila shook her head, and as she considered her pupil, her green eyes sparked with irritation.

"You have to be calm. The harder you try to force it to come, the less progress you'll make. Just close your eyes and breathe deeply. Don't try to draw on the sight; let it come to you."

Affaila continued to walk her through the steps again and again until at last Tsuga was able to open her eyes and see properly.

"Okay, I'm ready now." Affaila only nodded curtly, so the girl glanced down at the stone in her hands and then raised her eyes to look at the world around her.

She sent out her desire, as she had done before, and was delighted to see the tendrils of thought snake forth, their soft glow like that of a merry campfire. This time, Tsuga made sure to direct her will to several of the smallest streams and dipped into them tentatively.

Tsuga hadn't known what to expect the first time she accessed the power, but whatever half-form notions she might have had, none had been this feeling of immolation. She felt as though she flailed uselessly in an attempt to extinguish flames that threatened to consume her alive. Distantly, she could hear Affaila's voice.

"Pull back out. Do it slowly, one thread at a time. Be careful not to break concentration or sever any of the threads. Just withdraw them slowly. You know what magical backlash feels like now; no doubt you want to avoid a repeat of that experience. Be careful."

By the time Tsuga finally extracted the last thread and successfully drew them all back into herself, her entire body shook from the effort of such intense concentration.

Affaila watched the boy in concern. He'd touched the power successfully, but he'd been far too timid about it. The magic had sensed his hesitation and tried to overwhelm him. Affaila watched anxiously as she guided him through the process of withdrawing once again, careful not to let any of her anxiety show lest she disrupt his concentration. When at last Trag had successfully completed the delicate task, Affaila shook her head and allowed a lecturing tone to enter her voice.

"Magic is very finicky. It's almost as though it has a consciousness all its own. It will work for you and with you, but only if it knows you will force it to do so. You must be strong and decisive in your actions when dealing with wild magic. Once you've stored it in your stone, it becomes easier to use – even more so the longer it's stored. The more you use your stone, the more it tunes in to you and the less it will fight you, as well. That's why we're just trying to charge the stone today; I don't think you're ready to hurl fireballs drawing directly on the wild magic yet."

The boy's eyes widened at her explanation, and he shook his head vehemently.

"No, ma'am!"

As Affaila went into an explanation of what had just happened, Tsuga felt her eyes widen with each revelation. After having experienced what the healer was describing first hand, it made a good deal more sense than she might have expected it to. The older woman smiled at her sincerity and adjusted her position on the ground slightly.

"Okay, so let's try again. Be sure not to plunge into the river headlong, but don't do it as hesitantly as you did before, either. Just go into it steadily and confidently, and don't let it overwhelm you. It can be tricky to find the middle ground. Whenever you're ready, go ahead and give it another try."

Tsuga nodded at the healer's request and took a deep breath to calm herself. This time the sight came almost of its own accord, and she caught herself grinning at this accomplishment. She forced herself to breathe evenly and extended her will into and through the now-familiar inner recesses of the malachite and then towards the smallish river of new magic once again. This time, Tsuga entered the river of power the same way she might have a physical one: without hesitation, teeth gritted against the shock.

She could tell that she'd done something fundamentally right this time, for instead of the rage of an out-of-control wildfire she felt the slow, steady warmth of a hearth in the heart of winter flow around her and soak into her bones, where it soothed aches she hadn't known were there. When Affaila's voice came again, Tsuga could hear more clearly than ever before.

"Good! Now, slowly draw some of the power into your stone, as if you were drawing water from a well hand over hand. Do it steadily, and direct it into your stone until it fills."

For the first time Tsuga found herself enjoying a lesson in magic. This feeling of warmth and empowerment was heady, and as she followed Affaila's detailed instructions to charge her stone, she felt herself grin with the feeling of accomplishment.

Although she'd only had her mage stone for a couple of days, Tsuga had become so familiar with its feel that as the power began to siphon into it, she could sense the nature of the malachite change by degrees. As the green stone charged, it began to luminesce to Tsuga's mage sight. It did so sullenly at first, the quiet orange glow of a spent coal, but as the piece took in increasingly more power, the light it emanated grew steadily brighter until Tsuga thought it might actually burst into flame.

Affaila watched as Trag filled his stone. After several long minutes, the gem started to glow to her sight like a bonfire in the dark, and she began to grow concerned.

"Trag?" The boy shook his head absently.

"It's only half full." The healer made a noise of surprise. Already the malachite held nearly as much raw power as her amber could when fully charged. She spoke almost to herself, amazed at this show of strength by the small stone the boy had chosen.

"You chose a very powerful stone. Malachite is known for being a good vessel, but I never thought . . . my amber only holds about what you have now."

Tsuga only vaguely registered what Affaila was explaining about her stone; she was too entranced by the feeling of power and strength surging into her through the charging pendant in her hands. Time seemed to stretch endlessly as the stone's inner recesses were filled. Finally, Tsuga felt a sensation similar to that of carrying an over-full bucket and seeing water slosh over the sides.

Carefully, she stopped the flow of magic from the glowing rivulet she'd been drawing on and pulled the magical extensions of her will back into herself one thread at a time. Where the stone rested in her hand, it shone so brilliantly that Tsuga worried it might set her ablaze.

She blinked rapidly a couple of times to rid herself of the mage sight and looked again. She felt disappointment swell as she looked at the now-lifeless bauble in her hand. It seemed so . . . plain. But she could *feel* it squirm with magical life.

She had expected from Affaila's earlier description that this newly-captured magic might press against its restraints and try to break free, but it didn't. Rather, the power stirred but did not rage. It was like a flame in a lantern: secure in its confinement and content to stay within its cage.

Tsuga took the stone by its delicate copper chain to slip it over her head and carefully tucked it under her shirt, where it settled into place between her small breasts.

"Well, I'd say this was a successful day."
Tsuga jumped at the voice – she'd forgotten Affaila was there. The healer smiled as she stood; when she reached out to help Tsuga to her feet, the younger girl accepted the extended hand with a grin.

"Will we pick up here t'morrow?"

The healer seemed to consider for a moment before she replied.

"I think so. Once you've learned to draw on stored power, you'll have learned everything I can teach you. Healing and fire are vastly different, so I can only teach you the most basic of skills."

Tsuga nodded eagerly. As the two women parted for the day, the girl had the fleeting thought that she wouldn't sleep much tonight. She was far too excited by the power that radiated from the pendant hanging from her neck.

Between traveling, practicing her newfound magical abilities, and training in weaponry Tsuga should by all rights have been exhausted. She worked most of the day on her magic by making use of the down time when she did nothing but sit astride Devilsbane while the army marched to charge her stone and practice manipulating her element.

By now the entire unit knew of her new status, so the men were no longer alarmed when she suddenly produced a flame from thin air (though they did tend to edge away and make the sign against evil). It hurt her to be so feared suddenly (for the hatred bred into Devalians against the mages that had nearly defeated them in the Civil War was still strong), but there was nothing to be done about it.

Tsuga loved to coax the fire into shapes and designs. The more she worked at this, the easier it became. Affaila had warned her repeatedly that using magic was tiring, but with the addition of her stone Tsuga seemed able to draw on the power constantly and never feel strained. When the army stopped for the night, Tsuga would use what little daylight remained to practice her long-distance weaponry, such as archery and throwing knives, and after dark she would switch to those she knew by heart; she could dance through the forms of sword work and knife work, staff and spear, or unarmed combat blindfolded – and had, on more than one occasion. She would form small fireballs and set them in the air around her to follow her movements as she danced the forms long after the rest of the fighting men had sought their bedrolls.

By all rights, the busy routine should have so drained her that she collapsed each night into a deep and restful sleep, but the activity seemed to do just the opposite. The harder Tsuga worked, the more energy she seemed to have. It was not until months later, when she looked back on these days in retrospect, that she realized this odd period of excessive energy had come from nerves built up by unacknowledged tension.

Soldiers could often sense when a conflict approached. There was seldom anyone who gave voice to it, but weapons would be honed extra-sharp and men would become paranoid, jumping at the slightest noise. Brawls broke out amongst the men more frequently as the tension continued to mount. All summer, the anticipation of battle had been building; it eased little if at all in the wake of the frequent skirmishes with border patrols. The reason for the unease did not become evident until after the weather had begun to cool.

The day dawned clear, with a bite to the morning air that made the men shiver and energized the animals. Tsuga wasn't bothered by the slight drop in temperature; thanks to her strengthening bond to fire, she was now able to warm herself at will. It was a handy trick here in the heart of frozen Devali – especially now that winter was once again approaching.

Every soldier was on edge today; the atmosphere was disquieting now as the army rode through an unnatural silence. The animals spooked frequently, and even Bane seemed to shy at nothing a few times.

Something's not right here.

I know. What happened to the wildlife?

The birds and other wild things often fell silent as the army marched through their homes, but there was always something to see – one of the men would spy a deer in the underbrush, or a squirrel would chatter at them angrily from a high branch. But there was nothing here; not even a breath of wind stirred to move the leaves of the trees.

All down the line, shields came off of backs and were strapped onto arms as the men eased their weapons nervously. Several soldiers – Tsuga included – went so far as to draw their blades, as though the exposed iron could ward off the ominous silence. Her first instinct was still to draw the physical weapon, even with her strengthening bond to fire. The feel of the rough sharkskin beneath her palm gave her a sense of comfort as she rode through the eerie forest.

There was no shout, no cry of warning to alert anyone to what was happening. From nowhere, an arrow materialized in the neck of a man riding ahead of her and to her right. She watched in horrified shock for a split second as blood bloomed from the wound and the man fell from his saddle, and then instinct took over. She ducked behind her shield hurriedly, and only when a hail of arrows darkened the sky did she realize, as did the rest of the men, that her paltry shield was of no use.

Tsuga, burn the arrows!

Devilsbane's voice was forceful and full of authority, but the girl detected a note of panic beneath the calm surface of the command.

Desperate to free her hands – she had yet to master attacking without making a physical gesture of some sort – Tsuga threw down her shield and sheathed her sword. From beneath her tunic, she drew out the small malachite pendant and grasped it firmly in her left hand. By now, it had become second nature for her to draw on the stone's reserves and slip into mage sight. She clamped down on her panic and the sense of mourning she felt over the man who'd been the first to fall (though certainly many men had been hit in that first volley that she hadn't seen), and locked away all emotion for the time being. The sight settled over her between one heartbeat and the next. She breathed deeply and drew on the beacon of power she held clutched tightly in her hand.

A wave of flame – a technique that had taken her months to perfect – swept through the air, and the hail of arrows fell in ashes, the arrowheads thumping (for the most part harmlessly) to the ground. A few moments later, another volley followed and met with the same fate.

The Sennorrans, unfortunately, were accustomed to the use of magic in battle, and were not stupid enough to continue to waste their ammunition in a futile attack. The deadly rain of arrows stopped, and after a moment the enemy troops appeared from thin air and burst into action.

Tsuga cursed herself for missing the magical threads of illusion she now saw plainly as she dropped her stone to take up her reins. She drew her sword and charged into the fray, wishing briefly for the shield she'd discarded as she passed where it lay in the road. She spared the thought only a moment; that was all the time she had before the fighting joined around her.

Tsuga was, unfortunately, the only combat mage left with the army. The man who had tried to teach her had died some weeks ago in one of the many skirmishes with bandits. Against a strong magical assault, she would be worse than useless.

But nothing happened. No fireballs. No explosions of battle magic. Nothing but a normal, bloody battle where men fought and died by each other's hands.

In the ensuing chaos, Tsuga lost the tenuous grip on her sight. For her, the fever that accompanied battle did not meld easily with mage sight; she was forever forced to choose which she wished to utilize. It was for this reason that she did not at first notice the magical assaults that began to take their toll on the Devalian troops. It was only when a ball of fire nearly struck her full in the face that she took notice.

Tsuga's heart hammered in alarm, and she could feel Bane fighting down panic. She reached hurriedly to regain the mage sight, but the adrenaline pounding through her veins thwarted her first several attempts. Finally, she managed to calm herself enough to gain a weak hold on the heightened state of awareness; it flickered insanely, one moment flooding her vision with unearthly light, and the next leaving the world strangely dim. Meanwhile, men screamed in agony as they burst into flame. If she'd been able to listen to the men around her rather than struggle with her own inner battle, she might have known that they were blaming her, thinking these attacks originated from within their own ranks.

Another fireball impacted a man just to her left, and Tsuga snarled savagely. She gave up trying to stabilize her sight, as she no longer felt she had the time to waste trying to do so. She turned her prancing mount in a tight circle as she cast her gaze about desperately in search of the source of the magical assaults. Her eyes swept the rear of the enemy's line; she knew most mages hid behind the real fighting men to launch attacks from a safe distance while avoiding the dangers of the real fighting themselves. She was an anomaly, not the norm.

Tsuga fully expected to see five or more mages spread out along the line – in an assault of this scale, surely they would have committed a great deal of magical strength – but instead saw only one discernable magical aura, shining like a tiny sun that flickered in and out of existence with her unstable mage sight. All of the assaults seemed to originate from this singular source.

Time seemed to slow; in the space of a few breaths, Tsuga felt as though she had passed hours in the midst of the battle. She watched in horror as the beacon – the mage – gathered power for another assault. Desperate to give her friends a chance to defend themselves against the likelihood of death, she lashed out herself before the attack could be unleashed.

Either this enemy mage was poorly trained in battle magics, or he had assumed her dead when she had not begun hurling fire into the fray willy-nilly. Whatever the reason, Tsuga's attack seemed to take him utterly by surprise because, as she'd intended, the fireballs he'd been forming exploded in his face. She allowed herself a smug smile, imagining the pain such a backlash would have caused, not to mention the ringing ears and singed eyebrows he was no doubt suffering. Before the expression had fully formed on her lips, the enemy launched another assault, this one aimed directly at *her*.

Ramiq Nevarn was excited. He'd been anticipating this day for months, planning his own personal strategy the same way a general would plot the disposition of his troops. As apprentice to the Queen's Mage, he had the ability to mold raw power into any form of magic he pleased, and because of this he had to think long and hard about how he could best utilize his energy. Should he concentrate on attack, or defense? After all, even the Queen's Mage couldn't channel power endlessly; his ability to wield power was limited by the simple physical limitations of endurance and energy – and, until he had progressed beyond his current rank of Journeyman, the limitations of knowledge and what control he had so far learned. Ultimately he had settled on a many-pronged attack-and-defense strategy.

The Sennorran army would lie in wait while he blanketed them with illusion, and when the Devalians had ridden too far into their trap to escape unscathed, Ramiq would be given a command from the general (an arrangement he definitely resented) to drop the illusion and bide his time. When he felt it appropriate, he would follow up by hurling various forms of magical attacks into the fray, choosing his targets carefully to avoid hitting any of his own troops (yes, the eighteen-year-old noble considered the troops his, even though he was but a Journeyman mage who would not reach his full power for years).

Because he was still fairly inexperienced and could only handle one form of magic at a time in any significant quantity, he would be forced to choose his assaults carefully. When he reached the Queen's Mage's equivalent of Adept, he would be able to utilize as many of his magics as he wanted – or as his physical limitations would allow, at least – simultaneously, but for now he was limited to little better than a regular mage.

Ramiq, always one to make an entrance, was the last to arrive at the scene of the battle. A vain young man, he had spent hours perfectly grooming himself this morning, making absolutely sure that every sandy brown hair was in its place and that his robes (a brilliant royal blue trimmed with gold today) were spotless before he even considered departing. Lyra, the fox that Auriga had sent him as his guardian, slept in. Normally he would join her; Ramiq loathed having to rouse before noon. Today, however, was a milestone in his life: his first battle. For the first time, he would be trusted to accompany the army in the same position as he would be entitled to later in life as a full Queen's Mage (if he ever deigned to grace another battlefield; he rather thought he might leave that to those less important to the future of Sennor), so he had forced himself out of bed far earlier than he would have under normal circumstances.

The son of a fifth-generation horse breeder, Ramiq was a member of one of the lower-ranking noble bloodlines in Sennor. His family had earned their status by virtue of their unrivaled horseflesh; no one in Sennor bred better riding horses. By all rights, he should have ridden into battle on a well-bred white stallion like the mages of old.

However, the son of Sennor's best horse breeder had grown up with the insipid beasts around him. His entire life, he had been forced to clean up their shit and take care of the smelly vermin. Ramiq hated the animals, and he did his best to avoid them at all costs. So he did not ride onto the scene of their planned battle astride a proud stallion; instead, he simply teleported to the site of the ambush shortly before it was expected to begin. He was to be the next Queen's Mage, after all; he did *not* walk long distances. And besides, if he had walked – or even ridden – he might have soiled the fine cloth of the robes he wore. The mere thought was abhorrent.

His flamboyant arrival had upset the general. After an extensive screaming match in which Ramiq's sanity and competence were called into question for such a blatant use of magic and the general's wisdom was proclaimed to be flawed for screaming at the top of his lungs when he was supposed to be setting an ambush, the boy stormed off to await the battle and sulk for the rest of the morning.

When the scouts reported the Devalians' approach and returned with the captured Devalian outriders, Ramiq threw up the illusion he'd been practicing. Wagons became boulders, men shrubs, and mounted men small trees. Essentially, he created a perfect forest scene in a clearing where there should have been nothing but rotting leaves.

Unfortunately, he'd never been able to master the art of making the illusions move with the wind, and so the greenery stood stationary in the light breeze that danced through the clearing and cooled the men's sweat under their armor and padding. Ramiq had never tried this illusion on such a large scale, and it began to pull on his reserves a good deal more than he had anticipated as the army lay in wait.

The thwack of bowstrings signaled the joining of battle, and Ramiq looked up to see the first volley of arrows take down a significant portion of the enemy. He smiled grimly and watched as the second wave of archers knocked and loosed their assault. When every last arrow in this attack was swept away by a wall of flame, the boy let out a string of vile curses and stamped his foot in outrage. The Devalians weren't supposed to have a mage with them! When the same thing happened to the third wave, Ramiq prepared to tell the general to hold his fire; there was no sense in wasting their ammunition. The man was smarter than the mage gave him credit for, though: he blew the charge, and at this signal Ramiq dropped his illusion with a sigh of relief and sagged with exhaustion. The army would have to function without him for a while as he rebuilt his energy.

Ramiq watched the battle unfold through a haze of fatigue. He knew he should be trying to prove himself, but found he was unable to muster the energy to do so. After several long minutes during which he did his best to ignore the screams of the dying and the clash of steel, he was at last able to draw himself up to his full height and wrap one hand around the finger-length diamond he wore about his neck. It held a huge amount of power, and as the most versatile of stones, it was the perfect match for most any Queen's Mage. As he drew on the disconcertingly-depleted store of magic it held, Ramiq was forced to reach beyond the confines of his stone and into the rivers of power flowing around him. The wild magic fought him slightly, but he held firm until it bent to his will. Then, hesitating only a moment to select Devalian targets, he incenerated three men by enveloping them in a sphere of flame.

This kind of fireball was one of the easiest magical weapons to form; they took very little effort or energy because they took on a life of their own once unleashed – human flesh burned as readily as any other. Ramiq promptly launched another round of attack, and then prepared for a third. Unfortunately his fatigue and the chaos that surrounded his little island of calm at the back of the battle had cause him to forget about the fire mage that accompanied the Devalian force.

As he gathered the energy for this latest attack, the balls he held suspended before him doubled in size and quite unexpectedly exploded in his face. If he hadn't been properly shielded (as he always was), the incident may have singed him or afforded him some magical backlash. Instead, the explosion did little more than dazzle his eyes and insult his pride. Snarling, he turned his attention to seeking out the enemy mage, blood running hot at the audacity of the bastard.

The fire mage was easy to find: he was like a blazing bonfire walking through the battlefield. Ramiq allowed himself a moment to gloat; not only was the idiot risking a physical attack, he had not even bothered to shield himself against a magical assault! Before his foe had time to think, Ramiq lashed out with a long, slender tendril of fire – a Finger of the Sun. It moved much faster and with a good deal more force than a mere fireball, and he knew that there was no way his enemy could have ever seen one before, as he had invented it himself.

Tsuga felt her blood run cold as she saw a line of fire lancing towards her, ripping through the air so quickly that it pierced the men in its way before the poor souls had even seen their deaths coming. Frantic, Tsuga bent her will to the flames hurtling towards her, giving a desperate mental *push* so that the attack swerved aside and missed her by less than the space of her hand. She tried not to hear the scream of agony that came immediately afterwards, and instead forced herself to focus on the snake of flames that was already circling around to launch an attack from behind.

The Finger of the Sun was one of Ramiq's favorite things to do with fire. It was so much deadlier than a fireball, and it made him feel powerful to control such a large amount of raw elemental power. However, it was also a more advanced technique, and so required a good deal more energy and concentration than the simpler assaults he had been using until now. The pay off – aside from the sheer amount of destruction – was that it was all but impossible to counter; even if this amateur mage had been shielded properly, he would have suffered at the very least the effects of a powerful explosion. He would have had to have shields stronger even than Ramiq's own to avoid the pain and heat such an attack would cause when aborted.

The mage's jaw dropped open in shock when his attack was pushed aside with seeming ease to miss its target by a hand's breadth. He'd never seen anyone turn aside this attack; always it had at least had some sort of impact, even if it had only been to explode relatively impotently against a defensive shield and knock the scorched target back a few lengths. Ramiq blamed his failure on fatigue and the fact that fire was only his third-strongest ability, following closely behind healing and mindspeech. Irritated at this enemy's unexpected show of skill, Ramiq let his Finger wink out where it was and prepared to try something new. He had only just settled on what to do when the Devalian swine launched an attack of his own.

Tsuga was surprised when the hissing tendril of flame simply puffed out, but she didn't allow herself the time to wonder why its use had been abandoned. She'd seen how it had been formed and what the other mage had done to wield it. Now she planned to use it against him. Devilsbane responded to the unspoken command to stand and braced her legs so that she provided a statue-still base for Tsuga's efforts. The girl drew on the power stored in her stone and let it build in her until she could hold no more. The intense light and heat of it pierced her soul as though burning it clean. It was such an intensely euphoric pain that she merely stayed like this for a moment, reveling in it. She'd never tested her limits before, and she knew she held as much right now as she'd ever be able to. But she had a job to do. She tossed her head to regain her focus so she could give the power she held a shape and purpose. Then, she *pushed*.

The snake of flame leapt out of her so quickly that it took Tsuga by surprise. She desperately tried to steer it around her friends, but it had lanced through several Devalians by the time she managed to gain control. Like a physical manifestation of her will, it raced towards the enemy mage and impaled a few Sennorrans who stood in its way. Scarcely a full second later, the snake reached the mage – and disappeared. It simply fizzled out, as though it had been submerged in water. Tsuga swallowed convulsively at this show of strength. She could see, across the distance of the battlefield and even thrugh the dust raised by combat, the other mage preparing to attack her. She quickly assessed her energy levels and found herself already near exhaustion.

Never let it be said that I did not fight with every bit of strength I possess.

She braced herself and drew more deeply on her bond with the stone, drinking more power into herself through its dubious buffer.

Ramiq felt a surge of righteous indignation as the Devalian mage tried to attack him with his own invention. Though the only reason he'd attacked the fire mage with his own element was to inspire this same feeling of insult, Ramiq was highly affronted at having his own tactics turned against him. His noble pride made him a prime target for this kind of assault, no matter how inadvertently he had been wounded.

As the Finger of the Sun raced towards him across the field of battle he felt rage flood him, causing the blood to sing in his veins. The Finger dissipated harmlessly against his shields, as he'd known it would. His outer layer of shielding was designed to absorb an assault, and it did its job flawlessly as it took in the power that had formed the Finger and used it to grow stronger. Offended beyond rationality at the audacity of the stranger to attack him with his own technique, Ramiq abandoned the use of fire. There was little use in continuing in this vein, since the bastard seemed able to deflect such assaults with ease. He hesitated a moment, merely holding shapeless power within himself as he debated what to do. Finally, he let the magical energy ebb as he decided to try a different approach: psychological warfare.

Mind magic took a good deal less raw power, and it tired the mage using it in a completely different manner. He pulled back on the amount of magic he held until only a trickle remained of the torrent he had held previously. Ramiq had a hunch that this tactic would be a good deal more effective in this battle of wits than any further physical attacks.

So, little fire mage, who are you? Tsuga blanched at the unfamiliar voice in her head. Her face bleached white as she swayed as though from a physical blow. She no longer doubted who this mage she fought must be. She tried to hold her thoughts, to stop her racing mind, but failed.
What secrets are you hiding, hmm?

Ramiq regretted his decision almost immediately. Any Devalian should have been used to voices coming unexpectedly into their minds – Devalians were supposed to be inherently gifted in mindspeech – but this mage seemed to dissolve into a blind panic as soon as Ramiq made contact. The young Journeyman winced at the torrent of information that flooded him from the undisciplined mind and did his best to try to sort the words, images, and emotions into some form of coherence. He was about to withdraw in exasperation when one thought in particular piqued his interest.

Devilsbane, help me! He's IN MY HEAD! The horse snorted in alarm at this declaration and tried to speak to Tsuga to comfort her, but the Sennorran mage had shielded the two from mental contact immediately upon overhearing this plea. Tsuga could still feel the horse's panic rising to match her own, but there was no comfort to be gained without the ability to communicate.
Well, well, well, what have we here? Who, exactly, is Devilsbane? Tsuga tried not to answer, but her racing thoughts betrayed her. This time, she heard genuine surprise in the mage's mindvoice.
A Sennorran, fighting on the side of the Devalian army? My, that will never do . . . Tsuga.

She shuddered as he found her name, and he seemed to sense the reaction she had to it, for now he zeroed in on this topic.

And not just any Sennorran, but a woman! How did you manage that? . . . Oh, I see. They don't know, do they? Do you realize how much they'd hate you if they did?

The mindvoice laughed, and Tsuga became distantly aware of the sensation of tears running down her face.

Get out! Please, just leave me be! Devilsbane gave a little buck as the heat began to rise, trying to warn her bonded of the impending danger, but the girl was too far gone to notice.

What's the matter? Don't like having your secrets laid bare? What ever would you do if your friends found out?

Unable to control her panic any longer, Tsuga lashed out against the voice the only way she knew how: with fire. She felt her grip on consciousness loosen as energy flowed out of her, but before she could fall into blessed oblivion, the voice came again.

Oh, I see. Kill them before they can kill you. Is that it?

Tsuga opened her eyes with a great effort, and then closed them in horror at what she saw. The entire battlefield was engulfed in flames, and her friends ran screaming in agony as they tried to avoid the heat of the fires. An intense pain blossomed in her stomach, and then everything went black.

Ramiq did not consider himself a cruel man, nor did he think he was particularly vengeful. But as he rifled through the fire mage's thoughts, he could not resist giving her a few spiteful jibes. And that was something remarkable in and of itself: there was a female Sennorran in the midst of the Devalian army, and – as far as he could tell – no one was the wiser. He was shocked, but *her* reaction to his discovery was so violent that she lost control of her magic. He saw it coming from a while off, and could not resist egging her on, interested to see just what she'd do. Many mages would turn their power on themselves rather than lashing out at anyone else. He'd even known a few who would faint before they reached the magical breaking point. Which category would this child fall into? He didn't have to wonder for long.

Ramiq had anticipated a violent reaction when Tsuga lost control; he had bet himself that she was the type to strike out senselessly. What he had *not* expected was for the entire battlefield to be consumed in a towering inferno. The trees of the forest, dry from a long summer with next to no rain, ignited as though they had been coated in pitch. The flames raced through the ranks of men, and Ramiq knew that their cremation could only be moments away. As he felt the girl's consciousness begin to fade, he couldn't resist a parting admonition.

Oh, I see. Kill them before they can kill you. Is that it?

The girl blacked out, and Ramiq shook his head as the contact with her mind was severed and he came back to himself. He turned his attention to the flames to consider briefly the best way to quell them. Then, as was his custom, he opted for the most flamboyant method.

When he used his magic to pull the heat from the flames and dissipate it higher into the air, away from any available fuel, the fire snuffed out without a trace, leaving trees that had been blazing a moment before stone cold and men who had been rolling on the ground in a desperate attempt to extinguish their clothing relatively unscathed. The inferno vanished without smoke, leaving none dead from its sudden appearance (though many were burned quite badly), and the men who moments before had feared for their lives now raised a ragged cheer at this saving grace. Ramiq allowed himself a smug smile, and then turned his back on the scene of carnage. He would report to the general, and then go home. His plush feather bed was sounding better by the moment.

Tsuga came to herself slowly. She seemed to float in a gray haze; in one of her periods of partial awareness, she heard part of a conversation.

"She's a spy! She should be killed without question!" This voice she recognized as Seth's. She wondered idly who he was talking about.

"She saved your life; can you deny that? So what if she's a girl! Why does that matter?"

The second voice took her longer to place. It was female, and only when Tsuga heard the woman addressed by name was she able to identify the speaker.

"Affaila, step aside! I will kill her myself, if you will not!"

"You would strike down a helpless child? And what about a healer? You know the law as well as I. Do you care to explain my death to the king, Seth?"

The voices grew distant as pain and fatigue took over. She drifted in and out of consciousness, unable to judge how much time passed. Once, she managed enough energy to try sitting up, but found she was unable to move her torso. This failure inspired a bit of panic, and in this brief moment of clarity she recalled the rush of blood that had flowed out of her midsection moments before she'd passed out. She thought she remembered how it had happened, but the memory was lost as the drug-induced sleep took her under again.

"Blasted horse! Leave us alone!"

For the first time since her confrontation with the mage, Tsuga managed to open her eyes. What she saw would have made her laugh if she'd had the energy. As her mind cleared and her vision sharpened, she took in her surroundings. She was strapped to a makeshift stretcher of the kind used to drag dead bodies off of a battlefield. She could hear the impatient shifting of the beast pulling her, though she could not identify what kind of animal it was from her position behind it.

Affaila stood a few feet off. She was throwing stones at Devilsbane as the horse dodged out of the way like a skittish filly. It made for an odd picture, and Tsuga felt her lips stretch in a slight smile.

Bane.

She'd thought that she had sent the word into her guardian's mind, as had been her custom these past years, but Affaila turned as though she'd heard the name and smiled as she shoved sweaty red hair out of her flushed face.

"Oh good, you're awake! How are you feeling?"

Tsuga ignored this question, as its answer must be obvious, and instead looked to Devilsbane. The horse was still trying to edge closer to her wounded partner while avoiding notice from the healer.

"She's mine."

Her voice came out a hoarse rasp, but at least it came out. Affaila blinked in confusion and followed Tsuga's gaze, frowning when she saw the horse.

"She's been following us all night, and so far today, too. She broke her hobbles; look."

Tsuga moved her head slightly so that she could see where Affaila was pointing and smiled weakly at the sight of the ropes trailing from her guardian's legs. She tried to sit up, but her own restraints held her firm.

"She'd be more comfortable if you took those off." As she spoke something registered, and Tsuga cried out in dismay.

"Where are my things? My weapons, my pack, my saddle?"

Affaila smiled and shook her head.

"I can see where your priorities lie. Your saddle is strapped to the mule that's pulling you. Your pack and weapons are lashed onto it. And your horse is following us like a lost puppy."

Tsuga felt her body go slack in relief, and she sagged back against her stretcher to close her eyes against the glare of the sun. Her weak smile broadened at the image of Devilsbane shadowing them all night.

Can you get her to take these damned things off my legs?

"She wants the ropes off," Tsuga reiterated, eyes still closed. Then, almost as an afterthought, she added, "They've rubbed sores from walking all night, and they hurt."

"By Ketral's hairy ass, how could you possibly know that? Besides, I already *tried* to take them off, and she bit me!"

I did not! I snapped at her, but I didn't make contact! Wish I had, though; she shrieked like a little girl. She's been trying to chase me off ever since!

Tsuga shook her head and allowed herself to relax further as Devilsbane's odd sense of humor began to soothe her worries. "She'll behave. Just be careful when you cut the ropes." There was a moment of silence, and then came the rustle of cloth as Affaila moved away from the stretcher.

Tsuga opened her eyes and squinted against the brightness. She could see the light glint off of a small dagger in the healer's hand. She recognized it as the knife the redhead used for cutting bandages and cloth, and wondered briefly if it would be sufficient to slice through the thick ropes the Devalians used to hobble their mounts.

As the healer approached, Devilsbane flattened her ears and snorted as any wary horse would do. She was trying to keep up the lie of Tsuga's nationality, even though the girl was too tired to do so.

"Bane, stand."

At this weakly-spoken command, the horse stiffened and stood still as a statue. Her eyes rolled as Affaila sawed on the ties and cut the abrasive ropes free, but she made no move to attack.

"She's hurt," Affaila declared from where she was, and Tsuga tensed.

"What?"

"The ropes have rubbed sores."

She backed away from the horse carefully and rummaged in her pack for a moment before she came up with a jar of something. She moved back to Bane's side tentatively and crouched down as she removed the lid so that she could apply the ointment to the horse's wounds. When the healer had moved safely out of range and Tsuga had released her guardian with another verbal command, the beast merely stomped her foot in irritation.

Tsuga relaxed against the support of her stretcher as Devilsbane moved up to walk beside her. The sun was high overhead, and as it beat down mercilessly on her face, the girl judged the time to be early afternoon. She closed her eyes again to block out the glare. The healer must have assumed this time that she'd fallen asleep, because a few moments later she felt the stretcher lurch into motion. She winced as the left pole hit a rock, jostling her painfully. In an effort to take her mind off of the discomfort, Tsuga decided to try and figure out what had happened.

"So, you want to tell me what I missed?"

Affaila had been pleasantly surprised when the girl known to a good part of the Devalian army as "Little Brother" roused for the first time. It was customary for a healer – especially one who followed an army – to merely ensure the survival of an individual and leave the majority of the recovery up to nature. Consequently, Trag – until she knew the girl's real name, she would continue to think of her as the lad she'd helped train in magic – had been unconscious for nearly a week now.

She had been the one to discover the child's secret, and had told no one save the Captain. Seth had, of course, ordered the girl's execution, as was required by Devalian law, but he had done so almost half-heartedly. Although he had been outraged at first to learn of the girl in his ranks, he had soon seen the lighter side of things. After all, in nearly two years of living and traveling with the child, not a single person had so much as suspected the lie, so far as either of them knew. The Captain himself had sent the female into battle as one of his most skilled young men, and his most seasoned veterans had encouraged him to do so!

Desperate for a way to spare this brave and unique child, Seth had spoken privately with Affaila, and together they concocted a plan. The next day, Seth raged at the healer, making it abundantly clear that he commanded the liar's death. Affaila, just as publicly, refused to allow it, invoking the Law of Healers as she interposed herself between her patient and the Captain's wrath: that none may ever knowingly harm a healer, nor order another to do so, upon penalty of torture and death. This was an ancient law, a remnant from the time of Sennorra I, but it still held strong in both lands.

When Seth had again ordered the child's death, Affaila had called on another powerful code: the healer's oath, sworn by every person who dedicated his or her life to mending the wounds of others, stated that a healer was bound to help anyone in need, on penalty of a slow, agonizing death. Because she had sworn this oath, Affaila could not allow her patient to come to harm, lest the power she used to heal destroy her in turn. Since Seth could not legally cause her harm without signing his own death warrant, and he could not hurt the girl lest it cause the healer to break her oath, it was a stalemate, one law warring against another. Nothing could be done about the girl's lie until the child was well enough to no longer be under Affaila's care.

Because Seth had so publicly announced Trag's deception, he had been forced to consent to the healer's demand to carry her patient to safety – a precaution against one of the soldiers deciding to take the law into his own hands. Thus, the child's life had been spared. In all the confusion, no one had thought to wonder why the mule was already loaded, nor why their departure went so smoothly.

When the horse had first appeared, it had been dark. After leaving the army late in the afternoon, Affaila had walked through the night, pausing only briefly to eat or to relieve herself. The horse had seemed to materialize out of the shadows. At first, she'd thought she might have unwittingly stumbled onto a farm, but when the beast had continued to trail her, she became suspicious.

Being in Devali, she'd worried that it might have been one of the men in shifted form stalking her in the dark with orders to slay her charge, Law of the Healers or no. Weak in mindspeech, she was forced to stop and shift into her own animal form to attempt conversation.

Once she had changed her shape to that of the man-sized hopping marsupial that was her shift form, she had approached the horse and tried to speak. It had tried to bite her, and she withdrew in alarm to a safe distance, where she again attempted to make contact. Her mental probes had met with nothing more than the blank mind of a dumb animal, concerned with nothing more than its survival. Exasperated, she had shifted back to her human form and quickly donned her discarded clothing, which she had shed in order to shift without her altered proportions leaving her robes in shreds.

She'd attempted to chase the horse off, but it hadn't gone far before returning. When she'd begun moving again, it had continued to follow. From time to time, Affaila would try chasing it off again, but each attempt met with the same result. She'd been trying yet again when her charge woke. Affaila felt a surge of relief at this, the first sign of improvement the girl had shown after her healing. Although she could tell that her charge still lived, the healer had begun to doubt her own senses after so long with no indication that she was right aside from the slow rise and fall of the girl's chest.

When the child declared that the animal wanted the hobbles off, Affaila looked at her askance. In the daylight, she could now see the color and build of the horse and realized that it was indeed the beast Trag had ridden in the army. She'd assumed it belonged to the army – or more accurately, the king.

That the girl actually owned such a mount was a bit of a surprise, but not nearly so startling as the child's quiet declaration of the beast's feelings. However, this *was* Devali, and animal mindspeech was a common thing in these lands. It would certainly explain why the dumb creature was so determined to stay close to its master.

After she'd severed the beast's restraints and applied a healing salve (she was a healer, after all, and she could tell that the sores caused the beast pain) she retreated, only to find the girl drifting back to sleep.

So much for asking her name.

Affaila sighed and moved again to the head of their mule, where she clucked to encourage it into motion again. Presently, she heard a moan, and then the girl she'd presumed to be asleep asked a question.

"Well?" she persisted when Affaila didn't immediately answer. "What happened, exactly?"

Tsuga's eyes were still closed, but even if they hadn't been she would have been unable to see Affaila's reaction since the woman was leading the mule. The tone of her voice was amused, however.

"Lost your accent, I see."

The girl sighed and shook her head without opening her eyes. "No point in it anymore, is there?"

Affaila laughed. "No, I guess not." There was a brief pause, and then the healer followed with another question. "What's the last thing you remember? I can fill in from there."

Tsuga thought back to the battle and tried to pinpoint her last memory. She recalled the mage's mindvoice as he threatened to reveal her secrets, and then a sudden loss of energy.

"The last thing I remember is the voice in my head telling me I was killing my friends."

There was a pause, and then, "The voice in your head?"

Tsuga swallowed convulsively. "The mage's voice. He spoke to me, at the end. He threatened to –"

When she paused, Affaila finished the sentence for her. "Tell everyone you were a girl?"

Tsuga nodded, though she knew by the sled's continued motion that Affaila probably wouldn't see it.

"Yeah."

"I see. Well, what happened after that, from what I heard and what I know, is that you set the surrounding forest on fire. Nearly killed everyone – from both armies."

Tsuga winced, but the healer didn't see, and so kept talking. "Once you blacked out, that mage you were talking to put out the blaze. Just snuffed it out like the flame on a candle. Looked like the fire'd happened years ago. He was the only mage in the force, and since he was using so many magics, he had to have been the Sennorran Queen's Mage."

Tsuga shook her head in denial at this as she turned what she remembered of their exchange over and over in her head.

"No, he was too petty to be the Queen's Mage. And his mindvoice seemed . . . young. Powerful, but young."

"Ah. His apprentice, then? Still, if we could have captured him, it would have been a grand blow to strike. But that's past. Anyway, by the time you were brought to the healer's tent, you were nearly gone."

Tsuga groaned, and the mule stopped. She opened her eyes to see Affaila standing over her, looking concerned.

"Are you okay?"

The girl nodded and managed a wry smile. "Fine. I'm just getting really tired of almost-dying."

"Better than *actually* dying, wouldn't you say?"

Tsuga chuckled weakly. "True. But go on. What else happened?"

The healer sighed and sat down on the ground so that Tsuga could see her face. Affaila mopped her brow as she spoke.

"Well, someone had stabbed you just under your ribcage. Guess they figured if they killed you, the fires might die out. Even if you hadn't reverted to your instinct of drawing your vital energies, you would have bled to death in the next few minutes." At least now she knew why she felt so weak; merely fainting would not have left her feeling so drained.

"And why are we running away from the army?"

"Well, Devalians don't like it when we women don't know our place." Affaila rolled her eyes as she said this. "By all rights, you should be dead now."

Tsuga groaned again, and Affaila smiled in pity.

"Sorry, but it's true. Devalian law states that any woman who masquerades as a man is to be put to death."

Tsuga blanched. The older woman looked at her strangely, but didn't comment on her lack of knowledge about such a pertinent law.

"So? What are we doing way out here?"

"Well, I guess it won't hurt to tell you. You're not exactly planning to go around telling people you were in the army, I'm sure. Seth didn't want to kill you, so we devised a way to get you out alive. I left with you, and, well, here we are."

She shrugged and looked away. Tsuga remained silent for a while, lost in thought. After a moment, Affaila turned to face her again with a forcedly cheerful smile.

"So, you're obviously not a fourteen-year-old boy. Care to tell me who you *are*?"

Tsuga sucked in a breath sharply and hesitated. How much could she safely tell? Finally, she settled on the truth. Mostly.

"What's today?"

Affaila, not seeing where this was going, blinked in confusion before she answered. "The seventeenth day of the month of Novere."

Tsuga simply nodded; she had suspected something close to that.

"In that case, I am Tsuga Dafrin, a sixteen-year-old girl from the border, with no family and few options."

Affaila was taken aback by the revelation of the girl's name. From what her mother had told her, Affaila's father had been a healer from the Sennorran border. Their union was taboo, and as a half-breed Affaila was forced to hide her parentage.

Her mother was dead now, worked to the point of breaking over the years. But she'd told her daughter a bit about the man who was her father, in case she ever needed the knowledge. The fact that this girl-in-boy's-clothing not only shared his last name but had called herself by his first could not be a coincidence. But what were the odds that this barely-living creature was her half sister? Surely there was some other, more feasible explanation.

Tsuga didn't notice Affaila's reaction to her declaration. She'd closed her eyes against the glare of the evening sun, and as she lay in silence, she heard the soft rustle of robes as the healer stood. A moment later, her stretcher was being lowered to the ground. She opened her eyes to see Affaila untying the ropes holding her to the mobile bed.

"What's going on?"

Affaila looked at her and smiled.

"We're stopping for the night. I've been going since early last night without a good rest. And *I* haven't been just lying on a stretcher all that time." As she spoke, Affaila finished freeing Tsuga and helped her to a sitting position. "Come on. You're bound to need to take a piss, and it'll be good for you to get up and stretch your legs a bit."

The younger girl nodded, but as she tried to rise she found that her legs were not strong enough to support her. Affaila had to prop up a humiliated patient to help her take care of business before Tsuga could return to the stretcher and be lowered back down.

"Are you hungry?"

At the mention of food, Tsuga's stomach growled loudly; she nodded, eyes wide. The healer laughed and reached into one of the packs on the ground beside the mule. A few moments later, she handed her charge a wrapped bar that mushed in her hands as she took it up. Tsuga looked to the healer questioningly.

"It's chocolate," Affaila said, referring to the soft rectangle. "A bit melted from spending all day in the packs, but it'll still taste good."

She stood up as she spoke and began tearing up an ever-widening circle of the tall grasses that surrounded them to make a fire break.

"How are you feeling?"

Tsuga shrugged and peeled back part of the wrapper on the chocolate bar. "Okay, I guess. Weak. Tired."

Guilty. Traumatized. Lonely, and more. You have no reason to be, though. It's not your fault. Besides, you have me to help you through this, you know.

I know, I know. Thank you. And stop telling me how I'm feeling, if you don't mind.

Fine. Love ya too.

Tsuga sighed, and Affaila looked at her curiously.

"You okay?"

The girl nodded. "Fine. Just tired."

The healer nodded sagely. "With good reason. You just need to rest for a few days, and you'll be fine. In fact, you should probably try to sleep while I get a fire going. I'll throw some of the salted pork into a pot and make you a broth."

Tsuga nodded at this suggestion and stifled the urge to sigh. She hated being an invalid, but there wasn't much she could do about it now.

"So why don't you like to ride?"

A week had passed, and Tsuga and Affaila were traveling together still. The girl had recovered enough to ride – or at least, to cling to the saddle and let Devilsbane carry her – but though the mule had now been relieved of much of its burden (she, as well as her saddle, packs, and weapons were now all loaded onto Devilsbane), Affaila still refused to mount up. Their progress would have been a good deal faster if the healer had been willing to ride, and she wouldn't have been as tired at the end of the day. Even so, despite all of Tsuga's arguments she had adamantly refused. The younger girl was trying to understand what she considered to be flawed reasoning. Affaila looked up at the question and held silent for a moment before answering.

"I'd rather not have to trust my well-being to a dumb animal with more teeth than it's got brains. I'm perfectly fine walking, thank you very much."

Tsuga shrugged and shook her head – she still wasn't convinced, but she decided to let the subject drop.

Bane, however, was highly insulted; when Affaila stepped closer to her in an attempt to dodge an uneven part in the road, she snaked her head out and bit the healer lightly on the arm.

Tsuga gasped in alarm and scolded her guardian while Affaila cried out and leapt away.

If she doesn't want to ride us, maybe she should at least consider not walking on us and insulting us. More teeth than brains, indeed!

The horse snorted, and Tsuga tried to hide her laughter at the guardian's indignation.

Oh yes, and you biting her out of the blue will do much to change her opinion, I'm sure.

Bane laid her ears back and snorted at Tsuga's assertion. The girl did laugh then, and Affaila shot her a withering look from where she stood rubbing her arm and cursing loudly at the animal.

"What the hell's so funny?"

Tsuga choked off her laughter and cleared her throat in an attempt to regain her composure. "She says she takes offense to your opinion of her."

Affaila was a bit unclear on what exactly had just happened. She'd been talking to Tsuga, then had noticed a hole in the road ahead of her and moved to avoid it. Then . . ..

Well, now she stood wincing and rubbing her left arm where the thrice-damned horse had decided for no reason whatsoever to take a bite out of her. It hurt, but the tears welling in her eyes were as much from anger as from the pain. And the blasted girl was *laughing* at her!

"What the hell's so funny?"

Tsuga choked on her laughter and tried to look abashed (she failed miserably, in Affaila's opinion).

"She says she takes offense to your opinion of her."

This caught Affaila's attention. After seeing the way the girl and horse interacted, Affaila had presumed Tsuga to have a very strong gift in animal mindspeech. A bit of a misnomer, that; animal mindspeakers could not actually carry on a conversation with beasts. Rather, it was a rudimentary form of communication in which the human must form his or her ideas into the primitive thought patterns of animals. The fact that Tsuga claimed the horse had actually spoken therefore rang false to the ears of the Devalian healer, who knew the ins and outs of such magic.

"What did you just say?"

You've really stepped in it now!

Tsuga didn't need her guardian's assessment to know that she had just made a potentially fatal mistake. She felt her blood suddenly run cold; it was a very good thing she was mounted, because her legs had turned to limp noodles that would never have been able to support her weight if she were walking.

Well no shit! What do I do?

Devilsbane was silent a moment before she responded.

Might as well tell her straight out. You already spilled the beans. We're in the middle of nowhere. If she tries anything, you can more than defend yourself, right?

I'm still pretty weak. And besides, I can't kill a healer! That's as good as putting a price on my head!

Oh, says the Sennorran girl who convinced the Devalian army she was a native boy!

Tsuga frowned. The horse had a valid point.

Fine.

She took a deep breath and turned her attention outward again. Although her conversation with Bane had seemed to take minutes, it had in fact lasted the space of a couple breaths. Affaila was still looking livid and rubbing her arm.

"Well?"

Okay, here goes . . ..

Tsuga slowed her breathing and surreptitiously released the throwing dagger sheathed on her right forearm, just in case.

You'll be fine.

She hoped her guardian was right.

"When I introduced myself before? Yeah, that was kind of only half the story."

Affaila raised an eyebrow, but said nothing. Tsuga plunged on before she could lose her nerve.

"My Da was Trag Dafrin, a Sennorran healer. And this 'dumb animal with more teeth than brains' is my spirit guardian, Devilsbane. I'm Sennorran."

Tsuga braced for the explosion. She expected rage, denial, shock, or death-threats. She was ready for anything. Anything . . . except a dead faint. As she watched, all semblance of color drained from the healer's face, her eyes rolled back in her head, and the redhead crumpled to the ground in a limp heap.

"Goddess' tits!"

Tsuga launched herself from the back of the horse and hurried to Affaila's side. She felt panic rise along with her breakfast to choke her, and forced herself to swallow it back down. She'd never been on this side of the situation; she was always the one who woke on the ground in confusion. Even now, she had the distinct sensation that this was backwards. But at least she knew what to do; she'd been woken so many times and in so many different ways that she had a well-stocked arsenal of methods to try.

Affaila woke to the feeling of something cool and wet being dabbed on her face. It was the way her mother had comforted her as a child when she wasn't feeling well, and for a brief, disorienting moment she wondered what her mother's spirit was doing out here in the wilderness. Then she opened her eyes and saw Tsuga bent over her, using a spare shirt dampened with water from their sparse supply to pat the face of the unconscious healer.

And that in itself was an oddity; Affaila's place was on the other side of this situation. Healers were supposed to be stoic, unflappable beings. Not that Affaila was particularly good at either of those . . .. She shook her head slightly to clear it and reached up to shove the wet rag away.

As she sat up, Affaila's world dipped disorientingly. In an effort to cover her reaction, she spoke.

"So you're Sennorran. I guess I shouldn't be surprised; you've dropped plenty of hints."

Her words seemed to irritate Tsuga, because the girl's jaw tightened visibly.

Although Tsuga no doubt suspected that she had fainted because of the revelation of the girl's nationality, Affaila knew this wasn't the case. It was not this knowledge, but the realization that Tsuga was indeed her younger sister that had stolen her consciousness from her. For Affaila knew the truth of her own birth, and though the clues Tsuga had given as to her heritage had been enough to rouse the healer's suspicions, the all-out declaration of Tsuga's parentage was undeniable proof. Affaila had been traveling for over a year in the company of a little sister she hadn't known existed! Even as she contemplated this, she felt her head swim again.

Unlike Tsuga, who seemed always to rouse in confusion and with a need for explanation, when Affaila woke, the healer acted as though she'd never skipped a beat. She calmly reached up to push aside Tsuga's attempt at help and sat up slowly and carefully.

"So you're Sennorran. I guess I shouldn't be surprised; you've dropped plenty of hints."

Indeed, this declaration confirmed it: Affaila was capable of losing consciousness and still retaining both memory and composure. It wasn't fair!

Tsuga reached out to catch the healer as she swayed again, allowing herself a brief moment to feel justified that Affaila had not recovered as quickly as it had first seemed. She immediately felt guilty, but as the older woman steadied, the girl forced both feelings aside.

"Take it easy. You're going to be pretty dizzy for a while. . .. I've fainted enough times to know."

Though Tsuga had been completely earnest in this declaration, Affaila smiled as though it had been a joke.

"I take it you've noticed the irony here too, huh?"

Tsuga blinked in surprise at this comment, and then, as though a dam had burst, all of the emotions she'd been holding back for so long rushed to the surface. She collapsed in a fit of giggles.

Affaila watched as the girl seemed to lose her mind in the space of a breath. One second she was making sure the healer wouldn't crumple to the ground, and the next she was rolling in the dry grass, giggling inanely. Affaila frowned and looked up at the horse. Even if it was one of those guardian-things, she still thought of the offensive animal as a dumb beast.

"Is she okay?"

The question was completely rhetorical, so she didn't expect an answer.

"She will be."

The horse's lips moved oddly as they formed human speech, and as Affaila's eyes rolled back in her head again, her last disjointed thought was that she'd never in her life seen such a bizarre sight.

Tsuga lay on the ground, gasping for breath. She could not for the world remember what had seemed so funny, but she'd been incapacitated by laughter long enough that her sides hurt and her throat was raw. As her breathing came under control she sat up to look around, absently wiping her face clean of the tears her laughter had produced. She spied Affaila sitting on the ground a little ways off, darting her green eyes back and forth between Tsuga and Devilsbane, who was standing well away from the redhead. The healer, seeing Tsuga sit up, peered at her dubiously.

"What?"

The green eyes narrowed at Tsuga's question. "Oh, nothing. I'm just trying to figure out which one of us is crazy here."

When Tsuga simply looked at her in confusion, Affaila explained.

"Your horse spoke to me."

Tsuga snorted. This was a common occurrence for her, and she would think that a Devalian would be used to mindspeech. She said as much, but Affaila shook her head adamantly.

"No, I mean she *talked* to me. Opened her mouth and *spoke*."

This was unusual for Bane, and not as common in general as mindspeech; now Tsuga could sympathize a bit more with the healer's reaction. It might have been a bit surreal, at that.

"Really? She's never done that before."

Tsuga looked to her guardian questioningly and Bane, blunt as always, offered an explanation.

"There was never any need before. We share a mind, after all."

Affaila gave a little panicked giggle, but quickly cut it off.

"A talking horse. I've never seen the like!"

This observation caused Tsuga to giggle a bit herself, but this time she managed to keep the impulse under control and recovered quickly. She stood and dusted the grass from her clothes and shook the dead blades from her closely-cropped hair.

"We should probably get going. It's early, and we can still get a lot of distance. That is, if you're up to it?"

Affaila was having trouble grasping all this. Oh, she'd half-suspected the girl's nationality for a while, but somehow she'd never considered that this meant her sister would have one of the demonic animal-things, let alone that it would be able to *talk*! The reality made her shudder. However, when Tsuga asked if she would be able to keep the pace they'd been setting for their travels, she came back to herself enough to bristle at the insult.

"Of course I'm up to it! I'm not the one that nearly killed myself incinerating my friends a couple of weeks ago!"

Tsuga recoiled at the comment, and Affaila immediately regretted the outburst. She knew better than to take out her feelings on other people. She hastened to apologize.

"I'm sorry. It's just . . . I'm supposed to be asking you that, not the other way around!"

Tsuga, who had been laughing uncontrollably mere minutes before, now seemed to have withdrawn into herself. She muttered a half-hearted "whatever," and mounted the biting demon. Affaila blew out a frustrated sigh.

Damn. She'd only just found out for certain that Tsuga was her sister, and now she'd gone and made the girl clam up, when what she really wanted was to put her at ease.

Oh lovely. Nice job, genius. Maybe those stories are true, and the damn thing's bite is turning me into a demon, too! Wouldn't that be just wonderful!

Shamed into silence, Affaila stood and walked over to the mule.

"Now don't you start talking, too," she muttered. The pack animal just stared at her blankly, and she let out another little nervous laugh as she reached out to take up its lead.

"Great, now I'm talking to animals! Maybe I *am* losing it!"

The two women traveled without speaking for the remainder of the day. At length, as the light was fading, Tsuga broke the oppressive silence.

"This looks like a good place to camp."

Affaila stopped the mule and looked around. There were no trees in sight – the Dubai Plains were flat and covered in tall grasses, with only the occasional stand of trees to break up the scenery. They stretched a hundred miles, marking the ambiguous physical border between Sennor and Devali. The plains had few water sources, and so one stretch of grass was as likely to become their campsite as another; there was nothing to sway a decision one way or the other. After turning a complete circle, Affaila shrugged.

"Good as any."

Tsuga nodded curtly and swung down from atop her massive guardian. Since she'd been able to start making herself useful again, Tsuga had been helping Affaila with the necessity of trampling a wide circle of the shoulder-high plains grass to the ground so that they could see. The mounts "helped" by eating a mouthful here and there, and before long the agreed-upon area of forty paces was cleared in all directions, forming a rough circle around the small party.

Being surrounded by dry grass, it was obviously unsafe to start a fire, lest they set the entire plain ablaze. The tiny fire Affaila had made that first day had been an exception – and besides, they hadn't been truly into the Plains at that point. Luckily, Affaila had planned for the direction of their escape and brought plenty of trail rations to sustain them. Now, as she pulled out enough of them for tonight's meal, Tsuga frowned at the nearly-empty pack.

"So about how much further do you think we have? We've got about four days of rations left, and then I guess I'll have to start hunting. Hope you like raw pheasants."

Affaila grimaced at the suggestion, but before she could say anything Devilsbane ambled over and joined the conversation.

"That won't be necessary. Another couple of days, maybe three tops, and we'll be about to Lord Gregory's lands."

Tsuga shuddered visibly, but Affaila was so busy *not* looking at Devilsbane that she didn't seem to notice the girl's reaction. She did, however, notice when Tsuga began wondering aloud about how to avoid the place.

"And how long would it take us to get to Castle Lyshe instead?"

She could remember as a young child being taken to that estate when her father went off to war with Gregory's men. It was the nearest castle under direct protection from the queen, and as such was the haven for the women and children of the surrounding holdings in times of war. It was also home to one of the largest groups of healers in the country. They would be safe there, and much less likely to run into any unpleasant memories.

"About a week."

Tsuga frowned, thinking about their depleted supplies.

"We're pretty close to the edge of the Plains, then. The hunting should improve, and I should be able to cook anything we catch magically, if I'm very careful. I think I'm recovered enough now to manage that much. If we go to two-thirds rations, that combination should be enough to get us to Lyshe."

Tsuga was suddenly very grateful for all the boring meetings she'd played page for. She knew the numbers and how to stretch supplies in hard times. Granted, she wasn't provisioning an army, but the same principles applied. Affaila, however, didn't understand the need for this detour.

"What's so great about this Castle Lyshe? The holding is closer!"

Tsuga frowned, shying away from the memory of her shame and the reason she had left.

"Lyshe is one of the Queen's Castles."

Affaila looked at her blankly, and it was only then that Tsuga recalled the Devalian wasn't familiar with Sennorran customs. She decided to explain.

"Devali's monarch is the king, right?"

She didn't need Affaila's nod for confirmation; those tactics meetings had taught her more about Devalian politics than all the Sennorran scholars knew put together, she was certain. It occurred to her that this knowledge made her highly valuable to the Sennorran crown, but she shied away from the idea of betraying her Devalian friends by exploiting such knowledge to make a place for herself. It was with a great effort that she wrenched her thoughts away from her last memory of her comrades and continued her explanation.

"Well, Sennor is ruled by a queen, in honor of the peaceful reign of Sennorra I. Her husband, if she takes one, is not king, but rather her royal consort. The theory behind this, of course, is that a child's mother is undeniable, while the patronage is often questionable. Inheritance in Sennor passes through the female line, and only when there are no women left of a bloodline do the men have any hopes of inheriting."

Affaila looked poleaxed by this information, but now Tsuga had the bit in her teeth and was ready to run. History and policy fascinated her, especially when it came to the differences in the two countries that had resulted from the breaking of the one great nation that had encompassed so much of the known world those many years ago.

"The Queen's Castles are all over Sennor, though there are more of them near the borders and along the coast than in the middle of the country. These castles are safe havens for women and children in times of disaster. If there's a battle, or a fire, or anything like that, the women and children can go to the nearest castle and find refuge. They also serve as kind of permanent healers' tents; there are always several healers in residence, and anyone who is gravely injured can seek their help.

"Now, when times are relatively peaceful the castles are mostly deserted. But we've been at war for so long that they've become more like schools. After all, with so many women in one place, there are all kinds of petty squabbles if they're not kept busy. Lyshe, since it's so close to the border, is one of the largest healers' compounds in Sennor. Some of our nation's best healers are there, and there are forever sick and wounded flocking there – and not just women. Lyshe is the only one of the Queen's Castles that caters to men as well, and so it is the best place to seek healing and refuge, or even just trade. You would be amazed at all of the unusual things people turn up with . . .. Anyway, what with you being a healer, you may even find you want to stay there a while."

Affaila listened to all of this in silence as she chewed her trail bar thoughtfully. Finally, when Tsuga ran out of things to say, she smiled.

"I must admit, it sounds wonderful. And I'm sure I could learn something from the healers there. My curiosity has been aroused. Castle Lyshe it is!"

Tsuga heaved a sigh of relief and allowed herself a small smile.

"Alright then, it's agreed! We make our way to Lyshe!"

Affaila wasn't truthfully as comfortable with this decision as she sounded. For one, what were the odds that the Sennorran healers would be willing to accept her? Granted, they would follow the healers' oath, just as she did, but could she really trust her life to their hands? She may well have just agreed to seek her own death.

For some reason, Tsuga seemed anxious to avoid the holding of this Lord Gregory, though she hadn't said why. That, too, struck Affaila as decidedly odd; Tsuga had just explained how only women held lands unless there were none of the bloodline left. Did that mean that Gregory had no living women in his family? It must. She wondered if the reason was natural or something far more sinister.

That night, she had trouble getting to sleep. Though she usually slept like the dead, tonight she lay awake watching the stars. She thought it odd that these were the same ones she'd grown up watching in Devali; perhaps the countries were not as different as she'd thought.

Affaila startled when she heard a gasp and a soft whimper. She sat upright to see what was going on. Tsuga was still asleep, eyes closed tightly, but the expression on her face was one of stark terror. As the healer moved closer and reached out to wake her, the girl began to mutter as her head rolled from side to side.

"On fire. They're burning. All burning. It's my fault. I killed them. My fault."

Affaila cringed away from the girl's huddled form, for she felt as though she'd been approaching a roaring blaze. When the temperature continued to rise, though, Affaila braced herself and reached out to grasp the sleeping girl's shoulder.

"Tsuga! Wake up!"

At the contact on her shoulder, the Sennorran girl roused and sucked in a ragged breath. Affaila quickly pulled her hand away with a gasp and sat staring at her burned palm. She did not fail to notice that the moment Tsuga woke, the intense heat vanished. The only evidence of the girl's night terrors, aside from her haunted expression, was the crippling burn on the redhead's hand.

"I'm sorry about your hand." It was at least the tenth time Tsuga had apologized, and though Affaila had already professed forgiveness to her as many times, she couldn't help feeling guilty still. "You really can't do anything about it?"

Affaila shook her head.

"No. Like I said; a healer can't heal herself. It just doesn't work like that. And don't worry, I'll be fine. It doesn't even hurt that much!"

Tsuga could see the lie in that every time Affaila's bandaged hand hit against her thigh as she walked, but she said nothing about the healer's obvious pain.

"Well, when we get to Lyshe, maybe they can help. Until then, you just tell me what you need and I'll take care of it, okay?"

Affaila shook her head in exasperation.

"I'm burned, not bedridden! I'm fine!"

Tsuga frowned. "I know, I'm sor–"

Affaila turned on her then, green eyes flashing in anger. "Don't you dare say 'I'm sorry!' I've had more than enough of that! It's not your fault it happened, and I don't blame you! *Stop apologizing!*"

Tsuga cringed away from this tirade, dropping her eyes to the ground and pointedly *not* looking at the angry woman. When Affaila ran out of steam, Tsuga glanced up and nodded.

"Okay, I get it. I'm sorry."

She hadn't even realized the words had left her mouth until Affaila let out a frustrated cry and threw her hands up as she turned and walked away. Devilsbane, who had become accustomed to Tsuga's night terrors (though not happy about them, of course) was finding this entire fiasco highly entertaining. When Affaila stormed off, the horse snorted a laugh and tossed her head.

Real smooth.

Tsuga just looked at her guardian sadly and shrugged.

"Sorry."

From the other side of camp, Tsuga heard another frustrated sigh. When she looked, Affaila was throwing things angrily into a pack with her unmolested hand. Bane snorted again.

The gates loomed before them, dark and intimidating – a full twenty feet in height and nearly as wide. Affaila craned her neck back to peer up towards the top of the walls, where she could see men standing guard. After what Tsuga had told her about Lyshe, Affaila found it hard to believe that able-bodied men would stay here long. As a healers' compound, the castle was all but immune from attack. Curious, she called on her healer's sight. She felt somewhat justified for her feelings then, because to her enhanced vision, every one of the men showed recent signs of healing. Some of them still weren't in top form. Indeed, of the two guards that approached the pair of travelers on the ground, one had a half-healed scar on his face and the other winced from a painful limp that looked new.

"State your names."

It was the scarred man who spoke. Affaila opted to answer first.

"I am Affaila Dafrin. A healer," she added, as though her green robes were not evidence enough. Then again, stained as she was with travel dust, perhaps the color was not as obvious as it should have been.

Tsuga shot her a suspicious look at the declaration of her name, but Affaila ignored her. When the girl only sat in sullen silence, the healer sighed and shook her head.

"And this is my sister, Tsuga Dafrin."

The guard dipped a bow to Affaila and gave the mounted girl a cursory nod before moving to open the smaller door set within the huge gates. Affaila led the mule inside, but Tsuga hesitated. The Devalian turned back to summon her, but the younger woman was peering at the gate thoughtfully. Finally, she turned to the guard to ask a question.

"Why are the gates closed? I used to come here all the time with my Da. They were never closed then."

The older guard – the one with the scarred face, who seemed to be the one doing all the talking – nodded.

"Indeed, they didn't used to be. But these are dark times. We found a party on the road a few weeks back, shot full of arrows. There were healers with them."

Affaila felt her blood run cold at this declaration, and as she looked to her hands where they clutched the mule's lead, she realized they shook violently. Over the sudden roaring in her ears, she faintly heard the rest of the conversation.

"Who shot them? Do you know?"

"The arrows had white fletching. Completely unmarked." Affaila shuddered. "We have no idea."

"Dark times indeed, if men are slaying healers."

Affaila swallowed convulsively, and then Tsuga was through the gates and they had swung closed behind them. Somehow Affaila found herself mounted on the immense horse in front of Tsuga, still shaking like a leaf in the wind. It was the last thing she clearly remembered for days.

Tsuga was beginning to realize just how much she needed routine. It was always the times of transition or chaos in which she felt the most out-of-sorts. For their first week in Castle Lyshe, she knew no one and had nothing to do save to keep an eye on Affaila. The older woman had been severely shaken by the news of the healers' murder; she hadn't spoken a word in all this time.

Lyshe was home to the world's best mindhealers, but even with these men and women at their disposal, Affaila did not recover the power of speech for six days. It was the morning of the seventh, while Tsuga was getting dressed (an ordeal that took much longer for her than her traveling companion because of the small arsenal of weapons she kept secreted on her body) that the healer roused.

"What kind of man would kill a healer?"

Tsuga spun around at the quiet words, startled. She brandished the small dagger she'd been preparing to tuck into the waistband of her breeches as though against an enemy, but when her mind caught up to her instincts she sheathed the weapon and placed it where it belonged, feeling sheepish.

Affaila lay stretched out on the bed, staring steadily at the ceiling above her as she spoke. Tsuga frowned and moved to sit on the bed beside her, where she could better gauge how her friend was doing.

"A stupid one. And desperate. Everyone knows the law."

"Then why? Why would anyone *do* that?"

Tsuga shrugged. "Maybe it's a new war tactic: weaken the enemy by taking away the ones who keep them hale and healthy. Or maybe it was an accident."

Affaila shifted her gaze to Tsuga's face and gave her a wry look.

"When they used unmarked arrows? I doubt it was an accident. Healers aren't *like* other mages. There's no reason for us to hide our identities. If anything, we flaunt our rank because of the protection it affords us. Those healers would have been identifiable from miles off. Whoever shot them knew exactly what they were doing."

Tsuga sighed. "I know."

Affaila was silent for so long then that Tsuga finally gave up and rose to finish getting dressed. She was buckling on her sword when the healer spoke again.

"How long was I out of it?"

Tsuga turned back to face her at the question. The woman was now sitting up, and the combination of her wild red hair and pale skin made her look like a sprite as she stretched and stood up.

"About a week."

Affaila nodded thoughtfully at this, not seeming surprised, and looked around in confusion.

"Where are my clothes?"

Tsuga moved to the trunk at the foot of the bed and opened it to reveal their neatly-stowed packs. Affaila smiled and moved to find hers so that she, too, could dress in something fresh for the day. Tsuga politely turned her back.

"So, this is Castle Lyshe? I want the grand tour!"

Affaila still hadn't quite managed to recover from the news of the healers' murder, but at least now she could function. She was still haunted by nightmares of evil men killing her collegues. Who ever heard of such a thing? Why would anyone seek to murder the world's most benign mages? Such questions raced through her mind constantly, but she was now able to ignore them – at least for the most part.

When she had first roused, she'd been desperate to find work or amusement – anything to take her mind off of worries she could do nothing about. Now, largely sleep-deprived, the load she'd taken on was beginning to pull on her and wear her patience thin. This was why, when Tsuga confronted her one night about the introductions she'd made when they'd first arrived, tact was not the first thing on her mind.

"You know," Tsuga began, "I've been meaning to ask you something."

"Hmm?"

As a healer, Affaila had been easily accepted at the castle and promptly given her own work to do to help out. She had been somewhat surprised at first, but had settled into the routine of things gratefully. Now, she walked among the beds of her patients, tending to their afflictions. Those who came here often did so with week- or month-old wounds, many of which had long since festered. Some were only poorly healed. Still others ventured here for things such as leprosy or consumption of the lungs. Although a fair number of the patients suffered from immediately life-threatening ailments, most of them were things that would take a person slowly, rather than bleed him dry in a matter of minutes.

This resulted in an oddly relaxed, clinical atmosphere throughout the castle, and so Affaila was able to move sedately from the man with the broken leg that had set wrong to the woman pregnant with triplets as she spoke with her traveling companion.

"When we first got to the castle, and you introduced us? Why did you lie? You're a healer; you didn't need any more protection than that. At least, not from these people. So why do it?"

Affaila laid her hands on the pregnant woman's belly and checked her briefly to see how she was doing. All five sparks of life (for she was Sennorran, after all, and so held the life of her guardian in the balance as well as those of herself and her unborn children) were pulsating slightly, indicating a state of general well-being. Affaila gave the woman an encouraging smile and a nod of approval before moving on.

"I didn't lie."

Tsuga frowned and moved around the bed to follow her to the next patient.

"When you called yourself my sister and claimed my last name, that was a lie!"

Affaila sighed and shook her head when she saw that the man in this bed would not survive the night, despite her best efforts. All she could offer now was to ease his pain while he waited for death to come and find him.

"Keep your voice down. You're in a hospital!"

That word had been completely foreign to her a month ago, but after hearing Lyshe referred to as one so frequently, the term now slid off her tongue with ease. Tsuga grimaced, and the healer's expression softened.

"I told you, Tsuga; I wasn't lying."

The girl opened her mouth as though to protest, and Affaila held up a hand to forestall her. "We will not discuss this here. Come with me to my room, and I'll explain."

Tsuga followed the healer in sullen silence. Because Affaila had to be close to her patients, she had been given a room on the ground floor of the castle, just a short walk away from "her" ward, which was full of her personal charges. Tsuga had been given her own small room several stories up in one of the towers, but other than the view, there was little difference between the two. Tsuga turned to face Affaila once she was inside, and the healer closed the door gently before she did the same.

"Well?"

Tsuga had never been particularly patient, and her ire at Affaila's lie was not helping matters any. The healer sighed and moved to grasp Tsuga's hand so that she could pull the girl to sit on the bed with her.

"I told you, I didn't lie. My name *is* Affaila Dafrin. We're sisters. Well, half, at least."

Tsuga was already shaking her head in denial, a frown set stubbornly upon her face. "Even if I believed that, a name doesn't mean anything! Dafrin is a common enough name in Sennor, and I guess there could be some in Devali, too. That doesn't make us sisters!"

Affaila nodded, fighting to keep herself calm.

"You're right. There are many Dafrins in the world, and plenty of them are men. But how many could claim to be Healer Trag Dafrin of Sennor?" Tsuga felt her blood run cold. She'd never told Affaila her father's name.

"How could you know that? How could you possibly know that's who my Da was?"

Affaila smiled slightly. "Because he was my father, too. He never even knew about me, but he *was* my father."

Tsuga shook her head in adamant denial.

"No. That's not possible. Da was only ever with my mother. There wasn't ever any other woman." Affaila shook her head slowly with a sad smile.

"Tsuga, think about it. He was a man, after all. And before that, he was a boy, just like any other. Children don't *only* result from a union blessed by the gods. You're sixteen, right?"

She didn't wait for Tsuga's slow nod before she continued.

"Well, I'm twenty-one. Five years older than you. Our father knew my mother long before he met yours. He even loved her – or so he told her. But he was a healer, and a Sennorran besides. He left to see to his duties before he even knew she was pregnant with me. We *are* sisters, Tsuga, whether you want to believe it or not!"

Tsuga watched the world tilt distractingly as Affaila's last declaration registered. Try as she might to deny it, Tsuga had a sinking feeling that it was the simple truth; the older woman was, after all, her sister. Though their cultures were worlds apart and their nations at war, somehow the two had still managed to find each other. They'd even become friends, despite the twisted web of lies and deceit that separated them.

Her vision blurred, and Tsuga blinked rapidly. She felt hot tears rolling down her face, and then found herself gathered in Affaila's arms. Wrapped in the comfort of a sympathetic embrace, she sobbed noisily into the healer's shoulder.

When Tsuga started to cry, Affaila reached forward to gather the girl in her arms and cradled the young warrior as she sobbed brokenly. She had already come to terms with the emotions brought on by this discovery, but Tsuga's tears struck her deeply, and the healer soon found herself crying softly even as she offered comfort to the sister she'd never known. They stayed this way for an indeterminable amount of time until at last Tsuga pulled away and dried her eyes on her sleeve.

The only clothes Tsuga had been left with that weren't Devalian uniforms were the ones the army had found her in. After being worn for the entire journey between the two countries, the garments were more thread-bare than ever – and now too small, besides; Tsuga had grown several inches in the past two years. When they'd arrived at Lyshe, just as winter's grip began to tighten on the land, Tsuga had been forced to seek replacements.

Unfortunately, since everyone at the castle was essentially either a healer or a patient, and because Tsuga insisted on wearing men's clothing, she had been forced to accept the clothes of a deceased soldier who had been decently close to her size. As a result, her pants were barely held up by her sword belt and the sleeves of her tunic were rolled up several times so that her hands were free. The shirt was baggy and had stretched nearly to her knees before she'd cut off more than a foot from the bottom, leaving it with a shabby-looking hem where she'd attempted to stitch it.

If she'd been a better seamstress, she might have been able to alter the clothes to fit, but as it was she looked like a child playing dress-up with her Da's uniforms. At least these clothes were Sennorran, and though the stripes of ranking had been removed along with the stitching that denoted the Sennorran army, the colors and cut were still unmistakable. From a distance, she may have even passed as a native soldier. From a distance, and to someone with a very poor set of eyes . . ..

Affaila smiled at the image her sister presented, wiping her own tears away with the green hem of her skirts as she spoke.

"You know, we should really do something about finding you some more suitable clothes. I'd be happy to take those in for you a bit so that they'd fit better."

Tsuga glanced down at her outfit and laughed with a shake of her head. She'd forgotten just how silly she looked in this getup.

"That would be great."

She moved back from Affaila a bit to stand further away and smiled, a slightly wistful expression on her face.

"So, it's true? We're sisters?" Affaila's nod caused the younger girl to laugh again. "By the Bitch! Who'd have thought?"

Affaila looked surprised for a moment, and then a smile crept over her face. Soon, the two women were giggling together like a pair of young girls.

"Again?"

Affaila felt her blood run cold. The healer delivering this news was a shorter, wide-set man of middling years whose face was still flushed from his hurried walk to Affaila's small suite of rooms where she tended her patients. Affaila, on the other hand, was pale and shaking, utterly shocked by this announcement. The man nodded, his jowls wobbling.

"No sign of a struggle this time, though. They were traveling with a sizeable portion of the army. A good thousand or more armed men. Found 'em in the morning when they broke camp. Their guards were chopped across the middle, lying in pieces. The healers were just . . . gone. Looked for all the world like they'd gotten up and walked off. Except there were no footprints or anything."

Affaila shuddered. "And they've been found?"

Now the healer paled, leaving two bright spots of color on his cheeks.

"Only one. He was sliced open from sternum to pelvis, and his entrails were strung out in a wide circle."

Affaila staggered at this news as though under the force of a physical blow, but the man wasn't finished yet.

"They couldn't find the heart."

Affaila's breathing grew shallow and the world began to shrink, and then to expand wildly. She found herself shaking, and managed to aim her fall as her knees gave out so that she sat heavily on the edge of a bed. Though the other healer stayed until he was sure she wasn't going to lose consciousness, Affaila didn't notice. She also couldn't stop shaking for the better part of the evening, even after he finally left her to grapple with the myriad emotions the news of this newest attack had aroused.

In the months that followed this first grisly discovery, the reports began to come with increasing frequency. The states in which the healers were discovered varied, but always there was a missing organ. The first had lost his heart. Others were found without eyes, tongues, or ears. One was left to bleed to death from the hole where his stomach had been. The possibilities of what might be happening to these stolen body parts were sickening, and as the reports became more common, the mental state of the healers living in Lyshe became increasingly worse.

The men and women who lived and worked in the castle had always led a much less strenuous life than those healers who traveled with the armies. Their eyes were seldom ringed with the dark circles showing a lack of sleep, their skins always sported a healthy glow, and their faces were seldom lined with excessive worry or fatigue. This was no longer the case.

The strain of losing so many colleagues was beginning to take a toll on the surviving healers. They wandered the hallways as though lost, moving as silently as green-clad ghosts. The soothing words and comforting smiles they gave their patients now seemed less sincere, more forced. People whose lives were spent admonishing others for not taking care of themselves and warning them to eat and sleep sufficiently were now missing meals and avoiding sleep for fear of the nightmares it would bring.

Affaila was no exception to this rule, and her sister's deteriorating health was beginning to worry Tsuga. Finally, when the healer fell asleep over a quiet shared meal one afternoon, the younger girl decided it was time to confront her. She waited until one evening after the dishes from dinner had been cleared to raise the issue.

"You look horrible."

Affaila blinked at the bluntness of this statement and attempted to clear her fatigue-muddled thoughts. The insult should have irritated her, or at the very least inspired a sarcastic comment in response, but somehow Affaila couldn't muster either. She sighed heavily and leaned against the rigid back of her chair as though unable to hold herself erect any longer.

"I know. But what do you expect?"

Tsuga shook her head. "Fair enough. But I'm worried about you, Affaila. You're not sleeping, and I haven't seen you eat more than a few bites at any meal in weeks. You need to deal with this, or at least talk about it."

Affaila's eyes strayed from her sister's face as Tsuga spoke and focused instead on a swirling pattern in the wood of her small table. At the encouragement to face her fears, the healer shuddered and shook her head adamantly.

"I don't think I can."

Tsuga sighed and pushed her chair back from the table so that she could come around to gather the redhead in her arms, murmuring words of senseless comfort. Affaila pushed away in irritation – the first show of spirit she'd managed for days – but she was unable to keep her hands from shaking as she did. She wanted nothing more than to let Tsuga hold her as she wept out the tears of fear and mourning that seemed to be choking off her air. But she wouldn't. She couldn't. She was a healer, and as such she had to be strong. Besides, how would it look if she cried like a baby while her little sister offered comfort? No, she would swallow her emotions and go on as she had been, putting up a front to protect her image as an unflappable healer. Tsuga, however, didn't seem willing to let her push her feelings aside.

"Come on now, you'd never let me get away with saying 'I can't.' Of course you can deal with this. You have to. Affaila, look at yourself! If you keep living like this you're going to waste away!" Her tone changed, becoming softer and less frantic. "What are you so afraid of? I know it's not your mortality; you'd never have traveled with the army if that was an issue. So what is it?"

Affaila frowned, irritated at the question. Was she so transparent? When Tsuga only looked at her expectantly, face showing pity and concern, Affaila felt her irritation, along with her resolve, melt away.

It seemed that when she was around Affaila, Tsuga inevitably ended up in situations that made her decidedly uncomfortable. This one was no exception; when Affaila dissolved into tears and Tsuga rushed forward to gather her in her arms and offer comfort like a mother soothing her child, she had the distinct feeling of being out of place. She couldn't remember a situation like this in all her life, except for her time with Tau. Even then, Tsuga had been on the receiving end of offered comfort, not the one giving it. That woman had been the closest thing to a mother Tsuga had ever known. She still felt guilty for running off and leaving the kind widow with a squalling baby.

Affaila said something, but with her face pressed into Tsuga's shoulder her words were too muffled to understand. Tsuga merely shushed her before helping her stand and move to the bed so that she could sit more comfortably. The healer didn't even pause in her outburst.

In the sane corner of her mind, Affaila cursed herself for this loss of control. She was supposed to be the strong one; the rock, the unshakeable pillar. Yet here she was, unable to hold back her tears. After a few more minutes of helpless sobbing, this small, coherent part of her began to assert control once again. It didn't seem right for her to keep Tsuga here at Lyshe any longer; it was not safe for a healer on the roads any more, and she could see the hospital becoming a prime target for the attackers. She pushed the girl away gently as she reached this decision and gathered herself for the argument she knew it would ignite.

"You have to go."

Tsuga shook her head and pulled Affaila back into her embrace, stroking her hair comfortingly. The healer tried to choke back her sobs, but only succeeded in hiccoughing uncomfortably. She pulled away from the Sennorran and tried again to speak.

"You have to go."

Her words came out between sobs, but at least this time they came out. Tsuga just smiled and continued to shake her head.

"No, I don't. It's okay for once in your life to focus on yourself."

Affaila shook her head and dabbed at her eyes, still trying to control her outburst. "That's . . . not what I meant. Tsu, it's not safe to be a healer anymore. That's not going to stop any of us, but there's no reason for you to put yourself in danger."

Affaila was still crying, but she at least managed to quiet her sobs – for the most part.

Tsuga listened to her sister's explanation quietly until she had finished. Affaila did have a good point; it wouldn't be safe to be a healer on the road, and none of them were likely to hole up or travel in disguise. Healers were a notoriously proud and stubborn group. But that was all the more reason for the two women to stay together; splitting up made no sense at all. Tsuga shook her head firmly.

"You're hysterical. Why don't you just lie down and try to get some sleep? We can talk about this more when you wake up, okay?"

She stood up from the bed and turned down the covers, expecting the healer to yield to common sense and lay down. But Affaila didn't budge. She frowned and shook her head adamantly.

"I am not hysterical! And don't tell me what to do; you are *not* my mother!"

Tsuga groaned to herself.

"No, but I am your sister. And your friend. And I refuse to talk about this any more until you've gotten some rest!"

Affaila stood and planted her hands on her hips, face contorted into an expression of righteous indignation.

"You can't bully me into bed!"

Tsuga shook her head, frustrated with the healer's stubbornness. *I guess we really* are *related,* she mused.

"Fine. Then come find me after you've had a nap!" She spun on her heel and started for the door.

"Just where do you think you're going? This isn't going to just go away!"

Tsuga paused, doorknob in hand, and allowed herself a tight smile as she looked over her shoulder at Affaila.

"Well, that's good. That means it will still be here when you wake up!"

That said, she turned back around, walked out, and closed the door firmly behind her.

Affaila stood and glared at the closed door for a long moment, her green eyes sparking in anger. She kept expecting Tsuga to come back, but after several minutes she heaved a sigh and gave up waiting. She turned her back on the door and walked across the room to her bed, where she sat down with another exhalation of frustration. She *was* very tired, but any attempts at sleep lately had ended with her waking to her own screams in the middle of the night. Tsuga couldn't possibly understand what it was like to be afraid to close your eyes because of what you might see.

Affaila reached up a hand to stifle a yawn, and as she lowered it again found herself thinking that perhaps this time, with bright sunlight streaming in through her small window, it might be different.

She woke in a cold sweat, throat raw from screaming. The image of herself disembowled and hanging from a tree with blood streaming down her face seemed to hover in the air in front of her, and she felt herself shaking uncontrollably. The room was dark – while she'd slept, the day had faded into night. She had no idea what time it was, but there was no way she'd be able to get back to sleep after such a nightmare. Affaila threw back the covers – and how had she gotten covered? She certainly didn't remember that – and stood. The image of her death still hung in her thoughts, so she exited her room and headed outside in the hopes that she could dispel her horror in the cool night air.

The courtyard of Lyshe was well manicured; the snow was shoveled from the grounds, and though the traffic of many boots had churned the frozen earth to soup, the cobbles here allowed for slightly less difficult – though still slippery – footing. The healer stumbled slightly as the chill began to numb her feet. In her haste, she had forgotten to don anything sturdier than the slippers she wore in the hospital, let alone a cloak. Cold began to find its way in through the seams of her robes as she walked, but she was unwilling to retreat back into the warmth indoors just yet.

The sound of metal hitting stone caught her attention, and Affaila's eyes shot to where the sound had come from. At this time of night she had expected to be alone on her walk, but to her dismay there was a shadowy figure kneeling on the ground not a hundred paces from her. She looked about quickly for somewhere to hide from sight, but found nothing. Not wanting to be seen, she shrunk back into the shadows, praying for the darkness to shield her.

The figure was breathing heavily, and the soft moonlight glinted off the metal of a sword a few paces away. Affaila watched as the man – for surely someone so tall and honed by war could be nothing but – stood and retrieved his weapon. Moments later, he was dancing the forms again as Affaila looked on silently.

I know this person, she thought disjointedly. The movements were familiar, the way he danced out of the way of an imaginary blade and cut forward with an attack of his own almost in the same movement. But of course that wasn't possible. The only people she'd ever seen dance the forms were Devalian soldiers – most of whom were a hundred or more miles away, nestled snug in their bedrolls far from here. The few who *were* within the walls of the castle, she knew to be bedridden.

In the darkness, the patch of ice must have been hard to see: it caught the fighter unawares, and he sprawled onto the cold rock once more. Affaila winced, but the fighter didn't even cry out. Indeed, he did not so much as move beyond an almost imperceptible shaking of his shoulders. It was with no small surprise that Affaila realized he was sobbing onto the frozen ground.

Now less inclined than ever to intrude on what she was sure was meant to be a private moment, the healer stepped carefully backwards until she felt she was a safe distance away. Then, she turned and fled for the comfort of her work and the tentative peace that came from worrying over the problems of others, rather than agonizing over her own.

The day dawned warm and sunny. The wet season was all but ended, and the world was the lush green of a spring after months of rain. As usual, Tsuga had risen well before the sun to get in her morning workout. Since she was in a hospital, there really wasn't anyone to spar against, and dancing the forms alone grew to be a bit too routine after a certain point.

This morning, she had settled for an early run. The opportunity to view the world waking from its slumber was one she enjoyed, even in the pre-dawn shadows that hid the truly wondrous sights she now beheld as she walked back through the gates of Lyshe. Her shirt stuck to her back from sweat, but as the light caught the beads of dew and made the grass around her sparkle like a field of emeralds, she couldn't help but smile.

"Affaila?"

Tsuga swung open the healer's door and poked her head into the room before she entered fully. There was no answer, so she stepped further into the chamber and looked around. The healer was nowhere to be found, but as Tsuga examined the small space, she sensed something distinctly off.

Her sister had become somewhat notorious around Lyshe for her poor housekeeping; her bed was seldom made, and her room was always littered with various medicinals, bandages in various states of cleanliness and rolling, and other such paraphanalia. As Tsuga looked now, she saw a bed made with military precision, all of the potions bottled and tidily organized, and bandages that had all been rolled and stored away. The room was spotless – much like Tsuga's own – but the healer was not inside it. Tsuga shook her head in consternation and left, careful to close the door behind her to block out the eerie sight.

She felt fairly certain that she would find her sister in her ward, once again buried in her work. Sure enough, Tsuga found the older woman tending patients. Curious, she turned to one of the closest occupied beds. It was filled by a young man who was sitting up and looked to be in fine health – so long as one ignored his utter lack of a leg below the left knee. She moved to stand beside him and pitched her voice low in the hopes that Affaila would not notice her just yet.

"How long has she been here?"

The man followed her gaze and shook his head with a frown. He was a handsome young soldier, and had Tsuga had any inclination to pursue a bedmate, this dark haired, blue-eyed man would definitely have been worth a second look. He'd even tried to capture her fancy a few times, until Tsuga had grown frustrated with his advances and informed him in no uncertain terms that she was not interested. She'd rather spar a man than kiss one, and did not hesitate to point this out when approached. This particular young man – Roland, she thought his name was – hadn't seemed put off at all. In fact, he'd only set to pursuing her all the more eagerly.

"Hours. Pains in my leg woke me up in the middle of the night, and she was down here checking on us. She's made the rounds three times already. If she asks how my leg's feeling again, I may have to kick her!"

Tsuga turned to look at him in surprise. It never ceased to amaze her how a man whose life had been so drastically altered could have such high spirits. Roland laughed at her expression; the sound must have caught Affaila's attention, for a moment later a hand closed over Tsuga's shoulder and the healer's familiar voice came from behind her.

"So, Roland, how's the leg feeling?"

Tsuga hid a grin behind her hand and tried to cover her snort with a cough as the man adopted a sincere expression.

"Well, it feels great! My left one itches something terrible, though."

Affaila rolled her eyes and smiled at him kindly.

"Very funny. The itching means the wound's healing properly. Try not to scratch it, and I'll bring you a salve that will help with that."

He nodded, and when the healer looked away, he caught Tsuga's eyes and made a face. The girl laughed – until Affaila turned back around and she was able to have her first good sight of the woman.

She looked positively awful. There were dark circles under her eyes, which were bloodshot from lack of sleep. She was more pale even than usual, and had a haunted, haggard look to her that Tsuga had never seen before. They'd received news recently of yet another group of healers found slaughtered, and obviously Affaila had taken it pretty hard.

"Affaila? Are you okay?"

The healer turned to look at her, head tilted to the side, and smiled brightly.

"Of course; I'm fine! Why do you ask?"

Something about the tone of voice she used triggered an alarm in Tsuga's head, but she did her best to pretend she was convinced.

"Well, good! Do you have a few minutes? There's something I want to talk to you about."

The healer's eyes widened, and her gaze darted frantically around the room as she sought an escape. Seeing none, she stiffened her spine and looked pointedly away from Tsuga.

"For you? Of course. Come on – we can speak in my room."

Affaila opened the door to her room and gestured for Tsuga to enter ahead of her. Once both girls were inside, Affaila closed the door behind herself and stood facing it, trying to postpone the inevitable as long as possible. She could hear Tsuga moving about behind her, and then the clink of glass bottles as the younger woman rifled through her carefully-organized potions. The girl's tone was nonchalant when she finally spoke.

"This is a switch. Since when is it possible to see the floor in here? And I don't recall your potions ever being bottled before, let alone labeled or organized."

There was the sound of heavy boots moving across the floor, and then a hand was placed on her shoulder. Affaila shrugged it off and turned to walk across the room to her vials, checking through them to be sure Tsuga hadn't moved any. There was a sigh from behind her, and then silence.

Finally, unable to use the medicinals as an excuse any longer, Affaila turned to face her sister. The look of concern in Tsuga's brown eyes made her tremble; before she knew what was happening, the words came spilling out of her.

"I can't sleep, Tsu. The dreams are just so horrible! Sometimes they're my friends, but mostly it's me. And . . . I can't stand it anymore! I shouldn't be afraid to be a healer! I shouldn't flinch away from using my magic to help people!"

Tsuga crossed the room quickly to sweep her sister up into her arms and held here there while the healer continued to shake.

"It's natural to be afraid. It's okay."

Affaila shook her head adamantly. "No. Not for a healer. If healers were to show fear, do you have any idea what kind of panic that would cause in our patients?!"

Tsuga didn't dismiss this concern out of hand, like she'd half expected her to, but actually took a moment to consider it.

"Being a healer doesn't mean you can't be human, you know. I get that your patients might worry if you're not calm, but they worry more to see you in this state. They know what's going on. Light, Affaila, you're in the injury ward; your patients are mostly soldiers. Those men and women were prepared to die for their queen. They still are. They know that even if you patch them up good as new, they'll just end up hurt again – or dead. It's not their mortality they're worried about. They're more worried about you than themselves. Ask any of them. You have to take care of yourself, and part of that is letting yourself be human – and not trying to fight it."

The irony of this little speech distracted Affaila for a moment, and she barked out a laugh.

"Oh, and you're one to talk about accepting who you are!"

She pulled angrily out of Tsuga's embrace. The girl let her go. Affaila turned her back on her sister again and walked over to her bed. She tugged slightly at the covers to create a wrinkle, and then spent an undue amount of time smoothing it out again. Tsuga sighed, but though Affaila expected a retort, she ignored the barb completely.

"I've been thinking about what you said – about how it's not safe for me here."

This caught Affaila's attention, and the healer turned to face her sister with a frown, dreading what she knew must come.

"It's really not, Tsu. Not with people attacking healers on the road. Lyshe is a huge target now – it's only a matter of time before they strike at us directly. I think it's best that you leave."

"I agree."

Affaila felt the blood drain from her face at Tsuga's prompt answer. Yes, she wanted her sister safe, but never in her wildest dreams had she imagined that the girl would agree to it at all, let alone so easily. She hadn't realized until now just how much she had been counting on Tsuga's stubborn determination to stay by her side to prevent her sister from leaving. She was a bit taken aback, and it took several long moments before she was able to finally manage speech.

"Well, good." She walked over to the shelf holding her newly-organized potions and started pulling things down. "You'll want this one to extract poisons – from plants, or arrows, or just about anything. And this yellowish one here will help pull soreness out of muscles. The blue one will speed healing, and –"

"Affaila? I didn't say I was going alone."

"Oh, I know – you'll have Devilsbane, of course. But she can't protect you from everything, and last I heard horses still can't heal. So I think it's best if you take just a few of these to–"

She stopped when she felt Tsuga's hand on her shoulder, freezing in the middle of grabbing another bottle.

"Listen. I've been thinking a lot about this, and – would you *look* at me? There, that's better. I've been thinking, and I agree that it's not safe here anymore. For *you*." Tsuga emphasized this point by giving her a little shake. "So, *we're* leaving."

Affaila tensed and immediately began rattling off reasons this could never work.

"I can't just leave my patients –"

"There are plenty of other healers here to pick up your slack. They managed fine before you got here, and they'll do just fine after we're gone."

"Well, yes, but this isn't Devali! I'll stick out like a –"

"I've got it covered."

"How could you possibly –"

Tsuga gave the shoulder she held a firm squeeze. "I lived two years in the midst of the Devalian military with no one the wiser. I think I can sneak one woman past the Sennorran country folk."

"Well, but –"

"I'm not leaving unless you come with me. Period."

I don't see why I have to do this.

Why are you complaining? I'm the one that has to play translator!

Tsuga laughed at hearing Bane's side of the conversation and shook her head.

"You're the one that insists you could never pass as a Sennorran. So, we'll see how you do at being my guardian."

But you're *her guardian!*

There was a slight delay as Devilsbane relayed this message before Tsuga turned from cinching up the horse's saddle and faced the man-sized marsupial covered in red fur that was strikingly similar to the color of Affaila's unruly mane.

"She's a common-enough seeming beast. But how am I supposed to pass off a giant jumping rat as anything but my guardian?"

Affaila didn't answer – or at least, Bane didn't convey anything she might have said – so the girl turned back to packing their belongings onto the horse.

"Besides, this is just until the healers stop disappearing off the roads."

And who knows when that will be?

Tsuga sighed and shook her head without turning around. "I know it goes against the grain to just sit back and do nothing, but maybe this is the only way. There has to be a reason for this; Auriga is more merciful than Ketral by far. She wouldn't let this happen if she didn't have a good reason."

Affaila-the-rat snorted, and Tsuga laughed.

Your faith astounds me.

"What?"

I was never a big believer in the God – or the Goddess, for that matter.

"Then how do you explain the Devalians and their abilities?"

Easy. Years of inbreeding has resulted in everyone having similar attributes.

"Okay, then what about the guardians? Are they inbred, too?"

Affaila looked as though she were about to retort – but, upon remembering Devilsbane's sharp bite, she thought better of it.

Fine. We have no control over our destinies. We are the playthings of the Gods. Is that what you want to hear?

"Now, I can't say I agree with that, either. I think we make our own paths; the Goddess presents us with choices, and what we choose decides who we will be."

Whatever. Just hurry up, would you?

"What hurry? I'm done!" As she spoke, Tsuga swung up into the saddle with practiced ease and grinned down at her furry sister. "C'mon, let's go!"

So . . . where exactly are we going?

"Nowhere. Everywhere. Who knows?"

You mean to tell me you have no idea what you're doing?

Affaila halted her odd hopping gait, which forced Tsuga to halt Bane as well. Tsuga twisted in the saddle to look at the animal that had taken the place of her sister.

"Oh, come on! I'm a soldier."

That murdered her countrymen.

Tsuga wilted a little at that. Quick to contradict a thought that haunted her nights already, she hastily rattled off the retort she used against her nightmares.

"It's no different than one Lord's men murdering another's I didn't do anything wrong! In fact, I'll probably be welcomed as an expert in Devalian tactics and fighting styles!"

And are you confident enough in your welcome to travel to the capital and tell the king –

"Queen."

– Queen the whole story? Tsuga winced, and after a moment managed to respond.

"No."

Satisfied that she had made her point, Affaila set off again in her bouncy progress, leaving Tsuga and her real guardian to play catch-up.

So?

"So, what?"

Where are we going?

"This looks like as good a place as any for a test run, huh?" Tsuga sat atop Bane in the dim light of the setting sun, squinting to make out the picture on the sign in the fading light. There were no words, only the faded image of a dragon guarding her gold. Thus, Tsuga took the name of the place to be "The Wyrm's Hoard," or something of the sort. The light and laughter pouring out of the open doorway seemed inviting enough. Affaila hopped a little closer to the door and took an appreciative sniff.

I wish I could eat meat.

"Why can't you?"

The possibility caught Tsuga off-guard, and she forgot to have the question translated through Bane. Not that it much mattered; they were in Sennor now, after all. No one would think twice about hearing only half of a conversation.

My shift form is an herbivore.

"Oh . . . ."

It means I can only eat plants. I can't digest meat at all.

"I know what an herbivore is!"

Now . . ..

"You could always –"

No! I can't! You know that.

"Fine." Tsuga swung her right leg over Devilsbane's back and slid to the ground in one fluid, well-practiced motion. "Are you coming inside?"

I don't think I should –

Go. Two sets of ears are better than one. And you'll be able to hear the guardians. That's a definite plus.

Fine.

Affaila shot Bane a nasty look as a stable boy hurried over to take the horse into the barn.

"You take good care of her, lad; she deserves it."

Damn right I do!

"Oh, yessir!" The boy was gone before his words registered, and Tsuga was left to laugh at the misunderstanding.

Does everyone mistake you for a boy?

"Apparently. Come on, we'll get you a nice salad. Me, I think I'm going to have a big bowl of whatever's making that delicious smell!"

Affaila leaned back on her tail and aimed a playful kick at Tsuga's back, but the girl managed to dodge, laughing at the effort.

"Come on!"

Rather than spend more of their precious coin on a bed, Tsuga opted to spend her night in the stable with Bane. The stalls were large and roomy, and her guardian made for a good watchdog.

Affaila curled up in a back corner of the straw-lined stall while Tsuga positioned herself along one wall, feet towards the door – just in case anything did manage to get past the horse. Affaila watched the girl say goodnight to the demon-horse and tried not to acknowledge the pang of loneliness it caused.

It's a common enough thing, you know.

What is?

Wanting a guardian. Devalians that take the time to understand the bond often find themselves yearning for something similar.

What, a demon-beast to nag me all the time? No thanks! There was silence from the horse. When Affaila finally got up the nerve to sneak a peek towards the front of the stall where Bane stood, she saw the dim light reflected off of one large brown eye. She held the animal's stare for a moment before looking away in shame. She couldn't possibly want such a dysfunctional relationship . . . could she?

That night, she dreamt:

Affaila knelt in a puddle of blood. She had the distinct feeling that she was waiting for something to happen, though she had no idea what. She wasn't sure how long she remained there, hands folded in her lap and eyes fixed on the dark pool of liquid sitting atop the saturated earth. Gradually, she realized that she was crying, although she could put no words to the aching loss she felt.

"She is with you still."

The redhead startled and looked up. Before she could ask who, the sight of the creature before her stole her breath. Mere inches away sat the most immense wolf she had ever seen. From her position on her knees, the beast's head towered a foot or more above her own as it stared at her with unblinking golden eyes that seemed almost to glow in the darkness. The animal was completely black aside from those frightful eyes, and as her imminent danger registered, Affaila yelped and backed away awkwardly. The wolf lowered its head with a slight whine. The voice came again.

"She will guide your hand in this."

The words resonated within her soul, and Affaila's green eyes popped as she realized that the voice came from the enormous beast before her.

"Wha– who are you?" The wolf bared her teeth – for the voice had been decidedly feminine – and the healer cringed at the thought of what those powerful jaws could do.

"I am –"

"Affaila, wake up!"

Startled out of sleep, Affaila thrashed about, still expecting to find herself in human form. As the dream faded and she remembered where she was, the panic drained from her mind and reality settled in. The weak light of pre-dawn lit the stable, and the healer had to wait for her inhuman eyes to adjust before she could make out the features of her sister, who stood over her with an impatient posture.

"Come on! We have to get a move on if you want to eat before we go!"

Oh, right.

Affaila shook herself and rose to her full height, stretching out her sleep-cramped muscles.

"You okay? You seem kind of out of it."

Hmm? Oh. Yeah, I'm fine. I just . . . had the strangest dream.

"Oh, what about?"

I . . . it's gone now. I just remember that it seemed very important. It was so real . . ..

"Well if it's that important, I'm sure it'll come back to you when the time is right. Now come on; I'm starved!"

The day had started off with blue skies and a pleasant nip in the air, but some time around mid-afternoon the weather turned nasty. When sheets of icy rain began to pelt them, the three traveling companions increased their speed and made a mad dash for the nearest shelter: what appeared to be an abandoned house. As they drew close enough to make out more than just the vague shape through the driving rain, it became obvious that it had not been inhabited in a very long time. One corner of the thatched roof had completely caved in and the front door was missing. But the wall still stood, and it was the only protection in sight.

"Stay here. I'll check it out." Tsuga had to yell to hear herself over the thunderclaps that threatened to to deafen them all. Luckily, the bond she shared with Devilsbane saw to it that the message was conveyed despite the racket.

Already soaked to the bone, Tsuga swung down from the saddle and sloshed her way inside. The interior was too dim for her to see. Without thinking, she created a small flame to hold over her hand so that its dim light revealed the contents of the room. There wasn't much: small bones from dead rodents, a broken cup here, a forgotten toy there. Obviously, the family hadn't been in much of a rush to leave. The corner under the hole was flooding already, but the way the floor tilted allowed for the flow of water to go out the door. As a result, the other half of the old house remained reasonably dry.

"Looks good!" Out of habit she spoke aloud, though she knew there was no way either her sister or her guardian could hear her over the storm. Moments later, a rather large rat-like creature came through the door and shook violently, followed promptly by the horse, which did the same. Tsuga laughed and pushed her dripping hair out of her face with her free hand.

"Should we risk a fire?"

The rat – Affaila's shift form, though Auriga (or perhaps Ketral, in this case) knew why this form had been hers to wear – nodded.

You've already used magic, so if we were hiding from anyone, that's blown.

Tsuga winced at the mild reprimand, but her sister didn't dwell on it.

Might as well sleep warm and dry tonight. Tsuga nodded and started for the door.

Where do you think you're going?

She paused and turned back to face Devilsbane.

"If we're going to build a fire, we'll need wood."

The two "animals" exchanged a look – and perhaps some words – before Bane spoke again.

And just where do you propose to find dry wood in this weather?

"Well, I thought maybe under . . .. Oh, what's it matter if it's wet? I'm a fire mage." She waved the hand under her torch for emphasis, making the light dance wildly. "I can dry it off."

. . . Tsu, listen to yourself. You just said it – you're a fire mage. Look at your hand. You don't need wood at all.

That comment gave her pause. She stood for a moment, looking at the small blaze suspended over the palm of her left hand, and tried to imagine how much more of a drain a flame the size of a campfire would be on her energy.

"Well in theory, yes I could. But fire has to be fueled by *something.* If not wood, then some other energy source. Namely, me. How do you propose I keep us warm all night without draining myself dry?"

Well . . ..

"Well, what?"

Well, you do have a very powerful stone, and your connection with it is so strong, you're barely using any energy at all to draw on it.

"So? My stone only holds so much power. If I fell asleep and it drained, the fire would suck me dry before I even knew what was going on."

Tsuga got the impression that Affaila was heaving a sigh of frustration. The tone of her mindvoice as conveyed by Devilsbane only served to support this impression.

Connect to wild magic through your stone.

Her first question, of course, was if that was safe. She didn't voice it, though. Affaila was the senior mage here; surely she knew what she was talking about. Right?

"Okay, then."

She shrugged and opened the channel between herself and the stone about her neck wider, and then pushed further, beyond her focus stone and into the currents of wild magic that flowed around them. Presently, there was a merry blaze about the size of a large campfire hovering in mid-air in the middle of the dry half of the room. Both "guardians" made sounds of delight and moved closer to the warmth. Tsuga watched them for a moment, still uncertain about the wisdom of her choice. Finally, she shrugged off the feeling of foreboding and joined them.

She wanted to cry out. She tried with all of her might to scream, but when her lips parted, the sound that emerged was one of intense pleasure she didn't feel. The man on top of her – a boy, really; scarcely older than her own thirteen years – increased his efforts in response, renewing the awful pain inside her. When she found herself unable to fight him off, helplessness – a feeling she had never known before – overwhelmed her. Tsuga watched as her limbs moved of their own accord to wrap around the black-hearted, evil young man pushing himself inside of her like a crazed dog on a bitch in heat.

Detachment descended then. Her heart hammered madly in her chest as her mind retreated from the horror of the moment – or tried to. Something outside of herself had seized control not only of her body, but of her mind. She had never been aware that Elbon had such an ability. He had an iron grip on her thoughts, and though she tried to fight him, to at least pull back some part of herself and shelter it from what was happening, even this small mercy was denied her.

Affaila woke to a feeling of unbearable heat. She opened her eyes to see the comforting little fire she'd fallen asleep in front of transformed. In its place now raged an inferno. As she watched, the heat ignited the thatch of the roof, and acrid smoke began to fill the small dwelling.

Wake up!

She sent this desperate plea to the horse, and without waiting to see if she'd been heard, the healer shifted into her human form. Her bare skin immediately broke into a sweat. She coughed as she inhaled a lungful of smoke, and then fell to her knees so that she could crawl to her fitfully sleeping sister.

The girl was obviously trapped in a nightmare. She lay rigid – unmoving – so tense that Affaila's first panicked thought was that the child was several hours dead. But no – a quick look with her mage sight told her Tsuga was only dreaming. What Affaila saw surrounding the girl, though, horrified her.

Tsuga had fallen asleep without closing the link between herself and the wild magic. Normally, this might not have been a problem; the support of the stone may have been enough to keep the wayward energies in check. Unfortunately, Tsuga was anything but normal. One of her nightmares had taken hold, and the resulting weakening of concentration – even subconsciously – had given the wild magic just enough wiggle room to run rampant.

Affaila was horrified to realize that with every breath her sleeping sister took and exhaled, the flames grew hotter and brighter. She could now feel the skin on her own back beginning to blister, but not a bead of sweat marred Tsuga's face.

When she touched Tsuga (a hard thing to make herself do after the severe burn she had gained the last time), she recoiled in shock. The girl's skin was cold as ice. More frightened than ever, the healer reached out again to try and wake her sister.

Tsuga woke to a hand on her shoulder. Affaila was crouched next to her, and it took the girl's panicked mind several long moments to realize that her sister wasn't wearing any clothes. She found herself shaking from the memory of the nightmare, and she shivered as a chill ran up her spine. Only then did she notice how brightly lit everything was.

"Affaila? What's wrong? Why aren't you dressed?"

There was a look of fear in the healer's eyes, and as the horror of her dream slowly started to fade Tsuga felt the terrible chill she'd been suffering from begin to subside. Once the edge had been taken off, the temperature began to rise at an alarming rate. Her breathing quickened as she began to sweat, and she could scarcely make out the healer's words over the sudden roaring in her ears.

"You have to stop it, Tsu!"

At last she seemed to have come out of it. Affaila watched as the girl broke out in a sweat and began to feel the effects of the heat. Her frantic cry seemed to have no effect on Tsuga, however; she still didn't seem to grasp what was going on.

"Stop what? What are you talking about?"

Tsuga could see real fear now in her sister's eyes. It was then that she realized she couldn't sense her guardian. This sent a jolt of panic through her.

"Where is Devilsbane?"

Affaila's eyes widened, and now Tsuga realized that it was more than just sweat dampening the redhead's face.

"I don't know. But Tsu, you have to stop the fire!"

"You don't know? What do you mean you don't know? Where is she?!"

"Tsu, please! The fire –"

"What fire?"

It was only then that the pieces began to fall into place. The roaring, the light, the heat . . . the acrid smell she now recognized as smoke. Her breath quickened again as she looked over Affaila's shoulder to see the entire house engulfed in flames. When a surge of panic coursed through her, the blaze leapt higher, as though finding new fuel.

"'What fire?' What the hell do you mean, 'what fire?' Look around you!"

Another cloud of smoke blew into Affaila's face and made the healer cough violently. She could feel herself weakening, and knew it was only a matter of moments before the lack of air would steal her consciousness from her. Each breath hurt, almost seeming to burn her from the inside out.

"Tsu, please! I can't –"

Affaila's last words were cut off by a fit of coughing, but Tsuga scarcely noticed. Without the steadying presence of her guardian panic had quickly taken hold, and now she wanted nothing more than death – for what use was life, if she must endure it as only half a person? The temperature rose tangibly as the flames drew nearer, burning brighter in response to her decision.

Tsuga!

The familiar mindvoice jolted her to attention just before she could make the suicidal reach into the currents of old magic.

"Bane! Where are you? Where were you? What happened?!"

Not now. Tsu, you have to stop this! Stop the fire!

"I . . . can't!"

Indeed, even as she spoke she realized it was all too true. The fire had grown beyond her ability to control it. Her best bet would be to close her link to it, thereby denying it a great deal of its fuel.

Tsu, look at Affaila! She's not a fire mage; you're killing her!

The words sent a sharp stab of pain through her; for the first time since waking, Tsuga actually *saw* her sister. Her skin was blistered from the heat, and she was weeping in pain and terror. She was on her hands and knees, too weak to move, coughing violently. Bane's words echoed again in her thoughts.

You're killing her.

Tsuga stood and watched the glow of the inferno from a safe distance, what remaind of their scorched belongings scattered around her, some still smoking in the night air. She had managed to save her tack and weapons, as well as Affaila's pack – which, thankfully, held all of the healer's potions and medical supplies as well as her clothes. Luckily she had never removed the bags from the ties on her own saddle; her own clothes were safe, too. The rest had been too far gone by the time she had returned for a third trip inside the burning building.

Affaila had finally fallen into a fretful sleep after Tsuga's careful ministrations. As it happened, Devilsbane had been fine the entire time. She'd bolted in fear when Affaila had woken her and had taken a while to regain her senses – a consequence of sharing a mind with someone who was already thoroughly distraught. The girl stood now, one hand on her guardian's shoulder, the other clenching her pendant in a white-knuckled grip.

You're killing her.

The words still echoed in her thoughts, though she tried to keep them from Devilsbane. She had done this. Such destruction, all at her hands. Because of her ignorance. Her weakness. She had nearly killed her only living kin – nearly killed all three of them – because of her lack of self control.

"Never again."

What's that?

"I will never use my magic again."

But Tsu, it's a part of you! You can't deny it! You just have to learn to control it; it's like any other weapon.

"No. It is a vile and evil part of me. I refuse to indulge it any longer."

At the last, she tore the malachite from around her neck, snapping the delicate copper chain with one sharp tug. She considered, briefly, throwing the thing on the ground, but common sense won out. If she were ever to run into hard times, it might fetch a decent enough price to keep her alive for a little while longer. Reluctantly, she dropped it into the coin purse she wore about her neck – just in case.

The role reversal here was something Tsuga found quite ironic. When their travels had first begun she had been but an invalid, unable to even sit upright, and Affaila had tended her faithfully. Now, the healer was the one drifting in and out of consciousness while Tsuga sat by, unable to do much more than watch.

It was obviously painful for the woman to lie on her back, but her front hadn't come out much better. Tsuga tortured herself, watching the woman's face contort in pain at every small motion. The guilt ate at her more with each passing day. She felt responsible, and only the knowledge that she would no longer succumb to the temptation of her magic kept her from a descent into madness.

To fill the time while Affaila slept, Tsuga took to doing the small, mundane maintenance tasks that were often neglected in travel. She soaped and oiled her saddle and bridle (well, she had no soap, but she cleaned it as best she was able). After the drenching in the rain and then the rapid drying it had suffered in the fire, the tack desperately needed the care. She mended her clothes, which had holes in a number of places and looked little better after her ministrations. She even went so far as to craft herself another bow and some extra arrows, though she had neither steel for the heads nor guts for the bowstring, so neither was truly functional. At least it kept her busy.

Of course, she set traps and sought out vegetation (all of which was scarce this time of year) – she had to eat, after all. And as always, she danced through the forms of sword, spear, and her other weapons until she was able to collapse into a dreamless slumber – a sleep from which she always woke prematurely.

She was not used to this. No one told her what to do. There was no authority to answer to save that which she imposed upon herself. This was the closest thing to freedom Tsuga had ever known – at least at a time that she was not struggling for simple survival. It didn't take her long to decide she didn't like it.

Affaila drifted in a sea of pain. She'd had patients before tell her what it was like, but never had she expected to suffer such agony herself. The cold air against her inflamed and heat-damaged skin made it impossible to rest easily, for every breath she took sent another searing stab of pain coursing through her. And Ketral forbid she try to move – that brought on the queasy, lightheaded feeling that made her empty stomach churn and her head pound unpleasantly. She decided not to move. If she'd had the ability, she may have decided not to breathe, either.

In the years that followed, Affaila would often say that she could pinpoint the exact moment she realized she would live. Her skin, her lungs – all of her healing tissues – began to itch. The searing agony was washed away by this new, overwhelming urge to scratch. *Everywhere.* For the first time since the fire, she was able to think about something other than her pain.

"It itches!"

It had been five days. Five days with nothing to do; with Affaila showing no signs of improvement. Affaila always managed to swallow the lukewarm broth Tsuga made to give her some small nourishment, but beyond that, the healer did nothing but sleep. Tsuga was sharpening her dagger in the light of the pre-dawn of day six when the healer roused.

"It itches!"

Not exactly the profound statement of divine truth one might anticipate from a person who had survived a near-death experience, but at least it was a sign of life. Tsuga quickly set aside her task and moved to kneel at her sister's side.

"What does?"

Affaila's skin had blistered as though from the world's worst sunburn, and under the bandages Tsuga had been changing morning and evening, many of the blisters had burst and oozed over the past several days. The new skin underneath showed through pink and tender. The healer's eyes were open, free of fever-dreams now for the first time since the incident. Affaila rolled them as though in exasperation.

"Everything!"

Tsuga laughed with relief and reached out to the pack of medicinals she'd been rummaging through so frequently, holding out some small hope that she might find a miracle cure hidden away somewhere inside.

"Well, maybe you can tell me which of these creams and potions can help you with that." She produced a bottle full of a brownish-green liquid that looked too foul to be useless. "This stuff, maybe?"

When Tsuga produced her bottle of bugwort and asked if it would help with the itching, she had to laugh, even though the muscle spasm hurt her lungs.

"No, I don't believe bugwort will help here. That's used to treat a variety of things – sore throats, digestive problems, even helping nursing mothers produce milk. But not for healing burns." Tsuga's face fell.

"Oh." She quickly replaced the bottle and began digging for another. "Well, surely you have something that –"

"Oh, I do. Aloe vera. It's a bright, kind of clear green, and it's about like a jelly. There should be a jar of it –"

"This?"

Affaila nodded. "That's it. The leaf of the aloe vera contains a substance that has a cooling effect on burns. It also helps some with itching. I have other creams specifically for skin irritation during healing, but since it still hurts pretty badly, I think aloe will do nicely."

Tsuga tried not to let Affaila see her wince. The woman seemed to be taking her injury all in stride – even putting forth an effort to make light of the situation – but the comment about the amount of pain she was in only served to twist the dagger of guilt already lodged so firmly in Tsuga's gut. The girl tried to pretend nothing had happened and proceeded to smooth the gel over her sister's burns as gently as she could manage.

"I'm starved."

The statement should have been expected, but it took Tsuga completely by surprise. She couldn't remember eating since mid afternoon yesterday herself, and it took her a moment to think of what she had on hand in the way of food for the two of them. No doubt Affaila would want something more solid than a thin meat broth.

"I'm sure you are. You've been out cold for five days."

Again, the stab of guilt; again, she did her best to disguise it.

"We've got a couple of rabbits I managed to snare yesterday. It'll just take a bit for them to cook."

Affaila nodded mutely, and before Tsuga had even finished her ministrations, the woman's green eyes were closed once again.

Five days. Affaila closed her eyes against the words. She didn't want to believe it. Surely she had only been under a couple of hours? But no, the amount of healing her body had done told her otherwise. It was a sobering thought.

Tsuga left her sister to sleep and set off in search of firewood. She had not even considered using her magic since this latest incident, and the option was not one she contemplated now. Instead, she set about building a fire by hand. Her father had taught her this basic survival skill at a very young age, and even after the discovery of her magic, she had not stopped carrying the necessary flint and dry tinder to start a blaze. Once she had gathered enough wood, Tsuga returned to camp to find Affaila awake and watching her. As she dropped the dry limbs Tsuga managed a weak smile, which the redhead returned.

"Once I get this fire going, the rabbit will be done in no time!"

Affaila just nodded, so Tsuga set about her task. When she produced her flint the healer made a noise of surprise which the girl pretended not to hear. The first spark she struck ignited almost before it had left the stone, causing the kindling to burst into flame almost instantly. Tsuga cursed and backed away quickly, watching the fire calm as she retreated.

Every time she had started a fire after the incident – which she had tried to avoid, though hunger and the evening chill made it a necessity – she had met the same results. Though she tried to pretend she was not tied to the deadly element, the behavior of the campfire verified that the evil had its claws in her so deeply that she could not escape it. The thought was disturbing.

Affaila watched in silence as Tsuga started the fire. She was surprised to see the flint, but presumed that her sister's magical stores might have been so depleted by the burning that they had yet to replenish fully. When the fire leapt to life at the first tiny spark, she knew this assumption to be incorrect.

As her initial alarm at the sudden ignition began to fade and she watched the girl scurry away in haste, her eyes widened at the way the flames diminished in response to Tsuga's retreat. She had never seen such a thing, even with the most powerful fire mages.

Tsuga didn't hear her sister's faint gasp over her own string of curses, but once she'd assured herself that she wasn't on fire, she looked over to where her sister lay. She shrank away from the fear and confusion on the pink, blistered face and instead turned her attention back to the fire. She fed it wood carefully, trying to pretend it didn't surge to greet her when she approached. Once she was satisfied, she retreated to a safe distance to cut the rabbits into more manageable pieces. Affaila would doubtless be unable to handle anything heavy or particularly rich after being in recovery for so long, so although she had little to supplement it, Tsuga set about preparing a rabbit stew.

When Affaila was presented with the food, they promptly discovered a problem: her hands were so blistered that they were nearly impossible for her to bend. She was unable to hold anything. Tsuga, still fighting feelings of guilt, willingly neglected her own dinner long enough to spoon-feed her like an invalid.

"You know," Affaila said as Tsuga lowered herself to the ground with the bowl of stew, "I'm usually the one on the other side of the sickbed." The girl laughed weakly and shook her head.

"Well, now it's your turn to be waited on hand and foot. You certainly deserve it."

The healer smiled and obligingly opened her mouth for the first taste of food she'd had since the incident.

Almost as soon as her mouth closed around the first bite, Affaila's face contorted in an expression of distaste. She didn't spit the food out – she was, no doubt, far too hungry for that – but it took quite a while before she was able to swallow.

"What's wrong? Is it too hot?"

Affaila coughed a bit – painful, with her damaged lungs – and shook her head. "The temperature's fine, but I do believe that is the blandest thing I have ever tasted."

At the insult to her cooking, Tsuga couldn't help but laugh.

"Well, I'm sorry I'm not the great cook you are. I don't care much about taste, as long as it's not too foul. Maybe you can give me some pointers."

She was only joking, of course – she could care less if she was a good cook – but as she gave Affaila a second bite, the woman nodded eagerly.

"And as soon as possible!"

Tsuga laughed again and stuck out her tongue. "Fine, then. Tomorrow, if my food is so repulsive!"

"Deal!"

Once Affaila finished eating, the healer promptly returned to her fitful slumber. Tsuga waited until she was sure her sister wouldn't wake before she stood and walked away. She carried her own bowl of soup over to her small fire and stood staring into the flames. They surged higher at her approach, and as she looked she could see that they reached for her as though hungry for the power she held. She shuddered slightly at the thought of what they could do.

The first time she'd tried to extinguish a fire normally since the incident, it had instead burned hotter with her presence. Even when buried in dirt or doused with water, the flames would not snuff out. She had learned then that the only way to be rid of it was to let it burn away its natural fuel, and then leave it to expend itself harmlessly. Because the flames burned hotter in her presence, the wood was consumed more quickly the closer she was to the fire. So she stood, eating slowly, and watched the wood burn.

It's not your fault, you know.

Devilsbane's words broke the vision of the past she'd been watching and startled her out of her reverie. She looked to see that the horse now stood beside her. The flames of the fire reflected in the guardian's dark brown eyes, and Tsuga shuddered and had to look away, unable to meet that steady gaze.

"That's not what you said before."

The horse lipped at her collar, and Tsuga couldn't help but smile at the tickle of whiskers against her neck.

I didn't mean it. I was scared.

Tsuga sighed. "That's just it. You were scared because I lost control. Because I didn't know what I was doing. Because I was weak. Well, that's not going to be a problem anymore. I'm not going to be a mage."

Tsu, you're already a mage. Denying it won't make it go away. Your magic is still a part of you, even if you want to pretend otherwise. You know that.

"Yes, well there are a lot of parts of me I'd like to pretend aren't there. And who's to say I can't live a perfectly normal, non-magical life? I'll just have to be a little more careful."

A little? Tsu, do you realize what all this will entail? If you're going to pretend to be normal, you'll have to convince the rest of the world, too. You'll have to stay away from flames of any kind – torches, campfires, anything. You'll have to allow yourself to be cold and hot – your connection with fire ensures that you don't feel temperatures the same as the rest of the world if you don't want to. But even if you *are* able to convince the rest of the world, Tsu, you will never, for one moment, be able to forget that you are, in fact, a mage.

One of the logs settled and sent a shower of sparks cascading upwards. Tsuga shuddered at the memory conjured by the sight.

"Maybe not, but I have to try."

"I've never seen the like."

Tsuga shrugged and resisted the urge to look over her shoulder at their small campfire. She could feel the flames reaching towards her, could almost hear her name in the hiss and pop of the blaze.

"I'm sure it's just the wind. Maybe you have a fever still."

Affaila frowned at her words, obviously not convinced. "But I've never seen a fire follow someone like that! Not even an Adept!"

Tsuga tried not to betray how uncomfortable she was becoming because of this conversation. Her senses had begun to itch terribly from the desire to answer the call of the flames. But she wouldn't. She couldn't let herself give in, not even for a moment.

"I'm sure it's just your imagination. Now, eat, before it gets cold."

Affaila frowned and did as she was told, though her mind still raced madly. She'd regained enough strength over the course of the day to feed herself when propped up by drinking directly from the bowl, and the pain and stiffness had subsided considerably after repeated administration of a soothing cream meant to add suppleness back into her skin. She didn't even want to think about what a mess her head must look; she knew the hair had been singed, and in places had burned off all the way down to her blistered scalp.

She watched as Tsuga changed the bandages that concealed her blistered, weeping flesh and offered instruction and advice when necessary. There was no way she could be imagining the phenomenon with the fire; flames did not simply stretch towards a person like that for no reason. But Tsu didn't want to talk about it. Perhaps something had happened while she was unconscious. She would just have to ask Devilsbane when she got the chance.

The opportunity came sooner than she had expected. Apparently Tsuga had established a routine during the past few days of going out to check her snares every morning. When she traipsed off to do this as the sun began to rise above the horizon, she left the horse behind, presumably to keep an eye on the invalid. Once she was sure the girl was out of earshot, Affaila turned her attention to the guardian.

"You see it, don't you? The way the fire strains towards her?" *I'm not crazy, am I?* She certainly thought she might be – talking, as she was, to a horse.

"I see it."

Affaila startled. She'd only seen the beast speak aloud once, and that had been most unexpected. Now, it was just unsettling. And unnatural.

"You can't tell me she doesn't know!"

"Oh, she knows. More than you can understand."

"Then why does she deny it? It's a gift – she's very powerful. She should embrace this!"

"Affaila, how much do you remember about the fire?"

"All of it. I woke up, and the house was on fire. She was still asleep. I could smell my fur burning. I woke her up – she was freezing. I still don't understand how that was possible. But I woke her up, the fire got worse, and she got us out. I guess the pain was too much for me and I blacked out."

Bane tossed her head and pawed at the turf beneath her like any restless horse. She would have almost seemed normal, were it not for the human speech coming out of her equine lips.

"Nothing is ever that simple with Tsuga. You dismiss it that easily – smoke, a fire, some burns, and it was over. But not for her. She *caused* the fire, and she couldn't *stop* it; she panicked, and she *hurt* you. There is a part of her she can't control, and it causes people close to her pain. In her mind, it's tied it in with every bad thing that's happened recently – the army especially. She blames herself for putting you at

risk and pulling you away from the safety of your station with the army. And now this.”

“But it’s not her fault!”

“She doesn’t believe that. And now, she’s...”

“She’s what?”

“She’s turned her back on her magic.”

“She’s what?!”

“Look, when she comes back. She doesn’t even wear her stone.”

“But that’s really dangerous, especially for a fire mage! If she doesn’t give her power an outlet, it’ll find one itself – and usually it doesn’t end well. With someone as strong as she is, that’s a very, very dangerous thing!”

Are you two finished talking about me yet?

Yes, we are. Did you catch anything?

A couple squirrels. Nothing much.

Better than nothing at all.

As Devilsbane made this comment, Tsuga emerged from the trees with the field-dressed squirrels dangling from the rope she’d used to truss them. Such small animals didn’t boast much meat, but there was, at least, enough for another stew. She wasn’t sure Affaila should be eating much more than that at the moment anyway, although she did wish she had access to some sort of vegetable to supplement it.

Affaila had settled back in her blankets with her eyes closed as though asleep. Normally, Tsuga would have played along. Now, though, she was in no mood for playing nice.

“You may as well give it up; I know you’re awake.”

As she watched, Affaila cracked one green eye and looked at her as though to gauge her mood. After a moment she sighed and opened the other eye as well.

“Fair enough.”

“How are you feeling?”

“Pretty good, actually. The medicine dulled most of the pain; now there’s just that tight, itchy feeling that means it’s healing.”

“Well, that’s good.” As she spoke, Tsuga strung the squirrels up from a branch on the tree that sheltered them. Satisfied, she moved to her sister’s side and sat down. “Go ahead. Say it.”

Affaila looked at her consideringly for a moment before she spoke. “You can’t just stop being a mage, Tsu. It’s part of who you are. It would be like a fish refusing to swim!”

Tsuga shook her head. “A fish has to swim to survive. I don’t have to use magic – just because a person can do something doesn’t mean they must. And it certainly doesn’t mean they *should*.”

“Well, yes, but –”

"Magic has brought me nothing but trouble. It's almost killed me several times. And, more importantly, it's come damn close to killing people I'm close to on too many occasions."

"But, Tsu –"

"No; I'm much better off without it. And the world – at least the part of it I'm in – is much safer."

"I don't think you –"

"You're not going to change my mind, you know. Fire isn't like *your* magic. It is innately evil; it wants only to consume. It doesn't care what or who. It's driven by hunger, and will turn on its wielder as quickly as the enemy. It is *not* to be trusted."

With that, Tsuga drew her small belt knife and began cleaning her fingernails, determined to end the conversation. Affaila watched her in silence, obviously unhappy with the way the talk had gone. Tsuga didn't much care. She wasn't going to hurt anyone else – at least, not without giving them a fair chance to defend themselves.

There was honor in meeting a man face-to-face across the blade of a sword. She couldn't say the same for incinerating men with no warning and no hope to save themselves. It just seemed unfair, like killing a child – and there was something else she didn't want to think about. She saw for a moment the small boy dead in the road before she was able to push the memory away. She knew the child would haunt her dreams again tonight, as he did most nights.

The best she could hope for was to work herself to exhaustion so that she could, perhaps, steal a few hours of blissful unconsciousness before the nightmares woke her. With this in mind, she stood and brushed herself off. Though darkness would fall soon, she still had time enough to dance the forms of swordwork before the sun fully set.

"Well, glad to see you're feeling better."

Affaila smiled from where she sat. "Much, thanks."

She had been rifling through her pack of medicinals, taking stock of what she had left, but now she set it aside and stood. It felt good to be dressed in her healers' garb again. The green color was a universal symbol, and though her dresses were bloodstained and faded from much use (and a great number of wounded soldiers), they were still easily recognizable. It was as though she had armored herself against the world once more, and for the first time in months, she felt normal again.

Tsuga was frowning when Affaila looked back to her. The healer tilted her head to the side curiously.

"What?"

"Is it safe for you to wear that, considering?"

Affaila dropped her hands to the folds of her skirts protectively. She'd almost managed to forget about the brutal murders that had been plaguing the healers' ranks lately.

"But – what else am I to do? I'm still too weak to shift, and I don't have any other clothes."

She tried not to wince at the lie, but she feared Tsuga may have noticed. Shifting wouldn't be a problem, but she had just regained her sense of self, and she didn't want to lose it again so soon.

" . . . I have some extra clothes in my pack –"

"No."

"Excuse me?"

Affaila blew out a frustrated sigh, and then drew herself up to full height, as though steeling herself against an attack.

"I'm not changing. I'm tired of hiding who I am. I'm sick of being afraid."

Tsuga took a moment to truly look at her sister. Something had definitely changed. There was a strength and a determination there that she'd never seen before, and faced with this new Affaila, she found herself backing down.

"Fine. But if you're going to make a target out of yourself, you're going to learn how to protect yourself."

Affaila looked surprised that there hadn't been more of a fight, but after a few moments the rest of Tsuga's words seemed to register.

"What do you mean?"

"Get up. Come on; if I really wanted to kill you, you'd be dead by now."

Affaila spit out the mouthful of grit and blood that she'd been in danger of swallowing and levered herself up out of the dirt. "Did you have to hit me that hard?"

She stood and spit out more blood as she reached her hand up to her throbbing lip. Her entire body ached with fatigue, and she could count her myriad new bruises with her eyes closed.

"That was a love-tap, compared to what could happen. Come on now, hands up. Come at me."

It was her first lesson in self-defense. What Tsuga had meant by "protection" had turned out to be violence – something that, as a healer, she found very difficult to partake in. The girl didn't seem to understand this.

"You know damn well I can't. I swore an oath, Tsu! I can't go against that."

"You told me that oath, word-for-word. You swore not to raise your hand in violence, except to save a life. Your *own* life counts.

And if you don't do this now, you won't be able to protect yourself when your life really *is* on the line!"

Affaila's eyes flashed in outrage.

"I told you, I can't!"

Tsuga sighed.

"Fine, you can't *attack* me. How about defense? Can you stop me from giving you an eye to match your lip?"

The healer considered this for a moment before answering. "Well, I guess that would be okay, since I'd be stopping violence, not initiating it."

"Fine. Then get in your defensive stance again. If I have to beat you to a bloody pulp to keep you from getting hurt, then so be it."

Affaila groaned and heaved herself off the ground again. Every time Tsuga hit her, she crumpled like a tent whose ropes had come untied.

"Your stance is still off. You need a strong base to keep yourself from pitching over at the slightest push."

"But last time, you said I had to be more flexible, or I'd be dropped like a rock."

Tsuga sighed and ran her fingers through her short hair. Her sister was growing frustrated, and she was running out of ideas. Combat had always come so naturally to her that she had no idea how to explain something that was second nature, done almost without thinking.

"Okay, look at it like this: you have to have a sure footing and a strong stance so you don't drop like a sack of flour. But you have to be mobile and flexible, because the strongest oak can still be pierced by a well-placed arrow. You have to be able to know when to stand your ground, and when to retreat. It's like a dance – a give and take. Does that make more sense?"

"Not really."

Tsuga groaned and shook her head. "Alright, that's enough for today. You need your rest, and I need some time to think. We'll pick up again at dawn."

"Dawn?!"

"Yes, dawn. You're not ready to practice in the dark. Of course, I suppose we could always wait until the heat of the day...."

"Fine," Affaila groaned. "Dawn it is."

"Alright; so as important as hand-to-hand combat is, I think it may have been a bit much for you to start with. So today, we're going to do something different. We need to find something you're comfortable with. Since you don't like confrontation and you haven't gotten your stance down, I think it's best we stay away from the close-range weapons. Even though your belt knife will be one of your last lines of defense, you have to have the basics of stance and movement down before we can get to that. So we'll start with something a little less involved. These were a gift from a dear friend of mine."

As she spoke this last, Tsuga produced the throwing knives she'd received from Hari, the ex-thief-turned-assassin she had befriended during her time in the Devalian military. They were far better made than the first set she'd learned with, and she had grown accustomed to the balance and feel of them against her skin.

"And this is the set you will be practicing with."

She could see the disappointment in the healer's eyes when she produced the second set – a pair she had purchased for herself when she was only about ten. The balance was slightly off – nothing that would have much effect on a beginner, but could be highly detrimental to someone used to using truly well-made daggers – and they were nowhere near as beautifully crafted as the ones Tsuga now reattached to her own wrists. But they were well taken care of, and far less precious to her. If one of these blades was lost in the bushes during practice, it would be far easier to replace.

"Here; get a feel for the heft and balance of these. You wear them in arm sheathes," she explained as she pulled up the sleeves of her tunic to show how her own were attached, "and they slide in like this."

She demonstrated inserting the blades, then released them again as she continued to speak. "There's a catch that you can activate by pushing the blade further in with the heel of your hand, like this. That will allow it to slide down into your palm, and is an easy and subtle way to arm yourself, if you can pull it off. You just have to be sure not to drop them, because they will come right out as soon as you straighten your wrist."

Tsuga had actually spent a good deal of time studying the contraption, and knew quite well how it worked. It was set up with a pair of triggers – one at the top, where it would be depressed by the handle of the blade, and one at the bottom, set to keep the blade from sliding in the restraints. The knob at the bottom slid downward when the blade was pushed in further, causing the stop at the hilt to retract into the device so that the blade could slide back out of the holster freely and silently. It was quite ingenious, really.

"If you happen to release them and you end up not needing them after all, you can push them back in just as subtly by sliding them along your palm with your fingers, like this."

Again, she demonstrated as she spoke. She could feel the oiled metal pieces click quietly back into place against the sensitive skin of her arm, and showed that they were secure by shaking both arms slightly.

"Before you can throw them, you have to be sure to slide the knives all the way out of their sheaths so they don't get hung up on anything. Now, these are very sharp, so be careful."

She removed her own arm sheaches and demonstrated to Affaila how to put them on before handing the healer the second set.

"You just practice with those for a while and get comfortable putting them on and taking them off. Get used to the trigger and how much force it takes to engage it. I'm going to check the traps. After breakfast, we'll start with some target practice."

"The downside to distance weaponry like this is that once you've fired off your last shot, you're done. All well and good against one person taken by surprise, but it won't do much against a group – or someone with the presence of mind and the reflexes to dodge. Granted, arrows are better, but it's much harder to hide a bow and quiver than a pair of daggers." *Or ten.* "Not to mention, harder to learn."

Affaila nodded. She understood all of this, at least. And since she wasn't going to be practicing her aim on another person, she had no qualms about learning this particular skill.

"So, let me see you arm yourself. Don't worry about speed right now; I just want to see if you can do it correctly."

The healer nodded and removed the knives and sheaths so that she could put them on under her sister's watchful gaze.

"Good. Now, the throwing motion is a simple one. Slide the knife down until you're holding the end of the blade. Then it's a basic end-over-end throw, like this."

Tsuga demonstrated the motion slowly, and then released one of her own knives from its sheath, feeling the familiar chill of the smooth steel sliding against her skin.

"For now, we can aim at that fallen tree there."

Affaila looked to where she pointed and saw a rotting trunk that looked as though it had been struck by lightning in the last storm. She nodded. "Alright."

"Good. Now, I'm going to show you the motion one more time, then actually throw. Try and watch how I handle it – there's definitely a trick to these, and it's not as easy as it looks."

Affaila nodded and watched closely as Tsuga demonstrated again. Then, in one smooth blur, it happened – flick of the wrist, arm up, and the next thing she knew, Tsuga had returned to a normal standing position and was watching her expectantly. Affaila looked quickly to the tree and saw the knife neatly buried in the wood.

"I've seen people throw with an underhanded motion too, but I've never been able to make that one work correctly. There are different weapons – shaped like thin stars – that can be thrown sidearm as well, but I've never had the pleasure of using them. I suppose if it works for you, the knives can be thrown with a similar motion, though. Just find what is comfortable for you. Accuracy comes with practice. I'll give you what tips I can, but this isn't like sword work; there are a lot of ways to do this, and each person has to find what works best for them."

Affaila nodded again and waited until Tsuga had returned with her knife and backed away before giving it a try. She managed not to drop the knife in her maneuver, but the throw was short and sloppy. Tsuga shook her head, but didn't say anything. Affaila sighed and started to walk to retrieve the projectile.

"Hold on, there. You still have one more."

"But it's my left one! I'm right-handed; you can't expect me to throw with both hands!"

Tsuga just laughed. "If you can only throw with one hand, you're cutting your defense in half. It's the same with any weapon. I can use my sword left-handed or right. Granted, my left still needs some work, but if I were to lose the use of my right arm, I would still have a chance in a fight. I'm not expecting you to be perfect, and I'm not saying it's easy. I'm just saying that if you want to live, you have no choice."

Affaila winced at this reprimand and reluctantly did as she was told. This time she did drop the knife, and even when she managed a throw, it was erratic and well off the mark.

"Go find them, and keep trying. I want you to practice at least an hour a day, no exceptions."

Affaila groaned. An hour a day meant a lot of trips into the underbrush looking for wayward knives.

Affaila's breath hissed between her teeth as she inhaled sharply. The medication stung on the cuts she'd gained from the brambles, but she knew better than to leave a single one untreated. She'd seen soldiers lose limbs before from a nick or thorn prick they'd ignored.

Tsuga watched her, squinting in the half-light of dusk. She had not started their evening campfire yet – in fact, Affaila couldn't remember the girl starting a single one in the past few days; she'd gathered wood, but left building the fire and lighting the tinder to the healer. She also worried about the sudden silence of her sister's stone. When Tsuga had first begun to deny her magic, the stone had still pulsed with a quiet, benign life to her mage sight. Now, however, all semblance of power was gone from the piece. It was nothing more than a trinket – a discarded magical relic that, without the attention it needed, had become dormant.

When magic was denied, as her sister was doing with her fire talent, the power tended to build up, only to burst out in unexpected and uncontrollable ways. Had Tsuga stayed in contact with her stone, the malachite could have drained some of the excess energy and tamed it, shaping it into a safer, more benign form that would be easier to control. By refusing even this small concession to her magical needs, Tsuga was setting herself up for disaster.

If only she could be made to understand . . .. Since she knew Tsuga would not talk about the subject, Affaila firmly pushed such thoughts aside and kept the conversation this evening to safer topics.

"You know, even if I can get good with these things, I'm hardly going to be attacked by dead trees. I couldn't even bring myself to hit you, no matter how much you pissed me off. What makes you think that when the time comes, I'll be able to hurt a complete stranger?"

Tsuga shook her head. "I'm counting on your desire to live to win out over your irrational fear of causing harm."

Affaila frowned and mulled that over for a moment. Tsuga was a fine one to talk of irrational fears. Eventually, she shook her head to break the reverie and stood up abruptly.

"I'm getting cold; I'm going to start the fire."

When Affaila said she was going to start a fire, it took everything Tsuga had to keep from protesting that it was a warm night, or that the weather had been too dry lately, or that there was too much wind, or any of the other dozens of reasons that ran through her thoughts in those few moments.

"Alright. I'm going to go check the traps, then. Maybe we'll have some meat for dinner tonight."

Even to her own ears, the statement fell flat. They both knew she was using this as an excuse to avoid having to think about what she'd done. But Affaila didn't say anything; she simply began stacking wood. It didn't take long for the soft sounds of the other woman's labor to be beyond Tsuga's hearing as she stalked off.

You have to face it sometime, you know. You can't keep pretending it didn't happen.

Tsuga let out a string of curses as she slashed through a particularly dense patch of brush with her sword. Normally she'd try to leave the underbrush intact, but at the moment she couldn't resist the opportunity to express some of her anger and frustration on the innocent vegetation.

"What's to say I can't, hmm?"

Well, your nightmares say it pretty strongly. And you still think about it every time you look at her; obviously it's not as easy to forget as you're pretending it is.

Tsuga grunted. Even after having her guardian for the past few years, the thirteen years of having her head to herself before the horse came on the scene still made her expect to be able to have her own private thoughts from time to time. Obviously, that was no longer the case.

"Well, what's the big deal? I don't see why I can't just forget about it. Surely with time it'll get easier, right?"

Easier? Bane snorted. **Tell me, Tsu – how long has it been since you set the army on fire? Or since you were raped? Or since Da's death? Years. But you still think about all of them. You still wake up in a cold sweat crying just as hard as you did at five years old after you first heard the news. Do you honestly expect this one will be any different?**

Tsuga didn't answer – at least, not aloud. She knew the answer to that question – just as Devilsbane did – but she didn't care to think about it, let alone admit it to anyone. Not even her guardian.

"Well, even if it does become like the rest, it's nothing I can't handle. Been doing it for years, after all."

Even though Bane was well beyond her range of hearing, Tsuga knew the beast was snorting and tossing her head in irritation.

You hardly sleep anymore. You retreat more and more often from your own thoughts. I share your mind, Tsu. I know what a dark place it is. I can't blame you for wanting to hide from it, but you're driving yourself mad. Driving *me* mad.

This statement brought Tsuga to a stop, sword poised to make another brutal cut through the next clump of stickyvines. She sighed and dropped her arm to her side, her grasp on the hilt loosening as she felt the fight drain out of her. No longer possessed with the strength to support her, her knees buckled. She thudded into a cross-legged position on the ground.

Madness. It was enough to strike fear into even the most stalwart of hearts, and lately Tsuga's own had been anything but. She could feel her mind frozen as though she stood at the edge of a canyon, teetering between the safety of solid land and the endless abyss that fell away before her. One false move, and she would tumble into it, gone forever.

"What can I do?"

Months had passed since her near-death experience, and in that time Affaila had come to recognize changes in herself. She acted with more confidence, and even the way she moved and thought had changed. She no longer filled her arms with things for travel as she had before; she now kept at least one arm free at all times, just in case.

Though she still adamantly refused to wear trousers, she had consented to a few modifications to her usual get-up. The skirts had been slitted and seamed, so that they still offered the billowy benefit of concealment (especially of the small knives she'd taken to wearing strapped to her legs), while also providing for more freedom of movement than the traditional style.

She had become a very good aim under Tsuga's strict tutelage. Her sister rewarded this newfound confidence by allowing her some input in the travel plans. It had taken nearly two years and no few near-death experiences, but she had at last earned the status of equal in her little sister's eyes. Frustrating, that this respect came only in light of her supposed new-found affinity for violence, but who was she to complain? It seemed Tsuga had finally accepted her as something other than a tag-along. The horse, however, was another matter.

I still say this is a bad idea. What if she slips up?
"Then we'll all be killed. Or worse, imprisoned and questioned as traitors and spies."
Gee, I feel so much better. Devilsane snorted and tossed her head, eyes wide with worry.
"Would you calm down? I wouldn't be going along with this if I didn't have every confidence she can pull it off."
I still don't like it.
"Shh, here she comes!"
Tsuga was dressed in her usual costume, more-or-less. Ragged boots, poorly-patched pants and tunic, and a healthy layer of dirt, sweat, and horse. Conspicuously absent were her sword belt and the most obvious among the small arsenal of weapons she carried on her person. She had limited herself to a small, much-worn and utterly plain dagger, of the sort that any peasant might carry for mundane tasks. She'd recently taken a knife to her hair, which had grown to a horrific length, and now sported the boyish bob common among peasant lads.

Affaila, however, wore a dress fit to kill. As seemed to be her preference, she'd chosen green as the color of her outfit. Today, though, it was a deep emerald fabric with subtle but feminine embroidery in a darker, almost-black shade. Her slippers were the same color as the embellishments, and she wore a simple gold chain around her neck which traced a tantalizing line right down the center of her low, square-cut neckline. What might be on the end of that chain, however, was a mystery – it disappeared from sight in her cleavage.

She was laughing, dangling off the arm of a handsome man who, to Tsuga's critical eye, seemed entirely too full of himself for someone whose sword was so bejeweled as to be utterly useless in a fight.

"Oh Jeromae, you're terrible! Simply terrible!"

At least everything seemed to be going smoothly so far. From the toothy grin on his face, Jeromae seemed to be thoroughly smitten with the healer. He joined in the laughter while Tsuga moved around to Devilsbane's left flank and bent down to clean her hoof with the pick she carried.

I still don't like it.

Oh, shush.

The plan was going off without a hitch. Jeromae, as he called himself, had been in one of the most recently attacked parties. He was a noble – as evidenced by his rich clothing and utter lack of humility – who had been with his small war band and their accompanying healers when they were ambushed.

This particular raid had not gone like the others. That this group had been attacked at all was a surprise, with only two healers among the travelers. Recently the targets had been larger groups of the benevolent mages – at least five. The attack on Jeromae' party also had not been as absolute as the others. Besides the healers, only one man had been killed – his throat had been slit – and none were injured.

This meant one of two things. Either the killers were gaining skill, confidence, and support, or it had been an inside job. Affaila wasn't sure which prospect terrified her more, but she hoped that by gaining Jeromae' confidence, she might also gain some useful information.

She paused near Tsuga, using the excuse of admiring the horse to slow their progress.

"I heard about the attack last week. Absolutely horrible." She didn't have to fake her horrified shudder. Jeromae sighed and moved to stand closer to her, as though to offer comfort.

"Yes, it was truly tragic. If it hadn't been for the murdered guard, it would have almost seemed like an accident. Both were killed by their own potions, as though they were apprentices who simply mixed the wrong herbs together and stumbled onto a lethal combination."

Affaila shuddered at the thought, but shook her head adamantly.

"But that's simply not possible! Healers have an innate sense about medicines. If the mixture had been dangerous, they'd have known at once!"

Jeromae gave her an odd look, and Affaila immediately bit her tongue. She hadn't been hiding the fact that she herself was a healer lately, but in this particular exchange it was best that she not reveal that little tidbit of information.

But Jeromae only said, "Really? I hadn't been aware of that. Why, by the Goddess, would someone even bother with that, then?"

Affaila shrugged and reached up to pat Bane's shoulder. The beast snorted and laid her ears back, causing the woman to frown and back away. She could hear the smile in Tsuga's voice when "he" mumbled, "She don' much like bein' touched by strangers, miss. Iffin' y' don' mind m' sayin', it might 'ave summut t' do wi' yer perfume. 'Orses 'ave del'cate noses."

Jeromae bristled at the perceived insult, but Affaila laid a hand on his arm and mustered a cool smile.

"Indeed." She stepped away, pulling Jeromae along with her further down the aisle. Once out of earshot, she picked up the conversation where they'd left off.

"There are many reasons, I suppose. To discredit healers in general, for one. To make it look like a suicide, for another. Which it may have, had it not been for your poor guard. Or any number of other things. None of them good for the reputation of the profession as a whole."

Suicide, for example, was considered in Devali to be the ultimate sacrifice, something a man did in the hopes of sparing the lives of others. In Sennor, however, it was looked upon as an ultimate sin, something that would cause a person's soul to be cast out of the light of the holy Goddess, to perish for eternity in darkness.

If it were to come out that healers – the most cherished of Her children – had committed such a sin, the entire population of these mages would be cast out as heretics who had lost the way and turned their backs to Auriga's light. All of Sennor would then be left vulnerable to plague, injury, and disease, with no healers to tend the sick and wounded. Affaila's mind raced along this path, and she felt the rhythm of her heart speed up to match the pace of her thoughts.

"Awful," was all Jeromae said. "Simply awful. Why would anyone wish to discredit healers like that?"

Affaila shook her head sadly. "I don't know." But as Jeromae slipped her arm back through his, she had the disquieting thought that she did know – all too well.

"You and Mr. Pompous certainly seemed to be hitting it off."

Affaila shrugged. "He's a nice enough guy. I don't think he had anything to do with the attack."

"Well, that's comforting. What did you find out?"

The two women were on the road again, with no particular destination in mind. Autumn was coming on, and work would soon become extremely hard for Tsuga to find – but appallingly easy for Affaila.

If I live that long . . ..

"Only one other person killed. A guard. His throat was slit."

Tsuga nodded; she'd overheard this tidbit in the stables already and had had time to digest the fact.

"And it appears the healers were poisoned."

This Tsuga had not known, and she looked to Affaila now in shock. "You're kidding."

The healer shook her head. "I wish I were. But that's not even what worries me."

Tsuga frowned. "It's not?"

"No. They were poisoned with medicines from their own supplies. A lethal mix of their own potions."

"But that makes no sense!"

"Oh, but I'm afraid it does. Jeromae had the potions examined by another healer. Separately, the ingredients are actually very beneficial. But when mixed, they have a foul reaction that turns them toxic."

Tsuga was silent a while as she absorbed this information.

"So, what does this mean?"

"What it means is that someone screwed up. By killing that guard, they let on that something was amiss. Otherwise, it would have appeared that one of two things had happened."

"Oh?"

"Either that both healers were insufferably stupid and didn't know better than to mix the ingredients, or that they were bent on suicide."

Tsuga winced at the mention of the ultimate sin. She'd never been particularly devout, but certain things had gone so far beyond mere religious belief that they had become engrained in the very heart. Having attempted to kill herself once before, she still worried that she walked beyond the reach of Auriga's holy light. The only hope she had to counter this fear was that Bane had not cast her off . . . yet. Perhaps this meant there was still some small hope of redemption.

"I suspect if the plan hadn't gone awry, there would have been nothing whatsoever to arouse suspicion from any outside parties."

"You've obviously given this a lot of thought."

"I can't help it. It just keeps running through my head, over and over. It's all I can think about."

"And with good reason. So, any idea why?"

Affaila nodded as she stepped around a pile of who-knows-what in the road. "Someone wants to oust the healers. Not just kill us off, but completely destroy everything we are. Discredit us. See us cast out as sinners, to walk forever in darkness, cast out of the light. To completely eradicate us."

Tsuga shivered at this statement, suddenly cold despite the late summer sun.

"But think what that would do! All the pain! The illness! ...The death. Who would do such a thing?"

Affaila shook her head sadly. "I don't know."

"Are you sure splitting up is the best thing? I mean, with all that's going on?"

Tsuga was just finishing with loading her things on Devilsbane's back. Two months had passed since they'd heard of the last attack on the healers, and she had been offered a job as a guard on a merchant train traveling to the capital. Unfortunately, in light of recent events, the man had refused to allow Affaila to join them.

"We don't want any trouble," he had said. "Merchant trains always attract thieves and lowlifes as it is. We don't need to tempt the Goddess by having a healer travel with us."

The statement had saddened Tsuga; not long ago, a healer as a traveling companion would have been a priceless boon, not an unwanted burden.

Normally, she wouldn't have even considered taking the offer if it meant splitting up, but with winter only about a month away, she couldn't afford to pass up the opportunity. The weather would be turning any day now – the autumn rains always came this time of year, and the roads did not dry out until well into spring. The need for a hiresword would all but disappear during the colder months. The pay for this one job would be enough to get her through the entire winter, as well as the better part of spring. She had no choice but to accept. But she couldn't help worrying what might happen to Affaila if she weren't there to offer protection.

"Tsu, I'll be fine. I'm the only healer in the world who knows how to kill a man without getting a drop of his blood on myself. You've taught me well. I'll be fine." Tsuga looked at her sister dubiously.

"You've never had to put that to the test. You still can't even bring yourself to slap me, let alone try to kill me."

"I'm a big girl. When the time comes, I'll know what to do. Don't worry about me, Tsu. You're following your path; let me follow mine."

The two women embraced quickly, and then Tsuga swung into the saddle. Affaila watched for a few minutes until her sister disappeared around a bend in the road. Only after the younger girl was gone did she allow the tears she'd been holding back all day to fall.

The truth was, she was terrified. She'd been traveling with Tsuga for less than two years since leaving the army, but in that time she had grown to depend on her sister for much more than she'd realized. The girl was much stronger than she gave herself credit for, and through everything, she had remained a steadfast figure for Affaila. The healer never would have been able to cope with the loss of her job, her home, and her friends if it hadn't been for Tsuga's steadying presence. And she certainly wouldn't have survived the stress of the last several months without her.

"How will I ever do this alone?"

A light breeze kicked up, carrying the scent of rain. Affaila breathed it in deeply, and in that moment, she almost could have sworn she heard someone speak.

"She is with you still."

Tsuga waited until she had made it around a bend in the road and was hidden from sight before she pulled Bane to a halt and surrendered to the emotions she'd been holding back.

You'll be alright, Tsu. You were just fine before you met her; parting ways isn't the end of the world.

"It's not me I'm worried about." Tsuga sniffed and angrily swiped at the tears dampening her cheeks. "There's practically a price on her head, and she refuses to even defend herself! She's the only family I've got left! The only piece of Da I've got! What if she gets herself killed?"

Bane snorted and craned her neck around to lip Tsuga's trousers gently in sympathy. **You'll just have to have faith that what you showed her will be enough. Beyond that, all you can do is pray to the Goddess to keep her safe.**

"You mean the way She kept all the others safe?" Tsuga barked out a harsh laugh and tossed her head. "After all, she's done such a great job so far!"

Tsu, that's blasphemy!

"I don't care!" A breeze kicked up then, a light stirring of air that carried with it the promise of rain. Tsuga tilted her head back to look at the gathering clouds.

"Do you hear that, you bitch?" she shouted. "If you let my sister die, I swear by all that is holy, I *will* make you regret it!"

" 'Nother beer, lad?" Tsuga blinked in surprise and squinted in an attempt to focus on her empty mug.

Tsu, don't you think you've had enough?

"No." As the wench started walking away, she corrected herself – or tried to. "I mean, no, 'm not a lad. But yeah, 'nother beer."

The wench giggled, made her apologies, and obliged before flouncing off. Tsuga took a swig of the foul stuff and then went back to listlessly staring into its foamy depths.

Tsu . . ..

She could feel her guardian's worry pressing down on her, and
she took another long pull on her drink to push it aside. When
the weight didn't lift, she firmly clamped down on the part of her
brain where the thoughts and feelings of the horse resided and
closed herself off.

Alone in her head, though, she had nothing to distract herself
from her own dark thoughts. She finished her beer and thumped
the mug on the table to signal she wanted more. Distracted by
the pain, guilt, and worry that had been keeping her from sleep in
the week since she'd abandoned Affaila, she didn't even notice
when one of the younger male guards from her group sat down
beside her. At least, not until he spoke.

"Hitting the drink a little hard tonight, aren't you?"

His proper speech fell flat on Tsuga's ears. He wasn't of noble
upbringing – he didn't have the clipped way of speaking down
quite right – but the self-conscious lad fought hard to disguise that
fact. Tsuga scowled at him.

"What? Are you m' Da now, too? 'S my coin, an' I'll spend
it however I damn well please."

When one of the wenches came sashaying over with a full
pitcher, the man waved her away. Tsuga's expression darkened.

"What'd ya do that fer?!"

She felt a sudden weight on her shoulder and looked down in
confusion to see his hand there. She knew that she should object
to this – normally she would – but somehow she couldn't quite
form the words.

"Tsu, I'm worried about you. You don't strike me as the type
to usually drink like this. And I haven't seen you lay down to
sleep once all week. Are you okay? Is something wrong?"

Tsuga snorted sardonically – or at least, that's what she'd
intended to do. It came out as more of a wet sniffle, and she
realized that her face was soaked in tears.

"Wrong? What could possibly be wrong?"

Her voice sounded strange to her own ears. The use of her
nickname had triggered something unexpected, and now she
couldn't seem to stop crying.

In a distant corner of her mind, she registered that she was
being carried by someone, but she couldn't make out his face
through the blur of her tears. As he carried her upstairs –
presumably to one of the rooms – she could just make out a soft
"there, there" murmur over the din of the inn's other patrons.

Tsuga came awake slowly, her sleep-muddled mind slow to
rouse. She had the distinct feeling that something was horribly
wrong. She felt . . . alone.

Bane?!

She fought back panic when there was no response. The jolt of adrenaline cleared her mind a bit, and she realized that she had, for some reason, pushed her guardian out of her head last night and fallen asleep without reopening their connection. She hurriedly dropped the mental barrier, and was immediately flooded with a sea of emotions that threatened to sweep her under – worry, guilt, hurt, anger. She fought to keep her mind through all of this, but she must have stirred or made some noise, because suddenly an arm tightened around her and she was locked in an unexpected embrace.

Bane? . . . What exactly happened last night?

Before the horse could respond, the person next to her stretched and shifted positions. It was with considerable alarm that Tsuga realized all of her weapons had been removed. She was resting in the arms of a man, wearing only her thin tunic. She wondered what had happened to her pants.

"I see you're awake."

Tsuga tensed further – if that were even possible; she was already wound tighter than a bow string – when he spoke and turned her head to look at him. She knew that voice . . ..

"Charlie?" That was what his mates called him, at least. She had no idea if it were even his real name. "What, um . . .." She trailed off as she felt a hardness move against her in a way that she desperately tried not to think about.

"I brought you up here when you broke down."

"I did what?!"

He sighed and sat up. Tsuga took the opportunity to cast a frantic glance around the room in search of her pants.

"You were drunk. I mean, even more than you have been the other nights. I came up and asked if you were okay. You started bawling and jabbering something about someone named Affaila, and how you were a horrible person."

Tsuga grimaced. "I don't remember any of that . . .." She sighed, and then something he'd mentioned registered. "When you say 'brought me up here . . .?'"

He nodded. "Yeah. I mean, you obviously couldn't walk, so I carried you up here."

She was starting to get a really bad feeling about this.

"And then . . .?"

"Then I set you down on the bed and helped you get your boots off. The next thing I know, you're pulling an arsenal out of Auriga-knows-where. Then you passed out." As he spoke, Charlie gestured to where she'd haphazardly dropped her assortment of knives and daggers by the bed.

Tsuga nodded slowly, relieved to know that he hadn't gone searching after the weapons that she kept in some of the more personal areas.

"Okay. But, um . . . Charlie, what happened to my pants?" He blushed furiously, and Tsuga had the fleeting thought that he couldn't be more than a couple years her senior – about twenty, she guessed.

"Oh, um, yeah, about that . . . ."

Tsuga frowned and started to sit up, then remembered that she was barely dressed and promptly lay back down.

"Charlie?" There was a hint of warning in her voice, and the poor boy wilted further. "Where are my pants, and why were we in bed together?"

"Well, I started off on the floor. But you were mumbling and sweating and tossing in your sleep. I couldn't help it; I had to hold you. And when I did, you calmed down. So, I just slept next to you all night." Tsuga considered this for a moment.

"So nothing . . . happened?"

Charlie's blush deepened again, turning his face a fascinating shade of red. "What?! You think that I . . . that we . . . Goddess, no! No! I mean . . . Goddess, no!"

She blinked. "Good to know that's such a horrifying prospect for you. But if nothing happened, then where are my . . .." As she spoke, she caught sight of them at the foot of the bed, rumpled as though she'd kicked them off in the middle of the night. Now it was her turn to blush.

"Oh." She reached down to grab them and hastily pulled them on under the covers.

"Auriga's tits! I didn't mean it like that!"

He sighed, and Tsuga looked up to see him running his hands through his hair. He still had all of his clothes on – out of respect for her, she suspected.

"Goddess bless!"

Now fully dressed, Tsuga stood up and began tucking her tunic in. "Let it go, Charlie. I'm just screwing with you." She continued speaking as she began fastening her sword belt. "I know I'm not desirable; I've come to terms with it. No worries. Who'd want to bed a sword?" She added the last with a strangled laugh as she gestured to her straight, wirey frame.

She heard him moving, but didn't look up from fastening her belt; she assumed he was putting himself to rights as well. That was, until she found his hands on her shoulders. She tensed, but restrained herself from shrugging him off with great effort.

"Tsu, look at me."

She winced at the nickname and kept her eyes downcast. Charlie moved around in front of her and lifted her chin gently until she had no choice but to meet his gaze.

"Tsu, that couldn't be further from the truth. You're strong. You're smart. Goddess, you're the best fighter I've ever seen! And you're beautiful."

Tsuga could feel herself tearing up again, and she shook her head in denial of his words.

"No, I'm not." She swallowed hard around the lump in her throat, trying to fight back the tears.

"Yes, Tsu, you are."

"No, I'm really –" She wasn't able to finish her protest; his mouth cut off her words. She tensed and started to pull away, but something stopped her. The next thing she knew, she was kissing him back, completely lost in the moment.

Tsuga couldn't stop smiling the rest of the day. She'd never been kissed before – not that counted, at least – and certainly no one had ever complimented her on anything other than her fighting skills. She felt as though she were floating on air. She caught sight of Charlie a few times during the day, and knew she was blushing and smiling like a fool every time she caught his eye. She couldn't help it.

The other guards picked up on it, of course. In the week that she'd been on this job, she'd made a few tentative friends; they all took the opportunity to give her a thorough ribbing. By the time they finally made it to the next town and checked into the inn, she thought that her blush may have become permanent.

Desperate for some time to herself, Tsuga lingered in the stables long after the others had moved inside for dinner. She took her time grooming Devilsbane, brushing her coat until it shone with the care. When she had nothing left to do to pamper her guardian, she moved on to her tack, even though it was already in perfect condition.

She had just gotten everything taken apart and was beginning to meticulously clean the smaller bits when there was a soft knock. She looked up to see Charlie standing a few stalls down, watching her. She could feel herself blush, and she looked away quickly.

"Hello, Charlie."

She heard him moving, and then there was another stool beside hers. He sat down. Now, in addition to the comforting smell of horse and leather, she caught the sharper scent of human sweat and something she could only identify to herself as "man."

"You okay? I mean, this is the first time you haven't gone straight inside and started drinking."

She winced at the barb, and had the fleeting thought that she might have been on her way to developing an addiction. She ducked her head and kept her eyes on the strap of leather she was oiling.

"I'm fine, thank you. It's just been a long day. And I like it out here."

"Yeah, I guess a hangover does make for a hard day on the road, huh?"

Tsuga sighed and finally looked up to meet his gaze. *I never noticed before, but his eyes are exactly the color of fresh honey....*

"Charlie, why are you here?"

He hesitated a moment before answering. "I'm worried about you. I mean, I've never seen you get as bad as you did last night. Seems to me like you've got a monkey on your back."

Tsuga blinked in confusion. "What's a monkey?"

"Nevermind that. Tsu, do you want to talk about it?"

"I don't know . . .."

"Tsuga likes to pretend she doesn't have emotions."

Tsuga shot the horse a hard look. "You hush."

Bane just snorted and pulled her head back inside her stall. She turned back to look at Charlie, and then wished she could hide from the sympathy she saw in his expression.

"But everyone has emotions. Are you sure you don't want to – "

"Charlie, stop. I don't want to talk about it because I don't want to *think* about it. Why do you think I drink? To forget."

"Really? And how is that working out for you so far?"

"Not very well."

"Bane!" Charlie laughed at her exclamation, and Tsuga felt herself deflate in the face of their united front. "No, it's not working out very well at all. But I don't know what else to do about it."

"Well, I'm not sure what to tell you, since I don't know what's bothering you. But if it's any help, I want you to know that I'm here for you, okay? Anything you need. All you have to do is ask."

Tsuga nodded. "Thank you, Charlie."

From behind them, Bane snorted. Tsuga looked back to see the horse's head hanging over the stall door again.

"You really don't know Tsuga at all if you believe for one second she'd ever ask for help."

"Would it kill you to mind your own business once in a while?"

"Possibly." Bane tossed her head and directed her attention to Charlie again. **"On a lighter note, I can tell you what she's been thinking about all day, *and* why she's been hiding out here instead of inside, where she usually hides."**

"Oh, and why is that?"

Tsuga felt blood rushing to her face at the evident curiosity in Charlie's voice and expression, and she shot a frantic look at her guardian.

"You wouldn't dare!" The mischievous twinkle in Bane's eye spoke otherwise, and Tsuga looked back and forth between the two in desperation.

"If it's going to make you feel uncomfortable, maybe I'll just–"

Tsuga could feel the thought forming in her head. Devilsbane was about to tell Charlie that all she'd been able to think about all day had been him. Desperate to keep that knowledge to herself, Tsuga did the only thing she could think of to distract him.

She kissed him.

Tsuga woke to the unfamiliar feeling of arms around her for the second time in two days. This time, though, she came to as she usually did, with full memory of the night before. She tried to get up, but Charlie tightened his grip on her in his sleep. She stifled a frustrated sigh and looked around the dark interior of the room.

What time is it?

About two hours 'til dawn.

Tsuga groaned. The sound must have disturbed her bedmate, because he disentangled himself and rolled away. Tsuga took the opportunity to sit up and stretch out her stiff muscles.

"What time is it?"

Tsuga smiled at hearing him echo her own thoughts of a moment before. "Couple hours 'til sunup."

Charlie groaned and pulled his pillow over his head. "Goddess' tits! Why are you up so early?"

Tsuga laughed and threw back the covers so she could stand up.

"Actually, this is relatively late for me. Usually I only get a couple hours sleep, if that."

"You're insane, you know that? Absolutely insane."

Tsuga laughed again as she pulled on her boots.

"Go back to sleep, Charlie. I'm going to go down and get some breakfast and a quick workout."

"Hold on."

"What?"

Charlie took hold of her arm and gave it a gentle tug. With a smile, Tsuga obligingly leaned down so he could kiss her.

"Get some rest. I'll see you in a bit."

Tsuga pushed back an unruly strand of hair that had been itching horribly against her sweaty forehead and sheathed her sword. Despite the difficulty she'd been having with sleep – and, indeed, sanity – on this trip, she had not allowed herself to deviate from her routine.

Every morning when she woke, she would dance her way through the basic forms of the sword and knife before going to check on Bane. When the train would stop for lunch, she would spar anyone willing to face her. If there were no takers – though her banter usually succeeded in goading someone into action – she would practice unarmed combat alone.

If there was light when they stopped for the night she would run a mile or two, or else practice with her bow and arrow. Only when she had worked herself into a satisfactory state of exhaustion would she eat supper and attempt to sleep. Last night had been the first time that she had successfully slept – without being so drunk she couldn't stand – since she had abandoned her sister.

You didn't abandon her, you know.

Easy for you to say; you didn't even like her.

Bane didn't respond to that, so Tsuga let out a guilty sigh and drew the long dagger she wore on her belt opposite her Da's sword. The grip of this blade was as familiar and steadying to her as the other, and as she adjusted her hold, she smiled to herself at the comforting feel of the rough shark skin sliding against her calloused palm. After the first time the soldiers had rewrapped the hilts of her weapons, she had kept up with it; the shark skin truly did afford a more secure grip in a sweat- or blood-slicked hand. One blade in each fist, she settled down into her workout and let thoughts of the real world recede from her mind.

The sound of applause startled her out of her battle trance some indeterminable length of time later, and the red haze around her vision faded. The world suddenly seemed less crisp, and as the heightened sense of awareness ebbed, Tsuga became acutely aware of the sweat trickling down her back and between her breasts, and the beginnings of real fatigue in her muscles. As always, the sensations that made her mortal had been washed away in the battle fever, leaving only strength and focus.

Tsuga straightened from her final pose – a half-lunge with the knife extended in her left hand, her right arm grasping the wrist of her imaginary opponent (she had sheathed the sword at some point during her maneuvers; she couldn't have said exactly when).

Although this was a move every warrior prayed they would never have to use, it was a form that every fighter knew. In order to complete the thrust and kill her opponent, Tsuga would have to not only leave herself completely vulnerable to attack, she would also have to throw herself without a second's hesitation onto the opponent's outstretched blade, using her free hand to hold them pinned while her own weapon buried itself deep in the other man's ribcage. The move was suicidal, plain and simple. The only time it was used was by the stupid, the desperate, or those with no regard for life or death or what might be awaiting them on the other side of the veil.

Tsuga slid the dagger home in its sheath and swiped a hand across her sweaty brow.

"Charlie. What are you doing?"

The boy smiled and moved towards her. "Just watching."

"So I see. Well, did you learn anything?"

He reached out and swept her into his arms for a swift kiss. "I learned that I'm very glad you don't want to kill me."

Tsuga laughed and pushed him away gently. "You know, you'd be surprised how often I hear that."

"Not all that surprised."

"Don't gush. It's sickening."

Charlie laughed and ran a hand through his unruly blond hair.

"Fine. Well, I actually came to tell you that His Highness wants to get an early start today. Time to gear up."

Tsuga heaved a gusty sigh and rolled her eyes.

"High Highness my ass. But thanks. At least I got Bane polished to a shine list night. Assuming, of course, that she didn't decide to make my life difficult this morning by taking a roll?"

Of course not. You deserve a good day, for once.

Gee, thanks. As she spoke, Tsuga began walking to the stables. Charlie fell into step beside her.

"I'm guessing you haven't eaten yet this morning?"

Tsuga made a face. "For your information, I always eat breakfast before my morning workout. Though I wouldn't say no to a snack before we head out. Sword work does stir up quite an appetite."

He laughed. "Well, then it's a good thing I snuck through the kitchen on my way to find you. Here."

What he held out to her looked like an oddly-shaped roll, but when she bit into it she found it to be filled with meat and carrots and a few other vegetables cooked in a savory sauce. It was still so hot that it burned her mouth, but she didn't care.

"This is *good*!" She swallowed and grimaced a little at the pain, and then took another large bite, sucking air through her teeth in an attempt to cool it as she chewed. "What is this?" Charlie laughed again at her enthusiasm and shook his head.

"Don't know, but Cook was handing them out to the help, so I snagged a few.

"Damn!"

As they entered the stable, Tsuga was licking the last of the juices off of her fingers while Charlie watched, bemused. Bane was hanging her head over the stall door like any other eager young filly; when she caught sight of the girl, she whickered a greeting. Tsuga grinned and hurried her step until she stood in front of the oversized beast and could take the large, blocky head in her hands.

"Good morning to you, too. Ready for another day?"

"Are you kidding? That was the best night's sleep I've gotten in a while, too. Now hurry up; we're already running late!"

Now that they were no longer in hiding, Bane had become much more outspoken around the natives. No one in Sennor thought twice about a talking animal, and the one time Tsuga had commented on the sudden change, the horse had only said that it was more polite to those around to be able to hear both sides of the conversation. Tsuga could hardly argue, especially since Bane had the good sense to know what was best kept private. Most of the time, at least.

Their traveling companions must have decided that teasing her was much less interesting when she flatly refused to surrender up any details; by the time they pulled off the road for their midday meal, things seemed to be back to normal. No one had made her blush in the last couple of miles, and the day seemed increasingly bright. Her lunchtime sparring partner had been defeated easily, and once back on the road, Charlie even came to ride beside her. Bane adjusted her stride in consideration of his smaller mount so that they could converse more easily. The spotted house cat that was his guardian rode pillion behind his saddle.

"So what part of Sennor are you from?"

Tsuga had been forced to answer this question many times since she'd returned to her native land; over time she had crafted an acceptable answer out of part-truths.

"Close to the Devalian border. But I've been on the road for so long, I can't really call that place home anymore." Certainly not with Elbon still there, and everyone no doubt thinking her long dead by now. "How 'bout yourself?"

"I'm from the capital."

Tsuga noticed that his chest swelled with pride at this statement, and she couldn't stop what she asked next.

"Oh? So how exactly did you end up a mere hire-sword, then?"

He wilted and didn't answer, giving Tsuga immediate cause to regret her quick tongue. After a few beats of silence, she decided to volunteer an edited version of her own story in an effort to ease some of the discomfort that now hung between them.

"Me, I've always loved to fight. They couldn't keep me away from the Weaponsmaster. Eventually the old man kind of adopted me and started showing me the ropes when Da was gone." *Both before and after he was killed,* she thought to herself.

"I tried army life for a while, but I became compelled to travel, so here I am."

Compelled at sword point . . ..

Of course. But he doesn't need to know that, any more than he needs to know I'm talking about the Devalian army.

Of course.

Charlie was silent for a few minutes when she'd finished her story, and Tsuga began to think he wasn't going to respond. Just when she'd decided to change the subject to the weather or something equally as frivolous, he spoke up.

"My parents are dead. Since I was real little. Nice innkeep took me in – let me be a serf, more or less, filling in wherever I was needed. When the place burned down, I didn't have anywhere to go. Threw myself onto the mercy of the nearest man with a sword. He ended up being a retired Queensman, so of course he taught me everything he knew about fighting. And court politics. Fascinating stuff, that . . .. I was rejected from their ranks because I'm not of noble blood. That was pretty hard to take, especially since I bested all of them – both in combat and in knowledge of Sennorran politics."

Tsuga wanted to interject a question, but was afraid that to do so might prevent him from telling the rest of the story. She held her peace.

"So I ran away in shame. Promised myself I'd learn how to be noble, then try again."

Tsuga sighed sadly. That certainly explained his stilted way of speaking. She wondered fleetingly if he ever slipped under stress.

"Charlie, that's awful! I'm so sorry."

Although why anyone would *want* to be noble was beyond her. As was the logic that linked "nobility" to "hire-sword."

Charlie's jaw clenched and he shrugged without taking his eyes off the road ahead of them.

"It was a long time ago. And it's not like there's anything you could do about it."

Tsuga didn't argue this point; he was right, after all.

I could get used to this, Tsuga thought to herself as she removed the last of her secreted daggers and slid into bed beside Charlie. It felt good to snuggle herself up against him as he wrapped his arms around her. When she was comfortable, she looked up at him through her lashes and smiled.

"G'night, Charlie."

He reached a hand up to push back a stray bit of her hair, then pulled her towards him for a kiss.

She expected him to pull away after placing his lips on hers – he always had before – but he didn't. Instead, it was with no small amount of shock that she realized his tongue was sliding across her lips, gently probing. She hesitated a moment, unsure of what to do. But finally she opened her mouth, and his his tongue ventured inside.

Tsuga had a brief flash of the only other time someone else's tongue had been in her mouth. But this was nothing like when Elbon had forced himself on her; Charlie's touch was gentle, and as he continued to explore, Tsuga felt her body respond. A few moments later, his hand had found its way under her shirt and to her small breasts. As soon as he made contact with the skin there, a burst of heat surged in her gut.

The next thing she knew, both of them were undressed and his hands and mouth were everywhere, exploring her exposed flesh. He had begun to sweat, but she didn't notice, too wrapped up in the foreign sensations wracking her body. She couldn't help but gasp from time to time as he found a particularly pleasurable spot with his tongue or fingers, and she found herself completely in the moment – something that before had only happened when she feared for her life.

The world shifted abruptly, and he was on top of her. Tsuga tensed, freezing like an animal in the brush. Charlie reached down to slide his hand between her thighs and gently separate her legs. Instinctively, she clamped them more tightly together. His hands stopped. Tsuga couldn't see his expression in the darkness, but she sensed him looking at her.

"Tsu?" His voice was strained, but Tsuga scarcely heard him over the memory forcing its way to the surface of her thoughts. "Is something wrong?"

Why did I take off my knives? What am I doing? How did I get into this mess? And how do I get out of it . . .?

"Tsu?"

Tsuga swallowed around a lump in her throat and shook her head slightly, then realized that he couldn't see her in the darkness either.

"I –" She stopped to swallow again. "I'm fine. Why?"

Something in her voice must have given her away, because Charlie heaved a sigh and rolled off of her. She could feel herself shaking, but now that he'd moved away from her, her mind was no longer frozen in terror. She almost wished it was – now, she felt torn between the instinct to fear what had almost happened and an overwhelming sense of guilt for hurting Charlie. His weight left the bed, and she could hear movement and the sound of rustling fabric. Moments later, the door opened and closed, and then he was gone.

His mouth was pressed against hers to the point of pain. There was something foreign in her mouth – his tongue, she realized.

Tsuga woke to the sound of screaming, the sheets twisted around her and sticking to the cold sweat pouring off of her skin. When she realized that the bloodcurdling yell that had woken her came from her own throat, she cut it off and sat in silence, shaking.

"Charlie?"

There was no answer to her tentative inquiry, and Tsuga swallowed hard. After a moment of debate, she disentangled herself and stood up. She fumbled for a few minutes in the dark before she found the fire kit and lit the lamp by the bed, flinching when the flame surged far higher than it had any right to. She dressed quickly and didn't linger over adjusting all of the various-sized knives as she usually would have. Once fully clothed, she blew out the lamp and fled the chamber.

The common room was sparsely populated. Tsuga scanned the faces on her way to the door, but Charlie's wasn't one of them. There was a bite in the air that spoke of an early winter, but though the wind was cool, it raised no goosebumps on her tan skin; the fire within her saw to that. Still, she hurried her step and aimed herself for the stables.

The sounds and smells of horses hit her even before she walked through the doors and saw the dim lighting and sleepy-eyed mounts. Well, all but one. From a stall at the end, Tsuga could hear the sounds of a restless horse. Straw rustled as the beast turned, pacing the small space. Tsuga knew who it was. Sure enough, moments later a dark bay head appeared over the stall door.

Bane's eyes were rolling in agitation, and her nostrils were flared as she huffed out heavy breaths. Tsuga ran the last few steps and threw open the stall door. Her guardian surged forward, and Tsuga threw her arms around the thick neck and buried her face in the horse's shoulder. The beast was shaking as much as she herself was, and Tsuga felt that she could at last allow the tears to fall.

Um, Tsu . . .? Tsuga sniffed.

"What?"

"Maybe . . . um, maybe I should just come back later . . .."

Tsuga startled and whirled around, wondering how he had managed to get so close without her noticing. She sniffed again and swiped at her eyes angrily. She hated letting people see her cry.

"No, it's okay. I was actually looking for you."

"You were? Why?"

Tsuga took a step away from Devilsbane and wrapped her arms around her chest, hugging herself tightly.

"You left in such a hurry. I just . . . I just wanted to say –"

"Tsu, I'm sorry."

Tsuga choked on the same words and looked at him in confusion.

"Wait, *you're* sorry? Why?"

"I didn't handle things very well. I –"

"Charlie, there's something I need to tell you."

Tsuga watched as Charlie's face went from confusion to shock to horror during her story. When she'd finished, he blew out a sigh and scrubbed at his face with his hands.

"Goddess' tits. Tsu, I had no idea. Goddess, for you to have gone through that . . .. And then here I come along, and act like a complete ass . . .."

Tsuga smiled and shook her head as she reached out a hand to grasp one of his.

"You weren't an ass. You had no way to know. All things considered, if anyone's handled things badly, it was me."

Charlie shook his head in astonishment.

"But to go through something like that . . .. Goddess, I can't even imagine."

Tsuga tried to smile. She didn't know how well she succeeded, but Charlie's expression softened.

"I won't pretend I'm over it, or that it doesn't still bother me. But you didn't do anything wrong. And it's not like I don't . . . want to. I just . . .."

Somewhere during the course of her rambling, Tsuga must have looked down, for now Charlie placed a hand under her chin and gently lifted her face until she was forced to look him in the eye. He was smiling.

"You did seem to be enjoying yourself there for a bit."

Tsuga managed a laugh at that. "Well, maybe just a little."

Charlie's expression changed to one she didn't recognize, and he pulled her in for a kiss. When she pulled away some breathless moments later, she found herself flushed.

"Would . . . would you like to try again?"

Charlie's voice sounded strange, and Tsuga found herself excited at the prospect in spite of herself.

As they lay together, still somewhat breathless, Tsuga listened to the drumming of blood in her ears. It made an erratic counter-tempo to the rapid beating of the heart inside the chest on which she rested her head. She was thoroughly spent, and from the way the sheets were twisted, she judged she had good reason to be.

Her bedmate let out a contented sigh, and she glanced up at his face with a smile as he reached to run a hand through her hair.

"Wow."

Tsuga felt a jolt of shock at the voice. She had realized her bedmate wasn't Charlie – the chest wasn't nearly muscular enough – but had thought the man merely a figment of her imagination. The voice brought back a flood of memory, and suddenly she was watching again as she lit an army's worth of friends on fire.

"Tsu? . . . Tsu, wake up!"

As wakefulness returned to her, Tsuga fought to push back the memories of her past, beating back the image of her friends burning alive with determination.

"Tsuga, what's wrong?"

It was several long moments before she managed to reply to Charlie's question. "It's . . . nothing. Nothing. Just a bad dream, that's all. Go back to sleep."

As Charlie settled back against the straw mattress, Tsuga stood and began pulling on her clothes in the dark.

"Where are you going?"

"Shh. Don't worry about it. I'm just gonna take a walk. Get some rest."

Charlie mumbled a response, but she couldn't quite make out what he said – he was asleep before she had finished dressing. As she slipped out the door, she paused for a moment to look back at him. With a sigh, she turned and was gone.

For the past couple of days, Ramiq had found himself aroused at the strangest times. In the midst of a lesson, while bathing, and increasingly often in the middle of the night. While he often spent his spare time chasing the handsomer lads and ladies of court and dandling them at his leisure, such random and powerful moments of arousal were highly unusual for him. Now, as he stretched luxuriously under the down blankets atop his feather-soft bed, he felt grateful that for once, the stirring in his nether regions was gone, allowing him to relax and drift into a pleasant dream.

Ramiq lay stretched on his back, his latest conquest cradled against his chest. He could feel his heartbeat thudding rapidly, while hers made an erratic counterpoint. He grinned in spite of himself as he ran a hand through his sweaty, tousled hair.

"Wow."

She looked up at him and he smiled, thinking absently that she seemed vaguely familiar. He watched as her expression changed, and then the image was gone, and he found himself thrashing in twisted sheets that were not his own.

The rough wool caught on his calluses – but he didn't have any of those! – as he threw back the blankets. His heart hammered franticly, and he felt feverish – at once flushed and chilled to the bone.

Movement caught his attention; he glanced towards it, noting with some surprise that the naked man next to him was not as attractive as his usual choice.

"Tsuga, what's wrong?"

Ramiq woke with a start and lay staring at the ceiling for a few moments, listening to the wild beating of his heart. He quickly checked his shields to be certain they were all intact, and then let out a sigh of relief. They were as strong as ever.

Then how did I invade someone else's dream?

The only way for him to do that while shielded was through conscious effort. And he certainly hadn't been trying . . .. He hadn't really recognized the woman in his dream, though he knew without a doubt whose mind he had been in upon "waking." He would recognize that panicked girl anywhere; she was hard to forget.

Tsuga. The girl from the battle. He hadn't even thought of her in ages, so why was he now dreaming of her, and even being pulled into her wakeful moments?

Perhaps it had only been his imagination. Yes, surely that was it . . .. Spicy food before bed. Maybe the meat had been slightly rotten . . ..

Are you sure?

Tsuga scowled and heaved her saddle onto Bane with more force than was strictly necessary. The horse snorted and sidestepped in alarm.

"Yes, damn it, I'm sure! Now would you shut up and stand still?"

Bane didn't reply, so Tsuga quickly finished securing the saddle and her packs, then led the horse out of the barn and mounted. Desperate to be gone, she dug her heels into Devilsbane's sides and clung for dear life as her guardian flattened out into a ground-eating gallop.

When Bane could feel Tsuga's sense of urgency recede, she slowed to an easy canter, then a trot, and finally, to an ambling walk. There was no need to ask what had happened. Bane knew from the fear and self-hatred radiating from her human that Tsuga was, once again, running from who she was. It was a disconcerting habit – the more so because it tended to result in late-night departures and even more guilt to haunt Tsuga's dreams.

Tsu?

They had been riding in silence so long that the sound of her guardian's mindvoice startled her. She winced at the concern she could feel coming from the animal, and braced herself for the discussion she knew was coming.

"Mm hmm?"

What will we do now?

Tsuga sighed and ran her free hand through her shaggy hair as she considered the question. After a few long moments, she answered.

"We're two days' ride from the capital. Might as well go there. See if we can find some work."

But winter's just about a month away. Do you have any idea how hard that will be?

"Yes, I know."

And you don't have the coin from this job. How will we make it?

"We'll find a way, Bane. You know we will. Besides, I have half the coin. I made him pay us half up-front, remember?"

True. You have half the payment – minus what you spent drinking yourself into a stupor every night.

Tsuga sighed.

"Look, I know it's not going to be easy. But we've been in tough spots before, and we've always come out okay. Just have a little faith, hmm? Auriga will see us through."

Bane didn't answer, and Tsuga retreated gratefully into the uncomfortable silence of her mind.

Goddess, I hope you will.

"You, there! You look like you know your way around a sword! How'd you like to try your hand in the tournament?"

Tsuga's progress had been slowed to a crawl upon entering the marketplace. Throngs of people filled the streets nearly to the point of bursting, and peddlers took advantage of the delays to better hawk their wares. As she had next to no money, Tsuga ignored them – though she saw many men and women diverted from their tasks by pretty baubles here and there. But this particular call caught her attention. The words came not from some over-dressed merchant, but rather an older, grizzled man dressed in the uniform of a Sennorran soldier. Tsuga glanced down at her own travel-stained clothing, only then remembering that she herself wore the leftovers of a dead man.

She assumed at first that the man was speaking to the noble strutting through the crowds just ahead of her – tournaments were for those with money to pay the armorers and noble dignity to defend, not for a young sell-sword for whom honor took a back seat to the prospect of a full belly – but she soon found that he had made his way through the seething mass of people to walk by her stirrup.

"What say you, lad?"

Tsuga looked down at him and barked out a laugh. "Lad? Look again, sirrah."

The man peered up at her and then chuckled a bit himself.

"Beg pardon, miss. My eyes aren't as keen as they once were."

Tsuga smiled slightly, feeling an immediate liking for the man. "Would that all who made that mistake had the same excuse!" The soldier grinned and shook his head.

"Well, no matter. The question still stands."

Tsuga looked down at him, forced to squint in the bright light and the haze of smoke rising from the stalls of food vendors as she considered him. He carried himself easily and confidently as he wove his way through the crowd alongside her, moving with a casual grace that bespoke an intimate knowledge of the capabilities of his own body. He had no stripes of ranking sewn onto his uniform – an absence that Tsuga found odd – only the symbol of a shield emblazoned with a sword and spear crossed in the middle. She didn't recognize its significance.

"Does it now? Well, I've never had much interest in tournaments. All flash; no real merit to them at all."

"Ah, but this isn't your typical tournament."

Tsuga laughed again. "Let me guess, the winner gets a fat sum of money and a pat on the back from some noble or other? Or is it the hand of a desirable Lady?"

The man shook his head. "Neither. Actually, the winner of each event will become my next student."

Tsuga looked down at him again, intrigued by this statement.

"And who might you be, that I would risk being carved up for such a privilege?"

The man quirked an eyebrow at her. "You wear the clothes of a Sennorran soldier, and yet you do not recognize your nation's Weaponsmaster by the emblem he wears?"

Tsuga flushed a dark red, mentally berating herself. Now that he'd said it, she did recognize the symbol on his clothes. A smaller version – modified with a shield sporting that Lord's crest, rather than the royal one she now recognized on the emblem this man sported – had been worn by the man who'd held the same position on Lord Gregory's estate. How could she have been so stupid?

"Well, I beg pardon, Sirrah. I've only just arrived in town, and I'm not really –"

"– A soldier. Yes, I had guessed as much. I am Weaponsmaster Midan. And you are . . .?"

"Thoroughly abashed. M' name's Tsuga, Weaponsmaster. Perhaps, if I've not offended you too greatly, you would tell me more about this tournament of yours?"

"So, you want to teach people that are already masters in the art? Why?"

Midan laughed. They were sitting in one of the taverns a little off the over-crowded marketplace. He sipped a mug of ale, but after her recent experiences with alcohol, Tsuga had opted to stick with water.

"It does sound a bit odd when you put it that way, I suppose. But no, I want them to expand their horizons. To learn other arts, and master them as well. And to teach each other. This war is not going away any time soon. And it pains me to see the fresh-faced, inexperienced youths sent off to feed its insatiable hunger. I'm tired of it. I want to build a new kind of army, out of the best Sennor has to offer. Men and women who can fight with any weapon, in any situation. A group of elite warriors. Something to perhaps turn the tide of this war in our favor, at long last."

Tsuga took another sip of her water as she mulled over his words. It was a glorious thought, if a bit overly ambitious. But being part of such a group would ensure her food and shelter indefinitely. It would restore balance and routine to her unstable life. And – if this insane notion were to actually work – it would write her name forever in the history books. A very tempting offer for the vainglorious, indeed.

"How many events may I enter?"

The turnout for the day's events had astounded her. There were contestants of all ages, from scarcely entering puberty to ancient, battle-scarred soldiers with gazes like steel. And every one of them walked with an air of deadly confidence that made her shudder.

Do I look like that? she wondered idly as she watched the crowd part before a man with death in his eyes.

After much deliberation, Tsuga had entered herself in a total of four events: sword, mounted, hand-to-hand, and mixed weaponry, in which she could use any and every weapon at her disposal. The last was a category filled with thieves and street-fighters, but Tsuga felt that her cross-training and versatility would give her a reasonable chance. Four events would be extremely difficult for her, and infinitely taxing. She'd never been one to do things half way, though.

Tsuga had done remarkably well in all of her events thus far. She had placed in the top ten in hand-to-hand. Top five in mounted combat. She'd made it to the final round in swordsmanship, only to be beaten by a grizzled woman who moved faster than lighting and quieter than the wind. Now, she had only one hope remaining to earn her place as a pupil of Midan. If she didn't win this, the championship round of mixed weaponry, she would walk away with nothing to show for all of her efforts and bruises.

Her opponent for this final match was a starved-looking young lad that couldn't have been more than fifteen or so. There was a hunted, animalistic glint in his eye that reminded her of a wounded beast at the end of its rope and desperate to survive. Her heart went out to the lad, but she knew that if she wanted to claim her place as Midan's student, she must force aside her sympathy and defeat him.

At the call to ready herself, Tsuga drew her sword and the tiny knife she wore opposite it. The lad had a small dagger visible, which he switched rapidly back and forth between his hands. On the edges of the packed-dirt arena an assortment of weaponry lay scattered – everything from spears and staffs to nunchucks and maces, even ranging to chairs and other nondescript objects.

Tsuga lowered into a defensive stance and rocked her weight forward slightly so that she balanced on the balls of her feet. The bell sounded to begin the match, but Tsuga didn't move. She simply watched, waiting to see what her opponent would do.

The boy seemed to have the same idea, because he made no immediate move to attack. Instead, when Tsuga didn't budge, he began sidestepping slowly, circling her as though looking for an opening – a weakness of some sort. Tsuga turned herself gradually – just enough to keep him in her sights – still waiting for him to make the first move. He feinted towards her legs and danced back out of reach, but Tsuga didn't indulge him by engaging. She simply waited.

"Why are we here?" Ramiq's tone was whiny, and Lyra nipped at him in irritation.

"Because, dimwit, the Queen's Mage is here. Because you are his apprentice. Because you will be expected to attend these things when you take his place."

"But it's so *boring*. And dirty!" As he said this last, he wrinkled his nose and lifted his blue-and-green mages' robes to avoid dragging them through a pile of horse shit. Lyra sidestepped it agilely and shook her head.

"Stop complaining. You've already missed most of today's events. And the final round of this one has already started. Would you hurry up?"

Ramiq let out a heavy sigh and hurried his step. Before long, he was forcing his way through a crowd of spectators as Lyra darted easily in and out of the congestion, weaving through legs and around obstacles until she reached the platform where the queen and other high-ranking nobles sat to observe the proceedings. The fox settled herself in and glanced back over her shoulder only when a scowling Ramiq finally made it to his place to join her.

Bloody people. Blast it all, that ass spilled wine all over me!

Lyra just rolled her eyes. **And you already dried yourself off and wove an illusion. No one can tell. Stop bitching and watch the fight, would you?**

Ramiq grunted and cast his eyes to the arena, where a pair of boys were circling each other. Neither made a move to attack.

"Nice of you to join us, Journeyman Ramiq."

The young man winced at the quiet reprimand from his mentor and bowed his head. *Not Journeyman for much longer.* He was almost ready to test for his Master ranking. A few months away, at most.

"My apologies. I was . . . delayed."

"Meaning you couldn't be moved to get your lazy carcass out of bed, no doubt."

Ramiq flushed and kept his head bowed respectfully.

"Well, you're here now. May as well take in the proceedings. The *ground* certainly isn't going anywhere any time soon."

Ramiq nodded and lifted his head just in time to see one of the lads close for an attack.

The pair of combatants had been circling each other for several long minutes. Her opponent had made a couple of half-hearted feints, but had yet to commit himself to an actual attack. Tsuga had done little more than turn in a slow circle and shift her defense accordingly. She knew from the look in the lad's eye that he was waiting for her to initiate.

Tsuga had used what little spare time she was graced with between rounds to learn what she could of all the other participants. It was rare that she was afforded the opportunity to study her opponents before meeting them across the blade of a sword, and so she had taken full advantage of the chance in this competition. She had been lucky enough to watch one of this boy's matches a couple of days ago, early on in the tournament. She knew him to be a street urchin – a lad who lived his life by fighting for everything he had. But she had seen from his fighting style before that he was as non-confrontational as they came.

He had spent that entire fight dodging his opponent, dancing out of range and refusing to close. He had used the weapons at hand more as distractions and obstacles than anything else; the only time he had actually stood his ground was at the end of the match, when his opponent was frustrated and careless. Needless to say, the lad had won easily. Tsuga didn't intend to let the same thing happen to her.

She could see fear and confusion begin to take root in the boy's eyes when she made no move to attack him. He tried to lure her into action with a few more easily-spied feints, all to no avail. Finally, after what seemed an eternity, his anxiety got the better of him. He darted in low with a flurry of attacks, using both his small knife and his bare fist. Tsuga took a step back – not to retreat, but rather to give herself that extra half-second she would need to position herself and brace for the attack.

He was incredibly fast; she had to acknowledge that much. And if he left an opening for her to exploit, she couldn't find it, so caught up was she in fending him off. Tsuga took a deep breath and engaged her battle sense. Time seemed to slow. Her own breathing sounded loud in her ears, providing a steady accompaniment to the pounding of her blood.

She danced the forms, smoothly bringing her knife up to engage the boy's blade, using the edge of her sword to slash at his other hand, fending off the flurry of blows with the threat of dismemberment.

Once she had locked his blade against hers, Tsuga allowed herself a faint smile before twisting her wrist just *so*. His blade flew free, and her opponent gasped in shock and then ducked and rolled quickly out of reach. He came up with a staff, and Tsuga adjusted herself accordingly, settling in for a long and interesting fight.

Ramiq watched as one of the combatants was disarmed – only to duck away and come up brandishing a stick. He hadn't really seen what had happened; it had all been so fast that the flurry of movement had all run together. There was a cacophonous surge of cheers as well as jeers from the crowd of spectators. One of the older men sitting next to the queen made a sound of surprise.

"Something wrong, Weaponsmaster?"

"No, Your Majesty. It's just . . . well, I've rarely seen someone move like that.   Such deliberation in each movement, each maneuver planned and executed flawlessly, and in the space of only a couple of breaths."

The queen made some comment of approval, but Ramiq was no longer listening. Instead, he had called on his mage's sight and was aimlessly looking over the crowd. Here and there he saw a faint flicker, someone with just enough extra magic flowing in their veins to give their natural talents a boost, but not quite enough to make them a mage. There were a few genuine mages dotted throughout the throng of people, and Ramiq amused himself by taking the time to examine their shields and contemplate the best way to take each one down, should the need arise. A surge of power caught his attention just then, and he turned his gaze back in the direction it had come from: to the two lads circling each other in the arena.

A hunch. A feeling. A lucky guess. Tsuga didn't know how to explain it. In the heat of the moment, she didn't give it much thought. But when her opponent charged, she somehow knew that if she didn't move six inches to the left when he was two strides away, she would surely lose.

Sure enough, she followed her instincts – and when he charged, she stepped deftly aside, narrowly missing being struck unconscious by an unexpected blow on his upswing. A rush of adrenaline shot through her at the near-miss, and her focus sharpened even further. As her opponent stepped past her and turned back, Tsuga sheathed her sword, turned, and lowered herself to make a swipe at his knees with her leg in one fluid motion.

She could feel the success of the maneuver even before she realized she had decided to do it. When she made contact, the boy crumpled to the ground. Eager to press her advantage, Tsuga sprang forward from her crouched position, knife ready to press against his throat as she claimed victory.

At the last moment, her opponent brought up the staff he still held to block her. Tsuga cursed as her blade buried itself in the wood and he twisted it out of her hands. Not happy with how the tables had turned, Tsuga retreated and drew her sword again. The boy rolled nimbly to his feet and pulled the dagger free from the staff so that he could tuck it into his boot to use later. Tsuga made note of the fact as she lowered herself again to her defensive crouch and settled into the mindset necessary to endure a long fight. This promised to be interesting.

Ramiq whistled under his breath as the events of the fight unfolded. He watched with his mage's sight as one lad used a weak bit of fire magic to his advantage. Fire was chancy, and those with the ability to manipulate it often boasted other, less obvious gifts – not the least of which was a lucky streak to rival a God. Curious, he took a closer look at the boy.

He seemed vaguely familiar. Now that Ramiq was actively looking for it, he could see that the boy did indeed have some fire talent. Unfortunately, he couldn't pin down a strength to this youngster – his power seemed to wax and wane at random, never really settling down to anything like the stable range of a properly trained mage, or even an adequate trainee.

Is that even possible?

An untrained mage that no one knows about in the middle of the capital? Why shouldn't it be?

But Adain hasn't said anything!

Because Adain is watching the fight, not worrying about when he can go lure his next bedmate back to his chambers.

Ramiq blew out a frustrated sigh and ran a hand impatiently through his wavy hair.

If you'd been having the kinds of dreams I have been, you'd be pretty hung up on it, too.

I don't think so. The feminine persuasion has a great deal more control, thank you very much. You just need to learn how to handle yourself.

Tsuga twitched slightly as a crawling sensation made the hair on the back of her neck stand up. She felt as though someone were standing behind her, watching. Out of reflex, she glanced over her shoulder – just to be sure. That brief moment of distraction was all her opponent needed. He rushed her, taking advantage of this lapse by coming at her with a frenzy of blows.

The sensation forgotten, Tsuga returned her attention to the fight and parried his attacks franticly as she retreated in an effort to buy herself some time to recover.

Ramiq puckered his lips in confusion as he continued examining the mysterious mage. He reached out a tendril of magic and probed the lad to see what would happen. The oddly pulsating magic surged in response, and Ramiq pulled back, alarmed. He'd never seen power react that way. Perplexed, he settled back to watch the fight and see what happened.

Tsuga couldn't believe what was happening. She couldn't seem to recover; the smaller lad was quick, and – much as she hated to admit it – she had let her guard down. She could feel her control of the situation slipping through her fingers. Just as she realized this, she stumbled over an uneven bit of ground and found herself sprawled on her back, her own dagger pressed to her throat.

All she could think of was how badly she still wanted to win, and how all it would take was one split second of distraction for her to flip him over and claim victory – much as he had done to her.

What's burning?

Ramiq didn't even hear the smaller lad scream and drop his knife – he was too shocked that no one else seemed to see what was happening. Magic surged around the dagger the boy held, and again Ramiq had the strong feeling that he knew this mysterious mage.

He watched as the power flared and grew brighter to his sight, as though glad to have been released. Meanwhile on the field, the

tables had turned – the mage was now on top, fist clutched around the other boy's throat. At that moment, the world flipped upside-down on Ramiq, and *he* was on top of the streetrat, breathing heavily and suddenly painfully aware of everything around him.

Tsuga knew she had won. She could feel her opponent's pulse beneath her fingers, and as the adrenaline sang in her ears, she waited to hear the announcement of her victory.

Just then, the world dipped and spun; the next thing she knew, she was standing on a shaded platform, watching herself stand and be proclaimed the winner. She gasped, unsure what was happening, and blinked hard. Surely she was hallucinating.

Ramiq gave himself a little shake as he came back to himself just in time to catch the winner's name, and the comment Adain made to Midan.

"I'm not sure I saw that right. It looked as though the lad dropped his dagger for no reason at all."

Midan shrugged. "Looked that way to me, too. But I spoke to the girl, Tsuga. She's got a good head on her shoulders. Maybe we just didn't catch it."

Ramiq made an incredulous noise deep in his throat. "You've got to be kidding me," he muttered.

Adain turned to frown at his young pupil. "I'm sorry? Did you have something to say, Journeyman?"

Ramiq winced at the use of his title. Adain was plainly trying to put him in his place by reminding him of the company he kept.

The young man was still reeling from his revelation. He'd known there was something off about the fighter aside from just the magic. Now he knew what it was. Tsuga. The girl from his encounter with the Devalian army. Her magic was even more out of control now than it had been then, but he knew it had to be the same girl. What he didn't know was how she'd gotten here, or how he had suddenly seen through her eyes.

Everyone had turned to look at him – even Her Majesty was watching him with a bemused little grin. Ramiq coughed and ducked his head.

"No, sir. Only that it was an incredible victory. One could almost say it was . . . magical."

Adain quirked an eyebrow at him, but thankfully his mentor said nothing.

Tsuga scarcely registered what was happening as the announcer came over to lift her to her feet and declare her name to the masses. Her head was still reeling from her . . . out-of-body experience was the only way she could think to describe it. And aside from that, her magic had rushed to the surface in those last moments, and now it fought violently for release.

She knew that her calling it had resulted in the end of the fight. She had realized what was happening even as she'd done it. The taste of this victory was bitter. It had not been a clean fight.

What the hell just happened, Tsu?

I . . . I don't know.

Well, you got what you wanted. I just hope it turns out to be worth it.

Me, too.

Tsuga had been in the Warriors' Compound for a few weeks now. She couldn't think of a time when her life had been easier. Routine had always been good for her, and there was certainly no shortage of that as a trainee. Her days hadn't been this regimented since her time in the Devalian army. But this time, there was no lying about her nationality, no hiding who she was. It was . . . nice.

Every morning – as she always had – she rose hours before dawn and went for a run. By the time she returned to the Compound afterwards, it was time for breakfast, and then she was subjected to whatever Midan had scheduled for the day. Sometimes it was merely endurance training or repetitive drills. Once a week there was a lecture on tactics, provisioning, politics, or some other aspect of fighting that a "normal" soldier would not be expected to know. But some days, one of the trainees would be chosen to instruct their comrades in the art which they themselves had mastered. These days were her favorites.

Today, the skill of choice was archery. Pandi, the victor in the archery tournament, was a tall, muscular lad with a face that was particularly prone to smiling. His skin was a dark shade that Tsuga had never seen before, and he spoke with an accent she didn't recognize. He was the best archer she had ever seen, and he couldn't have been more than a few years her senior.

"The bow must be as an extention of your will, the arrow a physical manifestation of your sight. To hit the target, your will must be strong, your sight true."

As he spoke, he raised his bow and drew the arrow's fletching back to brush his high, exotic cheekbone. He simply held this position. Tsuga's lighter eyes darted to follow his line of sight, but she could not see anything at which he might be aiming.

"Your hands must be steady as you draw the bow. They must not shake from the strain. Take your time. Breathe. Concentrate on your target. And only when you are certain you are ready, release the shot."

But Pandi didn't let loose his arrow. Instead, he slowly lowered the longbow – nearly of a height with himself – to his side and turned back to face his comrades.

"A moving target is hardest to hit. Today, we will keep it simple. No arrows will be shot today." At the confused buzz that arose after this announcement, Pandi only smiled.

"You must first learn to appreciate your weapon. It must be a part of you. The wood of your bow should sing to your soul."

As he spoke, Pandi ran his hands lovingly over the intricately carved bow he held and smiled.

"I made this bow myself. Carved her with my own hands." He then lifted the arrow and twirled it between his fingers.

"I also make and fletch all of my own arrows. Granted, in the middle of a war, this is not always practical. And in a battle, I use what arrows are at hand. But these, these are specifically weighted and designed to fly farther, shoot truer, and hit harder than your typical arrow. With an arrow just like this one here, I have impaled a man's armored head from two hundred yards."

Tsuga whistled appreciatively, along with several others, as she took a closer look at the projectile. It was longer than her arm, and its length was covered in a spiral pattern carved around its shaft. She wasn't sure what good that did, but she trusted that Pandi knew what he was talking about.

"A longbow, as mine is, is the hardest bow to draw. It takes a great deal of strength and control. It is also the best for use against armored men. Only the best archers can properly wield such a bow. When we are finished, you will all be able to. Today, we will begin by learning how to craft one. You will all, eventually, be making your own."

That night, Tsuga dreamt:
She stood alone in the darkness, but she had the distinct sense that someone was there behind her. She could feel the age her body wore – hardened by years, her bones ached and her muscles lacked some of their usual strength and tone.

Suddenly, there was the touch of another's skin against hers, and she realized all at once that she was standing unclothed in an absurdly lavish room. The touch was familiar, and it lit a fire deep within her to which she was not accustomed. She turned, hungry for more, and looked up into his green eyes as he whispered her name.

"Tsu."

Ramiq awoke with a start and lay in the pillowy softness of his bed, heart hammering franticly. His own voice still rang in his ears, thick with emotion.

"Tsu."

He swallowed hard and looked to Lyra where she lay on the foot of his bed, watching him calmly.

Bad dream?

Ramiq shook his head in irritation and ran an agitated hand through his tousled hair.

"No, it was nothing. Go back to sleep."

"There's going to be a *what*?!" Surely she had heard wrong. Surely Midan had not just told them all that the queen was throwing –

"A ball. For all of the trainees in the Mages' Complex, as well as those of you here in the Compound. Her Majesty has upheld the tradition of encouraging friendships between the two, as you will all be working quite closely with each other for the rest of your lives."

Tsuga stifled a groan even as one of the other girls in the group chimed in with far too much enthusiasm, "Will we get to dress up?"

Midan laughed. "Of course. In fact, it's required."

Thank the Goddess, Tsuga wasn't the only one to groan at hearing this. Nor was she the one to ask the question she knew would come up.

"And how is a poor man's son to pay for such finery?"

Midan smiled and shook his head. "The queen has provided ample funds for that. No one need pay for his own clothes."

This time, it *was* Tsuga who spoke up.

"Do we have to go?"

This earned a frown from her mentor, but his voice was still light as he spoke.

"Of course you have to go. Consider it a hands-on lesson in diplomacy. Today you shall be relieved of your usual lessons so that you may go into town to find your outfits. Now, one at a time, come forward and take your coin; then be on your way, the lot of you!"

"Damn, you clean up pretty good!"

Tsuga made a face. Two of her good friends had come with her to help her pick out a gown, and neither of them was making the process any easier for her to bear. This particular comment came from Evan, a youngish man – maybe three or four years her senior – who had earned his place in their little group by being the best in mounted combat. He tended to speak his mind.

"Thanks. I, uh, think."

Kayla, the woman who had won the competition for the staff, laughed heartily. "Oh, Tsu, take the compliment. You really do look quite lovely."

Tsuga flushed and plucked at the burgundy fabric while she shook her head. "Good, then we're done looking for me, right?"

Kayla laughed again and moved to take her by the arm. "Nonsense. We still have to find you shoes and jewelry!"

Tsuga groaned. "Next you're gonna tell me I have to do something with my hair."

Evan snorted at the horrified look on Kayla's face.

"Oh, Tsuga, darling! Well, don't worry; I can help you with that, too. Now, go change so we can start finding you the rest of the things you'll need."

Would you stop obsessing? You look fine.

Ramiq scowled down at Lyra and shook his head.

"I am not obsessing. There was a loose thread."

Great. Well, it's gone now. Can we please enjoy the party?

The young mage sniffed and turned away from his reflection in the fountain he stood by. As he did his eyes swept past the door, and then lingered on a gorgeous young woman in a deep burgundy gown. She looked timid, uncertain – almost uncomfortable in her finery – and Ramiq caught himself smiling at the thought of what may be under the soft, flowing fabric.

Intrigued, he began easing his way through the growing crowd until he was close enough to the girl and her small group of friends to overhear their conversation.

"Would you stop worrying? I told you, you look fine."

Tsuga frowned and reached up again to try and relieve the pressure from the baubles holding her hair in place. Kayla swatted her hand away.

"Tsuga Dafrin, you stop that right now!"

The words had scarcely left Kayla's lips when there was an exclamation nearby. Tsuga turned just in time to see the navy and silver hem of mage's robes disappear into the crowd. When she turned back to her friends, Evan was leading Kayla off to dance; the next thing she knew, she stood alone by the door, surrounded by people she didn't know.

No matter. I'll just go find a quiet place to stand and wait out the night.

Ramiq had retreated to a dark corner – a secluded little alcove half-hidden by an ornate sculpture that he didn't take the time to examine. His heart was hammering wildly, and he couldn't seem to catch his breath.

Goddess' tits, what's she doing here?!

Well, she was invited for the same reason we were.

Ramiq jumped as something furry brushed up against his leg, but relaxed when he realized it was only his guardian. He gave her a withering look and opened his mouth to retort, but swallowed his words when he heard a gasp. He looked to the source of the sound and nearly swallowed his tongue when he realized who had made it.

"Sorry, I didn't think anyone would be back here."

Her cheeks were flushed; this close, Ramiq could catch the faint scent of horse about her. Despite his hatred for the beasts, on her he found the scent inexplicably appealing. When he couldn't manage to form a response, her flush deepened and she started to back away.

"I'll just be going, then. I – I'm sorry to have disturbed you."

Tsuga turned to leave, her mind racing. This had seemed the perfect hiding place. Little had she known it was already occupied. She had a sneaking suspicion that this young man's blue-and-silver robes were the same she had glimpsed mere minutes before, and she wondered why he was hiding here. He didn't seem to be all that intelligent, though; he'd been standing with his mouth agape since she'd stumbled across him, and had yet to say a word. Perhaps he was slow. Maybe he had come to look at the pretty baubles?

She had just stepped out from behind the statue when a hand closed around her arm.

Say something, you moron!

Ramiq gave himself a little shake, and then realized that she had turned away. Without thinking, he reached out to her and grasped her arm. He felt her muscles tense, and his empathic senses felt her jolt of adrenaline, but she merely stopped and turned to stare at him coldly.

This would be a good time to say something.

"I know what you are."

Tsuga's heart pounded at his words. Where a moment before his touch had warmed her inexplicably, now a cold fear spread throughout her body, paralyzing her limbs. Her voice was surprisingly steady when she spoke.

"I beg your pardon?"

Ramiq's empathic gift was being flooded with fear, and he suddenly felt like a cornered animal. This shouldn't be the case; he was thoroughly shielded, and the days when his defenses faltered enough to let in every stray emotion of the people around him were long gone. He released Tsuga and wiped his hands nervously on his robes – they were suddenly very sweaty.

I think you stepped in it.

Lyra's helpful comment served to spur him into action, and he licked his lips nervously before he spoke.

"I take it you don't recognize me. But then, why would you; you've never seen me. It's Tsuga, right?"

Tsuga was sure she hadn't done anything to give herself away. But he was backtracking fast now, with no sign of stopping. When he spoke her name, she almost thought her heart had ceased its beating in her chest. His voice – it was the one from the dreams. Younger, yes, but she recognized it all the same.

"Who are you? And how do you know my name?"

She still seemed suspicious. His empathic sense was going crazy, bouncing back and forth between terror, confusion, and a tangled jumble of emotions that he couldn't unravel. Her question put him on the spot, and he licked his lips again to buy himself an extra second to think.

"I'm in training to be the next Queen's Mage. I saw you in the tournament a while back. Very impressive, though using your magic may have been a bit unfair of you."

The world dropped out from under her. Tsuga staggered slightly under the weight of his words, and suddenly she realized why his voice *really* sounded familiar. It was the one from her dreams, all right. Her nightmares.

Ramiq watched her stagger as though from a blow and reached out a sympathetic hand to steady her. The next thing he knew, his face was pressed uncomfortably against the cold marble floor and she was on top of him, twisting his arm painfully behind his back until he thought she might pop it clean off. She bent low over him, and despite himself he felt a stirring in his groin as her lips grazed his ear.

"Listen, you. You tried to kill me. You exposed me to an entire century of Devalians who would not have hesitated to slay me on the spot. If you jeopardize my place here, I will relieve you of your entrails and cut off your dick so that you may shove it down your own throat. I am not a mage. Not anymore. What you saw at the tournament was a fluke, nothing more. You will speak of it to no one. Including me. You are to pretend you do not know me, have never seen me before in your life. Do I make myself perfectly clear?"

When the worm sputtered out a terrified affirmative, Tsuga stood – but not before digging her knee into his back for good measure. She left him stunned and gasping for air, and managed to keep her hands from shaking as she smoothed the velvet folds of her gown.

With a great effort, Tsuga pushed down her fear and plastered a bright smile on her face as she stepped out from the hidden alcove.

"Tsuga, there you are! Come on, we've a bet to settle!"

"Oh, and just what might that be?"

The voices faded as they moved away. Ramiq sat up slowly and checked himself for injuries. He was sure his back was going to sport a vibrant bruise from her knee. His wrist would probably darken as well. Nothing a touch of illusion or a session with one of his healer friends couldn't fix, to be sure.

We both know you're too prideful to let anyone know that someone got the best of you. Let alone a girl.

Ramiq scowled at Lyra, who had been notably absent during the incident.

"Yeah, thanks for all the help, you nappy old mutt."

The fox brushed up against him, tickling his hands with her soft red fur.

And what good would I have been to you, hmm? It's not like I've ever had any luck keeping your foot out of your mouth for you. Now pull yourself together, work your little magic trick, and let's get back to the party, shall we?

"Don't look now, but the handsome boy's staring again."

Kayla's eyes twinkled as she conveyed this information. Evan, who was standing behind them, leaned over so that his head was between the two girls.

"Ooh, really? Golly, he's so cute! Do you think he likes my hair?"

Tsuga laughed and swatted his head away playfully. "Hush, both of you. There's no way he's looking at me. Not with Kayla looking like that."

That wasn't true, of course. Though her friend truly did look stunning, the mage's eyes had been boring a hole in *her* all night. She could almost feel the resentment rolling off of him as he glared at her.

Well, did you think you could just offer to feed him his own genitals and then go on about your merry way as though nothing had happened?

Not exactly, but . . ..

Don't 'but' me. You can either deal with the situation like an adult, or avoid it, like you're doing. Either way, you're going to have to suck it up.

Tsuga resisted the urge to sigh – but only just – and came back to the conversation just in time to hear Evan say ". . . a cute couple. Maybe we should try getting him to ask her to dance?"

Tsuga felt the heat rising to her face. She was quick to protest.

"You know, I really don't think that's a very good idea. I mean, I don't even know how to dance!"

"Oh, well that's not a problem!" Kayla laughed. "After all, you're the girl. All *you* have to do is follow. It's *his* job to make sure you don't make an idiot out of yourself. Now, how shall we go about this?"

Tsuga could plainly see that her friends had no intentions of letting her have a say in this matter. While the two of them began plotting how to get him to dance with her, she began casting about for an excuse to leave before they figured something out.

Ramiq smiled and adjusted his position so that the light would better illuminate his sandy brown hair, thus catching the eye of the attractive young blonde who was standing opposite him.

"Kayla. You know, that's a lovely name. And historic, too."

She interrupted him. "Yes, the infamous Kayla, wife of the first king of Devali. Whore, more like. But she was remarkably lovely. You know, it's said of her that she could charm a bird from the sky to alight on her finger."

Ramiq snorted. "Of course she could. She was a mage. Animal mindspeech is almost as common in Devali as our guardians are here."

The lovely young woman rolled her eyes in an exaggerated manner. "Well, I never was much of one for history and politics; not my area of expertise. My friend, though – she loves it. Could talk your ear off about the inner workings of long-dead courts."

This piqued Ramiq's interest, to be sure. He'd always been fascinated with court intrigue. Aside from magic – and, admittedly, himself – it was one of the few topics of which he never tired.

"Well, your friend certainly sounds interesting."

Kayla beamed up at him. "Oh, she is! You should dance with her. She's too shy to say anything, but I know she'd be very flattered if you asked."

Ramiq chuckled, careful to keep the sound deep and hearty. Kayla's friend sounded like a frumpy intellectual, but the blonde woman was just the kind of attractive, brainless trollop he liked best for a meaningless tumble. Ramiq had no doubt that if he humored her and danced with this mousy "friend," she would be quite creative in how she chose to express her gratitude.

"Well, what harm could there be in one dance, right?"

Kayla had said there would be a signal when he said yes. She hadn't mentioned that the "signal" would in fact be the girl grinning and waving excitedly from half way across the ballroom.

"Tsuga, he said yes!"

Tsuga groaned and tried to pretend that she had neither seen nor heard her friend. She turned to disappear into the crowd, but ran smack into Evan – who, grinning broadly, took her by the arm and escorted her directly to Kayla's side despite her protests.

Ramiq froze. His heart hammered franticly in his chest, and he quickly scanned the room for the tell-tale velvet gown. Sure enough, there she was, being escorted to them by a strong-looking young man with dark hair and weather-hardened skin.

"You know," Kayla was saying, "I think you'll really like her. Tsuga is very strongly opinionated."

Ramiq shook his head, thinking to himself, *Yeah, no kidding.* He had scarcely finished the thought when Tsuga arrived with her smiling escort. Ramiq took a moment to appreciate the look of the lad, and then he was looking into her eyes, so full of ice-cold rage that they forced him to look away. Her voice was deceptively light when she spoke.

"Kayla, did you have to draw so much attention to us? You know I can't dance, and now everyone is sure to be watching."

Ramiq mustered what he hoped was a charming smile and extended his hand.

"Well, that will hardly matter. You look positively stunning. I don't doubt that you would attract stares whether you were dancing or not."

He was nervous. It was almost as though she could smell his fear. He managed something that was obviously intended to be flattering, but it served only to irritate her further. However, Tsuga didn't want to betray herself, so she mustered a tense smile and ducked her head slightly to hide the anger in her eyes.

"Well, aren't you just the smooth talker."

After that brief moment when she'd first approached, the boy had determinedly avoided meeting her gaze. He was currently fixated on a torch hanging from the wall behind her. She could feel it drawn to her, but determinedly pushed the awareness to the back of her mind. He chuckled and offered his hand to her.

"It's easy enough to find ways to compliment such a beautiful woman."

I think I'm gonna be sick. "Well, aren't you sweet."

Though it pained her, she let him take her hand as she managed an awkward curtsy. He brought her hand to his lips, and as he made contact, Tsuga felt a twinge shoot up her arm. She winced and jerked away hastily as she straightened.

Ramiq's heart jumped as he took her calloused hand in his. A strange sensation shot through him as he gave her a courteous peck. Her hand was gone from his before the feeling had even registered, leaving him to blink and look at her in confusion. She looked just as flushed as he felt, and in an effort to smooth things over, he blurted out the first thing that came to mind.
"Shall we dance?"

Kayla and Evan stood next to her, smiling and nodding like idiots. Tsuga knew she had no choice if she wanted them to leave her alone. It took everything she had not to grimace and grit her teeth, but she mustered a small smile instead.
"Very well. I can see that I am not to be given a choice. I shall follow your lead."
He took her extended hand while her friends grinned like fools. She could feel his reluctance in the stiff way he moved; in spite of herself, she found that she was making an effort to keep all of her own movements fluid and relaxed as he drew her into the small crowd of dancers.

She moved quietly and with a mysterious fluidity that reminded him strongly of smoke. He spun her out, unable to resist admiring her figure and the briefest glimpse of the line of her slender legs beneath the heavy fabric of her gown. She must have caught him looking; when he drew her close, she ground her heel onto his toes and elbowed him in the ribcage. He sucked in a painful breath and forced a smile.
"Just relax and follow my lead, and we can get through this with a minimal amount of pain." *I hope.*

Tsuga lost her balance as he pulled her to him, and in covering her stumble, she accidently stepped on him and landed a decent blow to his midsection. Not that she minded roughing him up a little, come to think of it.
Just as this thought occurred to her, she felt his hand slide to the small of her back and his fingers settle lightly against her spine. She forced her suddenly tense muscles to relax and glared at her dance partner, stubbornly ignoring the burning-bubbling feeling in the pit of her stomach.
"Watch the hands, unless you'd rather I relieve you of them."

When he took her into his arms and prepared to start the dance, Ramiq felt a sudden dizzying moment of disorientation. For a brief heartbeat, she was years older, dressed in a form-fitting red and gold gown with jewels set flatteringly in her hair, smiling at him with love in her eyes.

And then he was back, and she was once again threatening him with dismemberment. He shook his head slightly and dismissed the strange vision from his thoughts.

"This is how dancing *goes*. Of course, you'd know that if you allowed yourself to be touched without threatening to kill or maim your partner."

He snorted and took a step backwards, pulling her along with him as he turned to the right. She followed reluctantly, half a beat behind the music. He sighed and rolled his eyes.

"You have to relax and follow me. You're not in control here; I am."

The warm feeling inside of her ratcheted up a few degrees and heated into a slowly simmering anger. She frowned at his comment and followed him as he dragged her around the floor.

"I'm following you, aren't I? Aren't I supposed to?"

He shook his head as she was forced to take a couple of extra steps to catch up with him. "No. You're not *just* supposed to follow. You're supposed to let me lead. I'm telling you what I'm going to do. You're not paying attention."

Tsuga snorted. "All you're telling me is what I'm doing wrong, and it is certainly *not* helping."

The boy frowned and tapped his fingers lightly against her spine, sending an odd tingle down her back. She suspected him of using a small jolt of magic to gain her attention. The possibility only served to irritate her further.

"Just because I'm not talking doesn't mean I'm not saying something. If you'd listen to your body, you'd know exactly what to do."

Okay, so he'd given her a little jolt of lightning. Nothing harmful; just enough to get her attention. She frowned, and he could tell that she was actually considering his words. He applied a light pressure with his fingertips and guided her into another turn. She kept up a little better this time, and he smiled smugly.

"You see? You just have to listen with something other than your ears and stop resisting."

What he said made a certain amount of sense; after all, there were many situations in which a warrior had to trust in her body to know its own way. So, though it vexed her to no end, she tried following his advice. Sure enough, when she felt his hand adjust

on her back and moved in response, he moved with her. The turn
was far from perfect, but it was a vast improvement over her first
attempts. In spite of herself, she felt a smile tug at the corners of
her mouth. He was smiling, too.

"You see? Not as hard as it seems."

Tsuga could feel herself blushing, and she ducked her head
slightly to hide it. Her stomach churned with a confusing jumble
of emotions, and she was painfully aware of his body pressed
against hers.

Ramiq felt himself soften slightly when she flushed. It made
her seem human – indeed, almost feminine – and he decided he
rather liked it. As the dance went on she continued to improve,
and he found himself warming to her further.

"You know," he said, smiling at her, "when you're not
threatening to kill me, you almost pass for a beautiful woman."

She frowned and looked at him sharply, but something in his
expression must have convinced her that he meant no ill by the
comment, because she smiled and dropped her gaze again.
Something twisted inside of him, and before he even realized that
the thought had occurred to him, he had leaned forward and
kissed her. She was almost of a height with him, and it was
nothing at all to dip his head slightly to find her lips with his.

Tsuga felt completely off-balance. She was in close quarters
with someone who had completely destroyed her life once
already – and had the power to do so again if he wished. She
should be as far away from him as possible, keeping her head
down and flying under his radar. Instead she was in his arms,
letting him twirl her around a dance floor. What was worse, she
was actually enjoying herself. She looked at him askance when
he commented on her silence, but his expression was soft and
open. Suddenly all she could think of was how his green eyes
looked positively enchanting in the glow of the torch light.

She ducked her head as the heat in her gut rose up her neck and
into her cheeks. And then, between one moment and the next, his
lips were pressed to hers and the entire world had turned upside-
down. The heat in her stomach contracted, and then expanded
wildly. She suddenly felt very cold. Then, she felt nothing at all.

Thank the Goddess for the shields on this place.

Although Ramiq himself had been shielded against assault as
he always was, the explosion had come with such force and at
such an unexpected moment that he had been blown backwards a
good ten feet and landed on his ass on the cold marble floor. He
hadn't had time to erect a shield of absorption to prevent the effect
of her magic. His face felt tight – as though he'd been burned by

overexposure to the sun – and there were scorch-marks on his robes where he'd had to put out a small flame that had caught in the silk. He was sore all over; as he made his way stiffly to his feet, he became aware that everyone was staring at him.

He managed some comment about pranks and how they'll backfire, which illicited some laughs as the festivities resumed. The hall was none the worse for the wear, and it seemed he was the only one who'd gotten singed. Come to think of it, he thought he smelled burned hair . . ..

Ramiq looked to where they'd been standing at the time of the explosion, and only then realized that Tsuga was gone. Sore, confused, and a bit angry that she would disappear without so much as an apology, Ramiq strode stiffly out of the hall and into the cool night air. He wasn't sure where he was going or what he intended to do. He knew only that he had to leave the party before anyone started asking questions.

Tsuga woke to Kayla's face inches from her own, and she startled backwards and lost her balance. Strong arms surrounded her and held her steady, and she turned her head to see Evan's concerned face next to her. She could feel cool grass under her hands as she propped herself up.

They must have brought me outside, she thought.

"So, you want to tell us what happened?"

This from Kayla – who had, thankfully, backed away a few steps to give her some space.

"What do you mean?" Evan laughed and gave her shoulders a gentle squeeze.

"Come now, we were watching. Then we looked away for just a second, and the next thing we knew there was an explosion and you were on the ground. What did he do, try to blow you up?"

And then what had happened hit home. He had *kissed* her. She'd heard of sparks flying before, but they had set off an explosion. What did *that* mean?

"He kissed me."

Even to her own ears, her voice sounded dazed and distant. Kayla squealed, and when Tsuga looked to Evan, he was grinning from ear to ear.

"Tsu, that's great! So why the explosion, then?"

"I . . . don't know. Set him off, I guess?"

Kayla giggled infuriatingly. "Well, it wouldn't be the first case of premature eruption for an over-excited young mage."

Evan eyed them both with a look of long-suffering patience and extended his hand to Tsuga. She pushed it aside so she could hike her skirts up to her knees and stand on her own.

"Hmm. Well, we're going to go back to the party. Are you coming?"

"No, Evan. I think I'm just going to go back to the Compound and get out of this dress. You two go have fun, though."

Her two friends exchanged a look, and for a moment it seemed as though they would protest. Luckily, Tsuga's guardian chose that moment to emerge from the shadows and stand at the girl's back.

"Don't worry. I'll take it from here."

The two smiled and nodded before making their brief farewells. Once they had gone, Tsuga turned to bury her face in the horse's neck for comfort. The great beast stood steady for a moment before she twisted her head around to look at the girl.

An explosion, Tsu? Really? I thought you'd gotten this under better control.

"I know. I'm not sure what happened. It was all so sudden, and I was so flustered, and . . .. Light, Bane, I'm so confused!"

Shh, shh. Calm down. No one knows where it came from. Climb on. We need to talk.

Ramiq had retreated to the cooler air of the gardens as soon as he could slip away unnoticed, and now he simply absorbed the silence. A sound from his childhood caught his attention and he turned, seeking the horse that had just whickered. Sure enough, he spied a large beast standing patiently while a woman in a dark dress clung to it desperately.

"I'm not sure what happened."

Her words came to him clearly, carried on the light breeze that teased his disheveled hair. "It was all so sudden, and I was so flustered, and . . .. Light, Bane, I'm so confused!"

It's Tsuga, he realized, even as he felt an odd stirring and a strong urge to go to her. He stayed where he was, though, not wanting to startle her into trying to blow him up again.

She moved around to the side of the horse – her guardian, he presumed from the way she'd seemed to speak in response to something he hadn't heard. He watched as she deftly gathered her skirts and swung herself up onto the animal's bare back. The sight of so much toned white leg exposed gave him a far more familiar stirring, and though he knew he should look away, he couldn't help admiring her graceful, confident movements as she rode away.

If she could just learn to relax like that on the dance floor, she would be spectacular.

With a sigh of frustration he turned to go back inside, suddenly determined to find an outlet for his arousal.

Tsuga settled easily onto her guardian's back and let the beast pick her own way back to the Warriors' Compound. A few moments of silence passed, and then came the words she'd been dreading.

I think it's time to come clean, Tsu.

"About what?"

Don't play dumb. You need to sit down with Midan and tell him about Devali. You need to tell him you're a mage. It's getting dangerous, Tsu. If that boy had been anyone other than a Queen's Mage – if those people had been anyone but who they are – if you had lost control anywhere else, everyone in that room would be dead. Blown to bits. It's time to come clean with everyone, Tsu. Especially yourself.

"It has always been dangerous. And it has *already* killed people. They'll only train me to kill more. How is it fair to burn a man to ash? You can't fight against that kind of death. There is no honor, no skill, no challenge in killing that way . . .. I will tell him the rest, though – about Devali. But not anything that would put my friends there at risk. Never that."

Of course. Bane sighed. **There's something else, Tsu.**

"What is it?"

Are we going to talk about what happened with the boy? Or are you going to pretend that it didn't happen, either?

"I . . . I don't know. One minute, I could barely endure his touching me, and the next, he had kissed me. I have no idea what happened, or why he did it."

But you liked it.

"Well, I suppose I did . . .. But I nearly blew him up! There is no point in dwelling on it further after that."

At that comment, Tsuga was given the distinct impression that Bane had rolled her eyes. **If that is how you feel, then.**

"It is. Now let's go home. I can't wait to get out of this damned dress."

"Now, run this by me again. You were how old when all of this happened?"

"I was not yet fifteen when I was found by the soldiers in the woods. In fact, I had scarcely turned fourteen at the time."

Midan chuckled, and the other man – a general, from the knots of rank he wore – let out a low whistle and shook his head in wonder.

"Incredible. And this went on for two years?"

"Yes, sir; about that. They took me on as a stable boy of sorts, to tend their horses."

"And all because your guardian happened to be a horse. This is absolutely amazing. How ever did you keep it all a secret?"

"Men believe what they choose to, I suppose. My nationality was exposed before my gender – quite by accident, of course, and the soldier who found me out did me a great service by keeping my secret."

"And tell me again how it was you escaped."

"I was gravely wounded in battle – badly burned and sliced nearly in half. It was a healer who found me out. The same one who took me under her protection and declared me above the law until she deemed me fully recovered. By the time I was well, of course, we were far away."

The general was shaking his head again, but his gaze had sharpened, his expression become more direct. "You mentioned that they instructed you in the ways of war. Just what did they teach you?"

"Everything they could, sir. Every kind of weapon you can imagine. Several I'd never even heard of before. I learned to best men more than twice my size and strength; how to move, hide, and provision an army. I learned how they fight and think, how they set up their camps, how they spend their days. I learned what it meant to be one of them."

The two men exchanged a meaningful glance that made her want to squirm in her seat, but she forced herself to hold still. It was Midan who next broke the silence.

"Tsuga, how old are you now?"

The question seemed so off topic that it threw her, and so it was several moments before she managed to answer.

"I – I'm just shy of nineteen, sir."

Samuel was taken aback at the girl's age.

She's young. Maybe too young for what we're about to ask. But it wasn't as though they had any other options, really. The war was quickly killing off not only all of his leaders, but also many of the promising soldiers who might have been fit to take their places. And then, this child – no, this woman, this *soldier –* had come from out of nowhere, as though gifted to him by the Goddess Herself.

Midan spoke highly of her. She learned quickly and well, and had a mind particularly turned to the tactical and political. She was a better choice than any other he knew. But respect would be hard-won for one so young.

Goddess, but I hope she's up to the challenge. At last, he spoke aloud. "Tsuga Dafrin, you are to transfer your belongings to the Officers' Barracks on the north side of the Compound. As of this moment, you are Captain Tsuga Dafrin."

His words made no sense. For a moment, she had almost thought he'd said he was promoting her to captain. But that was ridiculous. She was too young. Too inexperienced. And besides that, she would be skipping several ranks with such a promotion. No; surely she had heard him wrong.

"I beg your pardon, sir, but I must have misheard you." The general shook his head.

"No, Captain, you heard correctly."

The world seemed to freeze for several seconds, and the simple exhalation of a breath to take years to accomplish. Her mind raced in those scant moments, and finally she managed to sort through the chaos of her thoughts and frame a question.

"General, are you sure about this?"

His newest captain seemed to freeze for several long moments before she was able to speak again. He had to smile at hearing her echo the very question he'd been wrestling with himself. When she didn't go on to try and dissuade him from his decision he nodded to himself, knowing now for sure that he had chosen wisely.

"Miss Dafrin, I am as sure as any leader can be in putting someone else's life in danger. Of course, as a captain, you will learn that fear and doubt for yourself soon enough. Now, do you have any other questions? I'm sure this is a lot for you to absorb all at once."

Tsuga sat back in her chair for a moment, as though by shifting her position physically she could settle her thoughts. She looked for a long moment towards Midan, and then back to him. He could see a question in her murky brown eyes, but the one she voiced was most unexpected.

"Does this mean I won't be in training anymore? Won't be part of the Elites?"

Where most her age would rejoice at the prospect of making their own schedules, Sam thought he detected a hint of fear in her voice, though her posture didn't speak to it. He started to answer, but stopped when Midan lay a hand on his shoulder.

"Tsuga," Midan said gently, "you will no longer be a trainee. In that, you are correct. And as captain of your own century, you can't be an official member of the Elites, either. But a good soldier – a good leader – never stops learning. Never stops training."

She nodded slowly as she absorbed this information. "But, Weaponsmaster, this means that I will no longer be training under you, does it not?"

Sam thought he saw Midan smile at that, but he couldn't be sure. He thought back over what he knew of Tsuga, and recalled that she had fought for her place among Midan's most advanced students. No doubt the thought of losing her hard-won place chafed. Certainly not a good way for her to go into her new position.

"Captain, it is my direct order that you are to continue your training with Midan so long as your company is stationed here in Sennor. Keep in mind, however, that you are also now in charge of overseeing the ongoing training of those under your command, as well as all of the other, less glamorous duties that go with assuming this new position. Those duties *must* come first. I trust you understand that."

A smile flashed across the girl's face for a brief moment before it was gone again. More and more, Samuel was beginning to feel that he had indeed chosen well.

Well, Captain, what will you do first? Shall we go pack?

"No. First, I want to meet my troops." *My troops! Goddess, but that sounds strange. I hope I can do right by them.* "I need to know just what I'm getting into."

Good idea. And don't worry, Tsu. I can't think of anyone who would be more suited to lead. You shall be firm but sympathetic; brave but cautious; cunning, yet strong.

"You have a poet's way with words, Bane! Goddess, I hope you're right!"

This is what I have to work with?

Tsuga was still mounted. She had found a page and asked him how best to summon the soldiers of her new command. The lad had spit and said "Just go to the third barracks. You'll find 'em."

Sure enough, she'd found them. They were a diverse group; many were her age and younger, but there were also several grizzled veterans in the group – and no few with malice in their eyes as they now stood before her.

When she'd first happened upon them, there had been a crowd around a handful of soldiers – two men and a couple of women she took to be their lovers. They all sported several cuts and bruises, but she was relieved to see that at least they had restrained themselves to a fist fight. Their weapons had been thrown down off to one side of the tangle. She wasn't sure if they had stopped fighting because she had commanded them to do so, or if it was because she – several years their junior, by the looks of them – had had the audacity to do so. Tsuga shifted her weight in the saddle and stared at the four troublemakers.

"So, which of you is going to tell me what happened?"

The four of them exchanged glances, and then the older of the two women spit out a mouthful of blood and glowered more intensely. "What business is it of yers, huh?"

Tsuga fought the urge to smile at her nerve and instead opted for a cold stare. "What is your name, soldier?"

This was apparently not the reaction the woman had expected, as she rocked back on her heels and hesitated a moment before answering. "Aluna. What's it to you?"

"And how long have you been fighting, Aluna?"

The woman didn't seem to have any idea where this was going. "Near an hour, I guess. Maybe less."

Tsuga shook her head. "You misunderstand me. You, Aluna. How long have you been fighting?"

Aluna blinked her gray eyes a few times as she mulled over the question before she responded. "Fifteen years. Maybe a couple more. Been so long, I can scarcely remember."

Tsuga nodded and turned her attention to the young blond lad who had been trying to break up the fight.

"And you, boy? How long?"

"Couple seasons."

Tsuga nodded, and over the next several minutes received answers to this question from every one of her soldiers. Not only had the fight drawn a crowd, but the little tableau of her interrogation drew the few who had not already gathered. By the time she had reached the last of them, she'd been assured that every one of her new charges was present. Their experience was as varied as the individuals themselves. She had a man who'd been fighting for thirty years – nearly twice as long as she'd been alive! – as well as several youths who had yet to see a battle. When the last soldier had given his information, Tsuga looked them all over again before she spoke.

"Many of you have fought longer than I have. Several of you have not even shed another man's blood. But I promise you, while your experience will be utilized and your knowledge sought out when appropriate, I have knowledge and experience to contribute as well. You have all told me your names. Now, hear mine. I am Tsuga Dafrin, native of Sennor. I was a soldier in the Devalian army. I have trained in arms for a good ten years. I have been admitted to, and now transferred from, Midan's small group of elite fighters. I have fought as a professional soldier and a hire-sword for a combined total of about three years. I am your new captain."

Though many had gasped or muttered at her admission about Devali, the announcement of her rank caused an uproar. Rather than try to shout over them, she simply sat calmly and waited them out. Finally, silence returned.

"I understand that many of you are alarmed or offended by my presence. As this is our first day together, I would start it well by granting each of you two boons. One: each person among you may ask me one question, of any nature you wish, and know that my answer will be nothing but the simple and complete truth. And two: any soldier among you may challenge me for my right to lead at any time. If I am defeated, I will go quietly and resign my position."

A bold statement.

We shall see if it pays off.

Tsuga draped Bane's reins over the horse's neck and swung herself to the ground before she turned to face her troops, one hand resting casually on the hilt of her sword.

"Now, who's first?"

Tsuga half expected them to swarm her all at once, but it quickly became obvious that a pecking order was already in place among them. The first to step forward was one of the middle-aged men. Twenty-two years experience, he had claimed, yet he still moved as though he were in his prime.

"Why should we believe someone from Devali shouldn't purposely lead us to our deaths?"

"A fair question. While I admit I left behind many good friends, I can assure you that my loyalty is first and foremost to my country and my Goddess. I fought for Devali because it offered me a secure place and an assured meal, but I am a Sennorran, not a Devalian."

He nodded thoughtfully and stepped back as the next question was voiced.

"What weapon do you favor?"

"I favor the sword. But I am reasonably skilled with every weapon I have trained with – which is to say, everything I've had opportunity to get my hands on."

"*Every* one?" someone scoffed.

"Yes."

"Who trained you?"

"I have had many, many teachers. My father. My Lord Gregory's Weaponsmaster. Fellow soldiers. Most recently, Weaponsmaster Midan."

"What makes you fit to lead us?"

"You do. I readily admit there is much I do not know. I will need all of your help to lead well, and I will seek the advice of each and every one of you without hesitation when it is needed."

"If you're a soldier, how come yer so well-spoken?"

"Lord Gregory treated me as his own daughter after my Da's death. He had me instructed in many things, including reading, speaking, and other courtly manners."

"What should we expect from you?"

"I'm very strict with myself. You can expect me to hold you to the same standards to which I hold myself. Constant training. Hard. In everything. You can expect for me to expect you to live, and to help you do so. I am not one to bark orders from the sidelines. My blood will be shed as readily as yours – as my brothers in arms, not as my underlings."

This time, there was a thoughtful silence before the next question was finally voiced.

"What do you expect from us, then?"

"Aide from what I just mentioned, I expect for my orders to be followed explicitly, but for even the most inexperienced of you to question me if my judgment strikes you as poor. And above all else, I demand your respect, as I will spend each day earning it."

The questions continued on long into the evening, with Tsuga laying down various rules for her company to live by. The topic ranged from "no woman may enter into battle if pregnant" to "no excuse save grave and life-threatening illness or injury shall suffice to spare you from training." By the end, Tsuga knew she hadn't even come close to covering everything, but there was only so much the mind could absorb at a time. When there were no more questions, she held up a hand for silence – and was rather stunned when she got it.

"I will leave you to your own devices for the rest of the night. Training begins in earnest tomorrow at dawn."

Tsuga had debated with herself over where to bunk. The general had told her to sleep with the other officers, but she wasn't comfortable in the company of men and women who had earned their place there by the loss of their own blood; not when her own title had been thrust upon her prematurely. Instead, she had begged permission to bunk with her own company. She felt an overwhelming need to earn her troops' trust and respect, and felt that living among them would help show them that she did not believe herself to be their superior.

Her night terrors would be more of a problem here than ever before. Not only would she rouse all of her command if she woke screaming, but she would have to face their questions afterward. In the end, though, she decided the potential gain was well worth the risk of a few hours' lost sleep and a bit of humiliation on her part, and had taken her belongings to her women's side of the barracks and claimed an empty bed among them.

The women left her alone this first night – whether out of respect for her fatigue, her position, or for dislike of her presence, she wasn't sure. Tsuga decided she didn't much care, either. They didn't have to like her. They had only to respect her.

Dawn came much later than it had any right to. Tsuga had been lying awake much of the night, making plans for the next day. At long last, she gave up the attempt at sleep and made her bed before quietly dressing and arming herself in the darkness. The unfamiliar room might have posed a problem to navigate without light, had it not been for the spark of fire inside her that even now made the room as bright to her eyes as though it were lit by a score of candles.

She took her boots in her hand and padded quietly outside. In the cool of the pre-dawn darkness, Tsuga paused a moment to lean against a wall and inhale the comforting smells of an army base – sweat, leather, unwashed bodies, and both human and animal waste. Once the sun rose this place would be swarming like a kicked anthill, but now, in the early morning, it was silent – like a great beast taking its slumber. Feeling invigorated by her anticipation of the coming day, Tsuga pulled her boots on and set off at a slow jog to wake her muscles.

Her company stood before her, half-heartedly assembled and none too silent. There were grumbles of "ungodly early" and "should be in bed," but she ignored them. She'd heard all about this company. They'd been out of combat for a couple of seasons because of the loss of their last Captain. In that time, it seemed, they had grown soft. Devilsbane stood at a distance, merely watching. She was there more for moral support than anything else.

Well, here goes.

You'll be fine. It's a good plan.

"Good morning!"

From the end of the line came a call of "Fuck you!" but this, too, she ignored.

"Today we will be cross-training. You will all need to sharpen your skills with your own weapons as well as with as many others as you can learn. The knowledge to use a spear when you've lost your sword in battle could well mean the difference between your life and your death one day. We'll start with a two mile cross-country run to warm up. Follow me. And keep up."

Without another word, Tsuga turned and set off at a steady jog. As agreed, Bane fell in behind the group of runners, keeping pace just behind the last in line. She would make sure no one fell too far behind.

The run took far longer than it should have. Only a handful of people managed to keep pace with her; by the end of it, even they looked worn out. She hadn't thought the exercise that difficult. After all, she'd gone slowly; a brisk jog, at most. She herself was barely winded.

They're horribly out of shape, aren't they?

When the last man had collapsed panting to the ground and Bane assured her that everyone was accounted for, Tsuga addressed them again.

"Well, I'm happy to see you've all been keeping in such good shape." The sarcasm was plain in her voice. "You can expect a short jog like that every morning, and another at the end of each day. Anyone who cannot complete the day's training will be set additional excercises accordingly until your fitness level increases sufficiently. Everyone line up."

There were groans and no small number of curses thrown her way, but they complied. When they had assembled to her satisfaction, she continued.

"Divide yourselves into the following four groups according to the discipline with which you are most proficient out of the following: sword, spear and staff, knives, and unarmed combat. We will cover all weapons eventually – four each week as we rotate through. If your weapon of choice is not a focus today, choose the group in which you feel you will do the best."

Several long moments passed, and no one moved. Tsuga scowled.

"Now! What are you waiting for, Mommy to hold your hand? GO!"

They didn't exactly jump into action, but they did begin to sort themselves out. There weren't many surprises in the way they positioned themselves, really. The majority of the larger men went to sword or spear. One huge man went to knives, though – but she shouldn't have been even as surprised at that as she was; he moved with the deadly silence and grace of a highly skilled assassin. Many of the women sorted themselves into knives and staff, though a few went to the other groups as well. When everyone seemed satisfied, she nodded and turned to the first group.

"And which are you?" As though she didn't already know.

"Staff and spear," someone answered, and she nodded before she moved on to the next.

"And you?"

"Sword."

The next responded unarmed, and she nodded towards the last.

"Which means you lot prefer knives. Alright. Straight lines, everyone. I will pair you off. First: you, and you." She pointed to the first person in the lines of both sword and knives. "You, and you." One each from staff and unarmed. She continued to pair them off thusly until everyone had a partner.

"Swordsmen, today you will be fighting with knives. If you don't have any, there are plenty that you can borrow – you have only to fetch them from the arms shed. Knives, you will of course be fighting today with swords. Unarmed with either a staff or a spear. And, as you may have guessed, staff and spear will be practicing in unarmed combat." When the protests died down a bit, she went on. "Is there anyone who has never used today's weapon at all before?"

Over half of them nodded or raised their hand, and now it was Tsuga's turn to groan. "Very well, we will start with a demonstration." She paused. "In fact, we will start with two. I need a volunteer from the staff and spear group, and one from the sword. I should practice myself."

She waited a few moments, and finally two soldiers stood up – a large, burly man with a sword at his belt, and a lithe woman holding a spear. Tsuga smiled and nodded.

"Very good. Come forward, sir. We'll begin with a demonstration of sword versus knife. I assume you can dance the basic forms? He nodded, and Tsuga allowed herself a small smile.

"Excellent. Do everything in slow motion, so that I can talk about it. Draw your sword."

He did so, reaching his right hand down to grasp the hilt. "Freeze." He stopped with the blade half drawn, and Tsuga examined his form with a quick glance. He would do nicely, she decided.

"Note the position of the hand on the sword, the angle of the arm, and the arrangement of the fingers and thumb. He has a secure grip, but not a tight one. His hand is protected by the guard, but not crowded up behind it. Draw."

He drew his sword fully, and Tsuga stopped him in the middle of bringing it upright. "Note how his wrist pivots and his grip shifts ever-so-slightly. Rest."

This command, of course, didn't mean for him to take a break. He was smart enough to know this, thankfully, and adopted the comfortable stance of battle rest – hilt at his hip, sword slanted so that the tip was protecting his left shoulder. This was the best defensive position.

"This is called 'rest' because it is the neutral stance. Same as with any other weapon. You can easily proceed to an overhead attack –" She gestured, and her man demonstrated before returning to rest, "– a low swipe," and again, he complied, "or a block. Thank you; you may sheathe your weapon."

As she spoke, Tsuga placed her hand on the long dagger she wore at her belt. "Those of you unfamiliar with knives, pay attention. There are two ways to draw a belt knife – the first is the same as the sword. However, if you are like me and wear both, your knife will be on the wrong side for such a draw. You may draw cross-body with your opposite hand, like so," and she demonstrated by drawing the blade with her left hand, "or with the same hand. The grip, of course, is different."

Again she demonstrated, holding the knife with the back of her hand to the outside, and drew slowly. "This draw requires one of two things – either an immediate overhead stab –" and she showed them before half-sheathing the knife again, "or else that you reverse your grip."

She showed them a couple of ways to do this – by tossing the knife and catching it, and then by rolling the hilt in her fingers.

"Rest is different for the knife, because the majority of your defense here comes from your speed rather than the length of your blade. Keep your arm close to your body, and position the knife either next to your hip, like this, or so that your hand is in front of your belly button. Either stance allows you to quickly attack or defend both high and low."

She once again demonstrated as she spoke, and then sheathed her dagger.

"A common pairing for mercenaries is a sword and dagger, with the dagger taking the place of the shield used by most foot soldiers. It is a pairing I myself favor in one-on-one combat, though it is not particularly practical on a battlefield. But we shall worry about that later. Today, each of you will be sparring with your partner using their own weapon of choice against them. Swords will use knives today, and visa versa. Now, for the benefit of those unfamiliar with any of the given weapons, I will also demonstrate a spar in each scenario. If you are ready?"

The last was addressed to her volunteer, who had been watching her intently. He straightened and gave himself a little shake.

"Yes'm. Ready."

Tsuga smiled. "Good."

By informing them that her strength lay with the sword and then choosing for herself the knife, Tsuga hoped to show that she was willing to follow her own rules. She dropped into a defensive crouch and watched as her opponent did the same.

Her shorter weapon put her at a distinct disadvantage, as it required her to focus primarily on defense, only striking back once she had engaged her opponent and could duck in close under his guard.

Unfortunately her opponent seemed to know this; he made no move to close for an attack, but instead only circled her warily. Tsuga turned, watching his movements, looking for an opening. His guard seemed pretty solid, but at last Tsuga saw a flaw, a way in which she might gain the upper hand. She began creeping closer to him, until she stood just beyond the reach of his sword. Still he kept his defense low, obviously expecting her to go for the large target of his torso. From that position, if she was fast enough and crafty enough, she just might manage to get a blow past him that landed on the extreme upper part of his body.

He chose that moment to feint towards her left arm, and in that small window of opportunity, Tsuga ducked low and moved forward, aiming a slash at his right hamstrings as she passed. At the last possible second, she flipped the knife from her left hand to her right and in one swift motion jabbed the pommel into the soft place in the back of his head where his neck met his skull.

She heard him cry out almost before she felt the impact, and as she turned, she had the pleasure of watching him crumple to the ground. Tsuga shook her head and sighed in disappointment. She had hoped for more of a challenge. She slid her weapon back into its sheath as she turned to address the rest of her troops.

"As you can see, it is not as impossible as it seems. All that is required is speed and cunning, and some small amount each of skill and luck.

"Now, my opponent here made several mistakes." She said this as she walked over to help him up. Once he had skulked back to his group, she went on.

"Who can tell me what they were?"

"He attacked first."

This came from someone in the sword group. Tsuga made a note of the face and that they would need to learn when it was best to take that kind of initiative.

"True; by doing so he gave me an opening."

"But the opening was already there."

Tsuga's eyes snapped to the woman who had spoken, and she nodded sharply. "Yes, it was. He expected me to strike for his midsection, and so left himself open to an attack on either his higher or lower extreme. What else?"

There was silence for a few beats, and then one of the older men in the unarmed group spoke up. "He expected your obvious attack to be your only one."

At this, Tsuga allowed herself a small smile. "Exactly. I could have followed through with the attack had it seemed worth it, but he had committed to it as the only thing I had planned. He thought he could predict me. Never expect an opponent to do what they should, or even what you would in their place.

"Now, madam, if you would be so kind, we shall move on to a demonstration of the spear."

Once again, Tsuga had her volunteer stand and go through some of the most basic moves and techniques of her weapon. When she was done, Tsuga demonstrated the fundamentals of unarmed combat in the same way. For the second time, Tsuga had purposely placed herself at the disadvantage for the spar. She now squared off against a woman of similar size and build, who brandished a weapon that would have been deadly enough even had it not been wickedly sharp on one end.

Tsuga had watched the woman closely during the brief demonstration, and so knew from the ease of movement and casual grace with which her opponent handled her spear that she now faced a formidable foe. Before she'd even been given a chance to settle herself into a defensive stance, the other woman was upon her, hammering her with a series of skilled blows that drove Tsuga back. She was forced to duck, dodge, and grapple as best she could to avoid being cut open. There were few set rules of form in this kind of unarmed combat – not when one's life depended on it – and Tsuga worried less about how the moves looked than how well they worked.

The woman was smart; she kept out of reach, using to her advantage the greater length afforded her by her weapon. Tsuga was all but impotent as a result, forced to focus on keeping her skin in one piece. After a series of near-miraculous dodges, Tsuga at last managed to grasp the shaft of the spear. She made the mistake, however, of allowing herself a moment to breathe a sigh of relief. In that space – that minute span of time between one breath and the next – the outcome of the match was decided. The spear shifted and spun in her hand, twisting her wrist painfully until she was forced to either surrender her hold or break the bone.

She decided that her pride was not worth the injury. Even as she let go, the butt of the spear twisted yet again; before Tsuga could react, it was buried in her ribcage. After this single blow, the other woman backed away and grounded her weapon, leaving Tsuga bent double as she tried to catch her breath. When at last she was able to breathe again, Tsuga straightened and extended her hand to the woman.

"You are quite adept with your spear. Remind me again of your name?"

"It's Derbaith, Captain. Derby, to my friends."

"Well, Derbaith, I must say it was a pleasure to spar against someone of your skill. Now," she continued, turning back to the rest of the group, "who can tell me what I did wrong?"

Today went well, I think.

"Oh, I agree. Minimal injuries, and everyone seemed to take to the exercises fairly well. They'll all sleep quite soundly tonight, I should think!"

Indeed. And what do you have in store for them tomorrow?

"A bit of a day off, I believe. Basic drills in their own weapons. I'm starting to get a feel for who has the most adaptability and the best instincts, but I still have nearly no idea how proficient everyone is in their respective disciplines."

They won't like it.

"Oh, aye. It'll feel like a step backwards, after today's training. But no matter the age or the skill of the fighter, the most fundamental strength – and weakness, for that matter – is rooted in the knowledge of the basics. If they don't know that already, they will by the time I'm through with them."

Ramiq lay in his large, overstuffed bed and gazed up at the canopy above his head. A few months ago, he had ensorcelled it with a simple combination of illusion, light, and water. Simple for him, at least; none save a person with the talents of a Queen's Mage could have accomplished it alone. Now, extraordinary patterns danced above him in an array of colors broader than human imagination could fathom. Even on his most restless nights – like this one – the quiet transformations soothed him. After some time the young mage was able to slip comfortably into sleep's warm embrace.

Fire blazed in her eyes when he looked at her, and Ramiq could tell that she was upset with him. He reached out a hand to her, and she turned away in disgust. He sighed and ran the hand through his sandy brown hair instead.

The anger she was projecting into the room battered his empathic senses, making it difficult for him to keep his calm. But there was an undercurrent there, as there often was with his wife. He forced himself to look beyond the anger and pry into her less obvious feelings. There was hurt there, like a festering sore too long ignored. A sense of betrayal came second, closely followed by feelings of guilt and inadequacy. Ramiq sighed and shook his head slightly to clear it before moving forward.

"Tsu, look at me. Please."

This time she let him touch her, and he gently turned her around to face him. He stood there for a few moments and simply studied her face with its sharp angles and weather-beaten skin. She didn't hesitate to meet his gaze, but instead stared him down, as if she thought doing so might change something.

"We are at war. As the Queen's Mage, it is my duty to do what I can to protect our people."

"Then protect them. Defend them. But must you attack the Devalians? They're good people. They have families, and lives that they deserve to live as much as the Sennorrans do. Who are you to take that away from them?"

"But Tsu, you used to face them in battle every season. You killed your fair share of them yourself. Why is this any different?"

"Because I fought them fairly. Face to face. You blow them up from the sidelines. How is that fair? You have so much political influence, Ramiq. You are second in that only to the queen. Can't you do something? Overrule the generals? Find a better way?"

Ramiq let out a long breath and reached out to gather her into his arms. She was tense, not relaxed against him as she usually was. There had been a time when what he had to do would have seemed to her to be perfectly reasonable. Lately, though, peace and politics had been all she could talk about. He couldn't help but wonder if the small child growing within her had a part in that. Was it possible that the life that grew there was one destined to bring a peaceful resolution to this war?

"I will do what I can, Tsu. I will only oppose other mages, and then only if they attack first, or if by taking on one or two, I can ensure the survival of many other lives."

Tsuga sighed and relaxed a bit. "I suppose that is better than nothing. Thank you, Love."

He lifted her chin and kissed her then, with the kind of tender passion born from the deep bond they shared. He felt her body respond to his, and almost with the same thought, they moved together to the bed and lay down.

Tsuga woke with a start, her heart threatening to leap out of her chest. She could still feel his touch on her skin, and she ran her fingers over her flat belly, almost expecting to feel the life that had stirred in her in the dream. She lay in the darkness and battled with the myriad emotions she'd felt in the vision, trying also to bring her feelings of acute arousal under control.

It had been weeks now that she'd been having these dreams – and every time, it was different – but this was the first time she'd seen the man's face for more than a fleeting second. The knowledge of his identity vastly disturbed her, and as she considered the implications, she decided that there could only be one explanation for these hallucinations.

He was obsessed with her. Either he so desired her that he was projecting these dreams onto her in the hopes of luring her to him, or else he found some twisted amusement in disturbing her sleep and playing with her mind. Either way, she was going to put a stop to it. But first, she had today's training session to take care of.

"Today will be a day off from training, of sorts."

Her company clapped and cheered, but when she held up her hand for silence, they obliged. Over the past few weeks, her place among them had become a little more stable; though they still teased her mercilessly, they at least didn't question her competance.

"That doesn't mean you get to go gallivanting around the taverns or dandling the local girls – or lads" and at that, she winked at the women in the group "– oh no. We're all going to play a little game. Who here is familiar with The Hounds and the Hare?"

A few people laughed and nodded, but for the sake of those who stared blankly she went on to explain.

"You will be divided into teams of four. You all are the Hounds. I am the Hare. You will be tracking me; sniffing me out, if you will. The four Hounds who find me must then 'kill' me by defeating me in battle. Simple enough, right?"

They all nodded and seemed to agree, but rather than let them feel too complacent, she gestured to a handful of ropes at her feet.

"You should know by now; nothing is ever that easy. Each of you will be tied to one of your teammates. And each of you will have one of two handicaps: blindness, or deafness."

At this, she pointed to a pile of rags and another of earmuffs. "You must work as a team; be each others' eyes and ears. This is an exercise in cooperation. Let us see how you all do."

Once everyone had been teamed up, "disabled," and lashed together, Tsuga looked the group over with a sense of anticipation. "Alright. You are to give me a five minute head start. You all know the rules. Good luck!"

With a sharp salute, she swung atop Devilsbane's back and set off at a brisk trot.

Let the games begin.

This should be interesting.

Indeed. It's time to have some fun with them.

In the two weeks that Tsuga had spent with her command, she had learned a great deal about their strengths and weaknesses, both as individuals and as a unit. She had learned the allies and the enemies, those who knew control, and those who had none. As a result, her teams – and yes, her choices of handicaps and the people she paired – had been well-planned and strategically thought out. Those who didn't listen had been blinded, so they must rely on what they heard. Those who were too cocky to accept what their eyes told them could no longer hear the sounds of their own voices. And those who got along the least would be forced to cooperate the most.

If there was one thing that every single person in her company lacked, it was a sense of unity. A glaring absence of cooperation and cohesiveness. She hoped that, through exercises like the one today, they would better learn to work together as a group.

There were no limits to what Tsuga was allowed to do to evade her pursuers. She was not confined merely to confused trails and hidey-holes, like the hare for which the game was named. She could climb trees, swim, brush away her tracks; any number of things, really.

She started by blundering into the woods, snapping branches and bending grass. Bane stomped her weight down with each step, leaving deep gouges in the soft earth. A toddler would have been able to follow such a trail.

Tsuga and her guardian wound through the woods this way for a few minutes until they came to a rocky outcropping that Tsuga often liked to visit during her morning jog. Here, there was no vegetation, no earth – nothing to betray their presence save an accidental scratch on the rock from a missed step. It was extremely exposed, but infinitely easier to hide her passage on the bare ground.

She spared a minute or two leaving false trails – a couple on foot, and some where Bane went out a ways alone to confuse matters further. All of them looped around confusingly before simply stopping when they backtracked. At last, satisfied that she had left a sufficient knot for the Hounds to unravel, she mounted again. When they started off this time, Bane stepped much more lightly, careful to tread on only the hardest earth on their path. Tsuga leaned low against the horse's neck and carefully moved branches aside as they passed to avoid snapping them.

Before long they came upon the small, clear stream that supplied the Warriors' Compound with fresh water. Bane plunged into the current, icy cold from the below-ground springs that filled it, without hesitation. Tsuga wrapped her legs around the horn on her saddle to keep her feet dry and the pair plunged upstream, doing their level best to confuse the trail further.

The day wore on without respite. The exercises had begun about an hour after dawn. It was now only a couple of hours before sundown, and still Tsuga eluded the Hounds. There *had* been a few close calls. A foursome would blunder along her trail while utterly lost, and she would hide well out of sight, watching and waiting for someone to spot her. What she observed, however, was that the pairs were far more concerned with who was right or who was better than they were with actually finding her. Once there was a fifteen minute argument over whether a patch of dark hair left on a bush was from Bane or a wild animal. It was Bane's, of course, and deliberately planted. Rather than looking for further signs (of which there were plenty), they chose to bicker loudly enough that she ultimately just slipped away under the cover of their screaming.

Overall, it was rather disappointing. She had expected the game to end somewhere around midday. It was now more than six hours past that, and she was beginning to wonder if she should just call them all in.

Give them a little longer. If they haven't found us by nightfall, I'll call to their guardians.

Well, alright.

"I'm telling you, that was deer hair!"

"I've never seen a deer so bloody clumsy in all my life! It looked like a herd of rhinos had blown through that forest!"

"What the hell is a rhino?"

"Oh, shut up! Goddess' tits, I'm getting tired of you and your bloody questions!"

Tsuga froze. It was one of the same groups who had almost found her earlier, now almost upon her again. They were screaming at the top of their lungs, presumably so that they could hear each other through their earmuffs. It seemed the argument about Bane's hair had never been resolved. The group of four stopped not ten yards from her, still bickering amongst themselves. All that separated her from them was a few scraggly bushes and the shade of the low-hanging branches that surrounded her. It was a wonder she wasn't spotted immediately.

She took quick stock of the situation, and then slid her feet out of the stirrups and up under herself on the saddle's seat. She stood carefully, once again infinitely grateful that Bane was her guardian, and not just any old horse. The animal stood rock steady, not so much as twitching her skin to shoo off the flies that pestered her. Once she had enough height, Tsuga grasped one of the heavy branches above her and, as quietly as she could manage, swung herself up into the canopy.

"What was that?"

"I didn't hear anything. You're both out of your mind. Deer hair. Hearing things. Next you'll tell me you smell a horse."

Shit. He heard me.

Nobody believes him.

"I'm telling you, I heard something!"

"Fine. We'll check it out. But by the Goddess, you'd better hope you're on to something."

Bane?

I'm on it.

The group began stomping through the brush in her general direction, as though to flush something out. They succeeded, all right. When they were only a few feet away, Bane plunged right into the thick of them, kicking and biting as she charged past.

There was a great deal of cursing and confusion; by the time they had straightened themselves out, Bane was already crashing away through the underbrush.

"I told you I heard something!"

"Shut the hell up and come on!"

Tsuga watched with a mixture of amazement and disgust as the four men blundered off after Bane. It seemed none of them had noticed that she wasn't in the saddle.

"Blood and war," she muttered under her breath.

"I heard her!"

"Well, where the hell is she?"

Tsuga let out another foul string of curses (this time purely mental) and looked down. Sure enough, the young woman who had heard her was standing almost directly below her, head tilted back as though she could search the treetops through her blindfold.

"It came from up there."

Tsuga only saw one pair – the young woman and an older man – and even as she wondered where the second pair had gotten off to, an arrow whizzed by a scant couple of inches from her face. It so surprised her that she lost her balance and didn't quite manage to grasp the limb in time to keep from tumbling to the ground.

"Shit!"

She grunted on impact, but didn't have time to take stock of herself for injuries. She rolled to her feet and drew her sword as she backed up against the trunk of her tree. The last thing she wanted was for them to be able to surround her.

"Congratulations. You whelps found the Hare. Now, can you keep me?"

Although the older man couldn't hear her, he snarled and drew his sword. When he tried to charge her, however, his blind partner tripped him up. Tsuga only just managed not to laugh as they collapsed to the ground in a heap.

"You won't get very far that way. Come come now, surely you can do better than that!"

About that time, another arrow flew within a foot of her head. Tsuga yelped as she ducked and spun to face her other attackers. She had expected the "deaf" man to be holding the bow, but instead found it in the hands of the young man wearing the blindfold. She gaped for a moment as the sighted man laughed and clapped his companion on the shoulder.

"Damn fine shot! That got 'er attention!"

As she marveled at the close call, the sound of a twig snapping behind her made her pivot again – just in time to manage a clumsy parry to her enemy's assault with his sword.

The scuffle that ensued was so chaotic that Tsuga found it difficult to keep up. Her attackers frequently ran into, hit, or otherwise hindered each other.

Just as often, though, one of them would come frighteningly close to lopping off her head. Finally, the man in the male-female pair succeeded in landing a blow to her back with the flat of his blade and she called a halt. It was a killing blow, and so she was at last forced to admit defeat.

"Very good. Head back to the barracks. Assemble for roll call. I'll be there soon, myself."

Call everyone in, Bane. Tell them to line up. Are you close by? She stifled a groan as she straightened and took stock of her lumps and bruises. *I could use a ride.*

Sure am. I'll be right there.

All in all, the day had been pretty successful. None of her soldiers had killed each other, though several sported cuts or bruises that no tree or bush could have inflicted. Tsuga pretended not to notice these things, though, and instead gave a brief lecture on the importance of trust, teamwork, and relying on more than just the senses.

After this, she dismissed everyone for the night. She still had to face the man who haunted her dreams before she settled in for the evening. But first, as her stomach loudly reminded her, it was supper time. She took a simple but hearty meal of beans and rice on a flat, round bread, and then swung atop her guardian, ready to get this confrontation underway.

What are you going to say to him?

"I don't know. Something along the lines of, 'leave me alone or I'll cut off your tiny, withered balls and feed them to you in bite-sized pieces.' Haven't really given it much thought, though."

Colorful.

They rode the rest of the way in silence, with Bane's swift trot swallowing up the distance between the two compounds. Tsuga used this time to take stock of herself. She was covered in cuts from the thorny underbrush she had torn through all day as well as covered in bruises from falls, tree limbs, and other such obstacles. Her clothes were torn in several new places and spotted here and there with blood and dirt. All in all, Tsuga figured she looked quite the mess. Not that it mattered; she hoped to present a frightening figure, not a pretty one.

As they neared the gates to the Mages' Complex, Bane slowed to a walk and ambled cautiously through the gilded and fantastically-formed entrance. They passed under the grand archway, and Tsuga felt a cold tingle dance across her skin, as though a thousand invisible snowflakes had hit every inch of her in a matter of seconds.

She shivered, knowing that if she were to engage her mage's sight, she would see all manner of shielding and protective enchantments set into and around the stone, no doubt maintained by someone nearby. She had the distinct feeling of being closely watched, and though she neither saw nor heard anyone aside from the one or two robed figures with which she shared the road, Tsuga was sure that her every movement – hell, every thought, no doubt – was being closely monitored and evaluated.

The pair passed unimpeded through the twisting and sloping streets, until Tsuga was so thoroughly turned around that she scarcely knew which way was up anymore. Finally, frustrated with her lack of progress, Tsuga dropped the reins and slipped into mage's sight. It was irritating how easily it came to her, after so much time trying to pretend she didn't possess the skill set of a mage.

When she opened her eyes, she very nearly fell off of her horse; only a lifetime of training and instinct kept her upright. There were so many lights and spells interwoven and twisted in with each other that it hurt to look at anything. As she grew accustomed to the jumble, she saw the tiny pinpricks of light on her skin – the afterglow of the spell that had hit her at the gates. She didn't recognize the magic, but knew it must be a spell of watching and protection. No doubt there was a great deal of invasion of a person's thoughts involved, too. The mere idea made her shudder.

As she adjusted further and began to make sense of the new information, Tsuga noticed directional symbols glowing in midair at the street corners – here one for north, there the symbol for "gates." She located the symbol for "sleeping quarters" and struck out in that direction, all the while hating the presence – and even more, her own use of – magic.

As they drew nearer to the long, low buildings that had been indicated, Tsuga began to notice more and more people glowing with power. She was sure that to them, she too was a shining beacon, though her lack of shielding – something she'd never really gotten around to learning – and the amount of time she'd gone without using her magic at all would mean the light was erratic, dimming and brightening at random.

Just let one of them try to tell me I'm a mage, she thought to herself. *Just let them try.*

"Rotten *bloody* light mage!"

Ramiq stood in his room, glaring at his reflection in the full-length mirror. Every half hour or so, his hair color would change; right now, it was the blue of a robbin's egg. In a few minutes, he was sure, it would change again. The bloody stinking bastard was a couple of years younger than Ramiq, but ages ahead of him in the study of magic. Of course, the worthless brat only had one skill to master instead of all of them, like Ramiq. He had to keep reassuring himself that this was the only reason he couldn't undo the spell. He was still seething and had begun to plot his revenge when someone knocked on his door. He swung angrily to face it.

"Listen you slimy little worm! If you don't remove this light-blasted spell, I'll make you wish you were never born!"

"What the hell are you talking about? Raving bloody lunatic. Open your thrice-damned door!"

He knew that voice. It wasn't that belonging to the blasted little light mage, but rather one that haunted his dreams more and more these days. Now more than ever, he was certain he didn't want to open the door.

"Oh great, it's you. What the hell are you doing here? Go away!"

"Ramiq, you damn well had better open this door before I break it off its fucking hinges! You've got a lot to answer for. Now open the damned door!"

Ramiq scowled. The door was solid oak; it weighed more than he did. He knew there was no possible way she could break it down. Just as he thought this he heard a thud, and his door shuddered. A moment later another thud came, accompanied by the sound of splintering wood.

"Auriga's tits, stop that! I'll let you in!"

The mage sighed and ran a frustrated hand through his colorful hair, taking a moment to compose himself. When at last he wrenched open the door, he was almost bowled over – as much by the sight of her as by the powerful presence she emanated.

Her short hair was disheveled – in the knots were even a few twigs and a leaf or two – and her clothes were dirty and torn. She had a few scratches on her face and hands, and one of them was coated in a decent amount of drying blood. But that wasn't what most drew his attention. As she stood there, silently glaring at him with fire leaping deep in her stormy gaze, she radiated power in a way that he had never felt before. Not only could he plainly see her scarcely-contained rage, but her unrestrained magic crackled, filling the air with a heat and energy that made him immediately break into a sweat.

She held herself with a confident authority that reminded him of a great cat before the attack. She knew she would win this easily; it was for her only a matter of how she chose to do so.

"Bloody crazy woman. What do you want?"

Tsuga's eyes narrowed dangerously at the greeting. Without waiting for an invitation, she pushed her way into his room. One scornful glance at the gaudy opulence that surrounded her was enough to turn her stomach. Incense and lush carpets, silks and fine furniture all crowded the little space until it became all but impossible for her to breathe. Suddenly wishing that she hadn't eaten so soon before seeking out the mage, she turned to face him – only to be nearly staggered again by the sight of him.

"Do I dare ask why your hair is purple?"

Ramiq scowled, but ignored the question. "What are you doing here?"

There was more than a hint of petulance in his tone, and Tsuga scoffed at him. "You know damn well why I'm here. I can't sleep without dreaming of *you*."

This was not at all what Ramiq had been expecting to hear. He blinked a few times, stunned, before he was able to form words.

"Excuse me?"

Never mind that he dreamt of her most nights now, too. The possibility that she may be having a similar experience served only to confuse matters further. She hated him, after all – he could feel the emotion rolling off of her in waves, buffeting him almost like a physical blast.

Tsuga's eyes narrowed, and she took a menacing step closer. "I don't know how you're doing it, but I know you're behind it. I do nothing now but dream of you – little moments together, sometimes, but mostly it's –"

"Sex?" Ramiq would have sworn that she growled at him. Her eyes narrowed, and he realized that he was sweating rather profusely.

"You would know, wouldn't you? Look, I don't know why you're doing this to me – and frankly, I don't give two shits. I just want it to stop. I want you to leave me the hell alone, got it?"

"Well, I hate to burst your bubble, but *I'm* not doing it." Tsuga *hmmphed*, but he shook his head adamantly.

"Really. I know you think you're Auriga's gift to the world, but you're nothing but a curse to me. I've been having what I'd be willing to wager are much the same dreams . . .. Nightmares, more like. Auriga's tits; it's like all I can think about lately is sex. More specifically, sex with you. I don't know what's going on any more than you do."

For a moment, Tsuga considered beating the truth out of the vile mage. She took a few beats first, though, to truly look at him. What she saw shocked her. He seemed sincere, in every sense of the word. He was just as frazzled and distraught as she was, and she could see quite plainly by the way his robes now hung that he was indeed thinking decidedly unclean thoughts – if not about her, then certainly about someone. Tsuga let out a gusty breath and ran a hand through her short brown hair. She came up with a leaf, which she dropped absently.

"Well if you're not behind this, then I'll admit to being stumped. So how do we stop it, then? I was pretty much counting on beating you until you fixed everything."

Ramiq grimaced. "Well, thank the Goddess that will no longer be the case."

"I didn't say I had changed my mind about the beating. I'm just not as sure that it will fix the dreams."

Ramiq felt his stomach drop at the last, and he swallowed hard. Tsuga held her threatening expression for a few more beats before she broke into a mischevious grin.

"Oh, come now; I'm not that bad. Still, I wouldn't mind someone to take out my frustration on . . .."

Thrown completely off-balance by this rapid emotional see-saw, Ramiq blew out a frustrated sigh and sat down on the edge of his plush bed.

"You're a crazy bitch, you know that?"

Tsuga simply shrugged – he supposed it was how she was trying to come across, after all. "But as to how we fix it, I'm not too sure. There are a lot of unknowns still. Are we having the same dreams, the same experiences? Are they happening at the same time? What do the details – if there are any – tell us?"

Tsuga frowned and shook her head. "So, what? We compare notes? I don't see how that will do us any good."

"Well you wouldn't, would you? It's not like you're a real mage, or even particularly insightful. And this *obviously* has its root in the mind magics. You're just going to have to trust me a little – this is my area of expertise, not yours."

Okay, so that might have been a little boastful – and quite rude – but she had been the one to come beating down his door and making wild accusations. He could tell that what he'd said didn't sit well with her, though; her arms were crossed over her chest, her feet set in a defensive stance as though she were braced for a physical assault. He let out a gusty sigh and tried a different tack.

"Okay, look. Neither of us wants this or asked for it, right? And we both want to get rid of it, don't we? Mind magics – empathy, speech, and such – are my strengths. I know this stuff. If we could fix this by stabbing or hitting something, I'd leave it up to you. But it's not that easy. So sit down, stop looking at me like I have horns and fangs, and let's start at the beginning. When did you have the first dream?"

Tsuga eyed the mage dubiously, then finally resigned herself to the inevitable. Rather than sit so close to him, though, she pulled over one of the ridiculously cushioned chairs and flung herself into it.

"Hell, the first time? I don't know. I wasn't even that close to the city yet. And the dream took place after I . . . well. Freaked me out. In fact, it affected me so deeply that I abandoned the company I was with and came straight to the city."

"But if your dream scared you so badly, why would you run toward the object of it?"

"I didn't know it was you. I'd never seen you before, and we didn't really talk much, in the dream. Remember, back then the only experience I'd had with you was during that battle."

"Yes, I remember. We didn't exactly exchange pleasantries."

"Precisely. You took *my* name from my mind that day, but I didn't know yours until the dance."

"Ah yes, the dance. I had a most . . . vivid dream that night."

Tsuga nodded, her thoughts haunted by her own rememberances from the evening in question. "Indeed. Look, I really don't see how this is going to help anything, and I have an early morning tomorrow, so . . .."

She started to rise, but he forestalled her.

"Sit down, Tsuga. Look, we both know that unless we figure this out, neither of us is likely to get much sleep tonight anyway. Now, what did you do just before you went to bed that first night?"

Tsuga sat back down slowly, lost in the memory of Charlie's hands on her body, his hungry lips against hers . . .. She felt herself blushing, and when she dared to look at Ramiq again, he was grinning.

"You're kidding me."

"He was very sweet, and it was a huge step for me. He was my first since . . .." She stopped herself short at that; there was no reason he needed to know about Elbon.

Ramiq couldn't believe it. So the she-devil was human, after all! And here he had all but convinced himself that her tastes ran more towards women. *Guess I was wrong there.*

"Well, isn't that charming. You dreamt about sex after having sex. So why should that have even bothered you, then?"

She glowered at him for a bit, but at last offered a reluctant answer. "It wasn't just a dream, though. I was completely aware. I knew that I was dreaming. I knew you weren't Charlie, even though you should have been. And as soon as you spoke my name, I knew who you were. I knew your voice." She blew out a gusty sigh and looked down at her lap. "It freaked me out, alright?"

Ramiq's heart went out to the girl, and he felt an unfamiliar urge to hold her and protect her from the world. He shook it off, though, and focused instead on the details of the dream she'd just given him.

"You know, I think I remember that night. I had a very similar dream – though mine was disturbing for an entirely different reason."

She didn't look at him, but he could tell he had piqued her interest when she voiced an inquisitive "Oh?"

"I was laying with your head on my chest after we'd finished, thinking how amazing the sex had been."

She flushed a deeper shade of red, and although he could see he was making her more uncomfortable, Ramiq pushed on.

"When I spoke, you stiffened and sat bolt upright. Then, instead of asking you what was wrong, I was you, hearing someone else – I'd be willing to bet it was this Charlie fellow – asking me – you – that very question. I had just enough time to realize all of this and what was wrong with it; then I woke up."

She was looking at him now, and he thought from the way she stared that she just might bore a hole straight through him.

"So this is a habit for you, to shove your way uninvited into my head?"

He at least had the decency to look abashed at that, though he was quick to deny the accusation.

"Look, I'll admit that on the battlefield, I invaded you and used your mind to my advantage. But as long as I'm properly shielded, I don't do that. Not by accident. It takes conscious effort for me to enter a mind."

"So, what? You're sleep-magicking?"

Ramiq sighed and shook his head. "So it would seem. But it's so improbable, when you add it all up. Why you? Why so carnal? And how and why am I projecting the same dreams to you, if that's even what I'm doing?"

"What do you mean, 'if?' Sounds to me like that's exactly what you're doing."

"Well, that's just it. If I were simply projecting my dreams onto you, then you would have the same experiences I do. You would dream from my perspective, not your own."

"Wanna make that sound a little less like gibberish?"

"During the dreams, I'm me; but you're still *you* when you dream. So I'm not simply pushing my dream into your head. I would have to have two separate dreams at once; your version, and mine. And I'd have to project yours to you all while *dreaming* mine."

"So, what? Is that hard to do?"

"It's impossible. No mage that I've ever heard of has been able to project two separate realities at once while awake, let alone while dead asleep."

Tsuga frowned. "So, what? You're the first?"

"That, or there is some other force at work here."

That gave Tsuga pause as she considered the implications of that simple statement. "That seems highly unlikely. From what you said, there would have to be at least two high-level mages involved, right? And they're accomplishing what, exactly?

Unbalancing our emotions? Playing with our minds? Disrupting our sleep? I just don't see it."

"Well, then where does that leave us?"

Tsuga looked at him; in spite of herself, her heart went out to the poor boy. He looked so defeated – so forlorn – that she couldn't help but feel for him.

"Right where we started, it would seem . . .."

Ramiq couldn't figure out if he wanted to scream or cry. It was all so frustrating; so confusing! Nothing seemed to be making any sense anymore. He must have presented a truly pitiful sight at that moment, for the brittle, thorny warrior softened before his eyes and offered him a sweet smile – the first sincere, non-threatening expression he'd ever seen on her sharp-featured face.

"Oh, come now. You act as though the world is crashing down around you. It's just a couple of uncomfortable dreams and some lost sleep."

"I know." Ramiq was mortified to hear himself sniffle, and as though that small sound had broken something inside of him, he felt his strength crumble. The next thing he knew, he was blubbering like a baby. "It's just so confusing, and I don't know what to do, and . . . and . . . and my hair is *purple*!" Tsuga's eyes flickered to his hair and back again.

"Actually, it's green."

Tsuga felt her heart twist in sympathy when Ramiq broke down. She'd been in that place no few times herself, and so knew just how he felt. With a small sigh, she stood and crossed to the bed. It took some maneuvering, but once her sword and dagger were situated, she was able to sink down on the pillowy bed next to him and draw him into a comforting embrace.

"There, now. It's not so bad as all that. What can't be cured must be endured. I've survived much worse, and I'm sure you have, too."

He didn't answer, but instead burrowed himself further into her arms. Despite herself, Tsuga pulled him in tighter, inexplicably driven to comfort and protect the young man she had come here prepared to beat bloody.

Ramiq didn't know how long he stayed there, his snot and tears adding to the blood, dirt, and sweat already soiling her tattered shirt. She held him patiently, though, one hand rubbing his back in a soothing motion while she mumbled calming sounds in his ear. Her embrace was oddly comforting. He found that he felt safe there, as though her arms could fend off all the troubles in the world.

At last, the tears stopped and he regained enough composure to pull away and sit up straight again. His back complained from the position he'd held it in for so long, and he grimaced. He tried to play the expression off.

"Sorry about your shirt."

She shook her head, and when Ramiq dared to look her in the eye, he felt his heart squeeze tighter in his chest. Gone was the fierce warrior girl who wanted to wring his neck. In her place was a friend – a confidant, someone who was there to comfort and protect him. It was something he had never expected from someone he had tried to kill (not to mention all of her attempts on his own life).

Tsuga glanced down at the damp piece of clothing and simply shrugged. "After what I put it through today, a little water is hardly going to make a difference." She stood and re-adjusted her sword belt, fidgeting as though uncomfortable. "Now, if you're going to be alright, I really should be going. It's getting late and –"

"Tsuga?"

She had made it about half way to the door before he spoke. Something in his tone of voice stopped her; she hesitated a moment before she turned around.

"Yes, Ramiq?"

He wasn't certain why he'd spoken. He really should have just let her go. But the sight of her walking away stirred something unnamable in him – to the point where he felt compelled to draw her back. He swallowed hard now, knowing what he wanted so desperately to ask her, yet terrified she would say no.

"Yes, Ramiq?"

What scared him even more than the prospect of her refusal was how much he yearned for her consent. Afraid to ask, but even more petrified of letting her go, he managed at last to give voice to the question.

"I'm sorry, I'm sure I misunderstood you. What did you say?"

This time when he spoke his voice came out stronger and more assured, though she still detected a tremor that spoke of – what? Nervousness? Hope? "Would you stay the night with me?"

All at once, the urge to run surged up inside her again. She felt herself start shaking and she took a frightened step backwards.

"Light, Ramiq, do you really think that's a good idea? I mean, we both have reputations to protect, and besides, our dreams drive us mad when we're separated by miles – by cities, even. What might happen if we share a bed?"

She could feel her heart hammering now; in response to her panic, she felt her long-ignored magic surging against her will, battering at her restraints. She forced it back, but it fought her, unruly and starving for the fuel so close at hand. His room was a deathtrap, from a fire mage's point of view. Fine silks and plush cushions were everywhere. The space was crowded with furniture, and there was only one window – too small to crawl through, should there be an emergency. The flame within her screamed for release; it threw itself ravenously towards the nearest silk hanging, but she hauled it back – barely.

Ramiq watched her struggle. He felt the temperature in the room rise significantly, and quickly redoubled his protective shielding in response to the uncontrolled surge of her magic. While she was distracted by this inner turmoil, he stood and crossed to her.

"Tsuga, I promise nothing will happen. I'll be a perfect gentleman. Like you said, dreams are just that – dreams. I can't explain it, but I just feel like I need you here tonight. What do you say? Will you stay the night with me?"

He could see her resolve crumbling, and before she could back away again, he drew her against him for a quick embrace, firmly ignoring the stirring in his groin as he did so.

"Come, now. There's no reason it has to go further than this. We can just spend the night talking, and leave it at that. Okay?"

Emotions warred within her. Her every instinct told her to run, to go as far and as fast as she could. Yet his arms felt strong and comforting around her, almost as though she belonged there. Still uncertain – and unable yet to commit to either course of action – she allowed him to draw her to the bed and numbly sat down beside him.

"You see? Nothing to be afraid of."

She wasn't sure she believed that, but as she sat with him her panic began to ebb until it had been reduced to a tiny, nagging sense of dread that was easily contained, if not ignored completely.

Without that fear pressing on her, Tsuga soon found that she *wanted* to stay with him – to forget her troubles and pretend, if only for one night, that the world was a safe place.

Tsuga woke to the unfamiliar feeling of bare skin under her hand. Using a trick she had mastered in childhood to fool her nurse when she looked in on her at night, she stilled her body and kept her breathing even as she opened her eyes.

She was unaccustomed to waking so sluggishly. Her awareness returned slowly, in bits and pieces. Her head was pillowed on Ramiq's bare chest, and she could tell from his steady breathing that he still slept soundly. She took in what else she could without moving: the silk bed sheets, the soft lighting provided by the enchantment on the ceiling. She also noted with some bewilderment that her magic had shrunk back and was no longer fighting her for release. It was a battle she had grown accustomed to, and now she found that she felt oddly incomplete without it.

Bane?

Yes?

What time is it?

Late morning. Approaching noon.

Tsuga absorbed this information, wondering how it was that she had slept so soundly – and so late. She could not recall doing so even once before this.

What is the company doing?

Enjoying a day off. What's say we give them this one?

Tsuga sighed. As though in response, Ramiq slid his arm around her shoulders and cradled her more closely against him. She considered, for a moment, what it might be like to simply stay in his arms – to see him come slowly to consciousness next to her, to experience the surreal peace of a day spent with him with no responsibilities to weigh on her mind.

On the heels of that daydream, however, came an immediate urgency from her bladder, and a nearly-as-pressing feeling of hunger. With a twinge of regret for what she had never had the chance to know, Tsuga slipped out of the man's arms and rose as quietly as she could from the plush bed. Ramiq mumbled something in his sleep and she froze, afraid she had woken him and would now have to endure an awkward conversation.

Much to her relief, he merely twisted the covers more securely around himself and sprawled out over the full expanse of the oversized bed. She couldn't help but laugh at this as she began buckling on her sword belt and tucking her assortment of daggers into their various hiding places. After she had finished dressing and had slid her feet back into her well-worn boots, Tsuga spared a few moments more to revel in the feeling of peace and well-being. Then, with a deep breath and the feeling of bracing herself for a shock, she slipped through the door and into the quiet hallway.

"Gone? What the hell do you mean, 'gone?'"

"Captain and her men left yesterday, with a couple other companies."

"But the fighting season's over. Winter's just around the corner!"

"Aye. On their way to the border, they are. Relieving the troops what been there all season."

Ramiq scowled, not sure if he was angry at her for leaving without so much as a "see ya 'round," or at himself for being so affected by her sudden departure. With a huff, he spun on his heel – forcing the soldier to take a step back to avoid being caught up in the flurry of fabric as he did so – and stormed off, glowering at any poor souls who crossed his path.

Tsuga had slept remarkably well that night in Ramiq's arms, but she found that the longer she was away from him, the more fitful her sleep became. As she traveled with the relief troops – some three hundred strong – she began to have fewer and fewer dreams of the mage, and more and more of the old nightmares instead. Before long, she was back to waking in cold sweats in the middle of the night, her every muscle sore from tension, and a scream of denial dying on her lips. None of her companions confronted her about this, though, for night terrors were common enough for a soldier – even one as young as she.

And so Tsuga endured as best she could in silence, as each day marked a further distance from the place she had come to call home and each night grew even more fitful than the last.

Winters in the heart of Sennor were miserable things, with freezing rains and stinging winds that found ways into every crack and crevice in existence. Here, on the northern border, they were hell. Snow blanketed everything, and even on the days when the sun shone and the temperature rose to something abouve bone-numbingly cold, the snow blindness still made being on watch almost unbearable. Tsuga did her best to keep the grumbles of discontent to a minimum by taking the worst post herself. In the wee hours of the morning, long before the sun rose, the world was at its coldest and least forgiving. The time of day made little difference to her – she scarcely slept at all lately, anyway.

Colder than Auriga's tit out here.

Tsuga pulled back painfully dry lips in a smile at Bane's comment and rubbed her hands together in a futile attempt to warm them.

"But so peaceful!"

Oh, yes! The drunken snores, the stench of human and animal filth. Quite lovely. At least it's not baking in summer heat.

Tsuga laughed, her hot breath fogging in the night air. The sound echoed eerily, and as she listened to the silence that followed, a feeling of dread settled over her.

It's entirely too quiet.

It's the middle of the night!

But listen. No owls, no sounds of wildlife at all. We haven't even startled a rabbit from the underbrush.

Bane snorted and tossed her head irritably. **On a night like this, I don't much want to run through the snow either.**

But it's not natural. Something's wrong. Come on, let's get back inside the walls. I have a bad feeling about this.

Bane turned, and the last thing Tsuga remembered before she hit the frozen ground and lost consciousness was the horse's anticipation of the warmth in the stables.

She came to slowly, as though she fought her way to consciousness through a thick muck. The first thing she noticed was that she was warm. This knowledge was followed closely by the realization that she was in a bed. It was not until she tried to sit up that she realized she was tied down on it.

"What the –?"

"Well, look who's up! You know, you'd think people would know enough not to shoot someone they want information out of. Bloody clumsy. Ah well, I suppose that's all that can be expected from their sort. Sorry about the restraints, by the way, but we can't have you trying to break free, now can we?"

The voice was male, and though he stayed where Tsuga couldn't see him, she could follow his progress as he paced the room by the shadow he cast in the fitful light of the fire. Tsuga restrained herself from asking any of the first questions that came to mind, such as "Where am I?" or "What do you want with me?" She remembered well enough her feeling of unease, and then the arrow that had taken her in the right shoulder. The wound was still painful, which meant she hadn't been healed – both a blessing and a curse, that.

In a reflexive action she sent her mind questing for Bane, seeking the stalwart guardian's calming presence. All she received, however, was a distant sense of fear, pain, and desperation. She'd never been so far from her guardian before, and found that she had to fight back a sense of panic when she discovered that she couldn't pinpoint the beast's location, let alone speak with her. All she had to go on was a sense that Bane was alive, if somewhat less than alright, and was in a general northwesterly direction.

The man came to stand over her, and Tsuga forced down her terror and made herself look at him. She wanted to take in every tiny detail about him, so that when she escaped – for she had no doubt in her mind that she would do so – she would know who it was she needed to kill.

He was neither particularly tall nor remarkably attractive. His hair was shortish and slicked back from his face so that she did not know if it were curly or straight. She thought it was black, though the combination of the dim lighting and the product he'd used could be blamed for that effect – so a dark brown or black, then. His nose was slightly off-center in his face, and was just a hair too short to truly suit him. His ears were small and feminine – so unlike her own – and *pointed*. They looked as though they had been *cut* that way. His face was a little too narrow, his chin and forehead a touch too long, and his chin hairless.

All of these details were filed away in short order, but his eyes were what held her attention the most. They were black as pitch and glinted with a look she recognized all too easily: madness. Whether that madness stemmed from power or something else entirely remained to be seen.

"Gone and gotten yourself a real prize this time, eh? A captain with no power and no influence. Congratulations. Do you honestly expect to gain anything from this?"

The man's eyes narrowed dangerously and he leaned closer to her, so that his rank breath came hot on her face.

"You think this is about some stupid war?!" He barked out a laugh, and Tsuga tried not to jerk as his spittle hit her face. "Hardly! No, Tsuga Dafrin, this goes far beyond the petty squabbles of a few overzealous religious nuts."

The use of her name unsettled her slightly, though the information would have been easy enough for him to glean.

"Well, since I hardly think you would have had me shot so that you could tie me down and rape me, I'm sure there is some motive to all of this."

"Oh, now in that, you are absolutely correct. You see, I have a great desire to find your sister. She has caused us a great deal of inconvenience lately. But she has proven remarkably difficult to pin down. So, I figure when she learns of her little sister's predicament, she will come right to us."

"You're the one that's been killing off the healers! Why? What did they ever do to you? To anyone?"

"Oh, it's not their fault. They are simply in the way. An obstruction, as it were."

"Obstruction? To what?"

"Never you mind about that. They are easily done away with. All that drivel about not causing harm to others makes killing them off as easy as killing a babe in its sleep. But Affaila threw a kink in everything."

"But Affaila's as passive as they come. How could she be causing you problems?"

"Passive? Little Miss Vengeful Goddess? Hardly! She's killed a fair number of my men, and consequently, she must be dealt with. Her and that damn overgrown mutt."

Tsuga was thoroughly confused by this, though she tried not to let it show. Last she had seen Affaila, the woman had been incapable of killing a rabbit for supper, let alone another human being. But if he was telling the truth and Affaila *had* finally found her nerve, then good for her.

"Well, I hate to burst your bubble, but I haven't seen or heard from Affaila in nearly two years. What makes you so sure she'll come to my rescue?"

"Oh, she'll come, Tsuga. You can be sure of that."

Tsuga's shoulder ached terribly, but the way she was tied made it impossible to ease her weight at all. She didn't know how long it had been since her keepers had looked in on her. The pair of men assigned to guard her hadn't seemed to be the sharpest arrows in the quiver – all brawn and no brains, to be sure.

She flexed her arms and legs experimentally, testing her restraints. She was tied expertly – securely, so that she could neither move nor shift, but not so tightly as to cut off her circulation or bite into her flesh. So Bigger and Stupider knew what they were doing in that department, at least.

"Hello?"

When her first attempt brought no response, Tsuga took a deep breath and tried again.

"Get your asses in here, you filthy stinking sons of swine!"

The door slammed open, and the one she thought of to herself as Bigger – for the obvious reason of his hulking frame – glared at her from the doorway.

"Shut the hell up, will ya? Ketral's balls, I'd think you'd be grateful. This is much better 'n how Misatt treats most of his prisoners."

"Well, don't I feel special. Don't help me much when I'm tied to a fucking bed and have to piss like I drank a barrel of ale last night."

From the other side of the door came a dim-sounding guffaw, and Bigger's head withdrew for a moment. There was a yelp, and then Stupider came in, glaring balefully at the floor. Bigger followed close on his heels.

"Don' see why we don' jes let 'er piss in th' bed. Might teach 'er a bit 'o manners, it might."

"Ah, but Misatt doesn't want to have to smell my piss on his daily visits, now does he? So I guess you boys are stuck overseeing my use of the chamber pot. Whose turn is it to dump it today? Might wanna be careful when you carry it – left a nice little surprise in there for ya this morning before the guard change."

Stupider snarled and landed one of his big, meaty fists in her unprotected stomach, causing her to wheeze as she tried to regain her breath, muscles spasming against her restraints when her body tried reflexively to curl around the point of her pain.

"Shut up, you filthy little whore."

Meekly, Tsuga bowed her head and waited for them to untie her before she again endured the humiliation of the men watching her take a piss. It had been awful at first, but she had come to take a kind of perverse pleasure in making the experience as uncomfortable for the two guards as possible. Let them think her crazy and afraid. She had only to bide her time until she could figure out the best way to escape.

Her weapons were her biggest concern – she had no idea where Misatt was keeping them, if he hadn't already sold them off. And it would scarcely do her any good to ask him. She didn't trust the bastard as far as she could throw him.

The time passed interminably, the only mark of the hours in the tiny windowless room provided by the arrival of her occasional meal – stale bread and whatever was left in the bottom of the cook pot – and the changing of the guards posted outside her door.

As the days stretched into first one week, and then two, Tsuga grew increasingly more antsy. She cared little for her own well-being, but she knew she had to free herself and find Affaila before her sister came for her. If the snatches of rumor she'd gleaned from her guards were even half true, then Affaila had been singled out to do Auriga's work. For that reason, even more than their close blood tie, Tsuga could not allow her to be killed.

Misatt grew increasingly troubled as well as yet another week marched by with no sign of her sister. Tsuga began trying to provoke him into telling her what she wanted to know. She had to be careful, though – agitating her captor was an exercise in suicidal stupidity, much like poking a bear with a table knife and hoping she could outrun it once it woke up.

"So, how is your most brilliant plan working out so far, Misatt? Didn't I tell you she wouldn't come? What use does she have for a half-sister she never even writes to?" Tsuga let a little bitterness creep into her voice on the last. Better that Misatt believe the two sisters to be distant and separated by a rift of resentment than to know the truth of their close bond. Anything she could do to protect Affaila, she would.

"What is it now, nearly a month later? And what do you have to show for all your efforts? A useless soldier tied to a bed? Someone you must either feed or kill?"

She barked out a harsh laugh, watching surreptitiously as his hands balled into fists and his jaw clenched.

"You'd better hope she comes for you soon. Because if she's not here before the new moon, I'll turn you over to my men, and they can play with you until they decide to kill you."

Misatt left then in a flurry of fine fabric, and Tsuga tried to fight back a shudder. She had absolutely no desire to throw herself upon the tender mercies of Bigger, Stupider, and Goddess knew how many others. She'd sooner kill herself. If only she had a way to do so. She only wished she could remember how many days remained until the new moon.

Tsuga had lain awake and restless for an indeterminate length of time considering her best course of action. She had no doubt that she could escape easily – they had stolen her every physical weapon from her, but they could not take her magic. Much as she hated and feared it, she knew it to be her best hope for salvation. It was what awaited her once she was free that posed the bigger problem.

Weakened as she was by her weeks in captivity, she couldn't run very fast or very far. She couldn't wander off too far, anyway – she had no idea where Affaila might be, or even where she should start looking. She would have to stay relatively near her prison and wait. Hopefully, she would be able to reach Affaila before anyone else – or before she herself was found and recaptured.

With no food, no weapons, and no spare clothes, her prospects in the harsh Devalian winter weren't good. She would have to rely on her instincts and her magic to keep herself alive. Death was not what frightened her, though – not now – only the prospect of failure. With her mind made up and a vague plan of action in place, Tsuga found it all but impossible to sit back and bide her time. She forced herself to wait, though, and the very next night, she was rewarded.

On this night, as on every other, the bawdy – and often drunken – conversation of her guards died off and eventually faded to noisome snores. She had no idea of the layout of the building, nor even of what awaited her on the other side of her own door. But she was done waiting; it was, at last, time for her to act.

With a deep breath, Tsuga closed her eyes and sought out the beast that slumbered within her very heart. Her stone was no help, now – it had been packed away in her belongings at the fort. She had only her own power to pull from for this.

Heat and fire roared to life, and she gasped as it fought her to be free. Shaking, she opened her eyes, regretting now that she had so long ignored her power. It was wild and unruly, much like a horse left too long to pasture without proper exercise and care. She forced such concerns out of her head with an effort and turned her attention instead to the ropes that bound her hands and feet. It was all she could do not to set the entire building ablaze, but somehow she managed to control the ill-tempered magic and bend it to her will.

The ropes fell away easily. Tsuga rose slowly to her feet, weak and unsteady from so much time abed. She forced long-unused muscles into action and made her way haltingly to the exit. Despite the weight of the door, it swung inward without a sound. Luckily, Misatt liked to keep his prison cells well-maintained. She stepped outside and looked around at the first different scenery she'd seen in nearly a month.

Her two guards had fallen asleep in their bedrolls. The stench of their unwashed bodies rocked her back on her heels so that she had to cover her nose before she could look around. *Some guards,* she thought. Not only were they asleep on the job, but their weapons were heaped haphazardly in one corner. None of the blades were hers, unfortunately, and they were all pretty poorly maintained. In fact, she noted as she buckled on a sword that was the approximate weight and length of her own trusty blade, the assortment was so mismatched that she'd be willing to wager they had been plucked from prisoners and victims alike. She considered the assortment for a few more moments, and then tucked away a few daggers on her person for good measure.

The steel weighed heavily on her atrophied muscles, and she found that she tired far more quickly than she'd anticipated. She stumbled her way down the hall, forced to use the wall to support herself. Her vision began to darken, and she had to pause for a moment to keep from passing out. The magic pulled at her as well, draining her energy still more quickly. The room began to spin disconcertingly, and as her resolve faltered, she felt the magic surge up against her weakening defenses.

Tsuga woke with a fit of coughing. The air was dark and thick; it was hard for her to breathe. She started to pull herself to a sitting position but found that she had no strength in her arms; instead she lay prone. As she tried to remember what had happened, she took in the smell of smoke and the haziness of the night above her. She could recall getting out of her room, and a bit of walking down the hallway. After that, though, there was ...nothing.

Her head throbbed as though she'd been kicked in it, and her mouth was as dry as she could ever remember it being. A light breeze stirred the ash beside her, and she shivered as the air cooled her feverish skin. It was only then that she realized she lay naked and exposed in the midst of what was once her prison. She grasped instinctively at her side, seeking the sword she'd taken, but found nothing. It was as though the inferno – for surely with her loss of control that was the only explanation for the state in which she now found herself – had burned away every vestige of her old self, leaving her as naked and vulnerable as the day she was torn screaming from her mother's womb.

The air stirred again, and once more she shivered at the chill it carried. *I can't stay like this,* she realized. Devali was still deep in the clutches of a harsh winter, and she would never survive laying exposed this way. She had to find some sort of shelter – soon.

And clothes. Clothes would be good. Light, while I'm wishing for the impossible, how about a sword and a rescue party?

She had to laugh at that. Even if someone *had* come looking for her, she'd been gone nearly a month. With the season being what it was, even *she* would have given herself up for dead by now.

Though she was unable to stand, Tsuga managed to pull herself up to her hands and knees, where she had to rest a moment while her stomach returned to its rightful place and the ground went back beneath her where it was supposed to be. Thus mobilized, she began to make her slow, painful way through the ashes and smoldering remains of the building and out into an unfamiliar and unforgiving wilderness.

Affaila stared in shock at the devastation that met her eyes. She had forced herself to stop and think after learning that Misatt had taken her sister; the amount of willpower necessary to keep herself from rushing off to rescue Tsuga had been great. Even once the relatively easy decision had been reached, it had taken over a month of tireless travel to search out and at last find his hiding place. The winter had made traveling on foot all but impossible, but still Affaila had braved the elements.

Now, she stood looking at a vast expanse of ash lightly covered by a sludge of gray snow. The immense black wolf at her side scented the air, and then sneezed as though something had tickled her nose.

"I smell magic here. Very powerful magic."

Hope dared to blossom in Affaila's heart, and she looked again at the scene, this time engaging her mage's sight. As Kisha had said, a thick haze of magic lingered over the place, an orangish glow like the last coals of a fire – the light left by residual power now beginning to fade.

"Goddess bless. I'd know that magical signature anywhere. That's Tsuga. Uncontrolled as always. In this weather, she can't have gotten far. Especially after a use of power of that magnitude."

Affaila sat down in the snow, not caring that the freezing wetness immediately began to soak through her thick winter furs. She slid her pack to the ground and closed her eyes to seek out other life in the area – a nifty little trick she'd acquired along with the imposing canine that now sat beside her, yellow eyes alertly scanning the area for any danger – or food.

"There." About five miles to the north and west of where she sat, a weak but distinctly human presence called to her.

Tsuga.

A year ago, the task of locating her sister wouldn't have been so simple. Affaila looked at Kisha, dutifully keeping watch over her as she worked, and smiled to herself. The Goddess had given her much that day. The responsibility weighed heavily on her shoulders, but the things she had gained – her guardian, a sense of purpose, and the means to heal the world – made it bearable. If only just.

She sighed, resigned to another couple of days' travel through the miserable Devalian terrain, and rose to her feet.

"Let's go, Kisha. She's in pretty bad shape."

Tsuga had been having a rough time of it. Her progress was excruciatingly slow, punctuated by many breaks. More than once, she woke from what must have been a faint of exhaustion to continue to crawl forward through the ice and snow.

It had taken her three days to gain enough presence of mind to light herself a fire when she stopped, so that she might have a chance at warming herself more effectively. Although the fire magic in her blood kept her from freezing to death, it never allowed her to feel fully warm as she dragged her naked body through the snow. The use of magic to light the damp wood drained her alarmingly, but the kiss of heat on her skin was so welcome that she didn't care.

It had been three days, too, since she had last eaten. Now, as she huddled as close to the flames as she could without sitting directly in them, Tsuga forced herself to look around and actually take stock of her situation. Even in the depths of winter, wildlife could be found here and there. And she was desperate.

"Snow hare."

Kisha was referring to the neatly-picked pile of bones they had found. No animal would have made such a stack, and the fact that Kisha told her they had been cooked first – an assessment supported by the dark smudge in the snow that betrayed the location of a now-cold campfire – further encouraged Affaila that they were indeed on the right track.

So, Tsuga had managed to find herself something to eat.

"She may yet be okay, if the elements don't kill her before she finds shelter."

Although the odd rabbit or squirrel that she managed to find should have helped her to regain some strength, Tsuga found that it wasn't much. She was now able to stand and stagger through the snow, but she still frequently collapsed in exhaustion.

She had come to rely heavily on her magic to keep herself alive, but such frequent use of it drained her far more quickly than normal in her severely weakened state. She needed to find somewhere she could hole up for a few days and regain her strength. Devali, unfortunately, was not a land of caves. The best she could hope for, really, would be a cliff or other such structure to back herself up against, where she might be able to fashion some sort of lean-to. Until such a place presented itself, though, she had no choice but to press on.

As best as Tsuga could calculate, she had been free now for almost a week. Her strength was returning, albeit slowly, and with it came her faculties. She had lost the option of staying near her prison when she'd burned it to the ground. If anyone came to investigate the magical surge, she didn't want to be anywhere nearby. As she observed the path the sun blazed through the sky, she realized that she had been blindly traveling northwest. Even in her delirious state, her heart had driven her to seek out her guardian.

She still couldn't sense the beast as more than a vague presence, but at least now she had a purpose to her struggles apart from her own survival. Since she had yet to find any suitable shelter, Tsuga at last gave up her hopes of doing so. She had to get to Bane – the sooner, the better.

"There's a storm coming."

Affaila tilted her head back to look at the sky. The stars were hidden behind a thick blanket of clouds, and the air held that uniquely metallic smell that meant snow – and lots of it. The healer shifted her weight on the rock she sat on, trying to ease the pain where an uneven patch dug into her backside.

"She's only a short ways ahead of us. We should be able to catch up to her by tomorrow night."

"By tomorrow night, we'll all be under two feet of snow; you mark my words."

Affaila frowned and looked around at the dark, slumbering wilderness around them. She had learned not to question Kisha when it came to such things; the wolf had an uncanny sense of danger, whether from the weather or less natural sources. The woman was no longer surprised; her guardian was a gift from Auriga Herself, after all, and as such possessed of certain abilities above and beyond those of normal members of her species.

"Well, then I guess we'd better get a move on. Is there any hope of shelter nearby?"

"I'm not sure. I'll go see what I can find. You go get Tsuga."

"Are you sure you'll be alright?"

Kisha's wise golden eyes looked at her reproachfully from where the wolf lay by her feet, glowing with an otherworldly light. **"I'll be fine. But we should hurry, if we want to beat this storm."**

The sun had begun its descent in the sky before Affaila finally spotted her. The snow had started to fall around dawn, and Kisha's bleak prediction was proving true. Affaila now floundered through the fresh powder as best she could, struggling to make forward progress.
"Tsuga!"
The shadow that she could make out through the driving snow faltered and then stumbled over some unseen obstacle to fall in a heap in the snow.

Tsuga staggered through a living hell. The snow blinded her and stung her eyes. Its icy wetness leeched the heat and energy from her body so that even the convulsions that had wracked her before took too much effort to sustain. Several hours ago, she had had the bright idea to draw on her magic as she moved to keep warm – her abilities innately kept her from freezing to death, but any sense of actual warmth was beyond her without actually engaging her magic – so now, although she no longer felt the effects of the blistering cold of the wind on her exposed skin, her stores of energy were so low that it was all she could do to simply place one foot in front of the other in hopes of one day reaching the shining beacon in the distance that was her guardian. Without that faint hope, she would have given up long ago.
She knew madness had set in when she heard the wind call her name, luring her down into its frozen oblivion. Her fatigue overcame her then, and she stumbled over her own feet. Unable to recover, she collapsed in the snow and simply lay there, waiting for the Goddess to take her into Her blessedly warm embrace. A figure appeared in the snow. After a moment, Tsuga realized it was walking towards her. Fiery red hair blew about a pale and wind-chapped face, and as Tsuga slipped beyond the realm of consciousness, she had the fleeting thought that it was somehow wrong for Auriga to be so afflicted by the elements.

Affaila couldn't believe it; despite all odds, she had not only found Tsuga, but Kisha had found them a copse of trees – the closest thing to shelter to be found in the Goddess-forsaken northern wilderness of Devali. She threw another wet, frozen log on her sickly fire and winced when it hissed and popped as the ice went from frozen to steam in a matter of moments. Tsuga sighed and shifted in her sleep, and suddenly the fire surged and heat – finally! – blossomed forth as flames licked at the fuel.
How her sister had survived so long with not a scrap of clothing on her gaunt body and no weapons to her name, Affaila

didn't know and likely would never fully understand. She had tucked the girl into her own fur-lined bedroll right away, and the fire seemed to be helping as well. As the wind howled through the trees, Affaila moved to her sister's side and sat down again.

Between one breath and the next, she slipped into mage sight and began looking more closely for injuries. She'd done a cursory check when she'd first discovered Tsuga, but hadn't had time for a proper healing session then, exposed as they had been.

Aside from starvation and fatigue, there was actually very little wrong with her sister. *Thanks be to the Goddess for that.* A few minor cuts and scrapes, a bruise here and there. *Not even the beginnings of frostbite.* Affaila was amazed by that simple fact, and as she went through Tsuga's body and infused it with life and well-being, she said another prayer of thanks to Auriga for sparing her sister that misery, at least.

Tsuga woke to the sensation of heat on her face and an unusual feeling of wellness. She looked around in the darkness – her fire-kin eyes granted her a clarity of sight that a cat would envy in this pitch blackness – and wondered distantly if she was finally dead. As she sat up, the furs slipped from around her shoulders.

I'm still naked. Is everyone naked when they're dead?

She recalled a fuzzy image of the Goddess before she had blacked out, and now as her eyes scanned her surroundings, she saw another figure sleeping restfully on the other side of the fire.

So not dead, it seems. Rescued, perhaps?

As she thought idly over what she could recall of the last few days, she reached a hand into the fire and took a small tongue of flame in her grasp. She played with and manipulated it without really paying attention to her own actions, using the motions to help stimulate her thoughts.

"You have quite a gift."

Tsuga startled and lost the flame in her alarm. She looked for the source of the voice but could see nothing aside from that same slumbering form on the other side of the fire.

"Who's there?"

Light glinted off of something, and then a piece of the darkness resolved itself into the most immense wolf she had ever seen. Tsuga gasped and fought the urge to scurry backwards as the huge beast came and sat next to her. It was unsettling, being on eye level with something that could bite her in two with scarcely any effort.

"There's no need to fear me, you know. Auriga did not send me to Affaila so that I might eat her sister."

The creature exposed her sharp teeth in what Tsuga supposed was meant to be a grin. The expression made her stomach turn.

"I'm afraid I don't understand."

"I will leave that to Affaila to explain. You should get some rest, Tsuga."

"Fine. But I expect a full explanation tomorrow . . . what was your name?"

"Kisha. Now, no more questions. Get some rest."

As the beast said this, Tsuga found herself stifling a yawn. *Perhaps not so recovered as I'd thought.* She lay back down and pulled the covers up to her chin once more.

"Very well. Good night, Kisha."

"Good night, Tsuga."

When she woke again, it was daylight. The fire still burned warmly on her face, and though the ground beneath her was cold, Tsuga felt as snug as could be.

"Good morning."

This time when she sat up, she remembered to hold on to her blanket for the sake of modesty. Another log dropped onto the fire and sent a shower of sparks flying towards the canopy that sheltered them. Though this display distracted her briefly, it could not hold her attention for long.

"Good morning yourself, stranger. If the rumors are true, I'd say you've been quite busy in the last two years."

Affaila blushed, and Tsuga found herself remembering the apparition from her fever-dream.

I should have recognized her for the hair alone, she thought ruefully.

"Well, I'm not sure just what versions you heard, but I'd venture they're true enough, most like."

"So you really run around with a giant wolf – whom I've already met, by the way – killing off bad guys?"

She couldn't keep the skepticism from her voice, but Affaila seemed to take her disbelief in stride.

"More or less." The healer shrugged. "We do as Auriga bids us."

"Do you now? But I thought killing went against your all-important oath? And since when do you worship Her? Sacriligious for a Devalian, don't you think?"

"Yes, well . . . it's a long story."

"Is it? Well, it just so happens that I've nothing but time. First, though, I would very much like to put some clothes on."

Affaila laughed – a light, silvery sound like the chiming of bells – and nodded. "Of course. I don't know how well any of my things will fit you, but you're welcome to try."

As predicted, Affaila's clothes proved a rather poor fit on Tsuga's taller, thinner frame. The skirts that drug the ground on Affaila scarcely covered her sister's knees, and the top strained across Tsuga's broader shoulders, though it sagged noticeably in other places.

All in all the girl looked a sight, but Affaila managed to keep her laughter in check – barely. Once they were both settled again, Affaila prepared herself to relive the tale. Tsuga – thankfully – waited patiently, so that she had some much-needed time to compose herself.

"I don't know how much there is to tell, really. After you and I parted ways, I took to the roads myself, traveling with various nobles and merchant trains as a healer. One of the groups was attacked in force – there were several other healers with them besides myself. Everyone else was killed or taken prisoner. From the amount of blood I woke up in, I should have numbered among the dead, too.

"I woke to a vision of the Goddess Herself, and She spoke to me. Told me the world was sick, and that it needed to be healed. More specifically, She said She needed someone who could cut away the infection and make whole what was left. She explained to me the deeper meaning of my oath, then, and asked if I was willing to take up the burden She offered me. I accepted, and here I am."

"And Kisha?"

Affaila smiled warmly and looked to where the wolf sat, staring out into the snow-covered woods.

"Kisha was the Goddess' gift to me; a companion to help me on my way, as well as a guardian to show me Her favor."

"Well, that's great and all, but it seems you've made some very powerful enemies."

Affaila shifted her position on the frozen ground and nodded. "Indeed. I had no idea how deeply this thing ran, Tsu. There is evil in the world that you've never dreamed of."

"And Auriga chose you to fight it alone?"

"But I'm not alone. She guides me. Her hand is in all things. And besides, I've got Kisha to help me."

Tsuga shook her head, and Affaila could see that she was troubled. "I still don't like it. It's an awful lot to ask of anyone."

"It's alright, Tsu. I don't mind, really. At least I have a purpose, now. And Kisha . . . I always felt like I was missing out on something, seeing you and Devilsbane together, you know? I just didn't realize how much."

Tsuga's heart dropped at the mention of her own guardian, and her mind instinctively reached out for the comforting presence of the horse. She was met with . . . nothing. Only a vague direction and a bone-deep need to get there as quickly as she could. Something of her pain must have shown on her face, because Affaila's expression softened.

"They took her from you, didn't they?"

Tsuga nodded, frustrated that she had to wipe tears from her eyes as she did so. "Yes."

"Is that why you're going deeper into Devali? I had rather wondered about that."

"Yeah. She's out there, somewhere. I can't even tell if she's okay; she's too far away. I just know I have to find her. I don't care what happens to me, as long as she's alright."

"I understand. And I wish I could go with you and help you on your way." Tsuga looked up, somewhat taken aback by Affaila's words.

"Why can't you?"

"My duty lies elsewhere, Tsu. The men who took you are only a very tiny part of what's out there. I still have a lot of battles to fight, and unfortunately this is where my path must diverge from yours again."

Tsuga nodded, though she fought back feelings of bitter disappointment. "I understand that, I suppose. Still, thank you for everything. You didn't have to come, you know."

Affaila laughed. "What, and leave you to wander about buck naked in the snow?"

Even Tsuga had to chuckle a bit at that. "Not my best plan, I suppose."

"I should say not!"

"All I could think of was that I had to get away. I couldn't bear the thought of you risking your neck for me. And I couldn't face the prospect of dying in captivity."

"So you decided to die alone in the snow, instead?"

The incredulity was thick in Affaila's voice, and Tsuga smiled wryly in response.

"Well, yeah. At least I would have died free."

Affaila shook her head in disbelief. "You are truly something else, Tsu. You know that?"

Since learning that they must part ways so soon, Tsuga had done her best to hide the fear and worry she felt. She was, after all, ill-equipped to face a harsh Devalian winter on her own. Without the malachite pendant, her magic was of next to no good to her. With only her own depleted energy stores to draw on for fuel and no physical weapons whatsoever, Tsuga fostered little hope for her survival in this frozen wasteland.

Now she stood, still clothed in her sister's ill-fitting garments, and faced Affaila. A small pack full of what little provisions the healer could spare was slung over her shoulder, and there was nothing left to say but goodbye. There were tears in Affaila's eyes; the older woman's speech was rushed – as though by hurrying the farewell, she could prevent them from falling.

"There's a town about two miles west of here. If the weather holds, you should make it in about a day at the pace you've been traveling. There's a bit of coin in your pack; it should buy you a meal and a place to sleep the night."

Now Tsuga felt her own eyes brimming with tears of gratitude. "Thank you."

"Now, stop. There's no need for that. What are big sisters for, right?"

"Right."

And now the tears did fall, tracing a hot path down her cheeks to drip onto the collar of her borrowed shirt.

"Affaila?"

"Yeah?"

And now she saw that her sister, too, had lost the fight, for she wiped dampness from her face as Tsuga watched.

"You will be careful? Don't do anything stupid, alright?"

Affaila laughed and pulled her into a tight embrace. "I won't if you won't."

"Deal."

Lie though they both knew it to be, Tsuga drew comfort from the promise, wrapping the warmth of it around her like a cloak against the winter's chill.

"Well, I don't suppose there's much left to say, is there?"

Tsuga knew that Affaila was trying to end their parting as painlessly as possible, so she went along with it.

"No, I guess not."

"Alright, then. Take care of yourself, Tsu."

"And you do the same."

Affaila nodded, and since she knew her sister would never muster the resolve to turn away, Tsuga forced her own reluctant feet to move and began trudging her way west through the snow.

Affaila watched Tsuga's slow progress until she had vanished out of sight behind a snow bank, and only then was she able to turn and begin picking her own path over the treacherous winter terrain.

"She will be alright, won't she, Kisha?"

"Tsuga is a strong girl. Don't underestimate her. I think you'll find she's quite capable of taking care of herself."

"You're right, I know. But still – I can't help worrying about her."

"I understand. She's your sister, after all. But don't forget you have other responsibilities now, too. You can't let yourself be distracted from them."

Affaila sighed. "I know, I know. How could I forget? But still, she *is* my sister . . .."

"What do you mean, 'no?'" The incredulity in her voice was plain. The innkeeper shook his head firmly.

"Look, I'm sorry. But we're full up. In this weather, everybody's dug in to wait it out. Ain't got no room."

Tsuga felt panic rise in her throat and fought it down with an effort. The Devalian winter was famous for its storms, and the current blizzard looked to be no exception.

"You can't turn me out in this; I'll die!"

The man looked sympathetic, but he only shrugged. "Ain't got nowhere to put ya."

"I don't need a room. I'll sleep on the floor, in the stables, anywhere! Just please, don't turn me out!"

He frowned. "Look, lass, yer not listenin'. There ain't no room. Not even on the floor."

Tsuga shook her head in disbelief. She hadn't anticipated this at all. She had no idea where to go from here. She felt deflated, as though all of her drive had seeped down through her feet and into the very floorboards beneath her. She must have looked truly wretched then, because the inkeep's expression softened.

"Well, now, there's no sense in sendin' you off without a decent meal to sustain ya. Find a seat, an' we'll get ya somethin' warm."

Tsuga nodded numbly and moved off through the crowded common room in search of a place to sit. Her usual preference was a corner table where she could position herself with her back to a wall so that no one could sneak up on her. Now, though, all such chairs were filled – mostly with gruff-looking soldier types who stank of ale, sweat, and piss.

Ultimately, left with precious few options, she settled nervously onto a bench between a grizzled but kindly-looking farmer type – judging from the dirt stains on his hands and clothes, at least – and a young soldier who was a little too far into his ale. Both seemed relatively harmless, though the man across from her leered at her in a way that made her extremely uncomfortable.

Once her bowl of unidentifiable mush had been delivered, her feeling of unease was proven prudent. The stranger leaned across the table; she caught a waft of opium as the material of his clothes strained against his excessive bulk.

"I can give you a place to stay the night."

His voice sent a cold spike of fear driving into her heart, but she forced her face to remain still. When she made no response, the man sucked his teeth and leaned even closer to her.

"You hear me, whore? Or is a filthy little bitch like you too good for my bed?"

Tsuga's blood ran cold at his words. In the space of a few accelerated heartbeats, she found herself drawn backwards in time to that night some seven years ago when Elbon's rancid breath had stung her eyes as he tore his way into her. With a great effort she threw off the memory and came back to the here-and-now – not much of an improvement, to be sure.

Despite her fear, she knew that she had to seriously consider his offer. She was dangerously weak, even now, and severely malnourished. Even with her survival skills and her magic she had no doubt that, if left to the elements in her condition, she would meet Auriga on the other side of the light in a matter of hours.

Still desperately hoping for some other option to present itself, she cast a hopeful glance around the room, pausing for a moment to look each of the men on either side of her in the eye. Both looked away and refused to meet her gaze. She couldn't blame them; they didn't know her, and her plight was not any concern of theirs. Resigned, Tsuga turned hopeless eyes at last on the man who was still leering at her from across the stained and beaten table.

"Thank you." The words tasted like bile in her mouth. "You honor me with your kindness, good sir."

The man grinned and leaned back, licking his chops as though savoring a tasty morsel of food.

"Well spoken whore, ain't ya? Hurry up an' finish yer slop then, bitch. Yer gonna need yer strength tonight!"

He laughed crudely, and Tsuga felt herself color uncomfortably as she ducked her head and did as she was told. The already-horrendous food now tasted like ash as she tried to swallow and her stomach turned unpleasantly, but she ate the swill all the same. He was right, after all: she did need the nourishment.

After two weeks – two long, miserable weeks – the storm had finally abated, freeing Tsuga to gratefully make her escape into the winter chill. Her time sequestered in the inn hadn't served to bolster her strength – in fact if anything, she felt even weaker than before.

The dark circles under her eyes had deepened in color and she had lost so much weight that she now seemed to be a living skeleton. Beneath the baggy sleeves and too-short skirts, her body was marked with myriad bruises from her nightly ordeal in the beds of the various men trapped at the inn along with her for the duration of the blizzard. She had scarcely slept – the horror of waking from one hideous nightmare to an equally miserable reality had kept her from any kind of restful slumber.

Now, as she trudged off into the waist-deep snow with no more supplies than she'd come with, she felt like a walking shadow: devoid of any emotion, lacking any thought save the placement of one foot in front of the other in the pursuit of her guardian.

In scant moments, the chill of melting snow soaked through her clothes and set her to shivering uncontrollably. Knowing the risks of winter travel – even if she wouldn't die of the cold itself, she could easily fall ill from exposure – she wove a thin net of fire about herself, using the inherent warmth of her magic to still the convulsions that wracked her body and dry her clothes.

Almost immediately, she felt the pull of the magic begin to drain her strength. She knew that by warming herself, she was cutting the distance she could travel each day in half, at the very least. Unfortunately, she also knew that if she didn't resort to this, the lack of protection from the harsh winter elements would surely see her dead. Her supernatural defense against the cold could only get her so far, after all. And so, growing weaker by the second, she trudged onward, placing one foot in front of the other despite her misery. The knowledge that Devilsbane was still alive and waiting for her somewhere was, at this point, the only reason she kept moving.

Even with some minor improvement in the weather, Tsuga found that the prices of the inns and taverns along her path were outrageous. The small purse Affaila had given her emptied at a remarkable rate; before she knew it, Tsuga found that she hadn't even enough coin on her to purchase a stale end of bread, let alone a bed for a night.

Had she been in Sennor she would have happily sold her services as a bodyguard, but in Devali women were seen as less than men. Here they were not allowed to enter into combat, nor even to train in the martial arts. Since she really had few other marketable skills – there were no crops to tend in the dead of winter, she was useless as a cook, and her stitches looked like the handiwork of a one-handed four year old – and all of the simple, menial tasks were already taken by those just as poor and in need as she herself was, Tsuga was left with only one option.

"Penny fer yer thoughts."

She was shivering on a dark streetcorner, staring up at the faded sign above her denoting the tavern's name. She jumped a little at the voice in her ear – though she had heard him approach, and even felt him step behind her, she hadn't expected him to speak in such intimate tones. She turned her head slightly to look at him, subtly cocking her hips to one side and adjusting so that her stance was a bit more provocative.

"For two silver pieces, you can get a lot more than that."

He wasn't bad looking; though his nose had been broken in several places and he was far from handsome, she had certainly seen far worse. And his smile seemed kinder than she was used to. As much as she loathed herself for what she was doing, she hoped he would take her up on the offer. He would likely be far more tolerable than any other man she might find inside the taverns. At least he wasn't drunk – yet.

"Yer awful scrawny to be askin' fer such a high price, lass."

Tsuga, sensing his interest, licked her lips and reached out to take him in her hand. "You won't be sayin' that once you see what I kin do."

The man swallowed, and Tsuga felt him harden under her ministrations. Unable to muster words, he simply nodded.

Tsuga continued to struggle her way north and west through the harsh winter weather, selling her body and her services to keep food in her belly and a roof over her head. Often, she found that she had to pay deeply to replenish her supply of the concoction that protected her from unwanted pregnancy; to prevent the conception or growth of a child was, while not unlawful, certainly taboo – especially in a nation dominated by men.

Black market preparations of the silphium plant were expensive and difficult to come by, but the prospect of having the get of some filth who rutted in her was unbearable. And so, despite the risk of putting her body through the trials of recovering from a lost pregnancy, she took the herb faithfully. The side effects were few and mild, and with her bleedings having always been irregular and unpredictable even before she had begun taking herbs in the army to help suppress her cycles, she felt that caution was the wisest route.

While the months changed, her scenery varied dismayingly little. In Sennor, she knew, the snow would already have melted into a miserable, unending rain. The snow melt and runoff would be flooding the rivers and streams, making travel all but impossible. But at least these were conditions she was used to, and could more easily survive (the temperature further south was much milder than this extreme northern waste through which she struggled). Here in Devali, she felt as though she trudged daily through an endless frozen hell.

For the past several days, Tsuga had begun to notice small changes in her bond with Bane. She now had a more clear sense of direction, and though she still couldn't communicate clearly with the horse, she occasionally found a set of emotions other than her own invading her thoughts. Though she drove herself as hard as her weakened body could endure, she still made next to no progress through the winter wasteland.

When she felt the cold of melting snow leeching the strength from her limbs, Tsuga called on her magic and sent heat coursing over her body. Steam rose from her filthy dress and hair, and when the use of so much energy caused her to stumble and fall to her knees in the snow, it hissed and melted away at the touch of her skin.

"What, by Ketral's sweaty balls –?"

Tsuga hadn't heard anyone approach, but at this exclamation she winced and released her tenuous grasp on the magic. She struggled to her feet and stood to face the person who had spoken. She swayed a bit before she managed to steady herself. Unsure what to expect, she gathered what little strength she had left and looked up to meet his gaze. But, when she did –

"Trag?"

"Sen?!"

"Blood and war, man! Er, I mean, ah . . . ."

Tsuga laughed and shook her head. "Reckon I look a far sight different than you remember me. What the hell are you doing in the middle of this blasted wasteland? Where's the rest of the company?"

Sen sighed and tapped the cane he leaned against on the ground. "Got my leg chopped off a few months ago."

"Oh Sen, I'm sorry!"

"Not your fault, and there isn't anything to be done for it now. Come on, you look ready to collapse. I've got a room in an inn not far from here. We can catch up there."

"So you want to explain what you're doing wandering through the snow in what are obviously someone else's clothes in the middle of Devali?"

Tsuga chuckled wryly and took another sip of her mulled wine. The warmth burned all the way down her throat and formed a little ball of heat in her stomach before slowly spreading outward. She sighed with pleasure and wrapped her hands more tightly around the mug before she spoke.

"You want the long version, or the short one?"

Sen cocked his head to the side curiously. "How about the abridged version?"

"Well, basically, I went home to Sennor and joined the army there. Made captain, in fact."

"Captain? That's great! Always knew you'd make something of yourself."

"Yeah, captain of the most ragtag band of misfits I've ever known." She laughed again. "But I wouldn't trade 'em."

"That still doesn't explain what you're doing in northern Devali."

"Well, when we got stationed at the border, I was abducted on one of my nightly rounds. They took my guardian from me, Sen. So, when I got away, I set off after her. And . . . here I am."

"Wow. You've been through quite a bit. How are you coping?"

"Alright, I suppose. Just doing what I have to to get by. I mean, Ketral's balls, I'm a woman with no money in the middle of Devali. I don't exactly have a lot of options . . .."

"Wait, are you saying . . .?"

Tsuga set down her mug and leaned forward across the table as she hunched her shoulders to make the neckline of her shirt droop and expose a little more of her pale skin.

Sad, she thought reflectively, *how easily this comes now.*

"That's exactly what I'm saying, Sen. I'm alone and without a means to make my way in the world."

She shifted in her seat and extended her leg under the table to run her foot along Sen's inner thigh. "What else is a poor girl to do, I ask you?"

Sen's face flushed a bright scarlet, and she could see his grip tighten on his drink. "I, uh . . .."

"Look Sen, I'll just cut to the chase here. You're a man. You have . . . needs. And for a hot meal and a bed for the night, I could help you meet those needs."

Sen shifted uncomfortably in his seat and refused to meet her gaze. "Look, Trag – er, ah, I mean . . .."

"It's Tsuga, Sen. My real name is Tsuga."

"Tsuga. I don't think – I mean, I can't – uh.... You're like a brother to me. Well, er, I mean –"

Tsuga sighed and shifted to sit up straight again, dropping the act as suddenly as though it had never been. "I understand. Shit, I shared a tent with you. Just wouldn't feel right."

Her friend relaxed visibly and shot her a grateful glance.

"Exactly. Besides, I'm not sure I could get past all those threats you used to make about cutting it off."

She laughed as her thoughts shifted back to that more pleasant time and allowed herself a small smile.

"Fair enough. And just to be clear, Sen: those threats still stand."

She could see him swallow nervously, but she was only able to keep a straight face for a few seconds before she broke out laughing again.

"Oh, come now. Can't I still give you a hard time? Just because you know I've got a pair of tits now doesn't mean I'm not the same person. I could still kick your ass in a fight, and you know it!"

Sen cracked a wry smile and took a sip from his mug to mask his discomfort.

"Always were one to cut straight to the point. Glad to see time hasn't tamed your tongue, my friend. Let me buy you a hot meal, and you're welcome to take my bed tonight. The floor is good enough for me."

Tsuga shook her head. "Nonsense. I will not accept special treatment from you just because I'm a girl. You will keep your bed, and know that I am perfectly happy with the floor. At least it's out of the weather, and it's more than I would have had otherwise."

And blessedly less, she added to herself, relieved beyond measure that she wouldn't be forced to perform tonight.

"Fair enough. Might have known you'd say something like that; you were ever the martyr."

"Not a martyr, Sen – only too proud to take charity. I won't accept help I haven't earned. It's not in me to be a leech."

Sen was silent for a few moments as he looked at her.

"How far is your guardian?"

"At the pace I'm traveling? One week; maybe two if the weather's against me."

He didn't speak for a long moment, and just as Tsuga had made up her mind to change the subject to something less painful, he looked up and met her gaze.

"Let me help you. I've got my discharge pay from the army, and I've nothing to hurry home to. I can make your travels far more comfortable, and I'd be grateful for the chance to reconnect with an old friend."

Tsuga shifted her weight on the hard wooden chair to ease some of the pain in her buttocks and frowned in thought.

"I won't have you spending your discharge pay on me, Sen. I just won't. You should be using that to buy yourself some land. Find a nice girl, start a life. I just wouldn't feel right, taking that from you."

"It's not like that at all. I can hardly let you continue to freeze to death. I wouldn't be able to live with myself, knowing I could have helped but didn't. And you can earn your way."

"How is that?"

"Well, I have a bit of a hard time getting around with just the one leg – let alone hunting or making camp. Puts me at a decided disadvantage should I be attacked, too. I could use a bodyguard."

"You could use a servant, you mean. I can hardly go around selling myself as a bodyguard in Devali."

"Well, the cover story is not important. We can work that out later. What do you say?"

Tsuga shook her head and searched his face with wary eyes. She knew him to be sincere, but still she hesitated to put him in danger for her sake.

"Look, Sen, I really don't think –"

"It's that horse, right?"

"Excuse me?"

"Your guardian. It has to be. That demon wouldn't let anyone touch her but you. And she was far too fine a beast for you to have had otherwise."

"Alright; yes, you're right. My guardian is Devilsbane. So?"

"So, how do you intend to get back through Devali – a lone woman with such a fine piece of horseflesh? Women have no property here. The first man who lays eyes on that horse will want it, and you'll be powerless to stop him from taking her."

Tsuga stiffened. "If anyone so much as tries, I"ll –"

"You'll what? Kill him? You're in Devali, Tsuga. You have no rights. If you kill, there will be no hesitation – no question. Your life will be forfeit."

"And just how will your being there stop any of this from happening?

"If we say she is my horse – I'm a discharged soldier; that would be believable – none would question it. I could get you back to Sennor safely, that way."

"I can't ask you to do that, Sen. Besides, what is to become of you, once you get me home?"

"I've always wanted to visit Sennor. I still have my voice and my instruments. I could pass as a traveling minstrel."

Tsuga looked at him again, still undecided.

"I'm not taking 'no' for an answer."

The nag that Sen had been traveling with didn't look like much, but the docile old beast was sturdy enough. Tsuga felt as though she were somehow betraying Bane by riding another horse, but it kept her out of the snow, which was something she desperately needed in her current weakened state.

Riding double with Sen also meant that she was able to share his body heat, thus further conserving her energy. For the first time in months, Tsuga felt safe enough to let herself relax. It wasn't long before the slow, swinging stride of the horse lulled her to sleep.

She came around slowly, disoriented by the swaying movement and the grip of Sen's strong arms holding her upright. It took her a few moments to get her bearings, but as her mind fought off the cobwebs of sleep she began to take in the details. She could smell horse, leather, and sweat – all comforting smells – as well as the less familiar smell of the coniferous trees native to northern Devali. The forest they rode through was full of them – towering giants with dark green foliage, the remains of which coated the forest floor in a thick and fragrant layer. It was an overpowering smell – though not altogether unpleasant.

Sen must have felt her stirring, because he adjusted his grip on the reins and shifted his weight. Tsuga sat up straighter in the saddle, moving forward so that she was no longer resting against his chest. She felt him suck in a breath behind her, and then reality settled in again.

"How long was I out?"

"Couple hours, I suppose. You must have been pretty tired."

"Yes, that. Still healing, too. And something about the feel of a horse under me . . . it's comforting. When I woke up, just for a moment, I almost thought –"

"That it was her?"

Tsuga choked off a strangled sound and simply nodded, unable to force words out of her tight throat.

"You'll find her, you know. A few more days – a week, at most – and then . . .."

"Finding her is one thing. But what then? I've no money to buy her. Stealing her would be a simple enough matter, but getting out of Devali with her after that, well . . .."

Tsuga trailed off as the despair she'd been fighting back welled up, threatening to choke her speech completely.

"It'll be okay. We'll figure something out."

"I hope you're right, Sen. I really do."

"Well, we found her."

Tsuga shot Sen a withering glance. "Yeah. Now how do we get her away?"

Yet another blizzard had slowed their travels, turning Sen's estimated week to nearly three. Although that extra time had allowed Tsuga to regain a great deal of her strength and conditioning, it had also given her far too much time to fret.

As they had drawn nearer, Tsuga had begun to reliably feel her guardian again. Two days ago, she had caught the beast's thoughts, and had seized upon this contact as a drowning person might seize upon a bit of flotsam. They had not broken the connection since, each taking stock of the changes in the other.

Consequently, Tsuga was now well aware of her guardian's situation. Frantic about her human, Bane had been wild and uncontrollable. The thieves had sold her, and after that the horse had changed hands several times before finally being confiscated by the army.

When the men had been unable to control the half-starved and wild animal, experts in animal mindspeech had been called upon to try and soothe her – such a fine piece of horseflesh was worth the considerable investment, after all. Bane had – wisely –

refused to communicate with them for fear of exposing her true nature. Tsuga knew any self-respecting man would be loathe to lose such a horse; predictably, Bane had been subjected to a number of cruel practices in an effort to break her spirit and make her more manageable.

Now, the once-proud mare stood tied to a tree, head hanging listlessly. Her coat was shaggy and dull, her too-long mane and tail in desperate need of grooming. Her hooves had lengthened and cracked painfully, so that it hurt her even to stand, and her ribs poked out at an alarming angle. The sight brought tears to Tsuga's eyes even as her blood thrummed with anger.

Don't worry, Bane. I'll get you out of there. I promise.

"So what exactly is the plan, here?"

Tsuga glared at her traveling companion where he crouched in the darkness. It was too dangerous for them to build a fire this close to the army's camp, and the lack of a hot meal made her stomach clench painfully. Although Sen had tried to persuade her to sleep, her mind had been racing too much to allow her any real rest. Now that darkness had fallen, Tsuga had grown restless and begun to pace.

"We're both familiar with Devalian military practices. There will be guards posted at every hundred paces, and half the guard will change every two hours, alternating groups until dawn. There will be a handful of guards patrolling inside the camp, but our main concern is the horse lines."

Tsuga moved closer to Sen and a tiny flame appeared just above the ground between them, smaller than her fingernail. In this dim light, Tsuga outlined a sketch of the camp and the positions of the guards in the trampled snow.

"Now, since Bane has been so unmanageable, she's not being kept with the other mounts. She's tied here, nearly out of the camp entirely. The men are so wary of her, they keep as much of a distance as they can get away with. We'll have to cause some sort of distraction to draw the guards' attention and allow us time to escape with her. Something that will hold their interest and keep them confused long enough for us to get some distance on them before they realize she's gone."

"You're not going to –"

Tsuga motioned sharply with her hand to cut him off. "Don't concern yourself with what I'll be doing, Sen. You just pack up and get that nag of yours as far west as possible."

"Why not south?"

"Because the border with Fardri is closer than Sennor. They won't risk an armed search for us there – it would start a war that Devali is ill equipped for, with so many of their forces already engaged in the campaign against Sennor."

The light snuffed out and Tsuga stood to move away again. The small use of magic wearied her, but she steeled herself against the weakness, knowing what was to come would be far more taxing. When Sen spoke again, she could hear the tremor in his voice that belied the bravado of his words.

"You are a better tactician than any I've met, Tsuga. And I know you can take care of yourself. The border is less than a day's hard ride, if the weather holds. But that's on a hale mount. I'll wait for you at the inn."

Tsuga nodded. "Wait no more than three days after you arrive. If we haven't made it by then, assume us dead and go your own way. They can't prove you've done anything wrong, and they shouldn't be hunting you. I'll give you an hour to get on your way before I start – that's between guard changes, when there will be the fewest men out and about. Be careful, Sen."

"I'll see you in a few days, Tsuga."

"Let's hope so."

You understand what's going to happen?

Yes.

Can you run?

Not well, and not for long. It hurts to even walk.

Bane, your life depends on this. . . . So does mine.

You think I don't know that? I'll do my best, Tsu, but I'm in pretty bad shape.

I know. I'm sorry. I'm just anxious for this to work.

So am I. You had better come out of this alive, you understand me?

Tsuga couldn't help but grin at the horse's threat even as she choked back her fear and worry.

Don't worry about me. You just run north and get as far as you can. I'll be right behind you. We can turn west once we're sure we're not being followed. Are you ready?

Yes.

Tsuga was only about fifty paces from Bane, belly to the ground. It was hard to see anything from this distance, but thankfully it was a clear night. The moon illuminated Bane's silouhette, and as the horse lifted her head Tsuga could see the outline of the rope that bound her. She took a deep breath to steady herself, and then summoned a trickle of magic – small enough that she hoped it wouldn't be noticed – and carefully bent it to her will. She thought she saw a wisp of smoke in the faint light, but there was no flame.

After what seemed like minutes, Bane threw her head back. Tsuga saw the rope break. She repeated the process with the horse's hobbles. She fought back a sigh of relief when the last rope snapped and turned her attention to the nearest dark shape in the night – one of the camp's outlying supply wagons. Although the wood and tarp were damp with snow, her magical fire found a foothold in the dry grain sacks inside.

Once the first small flame had taken hold, Tsuga turned her attention to a nearby tent, weakening the ropes that held it upright before setting a small flame to lick away at the canvas. She did this several more times throughout the camp, setting multiple small fires with no particular pattern so that all would draw attention at about the same time.

Finally, hoping she had set enough to create sufficient havoc, Tsuga slunk backwards until she was once again under the cover of the brush. Moments after she reached this relative safety, she heard the first shout of alarm. A gust of wind blew the scent of smoke in her face, and Tsuga smiled appreciatively. Fire and wind were old friends. The breeze would feed her little fires for her.

She felt as though she were made of lead weights as she stood and began to walk away. So much use of her magical energy stores had tired her a great deal, but she had kept her tricks small, and so was still able to break into a slow jog once she was far enough away to be sure that she wouldn't be spotted.

Bane?

They've pulled half the guard to fight the fires and search for the saboteur. I'm almost to the road. No one seems to have noticed.

Good. I'll meet you at the road. They won't separate us again.

"So how'd you two get separated, again?"

"We were being followed." *True.* "When her horse foundered, we split up to try and throw them off." *Sort of true.*

"You left your wife on her own?!"

Sen could tell from the way the man was looking at him that such a cowardly act was despicable in his eyes. The former soldier shifted uncomfortably.

"Tsuga can take care of herself. Better than I can, any more." He gestured vaguely to his missing limb. From the corner of his eye, he saw the innkeeper wince.

"Well, I s'pose . . .. Still, don't seem right to leave a lady on her own."

Sen sighed. He'd been thinking much the same thing since arriving in this place a week ago. He couldn't help but feel guilty for letting his friend undertake such a task alone while he skulked away like a coward. When the three days had passed with no sign of Tsuga, Sen had refused to give up hope, stubbornly staying put at the tiny inn and praying that he hadn't left her to get herself killed. It was getting harder to deny as the time passed.

"No, it ain't right to abandon a lady. But he didn't abandon me. And I ain't no lady."

Sen's head shot up at the familiar voice and he twisted in his seat, upending the tankard he'd been sipping from.

Tsuga shook her head sadly as she watched the drink spill. "Waste of good drink, that . . .."

She'd scarcely gotten the words out before Sen had knocked over the bench, too, and hopped across the small room to embrace her in a bear hug. Tsuga stiffened at the contact, though she couldn't help but be touched by this show of emotion.

"Tsuga! I thought you were dead!"

"And I thought I told you to be on your way after three days. Nice to know you don't follow orders. You always did make a poor soldier, Sen."

"And don't I know it! Come in, sit. Tell me what happened."

"All in good time. First, innkeep, I've got a horse in pretty bad shape. I need a ferrier, some warm meal for her to eat, and some grooming tools."

"Well, ferrier's just up the road. I can send a lad to fetch him. Stable boys can help ya with the rest."

"Tsuga, all that can wait." Sen had to reach out to grasp her arm as she turned to make her way out the door. "How long has it been since *you've* eaten something?"

"I don't know. A day. Maybe two. But that's not important. Bane's hurting, Sen. I'm fine."

With a sharp twist she loosed herself from his grasp and turned to address the innkeep again – a squat little man with a friendly face who was watching this little exchange with a look of bemusement.

"We will be in the stables. Please send the ferrier there when he arrives."

She didn't wait to hear his response, but turned on her heel and strode out, leaving Sen to struggle after her.

"So?"

"So, what?"

Sen had followed her to the stables. By the time he'd made it inside, Tsuga had already helped herself to the grooming supplies and was directing the stable boy in the concoction of a warm mash of oats and other things to help the horse process the nutrients more easily. Now, as Sen moved around to a stool placed out of the way and sat down, she shook her head.

"That's too mushy. She's a horse, damn it, not a suckerfish. Add some more of that ground meal to it. Should be like mud, not melted snow."

"So," Sen interrupted, "are you going to tell me what happened?"

Tsuga picked up a tool for picking debris and mud from a horse's hoof and lifted one of the emaciated beast's feet.

"Not much to tell, really." She *tsk*ed as she picked out a rock and a large clump of mud. "Poor baby; they really let you go, didn't they?"

Oh, they tried to take care of me at first. Guess I wasn't very cooperative, though.

Tsuga snorted as she set the foot back down and moved to the next. "Not surprising." Another large clump of frozen mud fell away as she turned her attention to Sen's question.

"Getting her free was the easy part. But she's in such bad shape she can barely stand, let alone run. So it was pretty slow going. We couldn't keep to the roads. Almost got ourselves into trouble a couple of times, but everyone burns." She shuddered. "That's the problem; every living thing will burn."

Her voice rang oddly in her own ears as she spoke. Those were not memories she was proud of. The ones she could get close to, she had killed honestly, robbed blind, and then burned to cover her tracks. The ones she couldn't . . . well, as she'd said, anything with a spark of life in it would burn.

"Guess that explains the wardrobe change." Tsuga moved around to Bane's left side and lifted her front hoof. Since she'd seen Sen last, Tsuga had patched together a reasonably well-fitting outfit from the possessions of the dead soldiers. The various articles of clothing differed widely in their states of wear, but they were warmer and far more practical than the ill-fitting skirts she'd worn before.

"Guess it does."

Once she finished with the last hoof, Tsuga selected a pair of shears and set about lopping off Bane's long, shaggy mane.

"There; that's starting to feel better, isn't it?"

Getting there.

Tsuga produced a small dagger from her boot then and set about pulling it through Bane's tail to cut out the worst of the knots and dirt.

"Looks like you found a few useful things, then."

"Aye. Sword. Couple of knives. Bow, but only a handful of arrows. Feels good to be armed again."

"I'm sure. Seems you've outfitted yourself pretty well."

"Tried to. But I'll still have to go through Devali to get to Sennor. Jilaed, the country just south of this one, is sealed to outsiders because of an outbreak of plague."

"Where'd you hear that?"

Tsuga returned the dagger to her boot and set about braiding Bane's tail into the traditional knot used in both militaries for its practicality.

"Questioned a few of them before I killed them."

"I . . . see."

Tsuga could tell from the tone of Sen's voice that something about this statement bothered him. She looked at him over Bane's rump and quirked an eyebrow.

"Out with it, then."

"It's just . . . you seem so calm, talking about it."

"And how do you want me to be, Sen? Emotional? Driven mad by remorse? We both know there is no place for that if we are to make it to Sennor alive."

Never mind that those deaths will haunt me for the rest of my life.

"You're right, I know. It's just disturbing, is all."

"Look Sen, we're both soldiers here. You were never cut out for it – I know that. But it's who I am. It's all I've ever known. It . . . suits me."

She finished with the tail as she spoke, gave a final nod of approval over the soft food mixture, and bent to retrieve a brush for her guardian's coat, choosing one with stiff bristles to get off what muck and excess hair she could.

"It twists my gut to hear that. I'm just glad you both came through it all in one piece."

More or less . . ..

" 'Ello?"

They both turned and looked up at the thickly accented greeting, and Tsuga moved around to get a better view.

"Are you the ferrier, then?"

"I am. What be you needin'?"

"She's in pretty bad shape. Hasn't been properly looked to in over a year."

"Alright. Tie 'er up, and I'll take a look."

Bane, who up until this point had been completely absorbed in the meal and unconcerned with the new arrival, snorted and raised her head to give the man a wall-eyed look.

"No."

"No? She looks to be a skittish one. I shan't work on a wild thing with no restraints."

Tsuga snorted. "Wild? She's docile as a lamb. Doesn't like ropes, though." *And I can't blame her, after what she's just been through.* "You've nothing to fear."

" 'Ow do you know that she won't get skittish-like?"

Bane, who was still looking at him warily rather than eating, flared her nostrils. **"Because I'm not some dumb beast, you lackwit. Now, if you would be so kind, my feet really *do* hurt."**

The man blanched, and Tsuga slapped her horse on the neck. "Real subtle, Bane. Nice."

Well, we're not in Devali anymore.

"Did – did that horse just –"

"Talk? Yes, I did. Don't look so surprised – haven't you ever heard of a guardian before?"

"Those – those demon-spawn that latch on to human souls and suck the life out of them while they sleep?"

Tsuga found Sen's hand on her shoulder, and only then realized she was shaking with rage. Having spent so much time in Devali, she'd heard many such falsehoods; she had never grown to tolerate them very well.

"That, good sir," she said through gritted teeth, "is a lie of the worst kind, and I will thank you not to repeat such in my hearing."

"I'm – I'm sorry, sir. It's just –"

"I'm well aware of the lies spread by our Devalian neighbors. Now, will you do the job, or not? Oh, and it's miss, by the way."

The man blanched again, but he set down the pack carrying his tools and nodded.

"It – it would be an honor, miss."

"So . . . wife?" Sen paused for a moment in unlacing his boots, and Tsuga could see him flush a bright red. He coughed and resumed his task, fumbling as he loosened the laces.

"Yeah . . . sorry about that. They asked who I was waiting for, and it just seemed simpler than telling them the truth."

Tsuga snorted and began removing her handful of weapons. "Yes, simpler. Except that now we have a room with one bed, and they expect us to act all lovey-dovey."

"Yeah, well . . .. Look, I'll sleep on the floor. No big deal."

Tsuga sighed and sat down to remove her own boots. She winced as she pulled them off, exposing raw and weeping blisters that had developed as a result of the poor fit.

"No, there's no sense in you taking the floor when the bed is more than large enough for both of us. Auriga's tits; we shared a tent for well over a year. We're both adults here, right?"

Sen offered a lopsided grin, though Tsuga noticed that he was still blushing.

"Right. Of course."

"Besides, I haven't gotten a decent night's sleep in over a year. I suspect I'll sleep like the dead, no matter where I fall."

So much for sleeping like the dead.

Tsuga stifled the urge to sigh as she lay staring into the darkness. Despite the softness of the bed and the quiet of the room, she found herself overwhelmed with an irrational fear that everything had been a fever dream – that by falling asleep now, she would only wake to find herself alone and fighting death in the snowy wilderness. Even though she had not loosed the contact with her guardian since regaining it, she couldn't shake the fear that Bane would be taken from her again.

At last, unable to quiet her worries, Tsuga slid out of the warm bed. She was forced to bite her lip to keep from crying out at the pain in her bandaged feet when she put weight on them. She left Sen sleeping in the bed and fled the room, bothering only to grab her sword and buckle it on as she made her way down the stairs and out into the cold of the night.

She immediately regretted not grabbing her cloak as the cold sank into her bones just as quickly as her feet sank into the churned snow in front of the door. She called on her magic to fight the shivering with an ease born of desperate, repeated practice and trudged through the darkness as quickly as she could.

Once she reached the stables she found the large doors closed and barred against the night, but as she'd expected there was a smaller entrance off to the side, which the stable boys could use to come and go without opening the main door. It was to this entrance she went and rapped softly. When there was no response, she gave the knob a try and found the door opened with a gentle push.

Not very concerned with security, are they?

And why should they be? They're not at war with anyone.

I wonder what that's like, she mused as she slipped inside and pulled the door closed behind her.

As her eyes adjusted to the dim light, Tsuga realized she stood inside the tack room, surrounded by saddles and bridles in various states of repair. She smiled to herself and paused a moment to inhale deeply the scent of leather, oil, and soap.

They were all smells from her childhood, associated with good memories from the time when her Da had still been alive and had taught her how to clean and mend the equipment. She held these good memories close as she stepped into the main part of the stable and made her way to Devilsbane's stall.

As instructed the stall door had been left unlatched so that Bane would not feel trapped or restricted. After what the beast had suffered, Tsuga certainly couldn't blame her for the paranoia. The horse, feet recently tended and freshly shod, had elected to lay down for the night to escape as much of the pain they caused her as she could. Tsuga smiled again and entered the stall to sit in the straw, where she took Bane's head in her lap and stroked the mare – as much to soothe her own nerves as to comfort her guardian.

With the physical contact, Tsuga felt the knot in her stomach begin to loosen. She could sense a similar feeling of relief in the horse. Before long she felt weariness settle on her, weighing her down like a heavy burden. She succumbed to a yawn as she moved around to Devilsbane's back, where she curled up to share the animal's warmth and promptly fell asleep.

"Tsuga? Ketral's balls! When I woke up and you were gone, I thought . . .."

Mind still addled by the clutches of her dreams, Tsuga blinked sleepily in the pale light of dawn. Around her, she could hear the familiar sounds of morning in a stable – restless horses eager for their breakfasts, the sleepy grooms calling to one another and speaking softly to comfort their charges.

As her eyes focused, Tsuga squinted up at a disheveled-looking Sen and sat up.

"You thought what? That I'd run off with my crippled and starved guardian and left you to rot?"

Stiff from her night spent curled up in the stall, Tsuga stretched her arms behind her before she stood, feeling her entire body ache from the cold. Without thinking she pulled on her reserves again, and though heat and life returned to her extremities, she paled from the effort it cost her.

"Well, no, but . . .. Blood and war; after everything we've just been through, I didn't know what to think!"

"Well, we're both fine. I just couldn't stop worrying that someone might steal her away from me again. So, I came out to check on her, and I guess I dozed off . . .. I can't remember the last time I slept through the night like that."

Neither can I.

Sen merely shook his head.

"Far be it from me to criticize something I don't understand. Come on inside; you must be hungry."

"By Ketral's hairy balls, what *is* this?"

Tsuga hid a smirk at Sen's horrified look as he pulled the leg of a beetle out of his bowl of stew and smoothed her expression before answering.

"Found it under a rotting log. Lucky for us; we need the protein, and this land has been so over-farmed and over-hunted there's not much else to glean it from."

Sen blanched, and Tsuga shook her head at him.

"Beggars can't be choosers, Sen. I'm sorry if a bug stew offends your delicate palate, but if you want to stay alive, you'll get past your squeamish stomach."

To prove her point, Tsuga took a large mouthful of the stew and choked it down, fighting back the urge to vomit as she felt something she didn't want to identify tickle the back of her throat on the way.

As she watched Sen take another mouthful and gag as he forced himself to swallow, she considered their options. Just over a month had passed since their escape from Devali. Two weeks' slow travel – the snail's pace necessitated by Bane's still-less-than-top condition as well as the unfavorable weather – had shown them that towns in the agricultural nation of Fardri were few and far between. Although on occasion a kind family would offer them food and shelter in exchange for labor, on this particular night the traveling companions found themselves without such luxuries.

The weather here had not yet given way to spring, but still Tsuga knew that the dreaded yearly floods grew closer with each passing day. When the snow melted in the foreboding mountains visible to the west, Fardri's rivers would overflow their banks, bringing with the influx of water the rich silt that made the land so fertile.

Unfortunately for the two of them, however, one of these raging rivers would be the Vitae, the Life-Bringer, which as the largest and longest river in Fardri formed the better part of the nation's border with Devali. As the snow melted from the surrounding fields, the Vitae would overflow her banks and submerge her many bridges. Passage would become impossible until the floods of spring had subsided and the river was once again slumbering peacefully between her banks.

Tsuga felt their time growing shorter with each passing day. She had no desire to stay away from her homeland for the additional months it would take to wait until international travel was once again possible. At their current pace, Tsuga calculated that they would reach the great river in another three or four weeks. She could only hope the weather would hold long enough for them to make the crossing in time.

"What's wrong?"

Tsuga startled and looked across the embers of their small campfire at Sen.

"Nothing."

"You're worrying again. Don't lie to me; I can see it as plainly as though it were written on your face. We're doing this together, Tsu. Which means you're not the only one who gets to worry here. Besides, maybe I can help."

Tsuga sighed and set down her empty bowl before throwing another log on the fire. Sen shrunk back from the scattering of sparks, but Tsuga merely watched them form and die in the cold night air.

"It's the Vitae."

"The river? What about it?"

"She's frozen now, but she won't stay that way. And when she melts, she'll be filled to bursting with runoff for hundreds of miles. Impossible to cross.

"And you're worried we won't make it in time before it floods?" Tsuga nodded, though she watched the ever-changing glow of the coals rather than meeting his gaze. "How far are we?" Sen never had been very good with navigation. Take away the man's roads and signs, and he was clueless. Tsuga cracked a small smile at the memories the thought brought to mind.

"At this pace, about three weeks. Maybe four."

"And you're worried that since it hasn't snowed in a week, the melt may have started already."

Tsuga couldn't bring herself to speak; she merely nodded.

"Well, sounds to me like it's a force of nature. You can't control nature; you can only endure her moods and pray you survive. Stop fretting, Tsu. I know you're anxious to get home again, but things will happen as they are meant to. Your losing sleep isn't going to stop the weather; nor will it get us to Sennor any faster."

Tsuga, stung by the harsh reality in his words, averted her gaze. "I never took you for a fatist, Sen."

"I'm not. I'm a realist. You can't stop the passage of time; you can only do your best not to be swept away by it."

Tsuga grunted and stood up, unable to remain still any longer. This worrying over things she couldn't change gave her too much nervous energy.

"Where are you going?"

"Sword practice."

With that, she left Sen sitting by the fire and stalked into the night.

"Can't you just . . . I don't know . . . freeze it back?"

Tsuga shot Sen a scornful look and ran a hand through her freshly-shorn hair.

"No, I can't. I'm a fire mage, not an ice mage. I can only heat things up, not cool them down."

"Huh?"

Tsuga shifted her weight in the new saddle Sen had purchased for her and plucked at the tunic she now wore. Knowing that they would again have to enter Devali, she had adopted a familiar disguise – dressed as a young man atop a now nearly-recovered and re-conditioned warhorse and armed with a stolen sword, she once again looked the part of a young soldier – this time, a mercenary.

"Fire and ice are like two sides of the same coin – each only half of the whole, but neither able to touch the other. My ability is to add energy to an object until it grows warmer, eventually bursting into flame. I can't remove heat from something once it's there; I can only move the heat to somewhere else or dissipate it into the air. It wouldn't be enough to freeze anything. Think of it like a campfire. You can warm yourself by it, cook your food over it, but the food will be too hot to eat unless you set it aside and let it cool on its own. You can blow on it, which will help dissipate some of the surface heat into the surrounding air, but your breath will never turn it to ice, no matter how long you blow."

"I'd have just accepted a simple 'no.'"

Tsuga shifted uncomfortably in her saddle and watched the bloated river's passage. As she'd feared, the water had thawed days before their arrival. The level of the river was rising steadily as the runoff from the melting snow and ice trickled in to swell it further. They stood looking at one of the many smaller bridges that spanned the Vitae, now rising less than an inch above the muddy, churning waters. It would take them at least a quarter hour to cross the bridge safely – they would have to dismount and proceed single file. With Sen's disability, what should have been a quick and easy passage looked to be all but impossible.

"Are you sure you want to do this, Sen? You don't owe me anything. You could stay and wait out the flooding."

Sen's expression hardened and he swung down from atop his horse. "Nonsense. I told you I would help you get home, and I meant it. Now come on – the longer we stand here, the less chance we'll make it across."

Tsuga started to protest, but she knew he had a point. "As you wish, then. But I'll lead your mount. Bane doesn't need to be guided, after all, and this way you have both hands free."

"Good idea," Sen agreed as he reached up to untie his crutch from his saddle.

"Bane can go first, then you. I'll follow you so I can help you out if you need it. Hopefully seeing Bane make it across will keep this nag moving."

"Yeah, hopefully."

With this simple plan set in place, Bane set off across the narrow, rickety bridge. When it came time for Tsuga to cross, she found the wooden surface of the planks slick with moisture. Sen's horse balked at setting foot on the bridge, but with some gentle coaxing the old mare ventured uncertainly forward.

The going was slow. Sen slipped often on the water-logged boards, and the nag Tsuga led was reluctant to move at all for the same reason. She supposed she could heat the wood a little – just enough to dry it off – but just a bit too far in the other direction and the boards may become brittle and dump all of them into the murky waters which currently lapped at the bridge and caused it to rock and sway uncertainly. They were less than half way across, and Tsuga was beginning to think that perhaps it would have been best for them to have waited, after all.

Up ahead, she heard – or rather, felt – Bane snort in dismay, and the little procession came to a halt as the bridge swayed alarmingly.

"What is it?"

She could scarcely hear her own voice above the roar of the water now beginning to lap at her boots. Luckily she didn't need to be heard for Bane to understand her.

There's a plank missing here. I just stepped through it. Can't see where the hell I'm going anymore. I'm fine, she added quickly, **but I'm not sure if Sen can get across it with the water like this.**

"He'll have to. Bridge is too narrow for you to turn around, and it's too far to back this old bag of bones." Though they both knew she was right, Tsuga could feel Bane's reluctance to move forward.

"Sen! Bane says there's a board out. You'll have to jump it."

Although she spoke with her hand on his shoulder, Tsuga had to yell to be sure he had heard her. She felt more than heard him suck in a breath as he nodded his understanding. She released her grip on his shoulder and stood back to allow him room as he slowly moved forward, probing ahead with his crutch to avoid falling through into the icy water that by now was half way up Tsuga's ankle. If they didn't hurry, they'd be washed away in a matter of minutes.

She saw Sen brace himself and stretch his crutch as far ahead as he could manage. He took a moment to adjust his stance – then he was over, slipping as he sought purchase on the other side. Tsuga let out the breath she'd been holding when at last he steadied and moved along out of her way. She was able to step across the gap with relative ease, but as the horse she led drew nearer to it, some manner of debris caught in the powerful current of the river struck the bridge, causing the rickety contraption to rock violently.

The horse spooked, rearing back and ripping the reins from Tsuga's grasp. She crashed down again, but lost her balance on the slippery wood and fell to her knees. Tsuga moved to help, but the beast was panicked and thrashed about too wildly for her to approach. The water was still rising steadily, and in the time it would take her to soothe and right the beast, they'd both be washed away in the flood.

Tsu, leave her.

"But Sen's things –"

Can be replaced. *You* can't. Now come on!

Tsuga heard truth in Bane's words, and Sen would understand, she knew. The horse was still thrashing wildly, making it difficult for Tsuga to keep her balance. Still, she couldn't see letting the animal suffer. Knowing the price she would pay for doing so, Tsuga opened herself to her magic and formed a blade of white hot fire as long as she was tall. With one quick movement, the horse's pain was ended.

With one final twist of will, the elemental sword became a blazing pyre which engulfed the body and consumed it almost instantly. Her conscience eased, Tsuga turned and released her hold on the magic. She staggered under the burden of exhaustion and stumbled forward, blinking rapidly to dispel the haze that had invaded the edges of her vision. The water pulled viciously, threatening to sweep her legs out from under her. With great effort she moved forward, dragging first one foot through the calf-high water, and then the other. She lost track of time; she no longer knew if days passed between each breath, or only seconds.

From somewhere beyond the one step in front of her that she could see, Tsuga thought she heard voices, but she couldn't make out the words. The jumble of noise came again, and Tsuga thought she heard her name.

She stumbled as she stepped unexpectedly out of the water and, unable to move quickly, lost her balance and fell forward. She felt a brief flash of relief that at least she wouldn't drown to death (though from what she'd heard, drowning was a peaceful way to go; far more so than, say, burning alive). Then, she felt nothing at all as the tide of weariness dragged her under.

Another full day had been lost to Tsuga's recovery, but at last the three of them (Sen now riding behind Tsuga on Devilsbane) resumed their journey, following the course of one of the river's offshoots in a rough south-easterly direction. Sen hadn't been thrilled about her burning all of his clothes and other possessions, but as Bane had said, all such things could be replaced. All that was required was money. Luckily travel, trade, and war all resumed with the spring thaw. Tsuga should have no problem finding work as a caravan guard – or even a personal bodyguard, the way things had been deteriorating with the war lately.

Travel through the mud and the few remaining piles of slush progressed unpleasantly and slowly, and Tsuga was subjected to a never-ending stream of complaints from Devilsbane. Tsuga knew that the nearest town – where she could seek hire, and the three of them could dry out and wash off the mud that had already coated all three of them – was two days' ride even in fair weather.

Tsuga shivered as a glob of muck worked itself free of Bane's hooves and landed on her cheek. While the natives of the northern reaches of Devali would already be down to their shirtsleeves and rejoicing in the relative warmth, Tsuga had grown up in Sennor, where even in the far north snows were brief and rare. By now it would be summer in Sennorra, the capital, and one would break a sweat merely standing outside.

Not so, here, she mused morosely as she listened to the sucking sound made every time Bane had to pull a foot free of the mire through which they rode. She knew that, all too soon, she would have to dismount and walk to allow Bane as much of a break as she could.

She chaffed her hands together and warmed them with magically heated breath to ease the cold-induced ache that made their use painful. Although the spare clothes they carried were no longer clean, they were at least dry. When they stopped, Tsuga would use them to scrape off as much of the mud from her guardian as possible and return some heat to the poor beast's limbs.

This is miserable.

I know.

How long until it warms up and dries out?

I have no idea, Bane. But at least we're going south. It's bound to get warmer soon, though I think they have a pretty long rainy season this far north.

Wonderful. The sarcasm was thick in Bane's mindvoice. **I can hardly wait.**

As Tsuga had predicted, the rains had started about a week after the river crossing. The small group was currently holed up in a little inn just off the main road. While they all knew that it would be impossible to put off their travels until the rains stopped, Tsuga was reluctant to drive them all back into it until she at least had a job that promised a fair bit of coin in exchange for their misery. The traffic through the inn was mostly lone travelers, but nonetheless Tsuga spent the majority of each day in the inn's common room, watching the door and listening to the various conversations.

Finally, early in the evening of the fifth day, her efforts were rewarded. A large group of men began to file in, all muddy and travel-worn. At least half of them were haphazardly bandaged, and Tsuga overheard words like "attack" and "double the fee." She waited until the group had divided themselves and settled in before she approached a table of the sullen fighting men.

"Dang'rus times, these."

She addressed one of the younger men in the group – one who had already downed a tankard of the swill that passed for Devalian beer and was half way through a second. He made a rude noise, and Tsuga took that as an invitation to sit down.

"Lemme buy yer next drink. I'd like t' hear what could take on such a strong group as thissun an' get the best o' ya."

The stranger's mug impacted the table with a thud loud enough to draw the attention of the others seated nearby.

"They didn't either!"

Tsuga made no move to argue with the youngster when he protested. Seeing that she wasn't going to take the bait, he subsided into bitter grumblings. An older man at the end of the table spoke up instead.

"Couple bandits, most like. But they been chasin' us for weeks, stealin' our supplies an' peltin' us wi' arrows an' the like. Can't pin down the bloody bastards."

"So ye'r jus' gonna quit in th' middle of th' job?"

The older man – Tsuga guessed him to be pushing his fourth decade – frowned. "Not at all. But that fat sod is whining about his safety and his goods vanishin'. Wants us to hunt down these thieves, like. Told 'im that'll cost 'im extra. Hired us t' be guards, like, not t' go lookin' fer trouble."

Tsuga nodded her understanding and gestured to the nearest wench to fill the man's drink, but he waved the woman away. Tsuga filed that fact away for future use.

"What makes you so in'erested, lad? You don' even look old enough t' know one end of that sword from th' other," he scoffed, gesturing to the stolen weapon she wore on her hip. "Haven't even got yer whiskers yet, have ya?"

Knowing better than to rise to such an obvious jab, Tsuga merely shrugged. "I use it well enough. An' I'm lookin' fer a hire," she added truthfully.

At this the man's expression became suspicious and he leaned forward to consider her more carefully.

"Are ya now? An' jus what could a li'l lad like yerself be able t' do? Our company's full, lad. Ain't lookin fer no li'l boys still stuck on their wet nurse's teet, like."

Once again Tsuga let the insult roll off her back, knowing it would be far wiser to encourage this underestimation of her skills lest her negotiations go south. If she found herself on the wrong side of any of their swords in the future, she would just as soon they assume her a poor swordsman. Taking her cue from the man she now presumed to be the leader of this small mercenary band, Tsuga leaned forward and pitched her voice conspiratorially.

"Way I hear it, yer men were hired on t' be guards, like, not t' go lookin' fer trouble."

The man barked out a laugh. "You mean t' say –"

"I mean t' say that yer employer may see th' wisdom in hirin' hisself a hunter an' tracker t' seek out these troublemakers 'f yours."

The man sat back in his chair and eyed Tsuga thoughtfully. "You've got balls, lad, I'll give ya that."

Tsuga merely shrugged and moved to stand. "If you'll 'scuse me, I need t' see a man 'bout a hire." She chuckled slightly at her own joke, but the older man stood and placed a hand on her shoulder. She tensed, prepared to cut him down if he moved to threaten her.

"Hold there, lad. No need t' be goin' t' him, like. Tell ya what: agree t' work fer me, an' we'll consider this yer trial period. Do a good job, an' we'll talk about takin' ya int' our comp'ny."

Tsuga shook him off and scoffed, "Thought y' weren't in th' business of mindin' chil'ren."

"We ain't. Prove to me y' can hold yer own, an' I'll c'nsider takin' y' on."

"Thought y' were full up."

The man shrugged. "Be a fool t' turn away a good man when 'e falls int' m' lap."

"Ya would, a' that . . ."

"Bryan."

"Bryan. 'Fraid I come as part 'f a package deal, though."

Bryan quirked an eyebrow inquiringly. "'Scuse me?"

"I travel with a friend. 'E'll need t' be 'comm'dated as well. Ya see, he – 'e's lost a leg."

Bryan frowned and considered her carefully."'E'll have to contribute. But yeah, yer friend c'n travel with us. What's yer name, lad?"

"Trag."

She didn't supply a last name, and he did not ask her for one.

"Trag, we leave an hour after dawn. Be ready t' ride out, or be left b'hind."

Rather than try to find a stable boy amidst all the confusion of a bustling stable yard, Tsuga retrieved her own equipment and let herself back into Bane's stall – where she had once again spent the night – and proceeded to check the mare over and load her up for the day's journey. The sun had just begun to peek above the horizon, but already the mercenary band's preparations for departure were well underway.

So you signed us up to be hunters?

Yes.

How do you plan on pulling *that* off? Your tracking skills are fair, but not great.

I know. I want to get an idea of what we're really up against. We can go from there.

As she worked, Tsuga listened to the sounds of a large group preparing for travel – shouts back and forth, restless horses, the jangling of harnesses as teams were hooked to wagons. She knew Sen would be helping to load the lighter of the supplies and hook in the mules who would be pulling the carts. He would spend his days with the wagons, taking his turn at driving as needed and helping with the chores around camp if they had to stop before they could reach an inn.

Although grooming and saddling Bane was relaxing to her in a therapeutic way, today she didn't linger over the beloved tasks, but instead made sure she finished promptly. As she "led" Bane outside, she looked around for Bryan and the other fighting men. She found them, already saddled and waiting, off to one side of the yard. She dropped Bane's reins to the ground and the mare stopped where she stood. This earned her a second glance from a couple of the men who knew how hard it was to train a horse that well.

"Bryan."

"Trag."

"I'll be following an hour behind you today, and will work my way around ahead of you before lunch. I want to see if I can spot these pests and get a better idea of what we're dealing with."

A few of the men scoffed at this, but Bryan merely quirked an eyebrow at her. She fully expected him to comment on the sudden loss of her accent, but he merely responded in kind.

"Is that so? And what if you do run into them?"

Tsuga shrugged, quietly amused that he had not only taken her trickery in stride, but had seemingly employed similar measures on her the pervious night.

"I'll be smart. And hard as it may be to believe, I *can* take care of myself."

Bryan did chuckle a little at that, but shrugged and waved her off. "Very well. Will you be joining back up with us tonight?"

"By evening meal. A lone rider can move much faster than a caravan. I'll scout things out during the day and join back up with you before we stop for the night."

"I expect a full report."

Tsuga, who had already turned away, stopped and frowned at him over her shoulder. "I'm sorry, but I was told I would be working independently – no help. You will be told what I see fit to tell you."

She walked the last couple of steps to Bane's side and threw the reins over the horse's neck. Bane snorted as Tsuga put her left foot in the stirrup and swung herself over.

"I'll see you tonight."

Tsuga was rather enjoying the liberation of not having anyone to bark orders at her all day. She'd never done any real mercenary work before; as she rode alone in the wake of the merchant train, Tsuga found herself enjoying the freedom. Although she knew she had a job to do, it was hard not to enjoy the weather. It had rained overnight, but the morning was sunny and warm. Though they slogged through the thick mud, even Bane's spirits seemed to be high.

They had been plugging along for a couple of hours with no excitement, Tsuga working her way off the road so that she could circle around the caravan, when she saw the first sign of something suspicious. The two figures were a ways off in the distance, but Tsuga found a pair of riders so far from the road to be unusual, no matter their proximity – or lack thereof – to the caravan. She trailed them for a while, trying to be as unobtrusive as possible.

Before long, midday had come and gone with no sign of anything malicious from the pair. She was about to give up on them when, between one minute and the next, the group of two grew to five.

"I wish I could get close enough to hear what they're saying."

For all we know, they're Bryan's scouts.

"No. I don't recognize any of their horses."

Neither do I, Bane admitted reluctantly.

As the day wore on, Tsuga grew increasingly suspicious. The group continued to grow, its numbers swelling to ten, and then twenty as the sun began to fall further and the sky took on an orange glow. From what she could see they were all armed, though the mismatched equipment looked as though it had been pieced together from whatever they could find.

As the sun dipped below the horizon, Tsuga reined Bane to a stop and considered her options. She had promised to rejoin the merchant train before dark, but she was reluctant to reveal her connection to them, just in case the mysterious group was watching her as intently as she had been spying on them. She didn't want to roast a couple dozen men if she didn't have to, and there was no way she could take them all on with steel and sinew alone. She swung to the ground and looked around to take stock of her situation. They were too far off the road to hope for a camp near water, but her water skin was still half full.

How are you for water?

I'll live.

Are you sure?

Yeah. I can make it until morning.

Alright. Then I guess we're camping here.

She moved to Bane's side and began removing her packs from the ties that held them to the saddle. When she slid her tack to the ground Bane shook herself, and when Tsuga turned back from setting the tack down and laying out the blankets so that they could dry as much as possible in the humid air, her guardian dropped to the ground to roll in the mud. Tsuga cried out in dismay.

"What did you do that for?! You're filthy!"

But it feels *so* good!

Tsuga shook her head and sank to the ground in exasperation. When Bane had finished, the horse lurched back to her feet and snorted in satisfaction.

It'll dry.

"You look like a walking mud monster."

As though to share the wealth, Bane gave herself a mighty shake, leaving Tsuga as liberally coated with mud as her guardian.

"Why, you worthless bag of meat!"

Tsuga flew to her feet and lunged at the horse, but Bane merely danced out of her reach. Laughter sparkled in her eyes as she and Tsuga engaged in a rousing game of chase until, exhausted, Tsuga collapsed on the ground and gasped for breath.

"Brat."

You're getting slow.

"Mud."

And fat. And lazy.

"Shut up." She sighed and rolled up to a sitting position. "I should eat."

Yes, you should. And then, **Hey!** when Tsuga pegged her on the hindquarters with a handful of mud.

Tsuga stayed up that night to watch the mysterious group. She didn't want to risk sleeping through all the excitement, so she kept herself awake by dancing the forms – first with her sword, the movements she could do in her sleep, and then with her dagger. She had moved on to unarmed maneuvers when her patience was finally rewarded.

Although the men moved quietly, it was a still night; the creak of leather and jingling of armor carried on the light breeze that cooled the sweat on her face and arms. Distracted from her practice, Tsuga turned to see the dismounted men moving with a silence and efficiency born of long practice. The group split in half, with about ten men mounting up and riding in the direction of the road. Not wanting to lose sight of them, Tsuga quickly tacked Bane – the drying and flaking mud caking the horse's hide forgotten in her haste – and set off after them.

Though she kept a safe distance, Tsuga knew that she had been seen. Her cover – if she had in fact ever had one – was officially compromised at this point, so she gave up trying to hide what she was up to. She eased her sword in its scabbard and listened to the sounds that told her the mounted half of the group was now trailing behind her.

Tsuga knew how difficult it could be to see the solution to a problem when one stood at its center, and so instead of seeking to warn the camp or to engage the bandits, she found herself an out-of-the-way place to hide and observe from a position of safety. She hoped that this way she might learn something more than what she had been told.

It should have gone against the grain to sit back when she knew an attack was coming, but she was a bit disturbed by how easily she set aside her compunctions and settled in to watch. She didn't know these people, after all. She had no allegiance to any of them. The only person among them that she cared at all for was Sen, and she knew he could keep himself out of trouble.

The camp was asleep save for a couple pairs of posted guards. The intruders did not bother with trying to take out the handful of men, as she had expected them to. Instead, the group of ten split so completely that, had she not known their numbers and that they were working together, she would have had no idea that they had a common goal.

Each person seemed to have a specific task; had she not been on the outside looking in, the confusion would have been such that she'd never have put two and two together. One man ran about lighting arrows – a mage? She saw no signs of magic about him; perhaps he carried a striker – and shooting them in every direction: onto wagons, though the thin canvas of the tents, even straight into the air. Another set about cutting the ties in the horse lines, while one man pilfered among the supply wagons that carried their food and water.

Tsuga watched all of this unfold, but none of it held her attention for long. None of it, save the man who walked through the tumultuous camp without being touched by the pandemonium gripping the mercenaries. He systematically went from one wagon to another, but she never saw him leave with any of the expensive bolts of cloth or other goods the train was carrying.

"What are you looking for, hmm . . .?"

The attack didn't last long. When the camp roused and began to fight back, the bandits withdrew while the other half of their party covered the retreat from the safety of darkness. Tsuga waited until she was sure they were gone before she stood and emerged from her hiding spot in the copse of trees. She walked through chaos, though order was quickly reasserting itself as the men found their bearings. The fires were being doused, the horses recaptured and soothed so that they could be hobbled again. And in the middle of it all, she found the one man she was looking for. The fat merchant was fussing over the contents of his carts, checking to make sure everything was intact.

The pompous idiot never saw her coming. When the hard wood of the wagon slammed against his back and the cold steel of her dagger touched his throat, he yelped in alarm and Tsuga's nose wrinkled involuntarily in response to the stench of his sweat. None of this distracted her from her purpose.

"Who – who are you?"

Of course he wouldn't know her. She had been recruited by Bryan, not this whimpering milksop. Somehow, she doubted Bryan had the information she needed.

"Right now, all you need to know is that if I think you're lying, I'll have no reason not to kill you. You know as well as I do that these are more than just the usual bandits. They didn't take anything. Didn't take it, because they couldn't find it. You're carrying something you shouldn't be. Something they know about. Something they want – badly. What is it?"

"I don't know what you're – okay, okay!"

His voice rose a full octave when her muscles bunched and she made as though to sever his jugular. She relaxed her grip slightly and let him speak.

"Jilaed is rich with stone mines. Everybody knows that. But what we get – what they sell to outsiders – are the rejects. The cast-offs. They keep the purest stones for themselves. All of our stones come from Jilaed. The Teeth don't have the kinds of veins their mountains do. The mages need the stones to use as their focuses. Pay top dollar for 'em. The better the stone – the larger, the less flawed – the better they work."

"So you're trading stolen mage stones to Sennor to make a pretty penny, right under the Devalians' noses. Looks as though you're not the only one with that idea, though."

Tsuga released the man and he crumpled to the ground, wheezing.

"Rather unfair of you not to tell your guards just what it is they're guarding."

Tsuga turned and left the man where he'd collapsed. It didn't take her long to locate Bryan – he was in the thick of things, helping to organize the clean-up now that all of the small fires had been doused.

"Bryan."

He didn't immediately turn around at the sound of her voice. In fact, he made a point of extending the conversation he was having before he finally acknowledged her.

"Thought you may have gotten yourself killed."

"Your concern is touching. I have information you'll want to hear."

Bryan let out a gusty breath as he glared at her, and Tsuga could tell he was fighting against his wounded pride. Luckily, his sensibility won out. Her opinion of him rose slightly when it did.

"Walk with me."

He didn't wait for her agreement, but rather turned and strode briskly off through the camp, leaving her to catch up or be left behind.

"This must be discussed."

Bryan ceased scrubbing at his face and dropped his hands with a sigh.

"Discussed?"

He cast her a sidelong glance at the surprise in her voice and shook his head.

"The Wandering Warriors are not an army, young man. I may be the one in charge, but my authority means nothing without the loyalty of my men. And so, I will discuss what you have told me with them and take their words into consideration before deciding how to proceed."

A democratic mercenary band?

Tsuga's opinion of the man rose again, and as he turned to walk away, she spoke to stop him.

"Mind if I sit in?"

Bryan shook his head. "You're not one of us yet, kid. The information you've given me is enlightening, but you still disobeyed orders."

"Orders?" Tsuga kept her voice even only with a great deal of effort. She paused a moment to calm herself before she said something she would later regret.

"If I am not one of your men, how can I be expected to accept your orders? And I volunteered for this, remember? I deviated from the original plan. Any decent commander knows that adaptation is key to survival. And you may think of something you wish to ask me. Wouldn't it be easier if I were already there, so you didn't have to send someone to fetch me and then waste time filling me in?"

Bryan considered her words for a moment, and then nodded curtly.

"Spoken with wisdom. Very well. Follow me."

Tsuga had never witnessed anything like the meeting that followed that night's raid. Although she had sat in on many war councils, those were always meetings of men who spoke for their underlings. But here the underlings spoke for themselves, on equal ground with their leader. Tsuga did not offer up her concerns or opinions – it was not her place to do so – but she found that she was frequently asked to re-tell her tale. She obliged as many times as she was bid, until at last it seemed there were no more questions.

She lapsed into silence as the discussion turned to finances and morals – the constant struggle between the need for survival and the desire to lead ethical lives. Not all mercenaries had such a hard time balancing the opposing demands, but it seemed most – if not all – of these men warred within themselves, fighting to find a balance between their senses of practicality and their consciences.

At long last, the decision was reached to finish the job they had agreed to. The mercenary band would continue to act as a caravan guard, but would not actively seek to engage or hunt down the bandits. As the group disbanded and Tsuga wandered to the horse lines, she considered the options now before her.

She could operate as one of Bryan's men and simply wait to be attacked – a scenario that did not greatly appeal to her. She and Sen could leave; since they'd never technically been hired on, it wasn't as though they'd be quitting in the middle of a job. But they were out of funds. The potential payment from this was something they needed in order to continue their journey. That left her with only one real option: work secretly.

While the rest of the camp made preparations to sleep, Tsuga took a detour to better learn the layout of the tents and wagons. She knew that if Bryan had anything to say about it, the layout would be much the same every night, set with military discipline and defensive strategy in mind.

As she wandered, she summoned her mage sight between one breath and the next. Though it irked her – now as much as ever – to have to use her magic and thus remind herself of the curse she suffered, she also knew this to be her best hope of finding the hidden stones. If they were indeed stolen mage stones, then there was a very good chance that some magical residue still lingered on them.

She glanced about her as casually as she could manage, taking in the by-now familiar threads of magic that ran through all things. As she had suspected, there were several places throughout the camp where the magic seemed to converge, its flow diverted by some outside force. Her memory wandered briefly back to those first months with Affaila, before she had known the other woman to be her own sister.

"Magic is an attractive force. The way our feet are attracted to the ground, or the way water will seek to pool and combine, so magic tends to draw magic to itself."

As Tsuga followed these small, unnatural diversions, she realized that the merchant had hedged his bets by secreting his loot in many places.

Wise, she observed absently. It would be almost impossible for all of them to be stolen in one sweep, as would have been the case long ago had they all been kept together.

She sought out each irregularity and took careful note of every hiding place. Her mental count had risen over twenty – together, that many stones valued enough to buy a small kingdom – when she caught her breath in surprise. There was a magical *tug*, a pulling at her very core that she knew all too well.

What, by the Goddess . . .? She stopped, confronted by the cart that carried the innocuous trappings of travel: rope, extra tents, emergency tinder, and the like. She could sense it, *there,* just on the other side of the plain wooden boards that composed the cart. It couldn't possibly be . . ..

"My stone," she breathed, amazed.

This changes everything. It must.

Tsuga lay wrapped in her cloak to ward off the damp and chill of the ground beneath her, with Bane standing guard over her.

Why must it?

It's mine! It was stolen from me. He has no right to –

So you would steal from the thief? How does that make you anything but a thief yourself?

Tsuga exhaled in frustration and rolled onto her back.

It doesn't. But he's hardly going to part with it readily, now is he? Even if he has no way of knowing how much power it can hold, just the fact that it is a serviceable mage stone makes it valuable enough for him to risk his neck transporting it.

True. Bane threw her head in annoyance. **But won't he notice it's gone?**

Not immediately. Not if I'm smart about when I take it. And even if he does, what reason does he have to suspect me, *and not the band of men seeking to relieve him of the lot?*

True. Why would he suspect the person he confessed to at swordpoint?

Tsuga couldn't help but chuckle to herself at that. *Well, then I'll just have to play the perfect little soldier boy, won't I?*

Tsuga rode with the caravan for the duration of the next day, allowing Bryan to order her about like an errand boy. She knew from the brief conversations with the various members of the mercenary band that if the weather held and all went well, they would reach the next town by nightfall. While the men spoke of how much they would drink, the whores they would tumble, and the luxury of a dry bed for the night, Tsuga's mind raced.

If she were leading the bandits' efforts, she would not want to make an open attempt in such a heavily populated place. Likely, one or two men would be sent on a quiet raid. They may even have planted someone at the inn as a servant.

While she and Bane ran themselves ragged riding up and down the caravan, Tsuga took note of how Bryan distributed his men and the alert wariness of each soldier. They all scanned the roadside, ever-wary of an ambush; never mind how relaxed their conversations sounded. These men were all disciplined and well-trained – even more so, she realized ruefully, than most of the military men with whom she had traveled in the past.

When her pacing next brought her abreast of Bryan – he rode
near the center of the caravan, she noticed, and not at its head as
a general might – she reined Devilsbane in to match his pace. He
didn't speak, but instead quirked an eyebrow at her inquisitively.
Tsuga took this as permission.

"What is the plan for tonight?"

When Bryan didn't answer, Tsuga gritted her teeth and
dispensed with the forced comaraderie. "The men talk of
whiskey and whores and soft beds. But surely you intend to post
a guard for the night?"

Bryan frowned, but didn't look at her when he spoke. "What
do you take me for, boy? I was killing men for money when you
were still at your mother's tit. You presume to know more about
what I should be doing than I do?"

Tsuga tensed at the insult, and her jaw clenched as she forced
her hand away from the hilt of her sword, where it had strayed of
its own accord. She tried to play off the gesture by adjusting the
way it rode at her side, but with little hope that she succeeded in
fooling the older man.

"No, sir. Simply volunteering myself as a guard."

This, at last, earned her Bryan's direct gaze. He seemed to
consider for a moment, and then nodded curtly.

"Fine. You can take the mid shift. With me."

Tsuga was roused from a fitful sleep by a knock on the stall
door. Her hand strayed to her sword where it rested in the straw
next to her, and she had the weapon half out of its scabbard before
the intruder spoke.

"Your turn for watch."

She nodded, now fully awake, and rose to her feet as she
sheathed her blade.

"You're not in your room."

"No." *Obviously.*

In the dim light offered by the lone lantern burning in the aisle,
Tsuga could only make out the outline of the man who'd roused
her as she buckled on her sword belt and adjusted her weapons so
that they sat comfortably. She recognized his voice, though – as
if his carriage hadn't been enough of a give away.

"Sir," she added belatedly. "Prefer it here. It's quieter, an' the
horses make good watchdogs. If something's really wrong, they
have a way of knowin' it."

Bryan nodded curtly and stepped aside to allow her to exit the
stall. "True indeed, if a bit unusual. Come – it's time to change
guard."

As Tsuga followed Bryan through the slumbering courtyard in
front of the inn, he gave her a brief run-down of their duties for
the night. Mostly, as she had expected, these responsibilities

seemed to consist of walking patrols through the carts and making sure everything stayed uneventful.

Once the preceding pair of guards had been dismissed and trudged off, yawning, to seek their own beds, Bryan and Tsuga began what would only be the first of numerous patrols through and around the loaded wagons in their caravan.

There would not be a better chance for her to put her plan into action, Tsuga knew. Even if the bandits did not make an attempt tonight, the carts would never be as lightly guarded as they were now. She had only to divert Bryan long enough for her to locate and reclaim what was hers. Luckily, she was perfectly equipped to do just that. After the better part of their watch had passed uneventfully, she set her plan into motion.

"Smoke."

Tsuga kept her voice low, but forced urgency into her tone as she pointed Bryan's gaze in the direction of the cart ahead of them that she had just ignited. Bryan cursed, and they both set out at a run. They had made it almost to the cart when another, further along, began to produce a curl of smoke as well. With a curt gesture, Bryan sent her off to investigate the second blaze. He drew his sword as she continued on, obviously expecting to run into trouble.

Once Tsuga was sure she was out of Bryan's sight, she ducked quickly into one of the carts – her target – and summoned a small flame in the air before her to light her way. She knew Bryan would be busy for a while – she had only lit tiny flames on the oiled canvas that covered the wagons, but the slick material would burn fiercely. He would have a challenge putting it out – especially if, as Tsuga knew he would, he first took the time to seek out the fire starter. She needed no more than a minute. Maybe two.

With mage sight, it was no difficult thing to locate her stone. As she had anticipated, the merchant proved wily. Tucked in among the coils of rope and folds of extra canvas was a small, nondescript leather bag tied with a thin strip of the same material. It was the type of pouch that nails or tent stakes might be stored in, but to Tsuga's magical senses, it blazed like a beacon.

Why no lock? she mused as she untied the leather thong and upended the contents of the pouch in her hand.

Locks imply value. If he didn't want anyone to know what he had, it makes sense that he'd try to make it as inconspicuous as possible.

Tsuga considered this as she dumped the handful of nails back into the little bag and replaced it just as she'd found it. The stone in her hand glowed brightly to her mage sight and felt slightly warm to the touch, as though it held a tiny inner flame of its own. She quickly tucked her stone into the coin purse she kept around her neck and stepped back into the night as she snuffed out her small personal torch.

She knew she had to find Bryan before he found her. Her story was already planned, and everything had gone off without a hitch. Now, her only remaining task was to make a place for herself in this small mercenary band.

Part Three: Tempered by Time

Time passes.
Time ages us all.
Only time will tell
Who will rise –
And who will fall.

Tsuga was confused – and more than a little suspicious.

"How do you heal a memory?"

The brunette healer cocked her head to the side and smiled, her silver earrings making a soft clinking sound with the movement.

"I don't heal memories – I heal the mind. If a person, say, has amnesia and they've forgotten everything down to who they are, it's usually caused by an injury to the brain – or sometimes a very traumatic event. By going into the mind, I can find the trauma and, once it's identified, heal the damage. If it's an event, I can help them cope better if I know what it is."

Tsuga listened to this explanation thoughtfully; after a few moments of silence, she looked up from her mug of ale. Her voice shook when she spoke.

"So you can identify troublesome memories. Can you . . . get rid of them?"

The healer frowned. "I'm afraid I don't understand what you're asking."

Tsuga dropped her gaze back to the table, listening to the general din of the tavern's patrons. No one seemed to be paying attention to the two women at a corner table. She missed Affaila – her sister would have been able to help her figure out how to phrase her question. Instead, she was on her own; Devilsbane certainly wasn't much help with delicate matters, as the horse tended to be extremely blunt.

"I've done some things I'm . . . not exactly proud of." She looked up to meet the healer's eyes again, and the woman gasped and recoiled slightly – probably at the utter lack of emotion in Tsuga's expression. "Had some things happen to me I'd just as soon not know. I want to forget. To start over. I want to be able to sleep."

The last word almost didn't come out, and in the shadows her face looked even more pallid and sunken than usual. The dark circles under her eyes seemed twice their size, and as she picked at her cuticles with her thumbnail, it became obvious that she must have a habit of chewing on her nails when she was worried. The healer frowned and shook her head.

"That's not usually the kind of thing I do, you know. I help people deal with pain, not block it. Now, if you want to look at your memories and figure out why they bother you, maybe we could –"

"No." The cold finality to the word cut the healer's sentence short.

"I'm sorry?"

"I don't want to look at them. I see them every moment of every day; they wake me screaming in the middle of the night. I

want to stop *seeing them. I want to forget. Can you help me, or
not?"*

"*Well, I suppose it might be possible . . .. There is an old
technique that involves locking memories into objects. They're
not really gone, just . . . moved. I've never tried it, but I know
how it's supposed to work.*"

"*Do you think you could do it?*"

"*I'm . . . I think so, yes.*"

"*Tonight?*"

"*Well, I . . ..*"

"*Can you do it tonight?*"

"*Okay.*"

Tsuga woke, as usual, in a cold sweat, tangled in her bedroll and fighting down a scream – all over a dream she forgot as soon as she opened her eyes. Even though she could no longer recall what had so terrified her, she knew that she would not be able to get back to sleep now. With a sigh, she wiped her sweat-drenched hair out of her eyes and swung her feet to the ground.

As she dressed – a process which consisted more of settling a small armory about her person than actually putting on shirt and pants, as she slept fully clothed – her heart rate slowed and she was able to breathe more regularly, though she still couldn't shake the feeling of dread.

Bane?

Tsuga wasn't sure why she always felt it was necessary to check on her guardian as soon as she woke, but just the feel of the animal's soothing mindvoice calmed her nerves and served to further relax her.

Two hours to dawn.

Tsuga sighed as she buckled on her sword belt and bent to pull on her boots. She couldn't remember the last time she had slept any later than this. In fact, there were a great number of things she no longer recalled, as though vast parts of her life had simply vanished into the mist.

At least I remember my training.

As she slipped through the hallway of the inn and down the stairs, Tsuga ran through a physical check of herself.

Her muscles were stiff and not yet awake.

Slower to loosen up these days.

Her eyes still felt too heavy to be open, but mentally she was alert and aware. By now, she was all too used to feeling this way – as though her mind were trapped in a body aging far too quickly. Each and every ache and twinge as she stepped into the muggy night air had a story to go with it.

When a stab of pain reminded her of the battle that had crushed her left leg – between Bane and a tree, to be exact – she had to smile slightly at the realization that she did in fact remember a great deal.

Tsuga walked out into the stable yard – not yet busy, as it would be in another couple of hours – and drew her sword. Although it was not the blade her father had left her upon his death, it was still a serviceable weapon and had seen years of heavy use. She took a moment to run her calloused hand over the worn shark skin she had wrapped around the hilt. The blade was familiar and comfortable in her hands, the balance well suited to her.

She'd had this one made after she'd lost Da's blade as the victim of a kidnapping. She could recall the months she'd been held captive, but she still had no idea of how she'd escaped – or how she had stumbled across Sen in the northern reaches of Devali. A tried and true friend, the man was now second in command of the Wandering Warriors, always by the side of the commander to offer another perspective.

Tsuga took a deep breath and stilled her thoughts. While she strove to set aside such distractions, she dropped into a basic defensive stance and began to dance the forms.

"Might've guessed I'd find you here."

Tsuga looked over Devilsbane's back and grinned at her long-time friend before she resumed brushing her guardian's already-glowing coat.

"You know, the commander of the biggest and most famous mercenary band in the world shouldn't have to bother herself with menial labor."

Tsuga made a face at the use of her title, but responded good-naturedly to the jest.

"'Never ask of another that which you are not willing to do yourself.' Bryan was a wise man, may the Lady bless and keep him. Are the others up yet?"

Sen moved forward and laid a hand on Bane's neck – one of the few people the horse allowed to do so – and shrugged.

"Still rubbing the sleep from their eyes, but yes, they're up. Do you ever sleep?"

Tsuga shrugged as Bane butted Sen to earn herself a scratch under her jaw. "I sleep enough. Once everyone's breakfasted, have them saddle up and meet in the yard. I'd like to get an early start today. We'll be crossing into Sennor around midday."

Home, Tsuga mused. She hadn't set foot on Sennorran soil in nearly eight years. In another couple of months, she would see her twenty-sixth birthday.

At twenty-three, she had become the first female commander of the Warriors – four years after earning her place among the other mercenaries in the band. She had, by that time, revealed herself as both a Sennorran native and a woman. Once they were safely out of Devali, there had been little serious danger to her; mercenaries were notorious for their tendency to accept someone despite their past and based primarily on their abilities. Now that she was surrounded by so many loyal fighters, the danger to her in crossing Devali openly was greatly reduced. She still kept a close lookout for any suspicious persons in the camp, though. It wouldn't be unheard of for someone to make an attempt on her life if they thought it a show of loyalty to their God, or a way to improve their own position.

The band's acceptance of her had proven to be a good decision; the fighters had flourished under her leadership in the intervening time, swelling in numbers until it had become an ordeal to oversee the upkeep and provisioning of over three hundred armed men and women. Ultimately, Tsuga had bowed to practicality and split the world's most elite fighting force into several smaller groups – about thirty fighters each – all of which worked as cohesive parts of the greater whole. It was easier to find a hire for thirty men than ten times that number; the only ones willing to pay for that kind of a force were those waging war. Tsuga had no desire to involve her men in the civil war between Sennor and Devali; she had men from both countries, and a few others besides. She couldn't ask such a thing of them, any more than she wanted to ask it of herself.

When Bryan had fallen in battle and the mercenary group – at that time numbering only a couple dozen men – had of an unspoken agreement begun looking to her for leadership, Tsuga had been greatly overwhelmed. As the only female member at that time – though not, as she had come to learn, the only Sennorran – her comrades' choice had come as quite a shock. She had reluctantly taken up the yoke of responsibility, and now, three years later, the Warriors boasted a military force of such skill and knowledge that they were rivaled only by the armies of the two greatest nations in the world: Sennor and Devali.

Up to this point, the mercenaries had managed to avoid any direct involvement with the war. None of the Warriors were particularly keen on political gain, and so most were satisfied with the odd jobs to be had as caravan guards, assassins, and body-guards. They traveled wherever they were paid to go, as the name of this band implied. Until now, that travel had not taken them into Sennor much at all. But Tsuga had recently received correspondence from the queen herself, asking Tsuga to come to her aid.

Tsuga was not a particularly patriotic woman. She had no undying loyalty to Sennor or to the queen. But the distress of a woman who worried for her people had touched her, and so Tsuga rode with the small group of men and women she traveled with (she made a point of rotating through the scattered groups every month or so, just to stay in touch with all of the fighters) to Sennorra, her native country's capital.

Tsuga stood alone in the midst of a violent inferno. At least, she had thought she was alone. Even as she had this thought though, she registered the horrified screams of those around her who were being consumed by the flames. The roar of the blaze was intense, and she could feel the heat buffeting her, more intense anything she had ever felt.

Why do I not burn?

She didn't understand what was going on, or why she could not sense her guardian. There was, however, another voice in her mind.

See what you do to them? They burn because of you, Tsuga. You are killing them.

Tsuga woke from the nightmare to find herself lying on the ground in her tent. She coughed, and then it turned into a desperate fight for air as she sucked in a lungful of acrid black smoke. She crawled forward blindly until she found the canvas wall of the tent and ripped it free of the ties that secured it to the ground so that she could struggle out into the cool night air.

As she teetered on the brink of consciousness, Tsuga collapsed on the ground and tried to regulate her breath while she sucked in the clean air. At long last, her breathing returned to normal and she was able to calm herself enough to sit up and take stock of what had happened.

The coolness of the malachite stone she wore around her neck was a comfortable presence as it settled back against her skin. As she tried to recall the disturbing dream that had woken her, Tsuga found the details once again slipping beyond her grasp. All she could recall was a sense of horror and the feeling of panic.

Bane?

Almost three hours before dawn. Any idea where the fire came from?

The fire . . . shit!

Tsuga looked to her tent, expecting to see the whole thing engulfed in flames. Strangely, aside from a few last wisps of smoke escaping from the gap she'd made upon her exit, there was no sign that anything was amiss. Tsuga scrubbed at her face in exasperation as she indulged in a rare moment of self-pity. She allowed herself only a moment to wallow, though, before she gathered her composure and rose to her feet.

Time to start another day.

"I feel ridiculous." Tsuga sat looking at herself in their vanity mirror. "I'm used to having short hair. I'm not made for this; I'm really not."

From across the room he turned to look at her. She could tell that he had to choke back a laugh as he crossed the floor to place his hands on her shoulders.

"Tsu, you look beautiful. The color flatters you. But it's true — you definitely don't look right."

Tsuga bristled, offended by his comment and stung by the thought that he saw her as sub-par. She closed her eyes and ducked her head to fight back the stab of pain she felt at his words, but before she could get herself under control he had swept her up in his arms and moved her to the foot of their bed. Despite her anger and hurt, she felt herself responding to his kiss in the same way a kicked dog responds to a gentle touch from the same abusive master.

"Now," he said as he pulled back, "sit still."

Tsuga huffed out a sigh and, despite her irritation that she was willing to pretend nothing was wrong, did as she was told.

Her skin tingled as he opened himself to his magic, but when she turned to see what he was doing, he took her head between his hands and expertly released her hair – longer than she had worn it since childhood; after losing all of it a few months ago in the blaze, she had been unable to bring herself to shear it off again – and the feeling of his gentle ministrations distracted her. When at last he stopped and allowed her to stand and face the mirror again, she could scarcely believe what she saw.

"Oh, Ramiq –"

"Wait. I'm not done."

He reached over the intricate updo he'd created with her hair – no easy feat with the added inches to her six feet of height; even her husband, who stood a few inches taller even than she, had to reach – and Tsuga gasped as he settled a simple gold necklace in the hollow of her neck. Her hand immediately went to the stone that glowed the color of the sun as it set, a perfect match to the dozens of tiny jewels now set into her hair as well as the many more which studded her gown. Each gem caught and magnified the light in the room until she seemed to glow like a candle in the dim space.

"There. Now you're perfect."

For the first time in years, Tsuga woke slowly. She blinked in the dim light inside her tent while the blissful feeling of her dream lingered. She allowed herself a few extra moments to languish under her blanket so she could replay it again in her mind.

Bane?

Mid-morning.

"What?!"

Tsuga sat up in her bedroll and threw back her covers, the relaxed feeling of a moment before forgotten as she began to hurriedly pull on her clean clothes. She would need to wear her most official-looking outfit today; she was meeting a queen!

"Why didn't anyone wake me?!"

I told them not to.

"What? Why?"

Her words came out muffled by the shirt she pulled over her head, but it hardly mattered since she and her guardian shared the same mind.

**There was no reason to disturb you. We're less than an
hour from Sennorra. Sen knows how to manage packing up
camp and running drills. And you needed the rest.**

"I'm fine."

I wasn't asking.

Tsuga huffed out a breath in irritation as she buckled on her
sword belt and settled it comfortably over her narrow hips.

"So everyone is ready to go?"

Everyone but you.

She scowled and tugged on her boots with a vicious yank
before stomping her feet to settle them into the sturdy shoes.

"Tell Sen to give everyone the half hour warning."

Breakfast?

"I'll eat while we ride."

"I am afraid I cannot make that commitment, Majesty."

The queen's bright blue eyes narrowed in annoyance, and her
chin lifted slightly in indignation, causing her sun-bright blonde
hair to flash in the light streaming through the windows.

"And why is that, Commander?"

Sennor's new monarch was young – Tsuga doubted the girl
had even seen her eighteenth summer – and so had not yet
mastered the art of concealing her innermost thoughts. As Tsuga
watched the queen's fear war with her wounded pride, she mused
over the danger an emotional young leader posed.

"Because, Majesty, it is not within my authority to do so."

"I'm afraid I do not understand you, Commander. You lead
the Warriors, do you not?"

Tsuga shook her head slightly. "I am the voice of my war
band, it is true, and I lead them to the best of my ability, yes. But
I do not command them so much as offer guidance and a pair of
shoulders to bear the responsibilities of leadership. Every man
and woman among us knows that he or she is free to leave the
band at any time, just as each holds the right to strip me of my
position if I am found by the majority to be unfit to retain it. Each
of my soldiers chooses for himself which jobs to accept and
which to decline."

The queen's shoulders slumped as a look of resignation came
over her face. "Then you cannot help us?"

Tsuga considered for a moment. The queen's genuine worry
struck a chord with her – better than anyone, she understood what
it was to hold the lives of others in her hand.

"I cannot commit to your service on behalf of the Warriors,
Your Majesty. I am sorry. But I will put your plea before them,
so that each man may decide for himself what he will do."

"And how long will that take?"

"My Warriors roam wide, Majesty. But messages will be dispatched immediately. Word will reach the captains closest to here by the end of the week. Those further out, I cannot say. I'm afraid that is the best I can offer you."

The queen nodded and rose, which out of respect and long-established custom forced Tsuga to stand as well. "It is a glimmer of hope, at least. I thank you for that."

Tsuga could hear the note of dismissal in the young regent's voice, and so inclined her head respectfully.

"Majesty? If it is allowed, I would like the chance to visit an old friend while I am here. Your Weaponsmaster, Midan."

The queen's expression fell, and Tsuga could have sworn she caught a tremor in the young woman's voice when she spoke.

"But surely you've heard, Commander. The Weaponsmaster has been dead these six years. Murdered in his sleep. Assassinated. At present, no one holds the position. I'm afraid we've not been able to keep any Weaponsmaster more than a few months since Midan's death."

Tsuga sucked in a breath. The news hit her like a blow to the gut, and it was several long moments before she was able to form words.

"Assassinated?"

"Yes. The same attack put me on the throne and wiped out many of my mother's most trusted advisors – including the Queen's Mage."

Tsuga shook her head, confounded that she had not yet heard this news.

"I am very sorry for your loss, Majesty. I had not heard."

The queen sighed and turned away to look out the large stained-glass window in the audience chamber, an immense room currently occupied by only the two of them and a handful of guards.

"The Devalians sought to leave Sennor with no one prepared to meet their challenge. They thought me a child, incapable of leading my people. They were wrong."

A note of steel crept into the queen's voice on the last, and when the fair-haired woman turned again to face her, Tsuga saw not a child, but a young woman thrust into adulthood before her time. The mantle of authority was a heavy burden to carry, but the queen, Tsuga knew, must bear it gracefully.

"Undoubtedly. If I may ask, Majesty, who remains to train your new soldiers?"

"At present, no one. The last Weaponsmaster left some weeks ago."

Tsuga absorbed this news, chewing over the implications in her mind.

"If it is alright with you, Majesty, my soldiers are in need of a good workout. I would request the use of your training grounds for the day."

The queen waved dismissively. "Yes, yes, of course. Someone may as well put them to use."

Tsuga inclined her head again and took her leave, mind still working to absorb this new information.

Tsuga lay awake that night, her body sprawled across an uncomfortably soft bed in a room too full of opulence to offer any peace. The smells overwhelmed her senses – clean linens, fresh flowers, and some odd smell that lingered from the last cleaning; a perfume of some sort sprayed on the pillows, she imagined. She would have preferred to sleep with her fellow sell-swords. She would have, had the queen not insisted on granting her a suite of rooms in the castle for the duration of her stay. In truth, though, all of these small annoyances could have been forced from her mind, save that dwelling on her discomfort distracted her from what was really worrying her.

She cared little for these days for political maneuverings – though she knew the ins and outs of most of the courts in the world, she kept current on this information primarily because it was prudent for a mercenary commander to do so, and not out of any genuine interest. Politics had lost their glow after years of fighting the wars they generated. Following such machinations came easily to her, but she found the subterfuge frustrating more than anything. In truth, the Devalian's strategy of assassination had, if not fully succeeded, at least dealt a grievous blow to the power structure in Sennor.

Six years.

The number still made her stomach churn. The Sennorran army still had trained, seasoned men to fight the many battles. But with no one to teach the new recruits, the army would become like a stream blocked by deadwood: stagnant and foul, with no way to replenish itself. Ultimately the flow of new blood would dry up completely.

She knew of only one solution to such a problem: Sennor needed a new Weaponsmaster. Someone experienced and reliable, who could guide the new soldiers and help them to learn as much as possible before they were sent off to bleed on the field of battle. And, while she could put this dilemma before her soldiers, she doubted any of them would be particularly keen on taking up a war which concerned them very little. She was not very fond of the idea, herself, and she was Sennorran. But talking with the queen today had touched her; she couldn't bring herself to simply leave her country crippled.

Her decision made, Tsuga at last managed to clear her mind and – finally – sleep.

"So, what? You're sleep-magicking?"

The young man sighed and shook his head. "So it would seem. But it's so improbable, when you add it all up. Why you? Why so carnal? And how and why am I projecting the same dreams to you, if that's even what I'm doing?"

"What do you mean, 'if?' Sounds to me like that's exactly what you're doing."

"Well, that's just it. If I were simply projecting my dreams onto you, then you would have the same experiences I do. You would dream from my perspective – not your own."

"Want to make that sound a little less like gibberish?"

"During the dreams, I'm me; but you're still you when you dream. So I'm not simply pushing my dream into your head. I would have to have two separate dreams at once; your version, and mine. And I'd have to project yours to you all while simultaneously dreaming mine."

"So, what? Is that hard to do?"

"It's impossible. No mage that I've ever heard of has been able to project two separate realities at once while awake, let alone while dead asleep."

Tsuga frowned. "So, what? You're the first?"

"That, or else there is some outside force at work here."

That gave Tsuga pause as she considered the implications of that simple statement.

"That seems highly unlikely. From what you said, there would have to be at least two high-level mages involved, right? And they're accomplishing what, exactly? Unbalancing our emotions? Playing with our minds? Disrupting our sleep? I just don't see it."

"Well, then, where does that leave us?" Tsuga looked at him. In spite of herself, her heart went out to the poor boy. He looked so defeated, so forlorn, that she couldn't help but feel for him.

"Right where we started, it would seem . . .."

"Of course Sennor would be honored to have you as our Weaponsmistress. But what of your Warriors?"

"They will choose a new leader from their ranks. It is their way. There are many fighters fully capable of stepping into my place."

"You are certain this is what you wish?"

Tsuga nodded. "Yes, Your Majesty."

"Very well. You will have to speak with the Queen's Mage about arrangements for sleeping quarters and training supplies.

He has been overseeing both training halls in the absence of a Weaponsmaster."

"But I thought you said the Queen's Mage was one of those lost in the attacks?"

The queen bowed her head and Tsuga wished, briefly, that she had been less blunt.

"He was. His pupil, Ramiq Nevarn, now holds that esteemed position."

The name struck her like a blow to the head, though she hadn't the faintest idea why. She tasted blood, and the room spun so that she was forced to reach out and steady herself against the wall. As she shifted, the weight of her malachite pendant settled back against her chest. Its familiar pressure comforted her, and her mind cleared as though by magic.

"I see. And where am I to find him?"

"It is late morning. He will be just starting his rounds in the mages' training yard, I believe."

Tsuga did not question how the queen knew this, but simply made the appropriate courtesies and took her leave.

It was odd, she thought as she walked through the vast corridors of the castle, that the mages' training began so late in the day. What on earth did they find to occupy their mornings?

She had not known a great many mages in her life, but those she had known were decent enough folk. Many of the ones she had dealt with less familiarly seemed to do nothing more than abuse their power over less gifted folk. Then again, she had known many non-magical people who acted similarly, so she supposed the weakness was in the individuals' minds and hearts, and not inherent in the magic itself.

As she drew nearer the Mages' Complex her skin began to crawl uncomfortably and a dull throbbing began in the back of her skull. She turned right down one of the twisting alleyways and as she did, she recalled the last time she had been here. Then, she had been a student of Midan. Now, her task was to settle herself into his former position.

Funny, the way the world works.

Although she did not remember being in this part of the Mages' Complex, Tsuga found that she knew her way almost instinctively as she strayed from the larger walkway down a narrower path to her left. As she continued to walk, the ill, clenching feeling in her stomach intensified. Mages always made her feel this way, it seemed, and so she knew she must be heading in the right direction. She followed the path around as it curved, and as she rounded the bend she heard a familiar voice.

"Magic flows through everything – from the dirt beneath your feet to the air you breathe, and even through each and every one of you. It is magic that holds the world together. It is our ability to tap into and use the inherent power in the world around us that sets us apart from the rest of the population. It is this ability which makes us mages."

Tsuga came to a stop at the edge of a broad, clear courtyard. There was nothing remarkable about it, really – a few trees, some rocks, a small fountain and a patch of dirt that showed the signs of a recent fire. Roughly a dozen people stood about in the robes that marked them as trainees, each in a place designated by some code she was not privy to. A man stood with his back to her and addressed them. The sight of his familiar outline – the shape of his shoulders, the way he carried himself – shook Tsuga to her very core.

Ramiq Nevarn.

Until now, she has not known the name of the man who had recently taken over her dreams. But she knew that voice – and oh, she knew *him*. No longer able to hold back the wash of emotions and sensations she felt, Tsuga swayed on her feet for a moment before her knees buckled and she crumpled to the ground in a dead faint.

For approximately the last week, Ramiq's sleep had been fitful at best. Every time he closed his eyes he was haunted by dreams of *her*, the woman who had once made his life all but unbearable. He had had dreams like this before, when he was still young and somewhat new to his magic. He hadn't known then what they had meant, and he was not any better informed on this matter now, nearly ten years later.

He dreamt of her. When he woke, he reached for her as though she lay beside him in his large, plush bed – but of course she wasn't there. She haunted his thoughts throughout the day and drove him to distraction, so that he grew increasingly agitated and became easily irritated.

Even with his power, his good looks, and his persuasive way with words, Ramiq had still not outgrown certain habits from his younger days – the foremost of which was his liking for numerous and varied bedmates. Unfortunately even these frequent escapades could not drive her from his mind.

He knew she was near. The wards he had placed around the Mages' Complex had alerted him to her presence, and as he continued his lecture to the assembled trainees, with his mind he sought her out and followed her progress. Her magical signature was not far changed from what it had been all those years ago – powerful, chaotic, and untrained – and the thought of what she could do if only she applied herself made his fists clench briefly in frustration before he regained control of himself and was able to force them to relax.

He sensed her come to a halt at the edge of the training grounds, and quickly redoubled his mental and empathetic shields. He had not forgotten what it was like to be inside that unsettled mind, and he had no desire to repeat the experience. As he finished the shielding process, one of his students broke in to his lecture about how magic affected and nourished life with a shout of alarm.

"Master Ramiq, sir! That man – he's fainted!"

Ramiq knew better than to show any sign of alarm to his students, and so he forced himself not to look over his shoulder. Instead, he addressed the boy who had spoken.

"The correct form of address is 'Queen's Mage,' or if you must, 'Adept,'" he rebuked gently. This particular boy was his newest student – a water mage whose power had brought him to sudden prosperity out of the life of a servant. He had meant no disrespect, and so Ramiq did not come down on him too harshly.

"But thank you for your vigilance. You all will excuse me for a moment."

Of course, the eyes of each of his pupils seared a hole in his back as he turned from them and walked at a deliberately steady pace to the crumpled form at the edge of the training grounds. It took every bit of restraint he had not to break into a run.

Tsuga returned to consciousness gently; she couldn't remember the last time she'd fainted this way, but she was pretty sure she had never roused feeling so . . . peaceful. When she opened her eyes, he was there, his strange green-gold irises staring into her own brown ones with a look of concern. Her head rested in his lap.

I must be dreaming, she thought idly as she floated in a sea of bliss. But gravel bit into her back, and sweat tickled her scalp. This was no dream.

"Tsuga. You're alright."

Ramiq refused to acknowledge the relief that colored his words when she opened her eyes and smiled up at him. Even through his redoubled shields, her chaotic emotions – surely he was not the one so awash in anxiety, worry, lust, fear, and uncertainty – threatened to overwhelm him.

"Ramiq."

On her lips, his name sounded like a prayer. The timbre of her voice made him burn. Then the moment passed – she tensed and pulled away, and he reluctanty let her go so that she could sit up on her own, even as he released his hold on the magic he had used to revive her.

"Ramiq?"

This time her tone was brusque, and he nodded at the implied question.

"I am Tsuga Dafrin." He didn't know why she bothered introducing herself – he felt as though he'd known her all his life – but he didn't ask, and instead let her continue. "The new Weaponsmistress. I was told you were the one to speak to about sleeping arrangements."

Ramiq went hot and cold all at the same time, and his thoughts tripped one over the other, each forming before the last had fully been recognized.

Sleeping arrangements? With me, of course. But why are you acting as though you don't know me? Haven't you seen what I've seen? Surely you have. Did you just say Weaponsmistress? That won't last long. Does that mean you're staying?

Tsuga took stock of herself. Her headache was gone, as were all of her other, more minor aches and pains. His gaze remained glued to her; she found, much to her dismay, that she was blushing. She had never seen this man outside of her dreams, and yet she felt as though she had known him all her life. She felt he was as much a part of her as her own leg. To cover her discomfiture, she grasped at the only thing she could: her reason for being here. Something in what she said must have thrown him, for he took several long moments to respond.

"Yes. I am. But I have a lesson to teach at the moment. You are of course welcome to sit in."

Tsuga laughed and shook her head at such a foolish suggestion. "I'm no mage."

His expression changed, and he looked at her oddly for a moment before he spoke again.

"No matter. This is their first class. Strictly lecture and theory. No magical affinity required. Come on."

Ramiq stood and automatically checked his black and silver robes for dust. Of course, there was none – the intricate layers of shielding and the magic he wove into all of his clothes insured that he always looked perfect and pristine. Reassured, he looked down at Tsuga – herself unable to boast his perfect presentability – and extended his hand with a smile.

"It won't hurt. And you just might learn something."

She bristled slightly at the implied insult but, as he had expected, didn't turn down the challenge. He shook his head when she insisted on standing without his aid, but did not comment. Instead, he turned and walked back to the place he had been standing to deliver his lecture. He made a point of addressing the brief lapse.

"When the magic in our own bodies waxes or wanes to an extreme, the body has a prompt and violent reaction, as the new Weaponsmistress has just shown us. Now, many of you have already used your powers in one way or another. After all, something had to have made it clear that you are possessed of the mage gift for you to seek out or be sent to this Complex for instruction. However, very few of you have had any formal training, and none of you have learned the basics.

"Mage sight, shielding, and self-control are three of the most fundamental skills in the mage's arsenal. A mage who lacks in any one of these abilities is a danger to themselves as well as others. Knowledge is your greatest defense – and your most valuable weapon. This skill set takes a lifetime to master, but here in the Mages' Complex, you will be given the tools with which you can hone your abilities over the course of your lifetime, so that eventually you will no longer require a teacher to do so."

Tsuga stood off to one side of the group and took in the mage's words silently. His students ranged in age from a child she guessed to be around nine to an elderly crone who used a cane to hold herself upright. They seemed also to come from all walks of life; although each wore a plain linen robe dyed in a color that she presumed had some meaning to them (pale shades of blue, red, and green, among other colors), which she took as uniforms, she had seen enough in her lifetime to be able to read people's stories in the way they conducted themselves. Nobility, slaves, streetrats – this class contained all of them and more.

She expected to have little interest in the mage's speech, but she found that this lesson, at least, could be applied to her own decidedly non-magical life. She found herself watching Ramiq intently as she absorbed his words. He was obviously in his element here; he lit up as he spoke, and his presence drew his audience in. While she could not utilize mage sight or shielding, the message to her was much the same as it must be to these students; after all, the abilities to see things clearly, to protect oneself, and to control one's actions and emotions were equally as vital to a warrior as they were to a mage – a fact that, until now, she had not given much consideration. Ramiq had not stopped talking.

"The way magic behaves and influences the world is hard to explain to someone who has never seen or felt it, so today you will be learning to engage your mage sense – that ability which allows us to see and feel the power around us. Without a good grasp of this ability, trying to grow as a mage is like trying to paint a masterpiece while blindfolded."

Each time he started a new class, Ramiq's thoughts went back to the first time he had given this lesson. Then, he had been in his early twenties – a child still, really – and newly thrust into a position he wasn't ready for. He had made a complete mess of that first lesson – and, honestly, a great number of the ones which followed – and his mouth still went dry every time he came to this part. He swallowed and plowed ahead.

"In order to engage your mage sense, you must master your emotions. Only a mind that is calm, clear, and focused can open itself to a higher level of awareness. So begin by breathing steadily and concentrate on your heartbeat. Close your eyes and listen to all of the little noises around you – and then tune them out. When you feel completely calm, slowly open your eyes. It may not work the first time. And even if it does, you will likely lose it between one breath and the next. You will have to master your frustration, ignore your excitement, and start over. Maybe a hundred times. Maybe a thousand. Do not let yourself become exasperated. Emotion will only make this process more difficult – indeed, nearly impossible."

Tsuga knew she wouldn't be able to see anything, but the exercise in relaxation and concentration couldn't hurt. She closed her eyes and listened to Ramiq's voice. She focused on the relaxed, even tone more than the words. It was soothing, hearing him speak, and she felt her breathing slow and her heart begin to beat more steadily. Tension and worry flowed out of her, and Tsuga opened her eyes with a feeling of peace.

The world was awash in light – reds, blues, greens, and hundreds of colors and blendings of colors for which she had no words. Ramiq, where he walked among his students, glowed in such a blindingly colorful mix of light that she actually gasped in surprise. She blinked, and then the vision – for certainly a hallucination was the only explanation – was gone.

Ramiq saw her face change. Even as he moved through his students, observing the efforts of each and offering words of encouragement or instruction where needed, he couldn't take his eyes off of her for long.

Tsuga was a mage. She knew it; so did he. But after the death threats she had made the last time, he had no desire to bring it up again. But if she knew, why had her mouth formed that little "O" of surprise? She seemed genuinely shocked when her mage sight worked, as though she had truly convinced herself that she was no longer possessed of her magical gifts.

He stifled a sigh as he paused beside a young girl dressed in the pale green of an apprentice healer and spoke absent words of encouragement to quell her frustration. He glanced again to Tsuga, and he knew that he would have to speak with her again about submitting herself to magical training. He was the Queen's Mage, after all. What did he have to fear from her?

The lesson only lasted about an hour. Tsuga figured Ramiq had cut it short on her account, but as this group left and another, smaller group – this one all wearing the same shade of pale yellow – filed in, she realized that he had simply kept to some predetermined schedule. He paused for a moment to exchange a few words with a woman of middling years dressed in a bright yellow robe the color of dandelions in the spring, and then he broke off and approached her where she stood off to one side.

"Dawn has a beginner's class for light mages now, so I won't be needed for a while. Come on; I'll show you what you'll need."

Tsuga turned again to look at the three students as their instructor started in on her lesson. When she turned back to Ramiq, he was already a couple of steps ahead of her; she had to lengthen her stride to catch up to him. He waited until she fell into step with him before he spoke.

"There is a room set aside for you in the Warriors' Compound, but it's not much. Just a bed, desk, and wardrobe. Pretty drab, by anyone's standards."

Tsuga had to laugh a little at that, and when he looked at her questioningly, she shook her head. "I've been living mostly in a tent for the last eight years. I'm sure whatever accommodations there are will suit me just fine."

Ramiq's eyebrows met his hairline, and he gaped at her for a moment before he was able to find his voice.

"A tent? For eight *years*? Why?!"

Tsuga smiled at his dumbfounded expression and shook her head. "I've been on the road with a mercenary band. You sleep where you fall – your tent, against a tree, in the saddle . . .. It's the way of life for a mercenary."

He shuddered delicately, and Tsuga couldn't help but compare him to a noble woman who had just sidestepped a pile of fresh, steaming horse shit. She bit back a laugh at the image and shook her head.

"Well, you'll have a room, here. And I'll introduce you to Jai; she's in charge of the servants over there. You can talk to her about your cleaning standards, meal schedule – things like that."

Tsuga considered for a moment, and then shook her head. "My trainees will be doing their own cleaning, cooking, and other chores. Tell Jai . . . I don't know. I'll find something for her and the other servants to do, I suppose."

Ramiq looked confused again. "But it's their job. Why not let them just do it?"

"Because there are no servants on the battlefield. Not for the common soldier; these men and women won't have someone to polish their armor and wash their linens for them. The trainees need to know how to pull their own weight. Might as well start sooner, rather than later."

Ramiq shook his head. "Well, it's your decision, after all, even if I don't understand the logic of it. But I'll show you the mess hall, the stables . . .."

Tsuga thought of reminding him that she used to live in the Compound, but she really had nowhere else to be, and his company wasn't *terrible*, after all.

Ramiq found that Tsuga was very easy to talk to. As he took her around the Warriors' Compound, he made small talk, all the while wracking his brain to find a way to bring up the subject of her magic. In the end, it proved to be unnecessary effort; Tsuga provided him with the perfect opening as they walked from the barracks to the training yard.

"I found your lesson to be quite enlightening. It would seem mages and fighters are not so far different, after all."

Ramiq laughed a little in surprise. "I remember a time when you would have sworn up and down that just the opposite was true. But you are right. Mages are only people, when it comes down to it – no matter how powerful."

She smiled at his words, and he had to look away from her to cover his sudden arousal.

"Sounds like you're well on the way to becoming a diplomat."

Ramiq ducked his head and took a deep breath to muster his courage before he spoke again. "Tsuga . . .." Something in his tone must have alerted her that his mood had shifted, because she stopped and turned to look at him with a quizzical expression.

"Out with it."

Her stance was defensive – he knew she had her guard up – but he plunged ahead anyway.

"It's hard for people without magic to understand the way mages view the world. It's like describing to a person from the southern reaches of Sennor what a blizzard is like. Telling someone they are a mage when they haven't yet figured it out for themselves is like telling that same person they are going to have to live the rest of their lives in the Crystal City. Of course they're going to rebel at first, until they have time to come to terms with the reality of their new situation."

"You're rambling." Although her voice held a note of irritation, her eyes danced with surpressed laughter. "Get to the point."

Ramiq blew out a frustrated breath and forced himself to meet her gaze. "Tsuga, a mage gift that is not trained is deadly. Not just to you, but to the people around you as well. It's my duty as the Queen's Mage to advise you to seek training immediately."

For a split second Ramiq held his breath, unsure what was going to happen. Her face froze, and the world around them seemed to stop as everything went deathly still. Then, she threw back her head and laughed.

"Me? A mage? You must be losing your touch. Or your mind. I am many things, Ramiq Nevarn – a mercenary, a former captain, and now a Weaponsmistress – but I am no *mage*! Auriga's tits! I've never heard such a ridiculous notion!"

Ramiq released the breath he had been holding in a sigh of frustration and frowned at her. Perhaps that old saying had some truth to it, after all. Some things really didn't ever change.

"Look, this whole Compound is made of wood. One false move, and you and everyone in it will go up in flames. I'm sorry, but I can't wait around for you to burn down half the palace. I'm afraid if you don't agree to – and stick with – lessons, I will have to advise the queen against her decision to appoint you to this position."

Tsuga felt as though she'd just been slapped in the face. Her jaw tightened as she fought back the urge to draw one of her weapons.

I can't believe I was starting to like him.

"You're *threatening* me? I already told you, I'm not a mage. You may as well give me flying lessons."

Ramiq shook his head throughout her outburst, and she realized now that he had somehow crossed his arms without her notice.

"You can deny it all you want; you can't make it any less true. I'm not trying to threaten you, but I can't let you put these kids in that kind of danger. Your other option would be to find quarters in the Mages' Complex, where I can personally ensure that you are properly shielded."

Tsuga frowned at him and shook her head. "You're telling me my choices are leave, live around mages all the time, or take pointless lessons and waste my time – which would be far better spent trying to keep these kids from getting themselves killed?"

Now Ramiq had that stern expression she knew all too well. She had seen it on her father, her instructors, and her commanders over the years. There was no getting around *that* look.

"That is exactly what I'm saying."

Tsuga blew out a frustrated breath and briefly considered her options. She could return to the Warriors, but she had already stepped down as Captain. She would be reentering the company as a peon, the lowest of ranks. She could always go it alone or try to establish her own company, but hire for a lone sword was hard to come by, and successful mercenary companies took years to establish.

If she agreed to live with the mages, she would be constantly surrounded by the magic that made her skin crawl and her head pound so unpleasantly. She already had enough trouble sleeping as it was; she had no desire to make things any harder on herself. Alternatively, she could agree to Ramiq's ridiculous lessons and waste an indefinite amount of her time trying to convince him that he was wrong. On the up side, though, once he saw the error in his logic, he would surely drop all of this nonsense and leave her be. She let out a sigh in resignation and glanced away from him for a moment before looking back.

"How often would these lessons have to be?"

For a brief moment, she thought she saw an expression of shock cross his features; just as quickly it was gone, replaced by that same serene facade he had maintained during the earlier lesson.

"Daily."

"Then you'll have to work with my schedule. I won't have this taking away from the time I need to spend with my trainees."

"I think I can manage that. You will have to come to the Complex, though, where there is less chance of you burning down a building."

Tsuga blew out a breath in frustration, but nodded her consent.

"Fine. But I will be holding training from sunup to sundown, so it will have to be after dark, or before dawn."

"You don't break for meals?"

"Alright," she consented grudgingly. "Lunch, then?"

Ramiq nodded. "Lunch. Starting tomorrow. Now, if you're all set here, I really should be getting back."

Tsuga shook her head absently, rather disliking this feeling of being trapped. "By all means. You have your students, and I have mine. I'll expect you at midday. Don't be late."

Tsuga sat atop Devilsbane, the ambling motion of the horse's walk easily mimicked by Tsuga's hips as she swayed with the movement. The heat of the day beat down on her from above; the sun was nearly at its zenith. As they rode along the road that connected the east and west sides of the castle – the Warriors' Compound and Mages' Complex, respectively – Tsuga felt the now-familiar headache begin to throb behind her eyelids.

She blew out a gusty sigh in an effort to relieve some of the tension she felt, but it had no effect. She had been coming to these fruitless lessons for over a week now, and still had not accomplished anything even remotely resembling magic. Not even another incident like that first day. She knew Ramiq must be growing frustrated with her lack of progress. She was quite exasperated herself with this collassal waste of time.

With a start, Tsuga realized that Bane had come to a stop by an unfamiliar building. Tsuga looked around, but she didn't recognize anything in this part of the Complex.

"What are you doing? This isn't the training yard."

Ramiq asked me to bring you here.

"What? Why?"

He didn't say.

"And you didn't ask."

It wasn't a question, but Bane blew out a quick breath – the equine equivalent of a shrug – and Tsuga rolled her eyes in response before she swung out of the saddle.

"Well? Where is he, then?"

"You're early."

Tsuga turned to see Ramiq standing in the shade of one of the large oak trees that sheltered this small courtyard. He was dressed in yet another of his fantastical costumes, complete with flowing robes, billowing sleeves, and a belt in a complimenting color. Today's outfit was a celebration of the color green; she thought she counted at least six different shades in the filmy folds of fabric. Nine days of lessons, and she had yet to see him wear the same outfit twice. This one made his eyes seem even more green than usual. She felt herself flush when he caught her staring and promptly looked up to the sun to cover her discomfiture.

"Actually, I am exactly on time. Just as I am every day. Why are we here?"

"Good day to you, too."

Tsuga resisted the urge to roll her eyes again – barely – and remained silent. All she could do was wait for him to get to the point.

"We are here because there is something blocking you. Whatever it is, it's keeping you from opening yourself to your power. It's time we begin working on removing that block."

Ramiq had known this would make her uncomfortable. Few people were okay with having their emotions laid bare. She was tense, and he was more than a bit nervous about opening himself to a barrage of her thoughts and emotions – though he wouldn't let himself aknowledge his fear, lest she sense his uncertainty.

They sat alone in the small, secluded courtyard that attached to his private chambers. There were certain perks to being the Queen's Mage, and this little retreat was one of them. The large horse stood nearby and watched silently. Under that calm brown gaze, Ramiq shifted uncomfortably.

"Alright," he began as he forced himself to look away from Devilsbane's stare and meet Tsuga's eye. "Now, the way this will work is that I'm going to open a channel between us that will allow me to feel your emotions and hear your thoughts. I want to ask you some questions and have you try a few things so that I can see how you react to them. Just the same things we've been doing, mostly."

When she didn't say anything, he shifted nervously and cleared his throat. "Alright, then. Here goes."

Tsuga hadn't been sure what to expect, but she didn't feel any great shifting of the world beneath her. She also didn't feel like she had when she'd first joined with Bane. There was no other presence in her head. The hairs on the back of her neck stood up, though, and she had to restrain herself from looking over her shoulder. She felt as though she was being spied on.

"Here goes what?"

"Just relax. Let's start with some questions. How does it feel when you're around magic?"

"It's hard to put into words," she began, forcing herself to stop searching behind her and turn back to face Ramiq. "It makes my skin crawl and my stomach churn. I get a headache, like there is a pressure building behind my skull that I have no way of releasing."

Ramiq nodded as though he understood; for all she knew, maybe he did. He said he was reading her mind, after all.

"That's your mage sense trying to communicate with you. It's been shut down and ignored for so long that it has had to find a way to make itself heard. The crawling you feel on your skin is the magic your power knows is around you. The headache is your mage sight, which for whatever reason you've been suppressing. As for the stomach ache, that's a physical reaction to the denial of an integral part of yourself."

Tsuga frowned; she couldn't help but be a little weirded out when she realized that Ramiq's posture and expression exactly mirrored her own.

"But I don't have any power. I never have. If I did, don't you think I would know? I'm twenty-six. Shouldn't something have happened by now if it was going to?"

Now Ramiq looked confused, though the only thing *she* felt was exasperation. "How is this possible?"

"How is what possible?"

"You're completely sincere. You're telling the truth . . .."

Ramiq flinched as her outrage struck him like a blow to the stomach.

"Of course I'm telling the truth! Why would I sit here and waste my time by lying about something like that?!"

He held up his hands in a defensive posture to try and placate her, but dropped them immediately when he felt her anger intensify in the face of his mollifying gesture.

"You don't understand. Even if I couldn't see the power you carry – the gift you possess – I would still know you're a mage. And a powerful one, at that. I've *seen* you use your magic. I've had you use it *against* me."

Tsuga shook her head, and he felt confusion flood her. "Not possible. I don't remember that. I've never even met you, until last week."

"You really don't remember . . .. Alright, I want you to try what we've been practicing. I'm going to check you over while you do – mage sight, healer's sense, all of it. I don't want to miss anything."

He could tell that the idea of not knowing herself as fully as she had thought she did worried her, but she took a deep breath and closed her eyes as he opened his magical senses to watch. Her breathing slowed and became more even. Her heart rate steadied as she gained control over her nerves with an admirable show of will. Her mind, which even as they had been talking had run numbers and made plans about her students and her own day, quieted.

As she went through the steps he had taught her to open herself to her mage sense, Ramiq monitored her progress. As she leaned forward and concentrated, her mage stone – for he could feel the power emanating from the trinket which identified it as such – fell forward to dangle in the air from its simple leather thong.

"You have to stop it, Tsu!"

"Stop what? What are you talking about?"

Tsuga could see real fear now in her sister's eyes. It was then that she realized she couldn't sense Devilsbane. This sent a jolt of panic through her.

"Where is Devilsbane?"

Affaila's eyes widened, and now Tsuga realized that it was more than just sweat dampening the redhead's face.

"I don't know. But Tsu, you have to stop the fire!"

"You don't know? What do you mean, you don't know? Where is she?!"

"Tsu, please! The fire –"

"What fire?"

It was only then that the pieces began to fall into place. The roaring, the light, the heat . . . the acrid smell that she now recognized as smoke. Her breath quickened again as she looked over Affaila's shoulder to see the entire house engulfed in flames.

As a surge of panic coursed through her the blaze leapt higher, as though finding new fuel.

"Tsu, please! I can't –"

Affaila's last words were cut off in a fit of coughing, but Tsuga scarcely noticed. Without the steadying hand of her guardian, panic had quickly taken hold in this situation. Now she wanted nothing more than death – for what use was life, if she must endure it as only half a person? The temperature rose tangibly as the flames drew nearer, burning brighter in response to her decision.

Tsuga!

The familiar mindvoice jolted her to attention just before she could make the suicidal reach into the currents of old magic.

Tsu, you have to stop this! Stop the fire!

"I . . . can't!"

Indeed, it was true. The magic had the bit in its teeth, so to speak. She had no choice but to let this fire run its course now. Her best bet would be to close her link to it, so that it could no longer draw on her for fuel.

Tsu, look at Affaila! She's not a fire mage; you're killing her!

The words sent a sharp stab of pain through her, and for the first time since waking, Tsuga actually saw her sister. Her skin was blistered from the heat, and she was weeping in pain and terror. She was on her hands and knees, too weak to move, coughing violently. Bane's words echoed again.

You're killing her.

Suddenly Tsuga was looking at herself, watching pain and fear play across her own face. Her heart pounded, the emotions overwhelmed her, and she felt a flash of panic as the temperature rose quickly. It was too hot. She – he? – broke out in a sweat, even as he – she? – shivered as though from a bone-deep chill. The pressure built behind her skull until she felt she must surely explode. Just before the pain reached the point of becoming unbearable, she lost consciousness.

Ramiq reeled from the magical backlash as the connection he had established was abruptly severed by Tsuga's loss of consciousness. He could feel the sweat beading on his brow and running freely between his shoulder blades and over his chest. As his head throbbed in reaction to his interrupted work, it slowly began to dawn on him that something was *wrong*. It was already well into the month of Oktum; it shouldn't be this *hot*.

He coughed as he sucked in a lungful of air that felt as though it must have come off a blasting furnace. It was only when this thought occurred to him that he realized the pair of them were surrounded by flames that had already begun to make the trees around them crack and pop loudly in the heat.

The matter was simple enough for him to fix; fire was one of his strongest elemental affinities, and under his scrutiny the flames quickly snuffed out to allow the cooler air to rush in and fill the sudden void. With the immediate danger averted, he shifted his focus back to Tsuga herself.

Although he was heavily warded against magical attacks, she wasn't. He still looked pristine and untouched, but where she lay crumpled on the ground, her clothes were singed. The smell of burned leather – her sword belt or her boots, he surmised – was strong in his nostrils, making him curl his nose in distaste. At first glance, she seemed to be fine; she was breathing evenly, and though she looked slightly flushed, she was not visibly burned. Still, he had to swallow a lump of worry as he crawled on his knees across the short distance that separated them and straightened her out so that he could pull her into his lap as he began checking her over with his healer's sense.

He was still checking her vitals when, of her own accord, she began to rouse. When she sat up and pushed him away, he let her go reluctantly – though he continued to urgently check her over visually as she raised a hand to her head and used the other to steady herself against the ground.

"What happened?"

Ramiq let out his breath and rocked back on his heels to look at her where she sat in the midst of the destruction she had caused. The ground was blackened and covered in a thin layer of ash that had been grass only minutes before. Soot drifted down on them from the branches of the tree that had sheltered them; it was split along one side from the rapid heating, and with each breath of air, more charred remnants of leaves drifted down to settle in her hair and on her shoulders.

"The second you touched your magic, you lost control and blacked out. And . . . well."

A wave of exasperation hit him before he remembered to reestablish his mental shields. He could tell she was shaken by what had happened, though she fought admiriably to hide it.

"How many times do I have to tell you? I don't *have* any magic. I don't know why, but every time I'm around any I seem to pass out."

Ramiq shook his head. Whatever breakthrough they had been approaching now seemed even further away.

"Tsuga?"

She had begun trying to stand, but at the sound of his voice, she relaxed back to the ground and turned to face him.

"What?"

She was irritated, he could tell; even without her thoughts and reactions threatening to overwhelm him, he could read the play of emotions on her face as plainly as words on a parchment. Still, he forged ahead.

"That memory, just before you blacked out . . . that's why you're so afraid, isn't it? You think you're going to hurt someone. But you won't. Not if you're properly trained. But don't you see? Ignoring it isn't helping; it's making things worse. You see what happened here; if this had been anyone else, if *I* had been anyone else . . .."

"What memory? Look, I don't know what you saw, but I didn't see it. I was doing the exercises you showed me, and then . . . well, there's nothing there. Not until I woke up."

Tsuga's head throbbed. Her mouth was dry, and every time she tried to move the ground dipped as though to throw her into the air. Her stomach loudly reminded her that it was lunch time even as she finally steadied her vision enough to look over her shoulder at Ramiq. His brow was furrowed so deeply that had she not felt so thoroughly miserable, she might have found it comical.

"You're telling the truth."

At this, she shook her head and rolled her eyes heavenward in exasperation – movement which she immediately regretted when the world dipped precariously again.

"A real genius, you are."

Ramiq shook his head. "But that's not possible. Last time you were in Sennor, you knew you had magic. In fact, you threatened to kill me if I ever mentioned it. You have fought me, will to will. You *know* you have magic. So how is it you can be telling the truth now when you say you don't?"

"I don't have any idea. And I don't have time for this right now. I have to get back to my trainees."

She tried to stand, but collapsed back to the ground when she discovered that she had no real strength in her legs. Somehow Ramiq's hands found their way under her arms; the next thing she knew she was standing, leaning heavily against him for support.

"You need to eat."

She waved off the comment, though she didn't push him away; she knew there was no way she would be able to stand without his aid.

"I ate before I came."

"Well, be that as it may, you used magic – and a lot of it."

"I don't –"

"You don't have magic . . . so you keep insisting. But someone set the courtyard ablaze. It wasn't me, and you're the only other one here. Just eat this. It will help, I promise."

He produced a clean square of cloth bundled around something Tsuga presumed to be edible. She took it, and the package fell open to reveal a tightly compressed bar of . . ..

"What is it?" She sniffed it dubiously, but still couldn't quite identify its contents. It smelled sweet.

"Think of it as trail rations, but for a mage. Oats, dried fruit, honey, almonds . . .. It helps restore your energy quickly. Soldiers rely on protein and healthy carbs; mages need sweets and fats. Just eat it."

Tsuga wasn't sure what to think of his offer, but she had to admit she was famished. She took a small bite of the strange rectangle and found it to be sticky and chewy, both salty and sweet. It was delicious, and the entire thing was gone in a matter of seconds.

"Better?"

Tsuga started to retort, but as she opened her mouth she found that she did indeed feel a bit more steady on her feet.

"Actually, yes."

She stepped away from him cautiously and found that she was able to stand unaided.

"Doesn't that tell you something?"

"It tells me I have a class to teach. Thanks for the food, Ramiq. I'll see you tomorrow."

While she had eaten, Bane had come to stand at her side, so that now Tsuga had only to turn around to put her foot in the stirrup. She swung herself into the saddle with practiced ease and managed to play off the dizziness from the sudden change in altitude by adjusting her position. Bane moved off at a measured pace meant to help Tsuga keep her seat with minimal effort. She did, after all, have students to attend to.

By the time they reached the Warriors' Compound, Tsuga felt more like herself. The headache faded with every step away from the Mages' Complex, and her strength continued to return with each passing moment. When at last Bane came to a stop and Tsuga slid to the ground, she was relieved that the world held steady. With a deep breath, she turned to face her pupils.

Unlike mage students, who came into their power at various ages, her trainees were all about the same age: headstrong youths, each of them. The life of a career soldier was often short-lived. Once a body lost its razor's edge and the reaction times began to slow, those who were not killed by a faster, younger opponent often moved on to a less risky career. If they were lucky, they moved up the military hierarchy and were promoted to a position of command, so that they were able to continue living the life they knew without having to put themselves directly in harm's way.

At nearly thirty years of age, Tsuga had chosen to make the move to a less perilous career path herself. Though she told herself it was a sacrifice to step off of the front lines and retire her skills to the capacity of teaching the next generation of fighters, in truth she could no longer deny that old injuries and the hard life she'd led had leeched her youth prematurely. It had started to grow increasingly dangerous for her to continue such a battle-heavy career. None of these thoughts had even occurred to most of the children she now taught, though. They only wanted the glory of battle, the thrill of bloodshed. It was up to her to make sure they survived as long as possible in such pursuits.

The students lined up as she had taught them; each stood straight and silent and looked to her for instruction. She took a quick tally; as Bane moved off to one side of the line, her gaze snapped to the empty position in the lineup.

"Where is Cain?" A few of them exchanged glances, but none answered her. "No matter. He knows the consequences of tardiness as well as the rest of you. Now, we've mostly been working on finding each of your strengths so far, and most of you have settled on a specialty. Being proficient in your discipline of choice is all well and good, but you must also be familiar with techniques your opponents may employ so that you can adequately defend yourself against any kind of attack.

"Erew," she said as she turned to face the pale-skinned girl with the long black hair and gray eyes that hinted at a bloodline hailing from the far eastern reaches of the continent, "what are the weakest points in a traditional suit of armor?"

Erew was young, and though she had been sold into slavery as a small child – as evidenced by the tattoos on the back of the girl's right hand – she had won her freedom through some means to which Tsuga had not been made privy. Just shy of fifteen, this particular child had shown a remarkable skill with distance weapons; most notably the longbow. Erew tensed and stood a bit straighter, though Tsuga was pleased to note that neither her hands nor her voice shook when she answered.

"Well the joints, of course. Everyone knows that. The eye slit in the helmet. Under the arms, if you're a lucky shot. The metal is thinner in any place that bends. If the armor is poorly made, it will expose gaps when the wearer moves in places such as the hips, knees, and elbows."

Tsuga nodded. "Very good. You know your target's weaknesses. What are yours?"

Erew opened her mouth as though to answer, and then closed it. This time she sounded uncertain when at last she did speak. "Well, archers don't wear much armor . . .."

"Braxton?"

Tsuga turned her focus now to a dark-skinned older boy – nineteen, she thought – who had the tall, muscular build that was the result of his fancy for heavier weaponry. He had been snickering at Erew's uncertainty, but at the sound of his name, he snapped to attention and sobered immediately.

"Ma'am."

"What is the best way to take out an archer?"

"Uh, well . . .."

Tsuga waited patiently for Braxton's mind to work through the problem he had just been presented. Many mistook the young man for a simpleton, but over the past weeks Tsuga had learned that he was in fact very intelligent. He took the time to look at a problem from all angles before taking any one course of action. He had the potential to make a great general some day – if his hesitancy didn't get him killed first.

"Numbers."

It wasn't the answer she had expected, but Tsuga was curious to hear his thoughts on the matter. "Go on."

"An archer has a finite number of arrows. Most archers don't have much else in the way of defense; few of them are skilled with close combat. So if you have more targets than arrows, the archer becomes vulnerable. It's just a numbers game."

Tsuga nodded slowly as she took in his words. "A very insightful answer. You are absolutely right. In the most straightforward way, numbers win. If there are more soldiers than arrows. If you are willing to sacrifice the first wave of your attack so that the second can have a chance at surviving. This is the crux of leadership. Who, after all, is fit to say if one life is worth more or less than another? The stripes on a man's uniform do not automatically make him fit to lead. Always remember that.

"Now, of course there are infinite variables on a battlefield: location, surprise, skill, strategy, provisions, fatigue . . . the list is nearly endless. So you see, every strength can be made into a weakness, and every weakness utilized to make it an unexpected strength. Today's lesson is about just that: turning what your opponent expects to be your weakness to your advantage. No weapons today; this will be theory only. Think of it as an afternoon off. Drop your weapons and find a seat."

When they all looked around in confusion as though seeking chairs and benches, Tsuga lifted her eyebrows and proceeded to fold her own legs and sink gracefully into a cross-legged position on the packed dirt of the training yard. The children – she couldn't help but think of them as such, even though a few of them were old enough to be considered adults by the rest of the world – quickly followed suit. She waited until everyone was situated before she began.

"Now, who can tell me the first step to combating a weakness?" Her students all exchanged puzzled glances, but when none ventured a guess she provided the answer to her own question. "The first step is knowledge. By knowing your own vulnerabilities, you can predict the thoughts and actions of your enemy. This simplest of changes turns any weakness to your advantage. Knowledge may only be the first step in this process, but it is what we will be focusing on today. If you want to stay alive on the battlefield, you must be able to think ahead and predict your opponent's next move. Erew, please stand."

The young archer did as she was told, though she looked puzzled by the command.

"You've all lived and trained with Erew for nearly a month now. You know her habits, her personality, the training she has received, and her skill with the bow. What are the chinks in her armor, so to speak?"

Erew paled at the question, and then flushed deeply as all eyes turned to her. The comments came quickly – though not all of them were what she was looking for.

"She's a clutz. Always running into things."

"Can't lift a sword."

"Or swing an axe."

"Distracted. I had to keep getting her to focus when I was trying to talk to her the other day."

"No, I wouldn't say distracted. More like she sees everything, and doesn't always focus on what the rest of us would."

"She's a fast runner."

"Aye, but no endurance. That run yesterday morning – what was it, three miles? – almost killed her."

Tsuga held up her hand, and the comments trailed off. "Erew?"

The girl had alternated between watching the ground and glaring at her fellows while they analyzed her. At the sound of her name, the girl looked up to meet Tsuga's gaze with eyes that blazed with resentment.

"What are your weaknesses?"

"I think that has been made painfully clear, Weaponsmistress."

"What has been made clear is that your peers do not know what they're supposed to be looking for. If you were an enemy trying to kill someone with your build, skills, and quirks, what weaknesses would you exploit?"

Erew paused for a moment as she digested what Tsuga had said and contemplated the best way to answer. Tsuga would have pitied the child, had she not gone through this same process herself many times over. It was an exercise in self knowledge, meant to build self-awareness and confidence.

"Well, I'm young. And female. Inexperienced; never killed before. Other than my bow and a couple of throwing knives, I'm usually unarmed. I occasionally get a little rattled, like when I think too much about the outcome of a single shot. I would be easily overwhelmed if an enemy could close with me before I could shoot him."

Tsuga nodded slowly until she was finished, and then gestured for Erew to reclaim her seat.

"Good. All good. Each and every one of you made a valid point, though not all would be of use on a battlefield. Matthew, stand. Who can tall me Matt's weaknesses?"

The lesson continued in this vein for a while, with each student having to lay bare their own limitations. When the last of them sat down in thoughtful silence, Tsuga stood.

"And me?" The trainees all exchanged worried looks, but none of them made to answer her. "Oh, come now, I know you're all dying to tear me apart. What are *my* weaknesses?"

"Well, you . . .."

"Um, well, there's . . .."

"Beg pardon, Weaponsmistress, but there's *not* anything."

Tsuga quirked an eyebrow at the boy who had spoken last. "Really? Come now. Everyone has weaknesses. Even me."

Erew – an insightful child, to be sure – was looking at her strangely, and when Tsuga met her gaze, the girl spoke up. "You have night terrors. I've heard you screaming in the night."

Tsuga went cold, though she tried to hide her reaction from her trainees. "That is true. But how could that be turned to my advantage?"

This time, it was Braxton who spoke up. "You use the time you're not sleeping to improve yourself."

"How so?"

"Well, I've seen you. Before dawn. You train; running, sword practice, meditation and the like."

"And if you've seen me dance the forms – as none of the other students seem to have done – then surely you have some other observations?"

Braxton flushed. "Well, I did watch you one night. I . . . couldn't help it. You moved with such fluidity, such grace . . .. It was as though your spear – that's what you were using – was an extention of your thoughts. But you favored your left arm slightly; the range of motion was not as free as that in your right."

Tsuga nodded. "Took an arrow to the shoulder a while back, and it never did heal quite right. Keen observation, Braxton. I've spend the better part of my life training myself to eliminate as many of my weaknesses as possible; but alas, some things simply have to be accepted." She paused and looked at her students as they nodded thoughtfully at her words.

"Alright, this concludes tonight's lesson. Get some rest.
Exercises begin at dawn tomorrow."

Tsuga watched as the trainees dispersed and then turned to face
Bane, who had found a groom and gotten herself unsaddled,
brushed, and fed during the discussion.

That Braxton's a sharp kid.

"Yeah. I had no idea he'd seen me. There's a lot more to him
than people think. He has a lot of potential. He could go far."

"While I'm sure you all want to learn the more advanced
fighting techniques, such skills will do you no good unless you
are proficient with the use of the basics. Stance, movement, basic
forms; these are the foundations upon which all great warriors
build.

"We have spent the last month determining each of your
aptitudes. And, while I would love to have you all cross train, the
purpose of this school is not to create legendary soldiers, but
rather to prepare you for war and give you the best possible
chance for survival. Therefore, from here on the focus is going
to shift from *finding* your strengths to *honing* them.

"We will begin rotating on a twice-daily basis through the
following categories: distance weapons, light weaponry,
unarmed combat, and heavy weaponry. I will not stop anyone
from cross-training in any of the other categories should you have
an interest in doing so, but no one is required to. Any student not
in the day's focus group will be doing fitness drills with
Devilsbane. Once a week, we will all come together to work on
mounted combat. Not all of you will be suited for calvary
positions, but those who show an aptitude for it will form a fifth
category.

"Now, I want all light weaponry to stay here; that's short and
half-sword, spear, staff, and knife. Everyone else, go with Bane."

Tsuga watched as the majority of her students trailed off after
her guardian, leaving her with a dozen youngsters who shifted
anxiously under her critical gaze. Five wore swords, six she knew
to be proficient with the quarter staff, and one – a former streetrat
– handled his knives as though they were a part of him.

"Now, I will be taking each of you aside one on one – but first,
I'm going to show you a few basic forms to practice in the mean
time." As she spoke, Tsuga drew her sword and took up a
relaxed, ready stance.

"By now, you're familiar with the rest stance: weight on the
balls of your feet, sword protecting as much of your body as
possible. For today's practice, you will return to rest after each
exercise.

"First and most basic is the move I know as Splitting the
Melon. It is a simple overhand blow. Were my opponent

standing in front of me, this maneuver would consist of my sword pulling to the side, rising above my head, and then striking straight down through his skull. It's a simple move, but must be performed quickly and with force because unless you are holding a shield, it will leave you completely exposed."

Tsuga demonstrated in slow-motion as she spoke, and then at full speed when she'd finished before she returned to rest.

"Second, a basic mid-level maneuver. From rest, raise your sword arm slightly and extend as though to touch your opposite shoulder with the hilt of your weapon. To strike, lead first with your pommel. Just before you reach full extension, snap your wrist and bring your blade forward to slash at your opponent's midsection. Complete the arc in a smooth, unbroken movement and then return to rest. This is known as Parting the Silk. This basic strike can easily be turned into a parry or into a variety of other maneuvers, which makes it an essential skill for any swordsman to know.

"Lastly for today, we have As the Moon Rises. This is a good move for when you have no time to recover from a strike such as Splitting the Melon and need to parry or even strike immediately. The point of the blade begins nearly in the dirt, and you should bring the sword upwards point-first in a backhanded motion. As the Moon Rises typically finishes at mid-level, but can be continued all the way up or paired with another form such as Parting the Silk."

Tsuga sheathed her sword with a grace born of long practice and made each of her sword students demonstrate the forms until she was satisfied that they were doing them correctly. Once the five had moved off, she walked over to the rack of weapons positioned to one side of the training yard and selected a quarterstaff.

"Now, many of the forms for quarterstaff and spear are very similar to the movements used with the sword. However, it is a lighter weapon with a greater reach and either two blunt ends, or a butt and a spearhead rather than a blade. The disadvantage of using a blunt weapon is countered somewhat if you choose to use a spear as opposed to a staff, and although we do not currently have anyone training in the spear or fauchard at this time, basic knowledge of the quarterstaff will allow you to function adequately with one in a pinch.

"A shorter spear allows for the bearer to use a shield, but a shaft of five or more feet is long enough to serve as both the weapon and the defense if the wielder is knowledgeable in the weapon's proper use. One major advantage of the staff is the speed with which you can change tactics. It enables you to attack or defend in every direction; high or low, or to either side.

"The most basic stance with the staff is a grip with both hands spaced well apart to allow for more strength in both attack and defense and help maintain your control. This is the grip we will be focusing on today. There is both good and bad to using a quarterstaff as your weapon of choice: it is more difficult to land a lethal blow with a blunted weapon than a bladed one. If you wish only to stun or bruise an opponent, this is a good thing. However, a well-placed blow with a staff can be an effective killing tool as well. These are strong enough to break bones, and a cracked skull can kill as easily as a sliced one."

Tsuga proceeded to demonstrate a couple of the most basic moves with the staff and walked her students through them to check their form. She checked in once more with her swordsmen, and once she was satisfied that they would not be practicing bad habits, she turned to the last remaining student: her street urchin.

"Now, you're already more skilled with your knives than any of my other students are with their chosen weapons, so I want to see what kind of bad habits you might have – things like sloppy form, poor footwork, or the like. The easiest way for me to do that is to see you in action. So, draw your weapon."

On the last, Tsuga drew her own dagger and dropped into a defensive stance.

"I just don't understand why we're not making more progress. You should have broken through this mental block by now."

Tsuga shrugged and avoided Ramiq's stare by looking over his shoulder at a small bird scratching in the dirt.

"I keep telling you; I'm not a mage."

Ramiq shook his head and frowned at her. "But you *are*. What I can't understand is what happened to cause you to be unable to remember. Not only that, but it's as though every time you seem to make progress, by the next day you've forgotten everything. It's almost as though you're under some sort of spell that selectively blocks your memory. But of course, that isn't possible. No mage has been able to perform a spell like that in hundreds of years."

"Look, I don't know what you want me to say. I really don't. I keep trying to tell you this isn't going to work."

Three more months had passed, during which time Tsuga had continued to faithfully attend her lessons with the Queen's Mage. Even after so much time, however, Tsuga was still at square one. Despite her sour attitude and lack of progress, though, Ramiq had not once suggested that they stop trying. Oh, he'd lost his temper – she knew he was often frustrated by her – but he had never given up. While she still did not enjoy her lessons, Tsuga found that she no longer experienced that sinking feeling of dread at the mere sight of Ramiq. In fact, she had even occasionally caught herself smiling as she made her way to the Mages' Complex each day.

"With your permission, I'd like to try something." Tsuga quirked an eyebrow and tilted her head to the side – wary, but trusting that he wouldn't intentionally set out to harm her.

"Like what?"

"Well, you remember that time I had you try some basic exercises while I linked to you magically?"

"You mean the time I blacked out?"

"Yes, well, that was unexpected. But I would like to try something else this time. Instead of reading your thoughts, I'd like to try and take a look at your memories. By establishing a link like I did before, I'll be able to see what you do and feel everything just as though it were happening to me."

Tsuga frowned. "So what do I have to do?"

"Well, I'll start by asking you about some recent events, and then we'll work back from there and see if we can't find the source of your block."

Tsuga doubted that any good could come of such an undertaking, though she figured that the worst outcome would be her fainting again.

"I guess it's worth a shot, if you think it'll help."

"I do."

Tsuga sighed. "Let's get started, then."

While the colder temperatures during what passed for winter in this part of Sennor had driven their daily lessons indoors, the milder weather of early spring now saw them back out in the secluded little courtyard. The pair was once again settled on the ground, though at this time of year they were cushioned on a carpet of tender new grass.

In the time that they had spent together, Ramiq had learned that Tsuga's real temperament was often hard to read without magical aid. Now she sat cross-legged across from him, hands folded calmly in her lap, and watched him with a serene, trusting expression that made him just a bit uncomfortable. In an effort to block that look of hers out of his thoughts and calm his mind, he closed his eyes and took in a steadying breath.

Opening this link would be risky. Unlike last time, today he would be not only taking on all of Tsuga's thoughts and emotions, he would also be letting her into his mind. She would be showing him everything she thought and felt, but he would be doing the same for her. There was no way to form such an intimate link without its going both ways. He had to calm himself; he didn't want to cloud her mind with his own feelings. When he was ready, Ramiq expanded the shields that kept his thoughts and emotions separate from the rest of the world to allow Tsuga – and only Tsuga – to share them.

Now, before they truly began, was not much of a problem. Both of them were reasonably calm, and the link was formed with relative ease. Ramiq watched as Tsuga's eyes widened slightly as she realized that she had another person sharing her mind. To Ramiq, the feeling was somewhat similar to the bond he shared with Lyra, though Tsuga was far less familiar to him. He firmly resisted an irrational urge to examine every corner of her mind and tamped out the desire to delve deeper into her consciousness to solve the puzzle she presented. She quirked an eyebrow in response to the echoes she caught of his feelings, but didn't say anything.

Before Ramiq could open his mouth to ask Tsuga to take him through her morning, she had already begun to think about the beginning of her day.

She had awoken in a cold sweat, choking on a scream that died in her throat. The cold stone of her malachite pendant thumped lightly against her breastbone as she sat up and fought down the feeling of panic that her dream had summoned. Even as she struggled to slow her breathing and calm her racing heart, the subject of the nightmare that had roused her escaped any attempts at recollection. Frustrated, Tsuga blew out a breath and ran an anxious hand through her short-cropped hair.

Bane?

About two hours before dawn.

I'm going for a run. You coming?

Even as she formed the question in her mind, Tsuga stood up and began changing out of her sweat-drenched night clothes and into one of her comfortably well-worn uniforms.

Wouldn't miss it.

As Tsuga opened her eyes and returned her mind to the present, Ramiq took in a shaky breath and tried to hide the trembling of his hands.

"Do you –"

"Have nights like that often? Almost every night."

Ramiq shook his head in wonder. "And you have no idea what the dream was about?"

"No matter how hard I try, I can never remember them. Not that I think I really want to, judging by the way I feel when I wake up." She paused a moment and made a face. "I don't need your pity."

Indeed, Ramiq now shared the ill feeling that his sympathy must have caused her. This exchange of emotions was beyond confusing; it was hard to extricate one person's consciousness from the other's, like this. He flushed.

"Sorry."

"Don't. Just . . . don't."

"Okay. Well, let's try going a little further back. To our lesson a couple of weeks ago, when you –"

"No, but I don't remember that. I never set you on fire! I couldn't have; I'm not a mage!"

"You really don't remember that? You almost burned down my bed!"

Tsuga knew Ramiq had to be joking. Or lying. Or . . . something. But she could feel him there inside her head, much like she felt Devilsbane. She knew his thoughts and how he felt; she knew that his right shoulder hurt from where one of his students had lost control of their earth magic and hit him with a rock, and felt when his stomach clenched because he had delayed his lunch in favor of their daily lesson. This time, she was the one to be pulled down into his memory.

"Just breathe. Relax. Watch the fire. Focus on the flames, and let go of everything else. Now, tell me what you see."

Ramiq watched as she stared into the campfire-sized blaze he had summoned in the air between them. The individual flames danced merrily, fed by his magic and teased this way and that by the various drafts in the room. Her face was set in concentration, her brow furrowed as she focused.

She was beautiful in the firelight. The heat had flushed her cheeks slightly, and the hair that fell across her brow was damp with moisture. As he breathed in, he caught the smell of her – sweat and horse and leather. She smelled like honest, hard work. If it hadn't been for the fire between them, he may have thrown caution to the wind and taken her in his arms; just swept her up and –

"What's that?"

"What?"

Shaken from this intense line of thought, Ramiq had to wrench his mind back to the here-and-now. Tsuga didn't move her gaze from the flames.

"That. There's a – a second glow. Kind of . . . rainbow-colored?"

Ramiq tried to keep the excitement out of his voice when he spoke; this was the first real progress they had made in weeks.

"That is my magic. Congratulations; you have just engaged your mage sight."

Now Tsuga did look at him, and her confusion was writ plainly on her face.

"But only mages have mage sight."

Now Ramiq could no longer contain the grin that split his handsome features.

"That is true. You are *a mage, Tsuga. Whether you want to believe it or not." For a brief moment, he thought he saw fear cloud her expression; then it was gone, replaced by her typical stubborn denial.*

"I'm not a mage. I can't be."

His flame flared, nearly doubling in size, and Ramiq promptly severed the magic that kept it burning – only to have the flame change from a tame little blaze to a chaotic fire whose heat made sweat rise on his skin as it popped and surged under an influence other than his own. Despite the imminent danger to his belongings, Ramiq felt excitement wash over him at this breakthrough.

"You see! This is all you, Tsuga! You are *a mage! Now, with a little practice I can teach you–"*

"I am not a mage!" Her voice had risen in alarm, and her expression was one that brought to mind a scared and injured animal.

"But you are*!"*

Tsuga had leaned forward so that her face was nearly in the blaze, and Ramiq worried in the back of his mind that her hair might catch in the flames. Her entire posture had changed, and she seemed in the wild light of the fire to have become a completely different person.

"Listen to me and listen good. I. Am. Not. A. Mage. I can't be. I won't be. Magic does nothing but hurt people. I do nothing but hurt people. How are you supposed to defend yourself from burning alive? There's no fair fight there, no chance for winning. I can't be a mage! I can't hurt anyone else!"

Her voice had continued to rise as she spoke, until she was screaming the last. As her emotions spiraled out of control, so did the fire – now a roaring inferno – between them. For the first time, Ramiq truly worried for her safety. He reached out to seize the blaze once more, but her strength overwhelmed him and the fire surged even more as she wrested control away from him. The fire continued to grow, fed by her panic, and Ramiq could hear the wood in his bedposts popping and cracking from the intense heat even as the smell of smoke began to fill his lungs.

"Tsuga, listen to me! You have to calm down. You have to control this. If you don't, we'll be the ones burning alive, right along with every other person in this building. Get yourself under control! Now!"

Her eyes rolled and she shook as though she were in the throes of a seizure or possessed by some otherworldy being.

"Tsuga!"

But she was gone; she had lost consciousness from the effort it had taken to sustain such a flame. And still the fire blazed, devouring the very magic that held her body together.

Ramiq opened his eyes and brought himself out of the memory. He was more than a little shaken – both from reliving the experience and from the emotions Tsuga's mind flooded him with. His student, however, looked as though she had just seen a ghost.

"I did that?" Her voice sounded strange – weak and frightened, and not at all her own. Ramiq could only nod.

"But I – I have no memory of that. I mean, I remember going, and I remember the lesson. But everything after you told me to look into the flames is just . . . not there. The next thing I remember is waking up . . .."

The young Queen's Mage shook his head, confounded as ever by this declaration. "But I simply don't understand how that could be possible. It's as though your memories have been tampered with; like everything to do with your being a mage has simply been removed. Do you have any other gaps like this?"

Tsuga shrugged, but when Ramiq continued to stare at her sternly, her show of bravado wilted and she let out a sigh. "Yes, of course I do."

"And how far back do they go?"

Tsuga thought long and hard on that one, but finally she shrugged.

"It gets hard to say, after a while, what exactly is missing and what has simply been forgotten. I guess . . . I'm missing most of my thirteenth birthday, and after that, the gaps become fairly frequent."

"What was so significant about that day, I wonder?" Tsuga shrugged, and Ramiq winced as he felt her pang of sadness and regret.

"I wish I knew." Ramiq considered her for a moment, and then spoke.

"Are you sure? Because if you're serious about that, I may be able to help. It will be a lengthy undertaking, but if it is in fact a spell of some sort affecting your memories, then once I figure out how it works, I can start to unravel it."

Tsuga didn't even pause to think. "I'm sure."

"Alright. Then we will begin tomorrow."

Last night had been one of the few through which Tsuga was able to sleep mostly undisturbed by her night terrors. It seemed strange, now that she thought about it, after what had happened with Ramiq yesterday. Although in all honesty, she could not exactly remember what had happened. The emotions remained with her, but the actual events were a bit foggy, as though she were trying to remember a dream.

As Devilsbane set a sedate pace along the road between the Warriors' Compound and the Mages' Complex, Tsuga swayed easily with the horse's ambling gait and tried to remember what had happened.

He thinks there's a spell affecting your memory.

"What? That doesn't make any sense. Wouldn't I know if I were under a spell? Wouldn't you? Wouldn't *he*?"

He didn't say.

Tsuga got the sense that Bane was being somehow evasive, but she wasn't sure why she felt that way. She decided, for the time being at least, not to push the matter.

Ramiq rounded the corner of the apprentices' bath house and saw Tsuga standing in the shade of an oak, leaning casually against the trunk as she idly observed the passers-by. His heart leapt into his throat as he watched her catch sight of him and trace his progress across the yard with her startling hazel eyes. Lyra, who padded alongside him, nudged against his calf.

You like her.

The words startled him so much that he missed a step and was forced to do an odd little hop-skip maneuver to regain his balance. The red fox was undeterred.

You're going soft, Ramiq. When was the last time you tumbled one of those pretty little lads? It's love, Ramiq. Admit it.

The mage looked up again to see Tsuga hiding a smirk at his display of clumsiness, and then found himself ducking his head sheepishly.

She's a student.

Never stopped you before.

Ramiq frowned at the truth of that statement. *She hates me.*

Nonsense. Look at the way she watches you; how her face lights up when she sees you. She may not admit it, but she likes you. The real question is, what are you going to do about it?

Tsuga hid her smile as she saw Ramiq across the small courtyard, and then had to bite back a laugh as he tripped over his guardian, who walked practically on top of his feet. His face turned a bright crimson when he realized that she had seen him, and then paled considerably as he came to a halt in front of her. For one brief, unsettling moment, she thought he was going to move closer – but he merely cleared his throat and gestured for her to find a comfortable patch of ground. By the time they were both settled, he seemed to have regained some composure.

"So far, our approach has been to try to access your magic. Obviously, that hasn't worked. So from here on in, I've decided to try a different tack. A more psychological one. I want to start by seeing if I can detect whatever spell – if that's what it is – is blocking you. Once we find it, I can start working on undoing it."

"But you've healed me before. Been inside my mind. Practically set up camp inside my head. I don't see how you would have missed a spell if it was there."

"Memory spells are tricky," he explained. "If you're not specifically looking for them, or if you don't look in just the right way, you may never know it's there. Especially if the mind mage was particularly skilled. The magic could have shields that turn the attention away. If this is the case the spell will be hard to detect, and even harder to undo."

"But you think you can do it?"

"I'm the Queen's Mage of Sennor. If anyone can do it, *I* can."

Tsuga rolled her eyes at the prideful tone in his voice and couldn't resist undermining his ego – at least a little.

"You're barely older than I am, and got your title through little more than the luck of your birth. You didn't work for it; didn't have to fight for what you have. If someone out there was able to work a spell that has taken you this long to even suspect, what makes you so confident that you'll be able to do all this?"

Ramiq flushed again, and when he spoke she reeled as though from a slap to the face.

"If you think a lifetime of magical training isn't hard work, you are in for a rude awakening, Tsuga Dafrin. I may be young, but I am not inexperienced. And I'm the best hope you've got. If this isn't fixed, it will kill you. So I'd be a little more careful about insulting the person who is trying to save your life if I were you."

Tsuga ducked her head. "I'm sorry."

Ramiq's expression changed to one she couldn't name, and he let out his breath with a gusty sigh.

"Let's just get started."

Ramiq had had an idea slowly taking shape in the back of his mind for a few days now, and as he watched Tsuga duck her head in an uncharacteristic show of submission, he decided that now was as good a time as any to give it a try.

"Since I haven't been able to detect any spells affecting you or your mind directly, I would like to try a little experiment. There is a small possibility that what is causing your block is not actually set into your physical and mental make-up. You may be able to shield against it."

Tsuga looked confused, so he spoke quickly to forestall any questions.

"Think of a magical shield like a suit of armor. It protects you from outside attacks, but if, say, you have an illness or an infection, it won't make that go away."

"Okay, but I can't use magic. How am I supposed to shield?"

Ramiq was growing excited now, and he had to slow himself down so that the words of his explanation wouldn't run one over the other.

"That's just it; magical shielding is only *one* kind. You can build mental shields – which require no magical ability at all – which, in your case, may be enough to weaken the spell's hold on you. Maybe not break it completely, but hopefully this will gain you enough wiggle room to allow you to study magic. It won't be easy, but . . .."

"Nothing ever is. Fine, I'll give it a try. What do I do?"

Tsuga could tell from the way Ramiq's eyes lit with excitement and the change in his posture that this was an idea he felt strongly about, so she decided to humor him despite her doubts. At her acquiescence, Ramiq flashed a bright smile and then settled down into what she had taken to thinking of as his "teacher mode."

"It's a little difficult to explain until you've successfully done it and can understand what you have to do, but I'll try. Basically, you have to close your mind off to anyone or any thing that may be trying to manipulate it. Some do this by imagining themselves inside a sealed room, or closing a door in their mind and locking it. You will have to find a way of visualizing your shield that works for you. And, at least the first time, it will be easier to do if you have someone specific you are trying to push out."

Someone like me.

Tsuga's entire body tensed at the unexpected and overwhelming *pressure* in her mind. Suddenly, she could not think her own thoughts, could not control her own body. Her heart beat and her lungs filled with air not of their own accord, but at someone else's whim. At *his* whim. She tried to form a coherent thought, but her mind was a jumble of emotions and she couldn't seem to find a rock to cling to in the flood of panic. Then–

I'm here.

Tsuga seized on Bane's presence as a drowning man clings to anything that might keep him afloat. She still did not have control of her own body, but at least now the small corner of her mind where her thoughts were still her own was a kind of haven from the overwhelming mental presence of Ramiq. Now she could think.

He had invaded her mind without warning; ambushed her in a way that was meant to unsettle her. But now, she had her wits about her. She didn't *want* him there. She wanted him *out*. So, she tried doing as he'd suggested: she imagined herself surrounded by high, impenetrable walls. When that didn't work, she tried locking herself behind a mental door – to no avail. Finally, in her frustration, she addressed him.

Why isn't it working?

Because I'm resisting you. You have the right idea, but what shields you have managed aren't strong enough to stand up to a gust of wind, let alone a deliberate attack.

Tsuga bristled at the implication that she was weak, and with a great surge of will, she burned him out of her mind with a ring of heat and flame that surged up within her and purged her mind of everything, leaving her alone with nothing but her own thoughts. It felt strangely empty. And then, as she directed her attention outward again, she saw what she had done.

Ramiq had expected her to struggle. He remembered all too well how she had reacted the first time he had invaded her mind. Then, she had nearly cremated two armies in the middle of a raging battle. It seemed that somewhere in the dark recesses of her mind she recalled it as well, because all at once a wall of flame appeared between them and he reeled under a wave of heat so intense that it nearly knocked him backwards.

Abruptly, he was intensely grateful that fire was his strongest elemental magic; he accepted the heat as part of himself and let the flames lick over his body and his clothes until the fabric – enchanted to resist all staining and magical attacks, but still unable to withstand this barrage – was consumed by the inferno before it passed him and expanded outwards, charring over half of the small garden before it died out, leaving a stunned-looking Tsuga staring agape at his naked, heat-flushed body.

"What . . . just happened?"

Despite the destruction of one of his favorite outfits, Ramiq couldn't keep a delighted grin from stealing across his features.

"What just happened is that you shielded yourself, and as a result were able to access your magic. *Now* do you understand why you have to learn to control this?"

Tsuga looked around at the blackened remains of the garden that had sheltered them, and then back at him. Ramiq was suddenly very aware of the grit digging in to his exposed buttocks. He flushed again – this time from embarrassment – and quickly bent light around himself into the illusion of clothing. Tsuga looked startled, and he watched as she blinked a few times as though she didn't quite believe her eyes.

"How . . . how did you do that?"

"It's an illusion. Magic," he added for clarification.

Tsuga's brow knotted, and he could tell that she was trying to wrap her head around this concept. "But if you can do that why not just –"

"Always walk around clothed in nothing but magic?" Tsuga flushed, and Ramiq chuckled slightly at her reaction. "Because I live in the Mages' Complex. Because illusions are stationary; unless I make a conscious effort to move the appearance of clothing with me, it stays put."

To demonstrate, he leaned forward, exposing a hand's width of his bare chest before he leaned back to his former position and the illusion settled over him again.

"And because of mage sight, to everyone here I would still be naked."

She ducked her head in embarrassment, but before Ramiq could steer the conversation to something other than his current level of exposure her head shot up. He could see panic plain on her face.

"Devilsbane! She's –"

"Not gone," Ramiq cut in quickly in an attempt to forestall any more uncontrolled conflagrations. "Only blocked by your shield."

"So as long as I'm shielded, I can't hear or feel her?"

"You just have to let her in."

"How do I do that? Wouldn't that compromise it?"

"Not at all. You can selectively choose to allow someone inside your shields. Think of it like the walls of a fortress, and you control the only gate."

"How?"

"Well, obviously your mental shield is fire. So imagine that your guardian can walk through the flames untouched – but that she is the only one. That should allow her to reside in your mind like normal without weakening your shield."

Tsuga was still struggling to choke back her panic enough that she could listen to Ramiq's words. She managed – barely – to keep her wits about her despite the gaping hole in her heart and mind where the guardian was meant to reside. She forced her breath to come evenly, and pictured the horse that was the other half of her life walking unharmed into the safety provided in the center of the imagined tower of flames. She had a feeling of something *shifting*, and then –

What the hell was that?! Where did you go? I thought you were dead! Are you okay? You're fine. What happened? Why did you do that?!

Tsuga reeled under the sudden flow of words and emotions. Rather than fight them, she simply steeled herself to ride them out. After the initial onslaught, Bane's mind calmed and Tsuga was able to focus on something other than retaining her sanity.

"You really think this is going to work?" Ramiq shrugged at the question and she found herself distracted by the brief flash of his bronze shoulders as they rose above the illusion of clothes and then disappeared again.

"We'll see. So far, you've had trouble remembering any progress in our lessons between one day and the next. Try to keep your shield up until tomorrow's session, and we'll see what happens. If all goes as I hope it will, then tomorrow you can start adding mage shield to your mind shield, and continue to progress from there."

Tsuga felt a feeling of dread begin to form a cold mass in her abdomen, but she knew she had to ask the question which she feared she already knew the answer to.

"Will I have to maintain this shield for the rest of my life? What if I get tired or lose my concentration? What happens when I need to sleep? What if I falter? Will everything I learn simply be forgotten?"

Ramiq's expression was a sympathetic one, but even so his words fell upon her ears like a hammer upon an anvil.

"With time, the shield will become second nature and you won't really have to think about it. But yes, you will likely have to maintain it indefinitely. I do not know what might happen if you allow it to falter, so perhaps it is best that you not do so."

Tsuga fought back a groan with great effort and framed a question. "What about sleep?"

"The shield should maintain while you sleep, unless it comes under direct attack or you somehow deliberately drop it while asleep."

She frowned. "And if that happens?"

"Then we will be no worse off than we were this morning. Now, that's all the time we have today, but I'd like to check your progress this evening. I'll come by the Compound tonight about an hour after nightfall to see how you're doing."

Tsuga absently nodded her consent to his proposed visit as she stood and dusted herself off. As she walked out of the little courtyard, she continued to worry over her shield, testing it and pouring more strength into it, imagining the flames burning hotter and higher in her defense.

After having spent nearly half of her life on the road without any place she could truly call home, Tsuga had grown used to living in a state of perpetual filth. A bath in anything other than a frigid stream was unheard of for a mercenary; a stable boy was lucky to have time for a quick dousing while watering his charges. She had lived under such conditions off and on for over a decade before she had taken on the responsibility of training Sennor's new recruits. With this duty, she had been given a roof and room of her own, complete with a copper basin large enough to submerge fully half of her body comfortably.

At first she had been reluctant to indulge herself by taking any such baths, but one of the older servants, upon seeing the effects of hard training and fitful sleep, had taken to drawing her a steaming tub scented with skin-softening oils and pain-relieving herbs. Though the gray haired woman had all but thrown Tsuga into that first basin, the Weaponsmistress had, since then, come to love the woman for her thoughtfulness. She now looked forward to her nightly soaks as a way to relax and soothe her tired body after a long day of administering bruises and lessons. Tonight was no different.

Just a quick soak, she promised herself. She still had nearly half an hour before Ramiq had said he would check on her, and the eucalyptis-scented water – a very expensive oil imported from the far southeastern reaches of Maelvin – steamed lightly, promising a blissfully warm temperature. Eager to submerge herself, she stripped off her sweaty, dirt-covered uniform, carefully removed and stored her personal arsenal of weapons, and lowered herself slowly into water just short of scalding hot.

Ramiq frowned at himself as he observed his reflection in the silver-backed glass that showed him his own mirror image. It was too bad that his favorite gold-and-brown robes now drifted as ashes on the wind. He felt slightly less than stunning in the pale blue-and-lavender robes he had finally settled on. Oh, he knew he was striking, to be certain, but still somewhat short of the stunning figure he preferred to present.

You love those robes. You're just nervous because you're going to see *her*.

Why should that make me nervous? I see Tsuga every day.

Yes, as her teacher. But you're going to check on her now, outside of your lessons, as just Ramiq, not as Queen's Mage Ramiq. You feel vulnerable.

Ramiq made an irritated sound deep in his throat as he turned to glare at the little vixen where she lounged on an overstuffed pillow almost half the size of Ramiq's bed, but she was not to be deterred.

She's already seen you naked, you know. Your outfit is hardly going to make a difference now.

Ramiq scoffed and strode briskly across his room and out the door without looking back. As he closed the door, he felt an immense surge of satisfaction as he heard Lyra yelp from her sudden dousing in icy water. No doubt he'd get an earfull later tonight for that prank, but she *had* brought it on herself, after all.

Under ordinary circumstances, Ramiq was loathe to walk any measurable distance – he greatly preferred to simply place himself wherever he desired to be by way of his magic. He doubted, however, that Tsuga would appreciate being popped in on in such a fashion. And so, out of consideration for her dislike of magic – and his fondness for his own skin – he set his feet upon the path that led east to the Warriors' Compound.

"Tsuga?" Ramiq knocked a little more firmly this time, but still there was no answer.

Lyra's tirade during the first part of his walk had ensured that he had blocked the fox from his mind until she calmed down. As a result, he now had no one to consult on his best course of action.

She knew the time. Surely . . ..

He opened his senses slightly, expanding his awareness of the people around him. He could sense her on the other side of the door. She was not under any duress, which relieved him somewhat, but she also didn't seem to be aware of his presence. Curious, he tried the door and found that it swung inward easily at his touch. Unable to stop himself, he stepped into the room and gently closed the heavy wooden door behind himself.

The room was tidy – almost sterile – though Ramiq wasn't sure why he should be so surprised at that. Tsuga led her life with such military precision that it only made sense she should do the same with her living quarters. He had been in this room several times before, and had seen the personality of the chambers change according to each new inhabitant.

The large king-sized bed from the last resident was gone, replaced by a standard-issue bunk like those in the trainees' barracks. In fact, most of her furniture was the standard issue found in each room of her Warriors' Compound. The wardrobe was polished and discreetly closed. The trunk at the foot of her neatly made bed was locked, and the immense desk – the one thing out of place in contrast to the other items in the room – was clear of any stacks of paper or other miscellaneous clutter.

Ramiq took all of this in with one casual look before his attention was drawn to the corner of the room concealed by the dressing screen. A bulky shadow spied through the opaque fabric hinted at a bathing tub, and as Ramiq heard the soft lapping of water, he realized that he had inadvertently intruded on a private moment. He flushed deeply at this insight and rapidy turned back to the door. His hand had scarcely touched the knob when a knife handle seemed to materialize in the door frame mere inches left of his head. The blade's handle was not the only thing trembling as he turned.

There she stood, as unabashed at her wet nakedness as she was at the way her body responded to the slight chill in the late spring air. The twin to the knife that had stopped him dangled from her right hand, and she looked none too pleased to see him.

"Do you make a habit of entering people's private chambers uninvited?"

Ramiq flushed at the insult and tried – but failed – not to look at her hard, glistening body. She was tall and slender, and he could not spy the slightest bit of softness on her; she was all lean muscle and quiet power. Her skin – pale where her clothing hid it away from the sun and weather, but leather-brown where it had been left exposed – was riddled with scars, new cuts, and fresh bruises that told the story of her life better than any words ever could.

"No. I mean, I knocked, but –"

"I didn't answer, so you just thought you'd let yourself in?"

She snorted, and then her eyes narrowed as she peered at him.

"Like what you see? Get an eye-full now; it may well be the *last* thing you ever see."

"Look, I'm sorry; I didn't mean to intrude. I just wanted to make sure you were okay. When I realized, I was going to leave, but you –"

Tsuga rolled her eyes and tossed her weapon casually onto the bed. Ramiq relaxed slightly, though he was still wary; he knew she could kill him with nothing more than her bare hands, if she decided to. He wasn't sure he could bring himself to magically restrain her, if it came to that.

"I'm not going to kill you. You're the Queen's Mage."

Her voice dripped with scorn the way her body dripped with fragrant water. She turned her back to him, providing a new view of her sleek body, and retrieved a towel from where she had slung it over the top of the screen. Once she had wrapped this securely around herself, she turned to face him again. He couldn't seem to tear his eyes away from her, even now. If he had thought she hadn't noticed, her next words dashed any such hopes.

"You know, usually you're supposed to pretend you're not looking. Not stare with your mouth open like some befuddled simpleton."

Ramiq promptly snapped his mouth shut and averted his gaze, though he could still feel her eyes as she crossed the room to stand before him.

"You came. You see that I am alright. My shield has – so far – held. So. Why are you still in my chambers, Ramiq?"

The sound of his name spoken in her voice, husky as it was from years of yelling orders across noisy battlefields, stirred him. He did his best to ignore the highly inconvenient pressure in his loins.

"Well, I – that is to say, I wanted – I had hoped, rather –"

He hadn't been so tongue-tied by a naked woman since he was a young lad barely gaining his whiskers. Apalled at his own clumsiness, he forced himself to look up and meet her gaze – only to find that she stood mere inches from him. When he breathed in, he caught the scent of eucalyptus on her skin. Before he knew what was happening, the small space between them was gone. His hands tangled in her short, wet hair, and his entire body seemed to hum as though he stood in the midst of a lightning storm.

At last, he had found the one thing on her that was soft and yielding: her lips.

Tsuga had woken at the click of the door closing to a tepid bath and wrinkled skin. She was immediately aware of another presence in the room, and she listened for sounds of movement so that she could locate the intruder. Mentally cursing herself for not having clothes – or at least her towel – closer to hand, Tsuga slipped out of the tub as quietly as she could manage.

She winced at the noise made by the water, but when she heard no reaction from her unwanted guest, she moved quietly to retrieve her throwing knives from their rack on the wall.

When she emerged from behind the screen, she was able to recognize the shape of Ramiq even from behind; unable to resist the temptation to teach him a lesson, she loosed the knife in her left hand and watched in smug satisfaction as the mage froze and stared at the weapon, which had hit exactly where she had aimed it: just to the side of his head.

It wasn't until he turned and started gaping at her that she recalled her current state of undress.

Well, nothing for it, now.

She proceeded to thoroughly reprimand him for his actions, but the entire time she had to fight the urge to cover herself. As soon as she could do so without seeming self-conscious, Tsuga turned and retrieved her towel, grateful to at least have some measure of modesty restored. Eager to truly drive her point home, she moved as close to him as possible, using her proximity to intimidate him further.

"Why are you still in my chambers, Ramiq?"

He stammered out a jumble of scarcely comprehensible syllables, and before she knew what had happened he was pressed against her. Her entire body began to tremble from feelings she scarcely dared to aknowledge as his hands gripped her hair, and where his body pressed against hers, her skin warmed as though by fire. She lost herself for a long moment before coherent thought began to return and she was able to push him away and break the contact.

"What –" the word barely came out, and she had to pause a moment to swallow before she could try again. "What are you doing?"

He was flushed, and she could tell that he was having as much trouble framing a full thought as she was.

"I – I just . . . I was just . . .." He gusted out a frustrated breath. "I'm sorry."

Her lips still tingled from the contact, and as much as she wanted to kiss him again, she held herself stubbornly apart.

"It's alright. Look Ramiq, you're a nice enough guy and everything, but you're the Queen's Mage. I'm the Weaponsmistress. It's not really appropriate."

Ramiq wilted at her words and backed away a step. Her heart went out to him, but she knew this was for the best. He was her teacher, and one of the most important people in Sennor. Nothing could ever happen between them. Knowing that hurt, but she had never been one to quell at doing something just because it was difficult.

"No, no of course not. You're right, I know." He sighed, and the pained look on his face tore at something deep inside her. "So, what? We just pretend it never happened?"

Tsuga managed a small smile and reached out to lay a comforting hand on his arm. "I think that's for the best."

Ramiq nodded, and she could see that he was having as much trouble getting his emotions under control as she was hers.

"Then I guess I should be going."

As he reached behind himself and turned the door knob, Tsuga had to clench her hands at her side to keep from moving to stop him. Instead, she placed one hand on the door and held it open for him as he backed through it.

"I'll see you tomorrow, Ramiq." To cushion the blow, she added, "Thank you for your concern."

She remained in the doorway and watched him retreat for a long moment – until she noticed one of her young students observing her.

"Weaponsmistress?" Tsuga stiffened and drew herself up to her full height as she fell back into her authoritative role.

"Can I help you, Jayden?"

The girl flushed and shook her head. "No, ma'am."

Tsuga watched as she beat a hasty retreat, and then backed into her own room and closed the door. She paused for a moment to rest her head against the comforting solidity of the cool oak and closed her eyes. She was still trembling – she told herself it was from the chill air on her damp skin, but she felt as though she had been emotionally beaten and then run through a laundry mangle. She felt sick and weak, and it was all she could do to cross the room and collapse onto her bed.

She felt his hands on her, and her entire body ached with pleasure. She leaned against him and breathed in his smell as his lips explored her flesh, making her skin flush with arousal. Sweat broke out on her face, and she became slick with moisture as he pressed against her. The warmth in her belly increased, and it grew difficult to breathe.

Tsuga woke in a fit of coughing and fought her way free of sweat-soaked and tangled sheets. Her over-enthusiastic efforts sent her crashing to the floor, where she lay stunned for a moment. It was easier to breathe down there, and as her lungs cleared and her mind woke, she realized why.

"Goddess' tits; not again!" She groaned, and then coughed again as smoke filled her nostrils.

With an effort, she snuffed out the flames, leeching the energy from them and taking it into herself until the fire died down. As she did this, she crossed to the window on the north wall and threw it open. Cool, clean air rushed into the room as the smoke billowed out, and Tsuga followed it by climbing through the opening and stepping down onto the dew-covered grass. She walked far enough away that she breathed clean air and then sank to the ground and leaned back against the cool wood of the barracks' wall.

In the two weeks since she had learned how to shield her mind, this had become an almost-nightly occurrence. Since she had made contact with her magic, incidents of uncontrolled magical outbursts had become distressingy common. It didn't help that her dreams were filled with Ramiq, nor that she hadn't been able to sleep for more than an hour or two at a time lately. Tsuga sighed as she fought back tears and dropped her head to her hands.

I can't keep doing this.

Two weeks had passed since Tsuga had broken through whatever spell or mental block had prevented her from progressing with her magic. In that time, her skill had grown in leaps and bounds. She breezed so easily through lessons in mage sight, mage shield, and the basic exercises he had set her that he could scarcely believe he taught the same woman. The only explanation he could muster was that her subconscious remembered whatever previous training she had received, even if she wasn't aware of it.

While he had thrilled to see her growing so quickly magically, it pained him every day to have to see her and speak to her, knowing all the while he would never be permitted to hold her. He couldn't sleep for dreaming of her, and even the delicious sweets he favored tasted bland and unappealing. He had lost a considerable amount of weight – he'd never been particularly bulky to begin with – and the dark circles under his eyes had raised so many questions that he had taken to wrapping himself in an illusion of health each day. While it wouldn't hold up to close scrutiny, it served to satisfy a casual glance.

Tsuga looked even worse than he felt, and her health seemed to decline further each day. He longed to take her into his arms, to heal her, to make everything better and make all of her pain go away – but he knew he couldn't. She wouldn't allow it.

Unable to banish thoughts of her – or dreams of that kiss – from his mind, he had tried for a few days to distract himself with whatever lovelies he could tempt into his bed. When he had found himself unable to hold his arousal one night, he had given up trying to forget her. The embarrassment had been such that he had not sought overnight company since.

Now, he lay on his back and watched the lights he had woven into the canopy of his bed tonight swirl lazily overhead. Usually the muted colors soothed him, but this evening they only sent his mind down paths best left unexplored. He gusted out a frustrated sigh and threw an arm over his eyes to block out the sight.

A knock on his door startled him, and he sat up as he expanded his senses to see who would be calling on him in the middle of the night. His first thought was that it was another emercency; the last time he had been so summoned, it was to put out a fire Tsuga had inadvertently started in her sleep and did not know how to extinguish. But she had mastered that lesson easily, and his sleep – or lack thereof – had not been similarly disturbed since.

A cursory scan of the surface emotions of his visitor revealed a sense of urgency in his guest, but not one of panic. Curious now, Ramiq rose from his bed and pulled on the silk robe that he kept nearby for such occasions – it wrapped around and belted loosely about his hips, making the simple garment one that was easily donned in a hurry. He was just finishing the knot as he opened the door.

"Tsuga?"

He was surprised – shocked, really – to see her, of all people, standing in his doorway, hand poised for another knock.

"Oh."

She dropped her arm and stood looking at him so long that he wondered fleetingly if perhaps he was dreaming after all.

"What are you doing here?"

She was dressed only in a well-worn and loose-fitting tunic that just brushed the top of her knees. She had no shoes, and from what he could see, she was uncharacteristically unarmed. She smelled like smoke, and he knew that it must be of her own making, for her to have come to him in the middle of the night like this.

"May I come in?"

"Oh. Yes. Of course."

Ramiq moved aside and she stepped into the room. She scarcely waited until he had closed the door before the words started tumbling out.

"I can't do this. I tried – I really did – but the dreams, and the lessons, and having to be around you and see you and talk to you . . .. I can't do it any more."

Ramiq blinked in surprise at the jumbled rush of words, and his heart leapt with a hope he scarcely dared to entertain at hearing his own thoughts so exactly spoken.

"Slow down. Come in and have a seat. What's going on?"

Tsuga shook her head, and it was with some alarm that Ramiq realized her eyes shone with unshed tears. He had never seen her cry before.

"I can't. I can't stay. Not any more. I just came to tell you that I can't do this any more. I have to get away. I'm resigning. I'm leaving tomorrow before first light. I just – I had to tell you in person."

The bottom dropped out of his world, and Ramiq reeled so badly from her words that he had to reach out and steady himself against the wall.

"What? Why? Why would you – where will you – what?"

Tsuga exhaled shakily, and as he watched tears dampen her cheeks, his arms ached to reach out and hold her.

"I don't know. But I have to. I can't sleep. I barely eat. I'm not able to give my students the kind of attention they deserve. All I can think about is you. I have to get away. Maybe if I leave, I'll be able to forget –"

"Forget me?" Ramiq tried not to let the pain her words caused him creep into his voice, but as he watched the worry lines on her face deepen, he knew he had failed. "Is that really what you want?"

Her voice was almosted choked by emotion, and he had to strain to hear her when she responded. "No. But what else can I do?"

"You could stay."

Tsuga laughed, but there was no mirth in the sound. "Not like this."

Ramiq shook his head. "You're right. Not like this. But –"

"Ramiq, we can't. You *know* we can't. And I can't be around you, knowing that."

"Well, by the Goddess, why not?" Anger crept into his voice, and she winced at the increase in volume. He took a deep breath and quieted himself.

"Why *can't* we be together? It's not like we're enemies. We're both adults. Whose business is it but ours?" Now he did reach out to her, but he forced himself to only place his hands on her shoulders. "Why are you so afraid to be happy?"

Tsuga had promised herself that she would get through this confrontation without faltering, but at the sight of Ramiq's pain, she felt her resolve waver. She didn't have an answer for his question – not really – but she knew she had to tell him something.

"I'm not afraid, I just –"

"Then whey are you running away from this?"

She tensed at this implication of weakness and pulled away from him slightly, all too conscious of his hands on her shoulders.

"Because if I don't, I might –"

"What? Be happy? I'm not going to hurt you, Tsu. Just seeing you like this is killing me; I don't think I could survive knowing I caused you pain. Please, don't fight this."

The desperation in his voice was plain, and she realized that she was shaking from the effort of resisting him.

Devilsbane – who had thus far remained blessedly silent on this matter – chose now to throw in her opinion.

You're the only thing stopping you. You do realize that, right? No one but you objects to this. No one would.

Tsuga's mouth dropped open at her guardian's words, and she snapped it shut again as soon as she realized that it had. There really was nothing she could say to that. Bane had a disturbing way of cutting directly to the heart of a matter.

With her guardian's words echoing in her mind, Tsuga looked at Ramiq's disheveled hair and agonized expression, and she felt something inside her give way. Before she could change her mind, she took the step needed to close the distance between them and pulled his head to her so that she could kiss him, just as she had been longing to since that fateful bath-time visit.

For once, Tsuga's thoughts did not drive her to distraction. She wasn't worrying about consequences or what anyone would think; she was simply immersed in the moment. She had no thoughts aside from the way his proximity made her feel and the thrill she felt at his touch.

When at last she was able to pull away and break the contact, she found herself breathless and flushed. His eyes were lit with a fire that made her blood run hotter. He spoke, and his voice was as breathless as she felt.

"I haven't been able to think about anything else. I can't sleep, I – I can't get you out of my mind. I think I love you."

Tsuga frowned slightly at this, confused by his choice of words. "You think?"

She immediately wanted the question back when she saw the agonized look cross his features again.

"I mean, how do you know, really? It's not like I've ever *been* in love before. I don't know what it feels like. But I don't have any other name for the way I feel."

Tsuga tried to swallow around the lump in her throat, but the attempt only made the tightness in her chest worse.

"I don't have any other name for it, either." Ramiq broke into a grin, and she found herself smiling in response even before she realized he intended to kiss her again. This time, it was Ramiq who pulled away first.

"Will you stay?"

Tsuga let out her breath in a rush and considered his hopeful expression and the comfort of his arms around her. "Well, those kids really do need a master to stay for longer than a few months. I suppose I *should* stay . . .."

Ramiq shook his head. "No. I meant . . . will you stay the night? With me?"

Tsuga, startled by this proposal, pulled away from him slightly as she felt the same old doubts gaining strength again.

"It's the middle of the night, Ramiq. I have to start the day's lesson in a few hours. You have your own students, and I'm really not sure it's a good idea for me to stay here . . .."

I can handle the lesson for the morning. It won't hurt you to take a morning off. In fact, I insist. You're barely functioning as it is. Take a break.

Her expression must have changed as Bane spoke, because Ramiq's face was as open and tender as she had ever seen it.

"I have other mages who can teach the morning's lessons. Your students can surely survive one morning without you. Just stay. Please."

The last was scarcely a whisper, and Tsuga felt her resolve waver – and then finally crumble when he reached up to brush her hair off of a cheek stained with soot.

"I suppose I can stay for a few hours . . .."

His smile quieted any doubts she still harbored, and as he pulled her in for another kiss, she felt her heart swell with happiness.

"The apprentice's exam is fairly simple." Ramiq stopped walking and turned to face his pupil, causing her to stop short in surprise. Tsuga rolled her eyes, and he smiled at her attitude.

"Your idea of simple is quite different than mine."

"No, really. All you have to do is demonstrate adequate skill in mage shield, mage sight, and basic elemental control."

"Basic elemental control?"

Ramiq smiled. "Creating a small fire and showing that you can maintain it, change its size, and extinguish it without losing control."

"Oh. Well, that does sound simple enough."

"It is."

Ramiq gestured around him to the bare patch of earth on which they stood. "This is the testing arena. In the case that a student does lose control, this arena is easy to shield because it is so used to being used this way, and there is nothing within it to be damaged. Now, let us begin with your sight. I will write a series of symbols like the ones used to give direction here in the Complex, and you will tell me what they are."

He waited until she had had sufficient time to clear her mind and engage her sight, and then he began. The skill of emblazoning symbols was not particularly complicated, and most mages were capable of learning it. It was, in fact, one of the abilities tested in the journeyman's exam. The first symbol he drew was the common cartogropher's mark for north. When Tsuga correctly identified this, he produced in turn the pictographic symbols for fire, wisdom, and strength. The last image was not actually part of the exam, but he felt his heart swell as she flushed in pleasure and named the symbol for love.

A handful of days had passed since she had come to him in the night, and they had not shared a bed since – even that night, both had been so exhausted and so terribly relieved to have at last acknowledged their feelings that they had simply fallen into a blissful slumber. In the interveneing time, they had restricted themselves to stolen moments at the end of their lessons; Tsuga insisted that her students must come first, and though he understood and respected her sense of responsibility, he longed to spend more time with her.

"Very good. Now, I can see that you have maintained your mage shield quite well. I am going to test its effectiveness by probing you, as I did in your lessons."

She nodded, and Ramiq felt an upwelling of pride at the calm and confident way she waited for him to proceed. It seemed to him that in the past weeks, she had become a far more stable and self-assured mage. He was used to seeing such poise from her when she had a weapon in her hands, but this new-found strength in magic seemed in some way to complete her. It rounded her out as a person and only served to increase his level of attraction to her. And it had been *he* who had brought her to this point. She was by far the most challenging student he had ever taught, but because of those early difficulties, she was also his most rewarding.

He examined her shielding closely, looking for cracks or weak points. He probed at it – gently at first, and then with more force. He examined the seal she had placed on it to tie it off, and pulled and poked at this as well.

"Good. A good beginner-level shield. In time, you will learn to layer your shields and create ones of varying strength and design, but this is a solid beginning."

She only nodded at his praise; any other student might smile or show some sign of pride, but not Tsuga. She was far too aware of the long road still ahead of her to enjoy any thrill at this small accomplishment.

"Now, let's see your elemental control. Start with a head-sized flame."

She did as she was told, and Ramiq observed the fire for several minutes to make sure that it held strong without pulsating or flickering. When he was satisfied, he nodded.

"Alright, good. Now, take it down to the size of a candle flame without letting it go out. Good. Now slowly increase it in volume until it is roughly man-sized."

She did so, and though he could see that maintaining such careful control strained her from the way she frowned and furrowed her brow and the way her body tensed, the flame held steady without popping or crackling. He made sure that she was able to maintain it for an adequate amount of time, and then nodded his approval. No sooner had she earned this gesture than he noticed that she had paled considerably. Although the air was not all that warm, he could see that she had begun sweating profusely.

"Alright. Now, extinguish the flame as you have been taught."

When she had first demonstrated this skill, Tsuga had snuffed out the flame with a wrench of will and a twist of power that had left a knotted blight in the flow of magic that *he* had then had to untangle. After that incident, he had made sure to teach her the proper way to remove the power from a flame and allow it to either flow into herself or back into the world without causing such a disruption.

He watched her do this now, critically considering her technique. The flame did not precisely shrink, but rather seemed to dim until it simply ceased to exist. The size of the blaze had been considerable, and by now Tsuga was straining to maintain her control. As her endurance grew – she had already reached her full strength, though she lacked the discipline to use it properly – this process would become so effortless as to occur almost instantaneously. For her current skill level, though, it was a disciplined and respectable showing. Ramiq grinned and stepped forward to embrace and kiss her.

"Congratulations, Apprentice."

Tsuga smiled as Ramiq released her and used her sleeve to wipe the sweat from her brow. The trial had been exhausting, but this sense of accomplishment was well worth a little fatigue. When he held out one of the honey-covered sweet buns favored by the mages, she accepted the messy treat gratefully.

"Thank you. So, what now?"

"Now, you are an official student of the Mages' Complex. Your training can begin in earnest."

Tsuga shook her head and spoke around a mouthful of the pastry. "What do you mean, 'in earnest?' I have students to see to, Ramiq. I can't just come practice magic tricks whenever you want me to."

"I don't expect you to."

It sounded to her as though the man was trying to backtrack, but she decided to let it slide. "Then what *do* you expect?" She swallowed with some difficulty – the buns really needed a glass of milk to wash them down – and promptly took another bite.

"Well, maybe you could attend a couple of the group lessons. It may benefit you to work with other fire mages, and maybe even to learn from a couple of the other instructors."

Tsuga shook her head. "That's all well and good, but like I said –"

"It can't interfere with your duties. Yes, I know. Would you just trust me?"

She flushed as she nodded and used the excuse of licking the remains of the honey off of her fingers to regain her composure.

"Alright . . . ."

Ramiq smiled and moved to pull her into his arms again. She let him, and smiled into eyes that were on a level with hers.

"Now, I have a proposal."

Tsuga quirked an eyebrow suspiciously, but decided to play along. "And what might that be?"

"Dinner. Tonight. Just the two of us. That won't take away from your students, will it?"

She smiled at him and shook her head.

"No, I suppose not. What did you have in mind?"

"Why don't you let me worry about that? How early can you be ready?"

She considered his words, more than a little curious now.

"Once the sun sets it gets too dark to do much, so that's usually when I dismiss them. By the time I get cleaned up . . . an hour after dark?"

Ramiq smiled and kissed her again. She was breathless by the time he pulled away.

"It's a date. Now go on; your precious students are waiting for you."

Tsuga made a face at his teasing tone, but in the end she knew he had a point. She gave him one final kiss, unable to resist the opportunity to do so, and then pulled free of his grasp and turned to mount Devilsbane for the short ride to the opposite side of the castle.

"I'll see you tonight, Ramiq."

It was times like this that Tsuga's utilitarian approach to her wardrobe was somewhat regrettable. She stood, wrapped only in her towel, and considered the clothes hanging before her. Her every-day wear was so worn and stained that none of it was good for anything but hard physical labor. Her dress uniforms weren't exactly appropriate for a date. And she really *had* nothing else to choose from. She was on the verge of turning away from her closet in exasperation when there was a knock at her door. She stole a glance at her window and made a sound of disgust.

"You're early. I'm not ready yet!"

"Mistress?"

Tsuga was surprised to hear the voice of the middle-aged woman who served the Warriror's Compound as a housekeeper.

"Come in, Ulna." Tsuga turned to greet the woman with a smile that faltered when Ulna started to drop into a curtsy and only belatedly remembered that Tsuga had asked her to dispense with such nonsense. "What is it?"

"Mistress, a package was left for you." Tsuga quirked an eyebrow, perplexed by this.

"By whom?"

"I do not know, Mistress."

"Leave it on the desk. Thank you, Ulna."

The older woman did as Tsuga bade her and departed without further comment. Tsuga crossed the room and considered the package warily. She wasn't expecting anything, and in her line of work it was as likely to try and kill her as to be an actual gift. Tucked on top under the simple twine knot was a small, folded piece of parchment with her name on it, which she removed and opened gingerly.

I suspected you may not have anything appropriate to wear tonight. Please accept this gift; I hope I got the right size. Ramiq.

Wary – but undeiniably curious – Tsuga cut through the string with her belt dagger and pulled back the simple paper that covered the bundle.

I could almost wish it had been a threat on my life, she thought in dismay as she pulled out the dress and unrolled a simple gown made of a durable homespun cotton dyed to an olive green. If she knew Ramiq, no doubt the color would bring out some supposedly marvelous feature of hers; her eyes, or her skin tone, or some other such silliness.

The lines of the gown were plain – a simple A-line cut with a square neckline and long sleeves that looked as though they would be just loose enough to allow for the daggers she kept strapped to her wrists. The skirt was divided for riding. As she examined the garment, she had to admit that as dresses went, it wasn't too bad.

At least try it on.

Tsuga rolled her eyes at Bane's encouragement, but reluctantly did as her guardian suggested.

I have to admit, it's comfortable . . ..

He obviously tried to find something you would be satisfied with.

As Tsuga pulled on her boots – freshly polished – and dropped the skirt back over them, she realized that Bane was right. The color, the fabric, even the cut of the dress all seemed to have been picked out specifically with her needs in mind. Even her clunky footwear looked delicate and feminine now that the dress mostly concealed her boots from sight. She proceeded to buckle on her sword belt – which she found sat where it should without causing the dress to bunch or snag at all – and strap on her other favorite weapons as she would with her normal wardrobe.

There was no reflecting glass in her room – her own choice – but she certainly felt more like herself than she had expected to in such a getup.

Well, I guess this is as good as I could have hoped for.

The ordeal of getting dressed and armed had taken up the remainder of her extra time. As this realization dawned on her, there came another knock on the door. She took a deep breath to settle her churning stomach and crossed to open it.

Tsuga opened the door expecting to see Ramiq – knowing the mage, he would be decked out in some flamboyant costume in colors similar to the plain green shade of her own dress. Instead, she saw . . . nothing. There was simply nothing there. Had she only imagined the knock?

She closed the door and turned back to her tidy room as she wondered what could be keeping Ramiq. Even as the question crossed her mind, a glint of color caught her eye. She walked the three strides to her desk and picked up the slip of parchment on which Ramiq had scrawled his note. Under his name, where before the paper had been blank, was one of the many symbols she recognized from her mage training, shining in a rainbow of colors that brought to mind the multi-hued signature of Ramiq's magic.

South. There was nothing else, though she checked the card thoroughly – and the remnants of the packaging as well. At last, she let out a sigh of frustration.

Fine, she thought loudly, trying to push the words through the fortified mental barrier she had built and all the way to Ramiq, wherever he was. *I'll play along.*

She crossed to her door again and opened it with a yank so that she could storm through it before pulling it closed behind herself with somewhat more force than was strictly necessary. She strode out into the night and set her feet on the path leading south around the castle.

She had no idea how far she was supposed to walk, but now that she had an inkling of what Ramiq was up to, she proceeded with her mage senses on high alert and watched for any other such magical displays. As it happened, she didn't have to walk very far at all before another small symbol materialized on the dirt path before her. *Water.*

Water? She paused for a moment where she stood and stared down at the three stacked squiggly lines that were the simplest depiction of the word. There was only one major body of water that ran through the city: a small tributary of the larger river that flowed into the ocean some hundreds of miles away. It flowed right through the middle of the city, then bent to run along the southwestern wall that surrounded the castle. Somewhat mystified by what he could possibly have in store for the evening, Tsuga shook her head and set off with considerably more purpose than she had had before.

She was nearing the river when yet another symbol appeared, hovering in the air less than a stride in front of her. She stopped dead and frowned slightly at this new apparition. *Bridge.* This was somewhat more problematic than the previous symbols; there were numerous bridges that spanned the small river, located all along its length.

"Which one?" she muttered in frustration, only to have the symbol shimmer and change before her very eyes.

"Follow? I've been following you all this way. This is growing tiresome, Ramiq."

She felt a little silly, speaking to a magic-forged symbol that only she could see, but as though in response to her tone, the apparition flared brighter and began moving away.

"What in the –" The floating pictograph paused about three strides away from her and, curious, Tsuga took a step towards it. It retreated another pace. Tsuga let out a sigh of frustration and set off to follow the blasted little thing.

Ramiq had fretted a great deal about every aspect of their first official date, from what he would wear to where they would go.

Of course, he couldn't simply show up at her room. He was determined to leave a lasting impression, and so he had decided to play to his two greatest strengths: magic and panache. So, when it came the appointed time, Ramiq triggered the first in the series of spells he had prepared. After that, it was only a matter of waiting for the proper time to activate each in succession until at last Tsuga reached the location he had chosen.

Had Ramiq not been on high alert waiting for her, he might have had no warning of her approach. She made almost no sound as she walked along the narrow dirt path beside the river, and at the particular moment when she rounded the corner that would have brought her into his line of sight, his back was turned. He sensed her, though; the feeling of her presence was unmistakable, and as he turned to face her he broke into a wide smile to see that she had accepted his gift.

He made a mental note to thank Lyra for that; the fox had refuted his desire for something more colorful and flamboyant, and had insisted that certain accommodations be made. Now, as he watched how Tsuga moved towards him, he was glad he had taken his guardian's advice.

Tsuga had, of course, come armed to the teeth.

Can't think of any other woman who brings over a dozen weapons to a date, he mused as she drew nearer. She moved with a quiet grace born from the intimate knowledge of the capabilities of her own body. The light fabric of the dress swayed with each long stride, an effect that flattered her movements and made her seem more feminine.

The look of irritation on her face, however, somewhat spoiled the effect. As she drew near she opened her mouth to speak, but Ramiq held out a hand to forestall her.

"I know what you're going to say, and I'm sorry I wasn't able to meet you, but I needed more time to prepare."

Tsuga crossed her arms over her chest and jutted her chin out in defiance.

"Why not just come out and tell me where to meet you?"

Ramiq frowned slightly. "You didn't notice the connection, did you?"

Tsuga scoffed. "What connection?"

"Don't you recognize where we are?"

"Of course I do. This is the White Lilly crossing, named for the flowering weeds that can't be cleared from the waters here."

Ramiq shook his head. "You really don't remember, do you?"

"Remember *what*, Ramiq?"

"I was standing on this very spot the first time I ever laid eyes on you."

Her expression changed slightly, though her voice was still full of exasperation as she spoke. "Well that's a sweet sentiment, but how was I supposed to know that? I'd never seen you until I took up my position at the Compound. Not aside from my dreams, at least . . .."

She flushed slightly, presumably at the content of those dreams. And no wonder; if she had seen anything like his own nighttime visions, she had good reason to color in embarrassment.

"I – I suppose that didn't occur to me –"

Now it was his turn to blush. He had in fact seen her several times before that day, but she persisted in denying all such encounters. The time he spoke of, though, was truly his own private moment. He had been standing near this bridge when she had first met Midan, back on her first visit to the capital city of Sennor. The sight of her had nearly stopped his heart.

"Until I saw you standing right over there," and he pointed, "I thought I was losing my mind, dreaming of you each night."

She was giving him a look he couldn't quite identify, and he found it difficult to meet her gaze under such an intent stare.

"I hadn't recalled it until just now, but on the road approaching Sennorra for that first time was when my dreams of you began. It seemed that the nearer I drew to the city, the more vivid they became. What is there that could do such a thing – make me dream of you without ever seeing you or knowing you even existed?"

Ramiq really had no way of answering her, because in fact they *had* had an encounter before either of them had been so haunted. He could only shrug helplessly and try to change the subject.

"Well, shall we begin our date?"

Tsuga looked perplexed when he extended a hand to her, but she took it all the same.

With her hand in his Ramiq stepped aside, and only when he gestured behind him did the scene he had concealed reveal itself to her. She couldn't help but gasp in surprise. Small lights played upon the surface of the water and dazzled her eyes as she took in the blanket spread on the riverbank and the meal laid out upon the fabric. More of the tiny golden mage-lights hovered in the air and on the grass around the scene, casting a soft enchanted glow over it all.

"Ramiq, it's – it's lovely."

She moved towards the blanket and gave a delighted laugh when a few of the lights moved to surround her as she walked. She turned back to him with a smile, only to see an expression on his face for which she had no name.

"It pales in comparison to you."

She flushed with pleasure at his words. Though she found it hard to believe anyone could find her attractive, the sincerity in Ramiq's voice and smile was undeniable. He moved to stand beside her, and she leaned against him and basked in the warm feelings bestirred by his proximity – which were further inflamed when he wrapped his arms around her. They stood like this for some moments before Ramiq spoke again in her ear.

"Are you hungry?"

Tsuga reluctantly broke their embrace and moved to sit on the blanket, only to find that her usual choice of positions was made highly inappropriate by her divided skirts. She made a sound of disgust and instead folded her legs to the side and tried to arrange the skirt discreetly. Ramiq came and sat beside her, and her discomfort was soon forgotten as he offered her a plate.

Tsuga was accustomed to simple fare; she had spent most of her life eating a soldier's rations and what meals she could catch and cook for herself. Bread was not a luxury she enjoyed often, and neither were the succulent-looking cuts of meat on the dish he held out to her.

She smiled as she took the platter of meats from him and selected a couple of slices for her own trencher, flipping them onto it with the use of the small table dagger she kept on her belt. She was somewhat surprised to see Ramiq produce a dagger of his own, though not at all shocked to note that it was excessively ornate. She hid her smile at this observation by reaching for one of the rolls, and when she looked at Ramiq again she was able – barely – to keep her mirth in check.

"You seem to have gone to a great deal of trouble here, Ramiq."

He made such a show of waving the implication away that Tsuga had to laugh.

"Nonsense. Who could ever think that you would be any trouble at all? It's not as though you go about lighting things on fire or throwing knives at people just for fun, after all!"

Ramiq managed to keep a straight face for a few seconds, but when Tsuga nodded solemnly, he burst into laughter.

"It's not as though you didn't deserve it, you know."

"You threw a *knife* at my *head*!"

"No, if I had thrown a knife at your head, you would be dead now. I threw a knife *near* your head to make a point."

Ramiq snorted. "No pun intended? And what of all the times you've set me on fire or tried to blow me up? Were those to make a point as well?"

Tsuga dropped her gaze and sobered slightly. "No, of course not. Those were accidents." She looked up when he placed a finger under her chin to find that his expression had softened.

"I'm sorry. I know that. I was only teasing." She nodded and managed a weak smile.

"I know. It's just . . .. To hurt a man with magic . . .. It seems so unfair. So unnatural. I don't like knowing I'm capable of such things."

Ramiq sighed and set his plate aside, and then took hers and moved it out of the way as well so that he could take her hands in his.

"Tsu, you have made your life by taking the lives of others."

She frowned, knowing that she must seem insane for her feelings, but still unable to get past them.

"Yes, on a battlefield. With iron and steel. Brawn against brawn. Those lives were taken honestly. Fairly. They had as much chance to kill me as I them. But with magic . . . what chance does any man stand against such power?"

Ramiq seemed to actually consider her words, but after a long moment he spoke again. "Such is the burden all mages must bear. Some powers are more given to destruction than others, it's true. However, just as death is a part of life, so conscience must be a part of magic. Just because you have the power to set the world ablaze does not mean you must do so. You have a choice, Tsu. You always have a choice. You choose to pull a bowstring or raise a sword. Because you have the knowledge and the skill, taking the life of another becomes a decision, not an uncontrollable impulse."

Tsuga squirmed, not liking the turn of this conversation. She pulled her hand free of Ramiq's and retrieved her plate of food.

"Of course. You're right." She feigned a light tone as best she could and popped a sliver of the juicy meat into her mouth. Thankfully, he let the subject drop.

As Tsuga closed the door in his face, Ramiq let out a tense breath and turned away to begin his walk. He still was not quite sure at what point he had agreed not to teleport in or out of the Warriors' Compound, but somehow the promise had been extracted, and he was determined now to hold to it.

It was a relief to step from the stuffy, closed-in space of the hallway into the open night air, even though it was not particularly cool out. As he set his feet upon the route back to the Mages' Complex, Ramiq allowed his mind to replay the night's events as it pleased.

She had looked truly lovely in the dress he had bought for her. Aside from the strange dreams, he had only seen her in a dress once. He determined, as he passed through the gates to the Warriors' Compound and out onto the street, to persuade her to wear them more often. The more feminine clothing made her appear somehow both softer and even more dangerous, like a dagger hidden in silk. The combination was intoxicating.

All in all, Ramiq felt that the date had been a success. He had managed to dispel her irritation and, despite a few rough patches in the conversation, had kept the mood light and intimate. He had almost thought he'd spoiled the whole thing when the talk had turned to morality, murder, and guilt. Luckily, she had guided the conversation neatly away from such dark thoughts; the rest of the night had been largely uneventful and pleasant.

I really must help her come to terms with her magic. She still thinks of it as a curse. Like it's an unfair way to protect herself, when it's really no different than what she teaches her students.

It will not be easy to change her mind on this matter, Ramiq. You must show her what good she can do with her power. Then, maybe she will be able to accept it in her own way, and in her own time.

Well, then that's what I'll have to do.

"Why are we here, Ramiq?"

Tsuga wavered between confusion and irritation, and – because she disliked the disadvantage confusion put her at – settled on irritation. He had teleported her to the middle of nowhere. There was nothing but ruin as far as the eye could see; charred tree trunks, ash blowing in a light breeze and coating the two of them in a fine layer of soot. Everything had been consumed by fire. She shifted uncomfortably at the knowledge that she was more than capable of such destruction and glared at Ramiq.

"What's going on?"

His expression was serene, and she found his calm demeanor only served to agitate her further.

"We are here for your lesson, Tsuga." When she looked at him askance, he went on to explain. "What you said last night really bothered me. You still see your gift as some horrible, uncontrollable force of death and destruction."

"So to convince me that I'm wrong, you brought me to the site of a forest fire, where everything has been destroyed by a horrible, uncontrollable inferno?"

Ramiq shook his head. "You're only seeing what's on the surface. Come here."

Tsuga moved towards him with some reluctance, and then followed his example and crouched down in the ashes. He brushed aside some of the powder-fine soot, and when the air cleared again, Tsuga saw the beginnings of new growth.

"What used to be here is gone, it's true. But new life lies just beneath the surface, ready to emerge and take root. Do you know that at the end of the growing season, many farmers will set fire to their fields? The ashes provide nutrients to the soil, and the burning of the remnants of weeds and withered crops prepares the field for the spring planting. You see, Tsuga, while fire can be deadly, it can also be a source of growth and life. Here; take my hand."

Ramiq stood and extended a hand to her, which she brushed aside so that she could rise unaided. He pushed his hand towards her again.

"Come on. There's more to today's lesson."

Although his words made her decidedly uneasy, Tsuga reached out and grasped his hand. She had scarcely closed her fingers around his before the world suddenly dropped out from under her. Things seemed to shift, and for one brief moment she could have sworn the world turned upside-down. When the ground once again stood solid beneath her, Tsuga swallowed the bile that had risen in her throat and took in her new surroundings.

"I'll never get used to that," she muttered as she shook her hand free of his. "Why are we at the foundry?"

Even discounting the proudly displayed mark of a master blacksmith, the purpose of the building was made obvious by the rhythmic ringing of hammer on anvil and the smoke billowing out of the multiple chimneys. Like most blacksmiths, this master had set up shop on the fringes of the town, where his noise and smoke would not be quite so bothersome. And, like every foundry she had ever seen, it was crowded up against a clean source of flowing water – the city's small river, in this case.

"Come on. Let's go inside."

Tsuga sighed, knowing this to be less of a suggestion and more of an order. She stepped into the smallish building and was immediately hit by a wall of heat. Ramiq followed her in, and she was a bit disgruntled to see that he did not so much as bat an eye at the high temeratures that had already caused her to break out in a sweat.

"Ramiq! Good to see you, good to see you! And who's this pretty young boy? Brought him here to buy him something shiny, have you?"

Tsuga choked back a laugh and cast a sidelong glance at Ramiq, who was flushing hotly as he grasped the hand of the enormous and heavily-muscled man who had greeted them.

"Oh yes, Ramiq, do! I do *so* like shiny things!"

She batted her eyes in her best impression of a vapid, spoiled brat and was rewarded by seeing the mage look as though he had just seen her turn into a toad.

"Um, Oro, this is Weaponsmistress Tsuga. She is an apprentice mage. We are here for her edification."

The large man blustered and wiped sweat from his brow with a brown, scarred hand to cover his embarrassment.

"Oh. Well, beggin' your pardon, miss. It's just –"

"It's just that our Queen's Mage has a well-known penchant for pretty young boys, and I look like one. Do not worry, Master Oro. The look on his face was well worth any minor offense I could pretend to take."

The big man offered her a lopsided grin, and she couldn't help but smile in response.

"Well, now, what can I do for the two of you?"

"I'd like for Tsuga to get a good look at your furnaces, Oro. Would you mind giving us a quick tour?"

The large man puffed up proudly, and though Tsuga had not thought it possible, she would have sworn he looked even bigger as he turned and gestured for them to follow.

"Of course, of course! Right this way."

As they neared the first furnace, Tsuga finally realized what was so strange about this particular foundry. "Master Oro?"

"What is it, miss?"

"Where are your bellows? And who minds them?"

Oro boomed out a thunderous laugh that startled her and gestured to Ramiq as the three of them came to a stop. "Why don't you ask Ramiq about that?"

Suspicious, Tsuga turned a cool gaze on the mage, but he merely shrugged and gestured vaguely at the furnace. "See for yourself."

Tsuga scowled at him, but when he made no move to offer a further explanation, she made a sound of frustration and called on her mage sight.

"Oh! It's magic! I – I can't quite understand all the workings," she added, almost to herself, "but I can see what the spell does. It holds the furnace at a precise and constant temperature."

"That's right." Oro rocked back on his heels and pushed his thumbs proudly into the tether that held his leather apron onto his barrel-like frame.

"Only ones like 'em in the whole city. Ramiq here set the spells himself. As long as they've fuel, they'll burn just the way I need 'em to."

"And why is that important, Oro?"

Tsuga shot Ramiq a withering glare, but his expression remained bland as he awaited an answer to his question.

"Well, for meltin' and purifyin' the ore, of course. You've got to melt and cool it several times, you know, and each time the temperature's got to be exactly right. Otherwise, you get flaws that could, say, cause that sword of yours to break in half if it were stressed in just the wrong way."

"And how many apprentices would you normally have to have tending your bellows?"

"Oh, dozens. And they're unreliable. They get tired, distracted . . . lots of errors, that way. Always having to refire things. Much fewer mistakes this way. Makes some of the finest metal you'll ever see."

As he'd been speaking, Oro had walked across the large room to one of the work stations, where he now retrieved something that he dropped into Tsuga's hands. It was the beginnings of a sword. The edges had not yet been honed, and the wrapping and decorating of the hilt had not even been started yet, but she could see no blemishes on the polished surface of the steel; though she tried, she could not find any fault at all with the fledgeling weapon.

"This is truly fine work, Master Oro," she said as she handed the unfinished blade back to him. "You are a credit to your craft. I shall certainly know who to commission for any new weaponry I may need."

The big man flushed with pleasure and used the excuse of replacing his project on the work bench to compose himself.

"Well, thank you, Master Oro. You have been most helpful, as always, but we must continue on with our lesson."

"Yes, yes, of course! And I've work to be done. It was good meeting you, miss."

"Please, Oro, it's just Tsuga."

If he made a response, it was lost to her, as Ramiq was already ushering her outside. As they turned to walk back towards the heart of the city, Tsuga sighed.

"Look Ramiq, I get what you're trying to do. You want me to feel more comfortable with my magic, so you're showing me that there's more to it than destruction and killing. I appreciate the effort, but –"

"Are you hungry?"

Tsuga broke off, dumbfounded by this sudden change of subject. "No, thank you. I ate already."

"Well, I'm hungry. I know a lovely little bakery a few streets over. Best sweet rolls you'll ever have."

Tsuga rolled her eyes, but followed him until he stepped inside a small shop that smelled of sugar and yeast.

"Ramiq! So good to see you!"

Tsuga's eyes adjusted to the change in light just in time to see Ramiq being enthusiastically embraced by a rather rotund woman whose hair was either dusted with flour or else going prematurely gray.

"Marci! You look stunning, as always!"

"Oh, you!"

As Tsuga watched the large woman flirt with the man she loved, she did her best to appear nonchalant. She knew this meant nothing – Ramiq was a hopeless flirt who would behave this way with every person he ever met – but still, she didn't like it.

Almost as though he knew how she felt, Ramiq turned and pulled her to his side with a smile.

"Tsuga, Marci here is the best baker in the city, but lately her ovens have been on the fritz."

Marci frowned. "You can say that again. The ceramic tile inside has started to crack from the heat, and now the ovens won't hold temperature properly. Takes twice as long for everything to bake, and it cooks unevenly, at that."

Tsuga leaned into Ramiq's embrace, subtly moving so that she was between the two of them.

"Why don't you just replace the tile?"

Marci shook her head. "It's not so easy, I'm afraid. Ceramic has to be custom shaped and fired, and then there's the problem of setting it . . .. I'd be out of production for weeks, and it's not as though I have any other source of income. I just have to make do."

Out of the corner of her eye, Tsuga saw Ramiq hide a smile. She turned to face him with a frown.

"Why are we really here, Ramiq?"

"I told you; Marci's skills with pastries are legendary, and I'm hungry."

"You had no idea her ovens were giving her so much trouble?"

"Well . . .."

Tsuga growled. "You're an ass, Ramiq."

He offered a shrug and a sheepish grin. "You could help her, you know."

Tsuga scowled again and shook her head. "I'm just an apprentice. I don't have the skills to do what you did at the foundry."

"It's actually very simple; all a matter of control, which you've been practicing for months now."

"You're an ass, Ramiq."

"Yes, you've said as much already." She made a sound of irritation and turned to face Marci.

"Where is your oven?"

The baker looked between the two of them in confusion, but finally gave herself a little shake and stepped aside.

"Through that door, in the kitchen."

"I can't believe I'm doing this," Tsuga muttered as she strode across the room, Ramiq and Marci hot on her heels.

The oven was immense, and the heat coming from it rivaled the blacksmith's enchanted furnaces. There were half a dozen workers in the small kitchen, putting things into the fires and kneading doughs and doing the usual cooking things that she supposed were commonplace in such kitchens.

"What's going on, Marci?"

The question came from an older man kneading a mass of dough on one of the long tables.

"They're here about the oven."

"Goddess bless! It's about time you took care of that!"

Tsuga shook her head and blocked out their chatter as she drew on her mage sight and delved into her powers, hand gripped tightly around the malachite stone that helped her to channel and control the magical currents around her.

"Alright, Ramiq. What do I do?"

"You figure it out."

"What?!" Tsuga tried not to wince at the high-pitched tone of her own voice.

"I told you as much as I can tell you. It's all about control. You know how to do this, Tsu; you just have to listen to your instincts."

Tsuga scowled at him a moment longer before she turned her attention back to the oven. The banging of pots and pans, the talking, and the general clamor of the kitchen faded to background noise as she narrowed her focus. She could certainly see what Marci meant; the heat in the oven was sporadic at best. More than half of it dispersed uselessly into the air, which no doubt explained the overwhelming heat in the kitchen.

"All the heat's just escaping into the air. It needs to be contained somehow, first, and then redistributed so that it cooks evenly. If I could reverse the effects of a shield so that it kept the heat in instead of out . . .. But to still let out the smoke, how to do that . . .? And I've never heard of a shield set on a thing, rather than a person. Your work at the foundry wasn't a shield."

There was one obvious way, of course; she could enchant the oven with mage fire. But Marci only needed to make use of the heat she was already producing, not necessarily to create more.

"And then there's the problem of putting things in and out of the oven. Even if I could figure out how to set a permanent heat shield – which in theory should allow everything else to pass through it, including the smoke – I'd still have to find a way to invert it . . .. And then there's the problem of regulating the heat so that it doesn't just burn everything up."

It took several tries and a brief discussion with Marci about the problems she'd been experiencing, but eventually she had a good idea of what was needed. The problem was that the heat was escaping through one side of the oven, which meant that if the bakers wanted the oven to hold temperature, they had to stoke the fires a great deal more than they normally would have. This made one side of the oven entirely too hot; food burned on one side before it cooked on the other.

After several long minutes of thought, Tsuga had an inkling of something that might work, but she had to consider the problem from a few other angles before she was sure that it would be feasible. Convinced that she had the solution, Tsuga gathered her magic and set to work. When she was finished, she had set up a small magical patch over the hole which was resistant to the escape of heat. It wasn't exactly a shield, though in a way it did have a similar effect: it kept the warmth from escaping through the cracked ceramic, and instead spread and redistributed the heat back into the rest of the oven.

She waited several long minutes more to be sure that it worked properly, and then tied it off the way Ramiq had shown her. She was sweating profusely by the time she finished, but when at last she released her magic and blinked away the mage sight, she was smiling. When she turned to face Ramiq, she found him beaming like a proud parent.

"I think that will hold nicely. Very well done, Tsu. Especially since I never taught you how to invert a shield; that's quite close to what you would have to do if you wanted to. Remarkable."

She flushed with the praise and shook her head. "It was simple, really, once I figured out what needed to be done."

"You see?" Ramiq pulled her into a hug and then released her. "I knew you could do it. And you used your magic to help someone. No explosions, no one burned to death, no disaster."

Tsuga rolled her eyes. "It was just an oven."

"It is a woman's livelihood. And an excellent first step."

They made their goodbyes, and Marci loaded them down with baskets of pastries and sweets as thanks for their help.

Tsuga was still having a hard time coming to terms with her magic. It had been several weeks since she had last lost control, but the worry that it would happen again weighed heavily on her mind. But on this late spring day, everything looked more promising; the warmer temperatures and clear skies lifted her spirits.

There really was nothing she could complain about, in truth. Her students were progressing steadily; she no longer worried that they would accidentally decapitate themselves. She wasn't setting fire to innocent objects, and though it frightened her to admit, her relationship with Ramiq filled a void that until now she had refused to acknowledge. As she dismissed her students for their lunch break, Tsuga found herself smiling.

You're in an awfully good mood.

"And why wouldn't I be?"

Indeed. Why not?

Tsuga laughed and swung herself easily down from Bane's saddle. Today had been a lesson in horsemanship, and of course the guardian had played a key part in her morning's demonstrations. She would not be needed for the trip to the

Mages' Complex, though – Tsuga planned to detour through the marketplace and check in with the bakery to see how her spell had been holding, and a horse would only get in the way in the crowded city streets. With a casual speed born of long practice, Tsuga untacked and groomed the guardian and set the horse loose to amuse herself until she returned.

A few short minutes later Tsuga struggled to make some kind of forward progress through the crush of people haggling and conducting their daily business in the market. With a sigh, she resigned herself to a snail's pace and turned her focus to people-watching in an effort to distract herself from her frustration.

There was certainly no shortage of interesting characters today; at a stall somewhere behind her, she could hear an old woman arguing vehemently about the value of the citrus fruits she wanted to buy. A bit ahead of her, separated from her by a few people, was a rather large man dressed in an elaborate costume that only a noble would be foolish enough to wear for any reason. Of course there was the usual mix of travelers, workers, streetrats, pickpockets, and beggars, in addition to the dozen or so wealthy men and women she could see.

There were also a handful of guards in sight, each doing his or her level best to minimize the crime happening, though the press of people worked against them. She was eyeballing a cobbler's stall – her boots were starting to wear through – when she overheard a question that caught her attention.

"Can you tell me how to get to the Warriors' Compound?"

Her head swiveled, and she shook her head sadly to herself at the sight of a scrawny young boy addressing one of the guards. The child was mostly unremarkable: brown hair, skin tanned from time on the road, back bowed under a pack that must be fairly burdensome by the way he carried himself under its weight. The guard's response brought a frown to her face.

"Little scrawny to be a trainee, lad. You looking for a job as a practice dummy?"

The boy was only a few feet to her left, so Tsuga turned and waded through the few people that separated her from the pair.

"We do happen to be in need of a new practice dummy, Jordan. But you see, I only allow my students to beat up blowhards who think they're Auriga's gift to Sennor. Can you report tomorrow at dawn?"

The guard flushed as his spine stiffened and he presented her the salute appropriate to her position. He had been one of the first students to graduate from her instruction after her appointment here – his training had been nearly complete by the time she'd taken on the position. He obviously had forgotten a few of the lessons he'd learned from her; perhaps it was time he was reminded.

"Weaponsmistress. I was just –"

"You were just insulting a boy who has done you no wrong. I will be speaking to your captain. Tomorrow, we practice unhorsing an opponent. My students will be delighted to have a real person to practice on, instead of the sand bags I had planned on. Dawn. Tomorrow. You won't want to be late."

"But Weaponsmistress, I was only –"

"That is enough, soldier. Your duty here is to protect the people of Sennor, not bully them. You would do well to remember that."

She waited until the errant guard had moved away before she turned her attention to the young boy, who she found to be gaping up at her in shock.

"You're the Weaponsmistress?"

Tsuga nodded as she took stock of the child. He wasn't malnourished, as his size had first lead her to believe; his build was lean, much like hers, though he lacked the power and muscle that he would undoubtedly gain as he matured. He carried only one weapon that she could see: a simple dagger, which she doubted he had ever used for anything more violent than skinning and gutting his dinner.

"I am. Are you interested in being a student?"

"Yes. Well, no. That is, not exactly . . .. I was looking for you."

Tsuga felt a cold sense of premonition stiffen her spine, and she surreptitiously released her throwing knives and slid them into her palms. There was no shortage of people who might have reason to want her dead, and none of them would be above hiring a child to attack or distract her long enough to make an attempt on her life.

"Were you now? And why is that?"

He fumbled at his belt for the knife and Tsuga tensed, knowing that she may well have to defend herself from this unlikely adversary. Her jaw dropped in shock, however, when he merely held the weapon up for her inspection.

"Where did you get that dagger –?"

"Trag," he finished for her. "My name is Trag Dafrin."

Her blood froze in her veins, and Tsuga had to restrain herself from looking around for another assassin hidden somewhere in the crowd. Around them life proceeded, unaware of the way her heart had stopped.

Trag is a common name. And Dafrin . . . that could *be a coincidence. But –*

"How did you get that knife, Trag?"

"I've always had it. My mother gave it to me when I was a baby. At least, that's what the woman who raised me said. It's

all I have of her. Well, that, and her name. Your name. I . . . that
is to say, I'm your son."

For the space of a single heartbeat, Tsuga couldn't breathe.
She couldn't think, and time seemed to stop. Then the moment
passed. She managed a sympathetic smile for the youngster.

"Look, kid, you seem like a nice boy. But I don't have a son.
I don't know how you got my Da's knife, or who put you up to
this, but –"

She broke off when the boy started crying – no doubt he was
exhausted, his nerves worn thin – and shaking his head
vehemently.

"But why would Tau lie? All the details fit. Your name. How
you act. The horse she said you had – though how it's still going
after twelve years . . .. You're a fire mage. And I even *look* like
you! It *has* to be true. It has to."

"Tau? . . . Where are you from, Trag?"

How does he know that name? I never told anyone about that
summer.

"I grew up on a farm on the border, just across the Bloody
Plains."

He slid the knife back into place on his belt and angrily wiped
his tears away with a dirty hand. Tsuga shook her head and
leaned forward to offer him the – mostly – clean cloth she carried
in her belt pouch. Her small malachite pendant dangled in the air
in front of her, and between one breath and the next, she was lost
in a memory so powerful it seemed she lived it again even as she
stood amongst the press of people in the marketplace.

She stood over the bed and looked down at the little screaming
thing that lay there, reminding her of everything she most wanted
to forget. It was a tiny, red, wrinkled thing, and as she watched
it squirm, the only emotion she could muster was a desperate
need to be rid of it.

Tsuga realized that she held her father's dagger in her hand,
though she didn't remember drawing the weapon. She ran a
thumb along the sharp blade and watched a thin line of blood rise
from the flesh.

"Tsuga? What are you doing?"

She couldn't muster any emotion at the sound of Tau's voice.
She only knew she couldn't do this. She had to get away. She set
the bloodied knife down on the bed and lifted her small pack of
belongings. She couldn't stay here.

Tsuga reeled from the power of the memory, and her breath
came shallowly. How could she have a son, when she didn't even
remember being pregnant?

There really is no telling what all I've forgotten . . ..

She had to fight back a sense of panic; the world was growing dark around the edges, and a maelstrom of emotions threatened to overwhelm her.

How can I have a son I never knew about? She shook her head to dispel some of her confusion, but the gesture only served to summon a wall of fire around her.

Is that real? Or is it my shield?

It was becoming harder to tell what was real and what she imagined. The flames surged when she looked at them, but she didn't flinch from the blaze of heat. In fact, she relished it. The temperatue was enough to catch the thin fabric of her clothes on fire, but the flames on her skin brought a feeling of pain that loosened the tight grip of panic on her heart and made it possible for her to breathe more normally.

Ramiq stood in the packed dirt area that served as the practice arena for all explosive or destructive magic. Today, he planned to put Tsuga through her paces and really test her control. He felt that she was nearly ready to try her hand at the journeyman's exam, and today's session would help him determine if he was correct. Impatient, he checked the position of the sun and realized that it was already well past the appointed time for them to meet.

Where could she be?

Even as the question crossed his mind, he spotted the familiar stocky form of a large bay horse. It was with some alarm that, as Bane drew near, he realized she not only lacked a rider, but was not even saddled. She came to an abrupt stop only a few feet from him, and he saw that the horse's neck was lathered with sweat.

She must have run the whole way here.

"Bane! What's happened?"

"Get on."

"Just tell me where to go; I can teleport there faster."

Bane was dancing in place, her eyes rolling wildly.

This can't be good.

"I'm going too. Get on. Now."

Ramiq grimaced. He was not a fan of horses, and was even less fond of giant, panicked, sweaty ones. However, since his concern for Tsuga greatly outweighted his reluctance, he clambered atop the immense beast. Though she stood rock steady to make his clumsy efforts less difficult, her muscles quivered with impatience. Ramiq was a tall man, in relatively good physical condition, but still he had to struggle to pull himself astride the warhorse with no stirrup for his foot and no mane to grip for assistance. Bane waited only long enough for him to find his balance once he finally made it up before she set off at a dead run, a sudden shift into movement that nearly unseated him.

At this speed, any words were ripped away by the wind of their progress, but luckily the Queen's Mage had more sophisticated means of communication at his disposal.

What is going on? Is she okay?

For now. She's in the market, and I'd wager she's minutes from burning it to the ground.

She's been doing so well . . .. What happened?

She just met her son.

Ramiq felt as though he'd been punched. *She has a son?*

Bane didn't answer – she was too busy maneuvering through crowds of panicked people running away from where they were headed. Ramiq's mind caught up to events belatedly, and with a *push*, he planted a certainty in the minds of the crowd by broadcasting it openly to the throng in front of him.

I should stop running and move to the side of the road.

Moments later, a path cleared before them and Bane was once again able to break into a run. It wasn't long before the inferno came into view, and Ramiq shook his head in disbelief as Bane skidded to a stop. His dismount was accomplished far more easily than the ordeal of getting himself astride the great beast; he flung himself down from the horse's back with little concern for his own well-being. He ignored the sharp stab of pain that accompanied his landing. Nothing was broken, he knew; he had simply jarred himself with the impact.

As he warily approached the flames, the heat grew uncomfortable – so much so that he had to pause long enough to accept the pain into himself as he had learned to do during his test for mastery of the element before he could go on without spontaneously combusting himself.

He stopped just short of the circle of fire and attempted to see through the conflagration. Several feet away, cowering beyond the reach of the flames, he could see a small boy huddled against the side of a building, staring in his direction with stark terror on his face.

Must be the kid.

"Are you okay, son?"

The boy didn't answer, but he was conscious and aware, so he would have to wait.

"Tsuga?" He raised his voice over the roar of the flames. "Are you alright?"

When his initial call failed to reach her, Ramiq tried to speak to her mind.

Tsu?

What he sensed of her thoughts sent him reeling. Her mind was scarcely recognizable. Merging with an element was a tricky business; in her inexperience, Tsuga was losing a battle of wills. If this was allowed to continue, the fire would kill her and leave nothing behind. Ramiq stifled a scream of frustration. He knew what he had to do – the only solution available to him – but she wouldn't be happy with him. In addition to a painful magical backlash, she would feel empty and used up. He well remembered the feeling, but sadly he had no other choice.

He cut his eyes to the right and saw that Devilsbane stood stock still, legs splayed and braced as though the earth might try to buck her off at any moment. Her eyes rolled, and her sides heaved as her head swung back and forth as though she searched for something. Ramiq took a couple of seconds to brace himself for Tsuga's reaction, then slammed a shield around her that cut her off completely from her magic. The flames died immediately and left Tsuga standing alone amidst the destruction, her weapons in a pile at her feet. They were charred and glowed with a sullen orange cast from the intense heat, but all were intact as far as he could see. Her clothes had long since burned away, so that she stood before him now completely exposed. Ramiq approached her slowly.

Her head swiveled and Ramiq shuddered as she turned empty, emotionless eyes on him. He worried that he had waited too long. Her lips parted, and when she spoke her voice was hollow and distant.

"Ramiq?"

Tsuga's mind was awash in chaos, just as her body was awash in heat. She felt no pain from the flames that licked over her flesh. In fact, the sensation of a thousand tongues exploring her exposed skin aroused her, a state which only served to add to her confusion. How was it she had a son that she only now recalled?

How does one forget an entire pregnancy?

Somewhere in the back of her mind, she thought she heard Ramiq's voice. But that wasn't possible, any more than it was possible that Bane should be frantically invading her thoughts. As Tsuga continued to bask in the heat of the fire, her life seemed to become more of a dream than a reality. The longer she stood in the warm comfort of the blaze, the more she began to think that perhaps this was where she belonged. Being here just felt . . . right. Nothing to worry about. No pain. She could simply let the flames consume her earthly body, and then she would be free to join them and become pure, elemental power.

Abruptly, that feeling of freedom was gone. She crashed back to earth, suddenly fettered to a body that felt too heavy for her spirit of smoke and fire. She staggered under the weight of the unwanted flesh, and when she lifted her gaze to look for the source of her chains her too-mortal eyes lit upon Ramiq. *Ramiq.* Here was a reason for her to stay. Here was something that could make the pain of this clumsy body worth bearing.

"Ramiq?"

Between one breath and the next, she crumpled. He winced to see her fall among so many sharp – and hot – blades and hurried to her side. As he pulled her gently away from the pile of heated metal, he was startled to find himself suddenly cast in shadow.

"Is she dead?"

He had forgotten about the boy, who now stood awkwardly in front of him, pale and visibly shaken by what he had just seen. Ramiq shook his head and did his best to provide Tsuga some measure of modesty by covering her with the flimsy shield of his own body.

"No, she's not dead. She fainted."

"So she's going to be okay?"

Ramiq tried to offer up a reassuring smile, though he wasn't sure how successful he was.

"Yes, she'll be fine. But I need to get her to a bed. Are you alright, son?"

The boy swallowed and Ramiq could see that the child – he looked to be about twelve or thirteen – was struggling to hold back tears as he nodded.

"Yessir. But where are you taking her? She's my –"

"Mother. Yes, I know. I'm taking her to the Warriors' Compound. Do you know where that is?"

The boy shook his head no, and Ramiq let out a gusty sigh – then looked to Bane as an idea occurred to him.

"You see that horse? The one I rode up on?" The boy nodded. "She's Tsuga's guardian. She will make sure you get there. Why don't you go introduce yourself?"

That should help keep Bane grounded and calm.

Ramiq waited until the boy had turned away and taken a few steps towards Devilsbane before he gathered Tsuga in his arms. He pictured her room clearly in his mind, neat and tidy, just as he knew it would be. With a *twist* and a *pull* of his magic, the world shifted around them, and abruptly the pair of them were alone on Tsuga's floor. Ramiq struggled to his feet with her still in his arms and carried her to the bed, where he gently laid her down and covered her with the coarse wool blanket before he sat down beside her and took her hand in his.

"Oh, Tsu . . .. What else don't I know about you?"

Tsuga drifted near conciousness, her thoughts disjointed, her mind working sluggishly through what she knew.

I'll need to give the trainees a final exam soon; they're about ready to enlist in the army. I need to put in an order for new boots with the cobbler. And what time is it? I'm late for my lesson with Ramiq!

This last thought jolted her awake, and she immediately wished that it hadn't. Her entire body hurt as though she had been beaten bloody and her head throbbed painfully in time with her pulse. She groaned and put a hand to her temple in a vain attempt to reduce the pounding.

"You're awake!"

She winced at the flash of pain the too-loud words caused her and forced one eye open despite her discomfort.

"Ramiq?"

Even the hoarse sound of her own voice caused her to wince, but still she opened the other eye and slowly turned her head in the direction from which his voice had come. He sat beside her on the bed – her bed, she realized – and he smiled down at her with such relief that she had to wonder what had happened.

"How are you feeling?"

She made a face. "Like death."

"I'm not surprised. Gave us quite a scare, you know. What were you thinking, trying to bond with fire in the middle of the market? With no training in how to do it successfully! You're lucky to be alive!"

Tsuga absorbed this information in silence as she tried to remember what had happened. She could recall thinking that she had needed new boots.

"I was going to check in with Marci at the bakery before our lesson. The market was so crowded, I could barely move. I overheard a young boy asking one of the city guards how to find the Warriors' Compound. The next thing I knew, he was showing me my Da's dagger and saying he was my son. And then . . .."

"And then you tried to burn yourself alive. I know that part. Tsuga, why didn't you tell me you had a son? Did you think I would think less of you? That I wouldn't love you as much?"

Tsuga shook her head and immediately regretted the action when the movement set the room spinning. She had to hold herself very still for a long moment until the world settled down again before she could speak.

"I didn't know."

Ramiq's eyebrows disappeared behind his bangs as his expression changed to one of incredulity.

"Tsu, that doesn't make any sense! You gave birth to him. Hell, you were pregnant with him for nine months! It's not as though you could simply not *know* you had him!"

Tsuga scowled and felt her shoulders tense in indignation. "I'm missing fully half of my life, Ramiq. I don't know why I don't remember these things – only that there are large gaps in my head, and I simply *don't know* what is supposed to be there."

Emotion lumped in her throat, and Tsuga was dismayed to find hot tears on her cheeks before she had finished speaking. Ramiq let out a sigh, and his arrogant posture seemed to deflate with the exhalation. He took her into his arms and cradled her head against his chest.

Ramiq held her until her sobs subsided, and then for a long while after. He kept expecting her to push him away, sit up and swipe her eyes dry, and adopt her usual attitude of imperturbable toughness. She never did. Eventually, when she had been breathing evenly and without moving for some time, he realized she had fallen asleep.

What do I do now?

Stay with her.

Ramiq frowned; he had merely been wondering to himself, but Lyra had, as always, chimed in an opinion.

But —

Don't question me. She's sick, distraught, and exhausted. She will be grateful for your support.

Ramiq stifled a sigh and gently pushed Tsuga away from him and laid her back against the pillow so he could pull the worn wool blanket over her. He had never managed to get her clothed, and he worried now how she would feel about his staying the night with her current state of undress.

He stood at her bedside for a few moments longer and watched her as she slept. At last, he let out a sigh and bent at the waist to pull off his boots. His robes promptly followed, and then, with no other delays forthcoming, he finally persuaded himself to pull back the old covering and settle in next to her on the narrow bed.

Normally, the proximity of a warm body and the feel of her bare skin against his would arouse him, but an entire day spent fretting over her health had exhausted him. His last thought before sleep pulled him under was a longing for his overstuffed pillows and silk sheets.

Tsuga came awake all at once, but her mind could not immediately make sense of what was happening. She came to several realizations in the space of a couple of breaths. First, that she was naked. Then, that she was not alone. That her bedmate, whose strong arms held her against him, was Ramiq, who was also nude. And lastly, that there was a not-alltogether-uncomfortable hardness pressing against her buttocks. The hardness moved, and Ramiq mumbled something unintelligible in his sleep. Her heart raced, and she flushed as she realized what it was, and in what manner of situation she now found herself.

Bane?

Just before dawn. He stayed to make sure you would be okay.

Tsuga considered this information for a moment. *So . . . .*

Nothing happened.

She let out a sigh of relief, and Ramiq shifted slightly in his sleep and pulled her in closer in response. Admittedly, being held against his body like this felt good, but the lack of clothing between them – not to mention his obvious arousal – made her stomach churn uncomfortably. It was not a difficult decision to get out of the bed and start the day. Actually disentangling herself from Ramiq proved a bit more of a problem.

For an out-of-shape mage, he's certainly got a strong grip, she mused.

At last, she succeeded in freeing herself from his arms and slid out from under his leg. Unfortunately, she misjudged her location on the bed just a bit, and as a consequence lost her balance and landed in a heap on the floor. She lay there for a moment, cursing her stupidity under her breath, and then was surprised to see Ramiq's head poke over the edge of the bed.

"Tsu? What are you doing down there?"

She had to admit he looked quite adorable in this sleep-muddled state. Softer, somehow. Less perfectly manicured, what with his mussed hair, groggy expression, and the large red mark on his cheek where he must have been cushioning his head on his arm while he slept.

"I fell."

He gave her a drowsy, crooked smile and patted the thin mattress beside him. "Come back to bed."

Tsuga shook her head and stood, and only then recalled that she was still undressed. She grabbed at the nearest covering – a corner of the blanket – and held it in front of herself.

"I have students to attend to. And I need to eat," she added as her stomach rumbled noisily.

Ramiq sighed, and Tsuga thought fleetingly that he looked like a kicked puppy. "Do I have to get up?"

This startled a laugh out of her, and Tsuga shook her head. "No, you don't. Sleep your day away. But I have things to do. I need to get dressed. I need new boots, after yesterday's . . . incident. And – wait. Where are my weapons?"

Ramiq just looked at her blankly, and Tsuga shook her head in exasperation and cast her eyes about the room. "My weapons, Ramiq. My sword and knives. Where are they?"

With your son. He had the forethought to bring them in off the street.

She cringed at the mention of the boy she'd met yesterday, though knowing her weapons were safe helped to ease her nerves slightly.

"Never mind," she told Ramiq, who was still looking as though he hadn't fully processed anything she'd said.

He shrugged and collapsed back against the bed and pulled her pillow under his head. She found it hard to believe that he fell back to sleep so easily, but when she watched him breathe evenly for several long moments, she finally had to conclude that perhaps he had never truly woken up to begin with. She shook her head in wonder and moved to her small standing wardrobe to pull out her clothes for the day.

So, she began as she pulled on and laced her trousers, *where did you put him?*

She would, after all, have to retrieve her weapons before she could begin her day. Even once she had pulled on pants, a loose tunic and her pair of dress boots – the only other shoes she owned – she still felt uncomfortable and vulnerable without her sword and other various blades.

He's in the boys' barracks. Told him to sleep there for the time being, until you decide what you want to do with him.

Tsuga slipped out of her room and closed the door behind herself. As anxious as she was to arm herself again, her stomach made it plain that her first priority would have to be breakfast.

The Warriors' Compound had a simple, militant layout. Two long buildings on the north and south sides of the packed dirt training yard made up the boys' and girls' barracks, respectively. There was a separate room in each building furnished for a Weaponsmaster of either gender; Tsuga, of course, slept on the women's side. The boys, who were just as much trouble as – though certainly no more than – the girls, were under the careful watch of Bane, who could easily observe the building and its comings and goings from her stall in the stables where they backed up to the eastern wall of the Compound. The stable sat tucked beside the equipment shed that housed the practice weapons, spare swords, and the tools necessary for mending and maintaining one's weapons, and opposite the mess hall and servants' quarters on the other side of the training yard.

At this time of day, the mess rang with the sounds of trainees eating and conversing – none too quietly – and the first few students had begun their warm-up exercises along the edges of the packed dirt yard.

Tsuga paused at the door to the boys' barracks and took a moment to gather her thoughts before she swung the door inwards and stepped into the long single room that housed the tidy rows of bunks on which the trainees slept. By now, most of them were already out preparing for another day under Tsuga's strict tutelage. After his trauma yesterday, Tsuga was not at all surprised to find that Trag was still in bed. Her eyes went to the racks against the western wall, arranged there next to the door through which she'd entered. Near where he slept, placed carefully in slots affixed to the wall that were appropriate to their sizes, Tsuga found her weapons.

She lifted her sword free and sighed with regret at the ruined remnants of the shark skin that still clung to the hilt. While not impossible to replace, getting her hands on enough to re-wrap the grip would not be easy. She was just grateful that the weapon had survived the intense heat without being warped or damaged. As she held the sword up to the light that filtered in through the open doorway, she noticed that the blade had been polished and sharpened. The metal seemed slightly different, too, though she couldn't quite put her finger on what had changed.

"Sorry."

Startled, Tsuga turned, sword in hand, to find Trag standing behind her in his night-shirt – still sleepy-eyed, but awake.

"What's that, Trag?"

"I couldn't help myself. They were all dirty, and they were just . . . wrong. So I fixed them." Perplexed, she quirked an eyebrow at him.

"What do you mean, 'they were wrong?'"

Something brushed between her legs, and Tsuga looked down to see a wiry wild dog move to sit beside Trag. The boy smiled down at the animal and gave its ears a scratch as it spoke to her.

"Trag is a metal mage."

Tsuga felt her other eyebrow join the first as it raised towards her hairline in surprise.

"This is Temalon," Trag announced proudly. "He found me when I crossed the border. And he keeps saying that, but I'm no mage."

Temalon gave his head a little shake and thumped his bushy black-flecked tail.

"You're young. You haven't really matured yet. But you will be."

Tsuga looked at her sword more closely. There was definitely something different, but she couldn't quite tell what it was.

"You know," she mused, "I'm not very familiar with the workings of magic. It's not my area of expertise. I have to tend to my trainees today, but why don't you take a trip to the Mages' Complex this afternoon? I want to talk to you some more this evening when you return, but I'm afraid I have to get to the day's training session."

He frowned and looked down at the animal by his feet.

"What do you think, Tem?" The canine let out an odd kind of yipping bark and hung his tongue out to one side of his pointed snout.

"I think it's a good idea. Besides, a little sight-seeing couldn't hurt."

Trag shrugged. "Okay, then. I guess we could do that."

Tsuga nodded curtly and returned her sword a bit reluctantly to its place on the wall rack; it wouldn't do her any good to carry it in its current condition, after all.

"Alright, then. The mess is to the west of the training yard. If you'd like to borrow a horse for the trip, you can talk to the stable master."

Trag nodded, and Tsuga stepped through the door. Once she was out of sight, she heaved a sigh of relief and leaned against the wall. She was shaking from the strain of feigning calm, and really had no idea what to think about the whole situation.

What am I supposed to do, here? I don't know how to be a mother!

Then don't. Just spend time with the kid. Figure out who he is, and go from there.

Tsuga shook her head and pushed away from the wall. As much as she wanted to worry over the problem some more, she had a job to do. She couldn't allow her personal issues to interfere with her duties.

Are you planning on working today?

Ramiq groaned and pulled the pillow over his ears, though he knew full well it would do nothing to block out his guardian's mindvoice.

What time is it?

Time for you to get up and stop lazing about in bed.

He grunted and cracked an eye. Light streamed in through the crack in the shutters, and the enthusiastic sounds of activity outside told him that Tsuga's poor students were already hard at work swatting at each other with wooden sticks, or whatever it was that she had them doing this morning. With a sigh, Ramiq rolled himself out of bed and looked around the chamber.

Yesterday's robes were in a heap on the floor. His shoes had been carelessly discarded half way across the room, and somehow Tsuga's threadbare blanket had been twisted and now lay half on the floor. No doubt Tsuga would take the time to tidy up and make the bed, were the situation reversed, but Ramiq disliked mornings and would not be fully himself for several hours yet. He made a sound of disgust and turned his back to the mess as he took hold of his magic and *twisted* the threads that held the world still around him. There was a brief moment of disorientation, and when he blinked it away, he found himself standing in the middle of his own rooms.

Lyra looked up from her overstuffed silk pillow in the corner and watched him as he crossed the short distance to his open wardrobe and pulled out an outfit in various tones of gold that he'd had made to replace the one Tsuga had burned. He pulled on the darker pants and the softer-colored tunic, followed by a thigh-length, long-sleeved robe that belted at his waist with a shimmery, pale gold sash that matched the sleeveless sheer robe that completed the ensemble and fell just short of skimming the ground.

He turned a critical eye to his reflection in the mirror and ran his silver comb through his hair. He dipped it in his washbasin and used the clean water to help smooth out the wispy not-quite-curls that had snarled while he slept.

Satisfied with his appearance, he stepped into his matching boots and looked down to Lyra, who had abandoned her bed during the entire process and now sat impatiently by the door.

If you're ready, Your Highness? You're already late for the day's first lesson.

Ramiq waved this statement away as he breezed through the door and out into the hallway. Mage students were each given their own room – small ones, mind, but they were not forced to suffer the same barbaric conditions as the warrior trainees. As he walked by the closed doors and stepped outside, he glanced down at his guardian, who padded beside him.

"I'm always late for the first lesson."

Yes, and that makes you late all day long. Ramiq *tsked*.

"Nonsense. I am the Queen's Mage. I am always on time. Everyone else is simply early."

Lyra sneezed – the vulpine equivalent of an eye roll – and Ramiq pretended not to notice. His first lesson today was with three apprentice earth mages who would be learning how to listen to the earth around them to glean knowledge. Not his strong suit; he was not a good listener, and patience tended to elude him. Earth had, in fact, been one of the elemental magics with which he had struggled the most as a student, due in large part to his flamboyant and admittedly hot-headed nature.

As he drew closer to the dirt-packed area that was set aside for earth mages (and fire mages who tended to inadvertently burn anything around them), Ramiq made out four figures standing and talking amongst themselves. Three of them wore the pale brown robes that marked them as earth apprentices, but the fourth wore a loose tunic and pants. It was only when he drew near enough to make out their faces that Ramiq recognized the boy from yesterday's incident in the market. The mage stopped when he reached the small group.

"Good morning, trainees."

His three students mumbled a good morning in response, but Ramiq's focus was already on the child who claimed to be Tsuga's son. He had no reason to doubt the boy, really – and Tsuga had not actually denied the relationship – but still Ramiq found it hard to believe. Tsuga simply wasn't the motherly type, and he certainly couldn't imagine her ever having been married –

or in any kind of relationship that would have resulted in a child. The realization that he knew so little about her was disconcerting, so he tried not to dwell on it overmuch.

"And hello again to you, young man. We never had a chance to make introductions yesterday. I'm Ramiq Nevarn, the Queen's Mage."

The boy's jaw dropped in shock, and it was only after the coyote at his side nudged him that he snapped his mouth shut and managed a response.

"It's an honor, sir. I'm Trag Dafrin. And I'm not anything special."

His guardian let out an odd barking yip in protest. **"Nonsense. Of course you're special. Now tell the Queen's Mage why you're here."**

The boy flushed and ducked his head. Ramiq was having a hard time seeing a connection between this timid child and the strong-willed, self-assured woman he had come to love.

"Temalon has it in his head that I'm some kind of mage or something, but I don't know about all that . . . but Tsuga told me I should come here and look around."

Ramiq raised his eyebrows in a show of interest. "Is that so? Well, there's a pretty easy way to find out. Do you know what kind of magic you have, Trag?"

The boy shrugged and scuffed the toe of his boot in the dirt. "Metal. 'Least, that's what Tem tells me."

Ramiq nodded slowly and managed a warm smile at the boy despite his own confused jumble of thoughts.

"And is there anything you've noticed recently that might support that?"

"Like what?"

"Well, like an increased interest in things made of metal, or sudden, unexplained knowledge about it."

Trag's face brightened and he looked up from the ground at last. "You mean like how I fixed her sword and all those knives yesterday?"

Ramiq nodded. If he thought of the boy as just another potential student, it made it a little easier to pretend that everything was normal.

"Yes, Trag. Exactly like that. How did you fix them?"

The boy shrugged again, but this time held Ramiq's gaze. The man recognized the look on Trag's face – he was passionate about this topic as only a mage could be when talking about his magic.

"Well, they were just . . . wrong. Not *really* wrong, like some things are. Just a little wrong. I don't know what I did, exactly. I just held them and got them all polished and sharpened, and the whole time I kept thinking how they didn't feel just right. And somehow, when I was finished, the wrongness was gone."

"Well, Trag, that certainly sounds like the early development of a mage. If you'd like, I can use my mage sight and tell you for sure."

Ramiq had scarcely gotten the sentence out before Trag nodded enthusiastically. The man chuckled slightly and slipped easily into the sight. Sure enough, Trag glowed with the steel gray aura of a metal mage. The light was weak and irregular, meaning he had only just begun to come in to his powers and was as yet untrained; at this early stage there was no way of knowing for sure how powerful the boy may become in his element, but the fact that he had magic was undeniable.

"Looks like your guardian is absolutely right, Trag. You're a budding metal mage. Your magic will grow naturally over the next year or two until it reaches its full strength. With proper training, you can learn to use it safely."

Trag's face fell. "Two years?"

Ramiq laughed again at that and reached out to ruffle the boy's hair. "That's if it is left alone to grow at its own pace. The more you are around magic and the more you exercise what abilities you have with it, the faster it will mature. If you'd like, we can set you up with a room here at the Mages' Complex and enroll you in some of the theory and basic classes until you're ready to begin in earnest."

The boy's face lit up; all at once, with his ruffled mouse-brown hair and mud-colored eyes, he looked a great deal like Tsuga did when she was excited. Ramiq's heart constricted at the thought.

What have I just done?

"Oh, yes, sir! I would like that very much."

"I didn't know at first how I was going to get through seeing him every day, but he's a pretty good kid – and a joy to have in class."

Tsuga sighed and looked up from the saddle she was cleaning at these words from Ramiq.

"I had hoped he would stay here so that I could get to know him. I've scarcely seen the boy. Here this long-lost son drops into my life, and after a month I still know next to nothing about him."

Ramiq sighed and pushed away from the wall he'd been leaning against to place his hands on Tsuga's shoulders as she resumed the tight circular motion she'd been using to polish the saddle's cantle.

"He's just on the other side of the grounds, you know. You can see him any time you want. He talks about you all the time – always asking how you are and if you've asked after him."

Ramiq lifted his hands and walked around her until he could see Tsuga's face.

"He left everything he knew to come find you, Tsu, but he's afraid you don't want him around."

Tsuga looked up in alarm. "Why would he think that?"

"Well, let's see. You abandoned him and never made an effort to see him again. And since he's been here, you've scarcely said two words to the boy. I think I can see where he's coming from."

Tsuga's shoulders slumped and she stopped polishing again. "I don't know how to handle myself in this situation, Ramiq. What am I supposed to say to him? How do I act around him?"

"Like yourself."

Ramiq reached out and took the oil-soaked rag from her numb fingers. Tsuga looked up at him, feeling at a loss. She watched as he set the rag on an empty wooden stool and then let him pull her to her feet.

"Come on."

"Where are we going?"

"I have an idea."

Tsuga sighed and allowed herself to be pulled along as he led her out of the tack room and then outside. She blinked as her eyes adjusted to the bright sunlight of the early summer afternoon. Each week, she gave her students a day off to rest and enjoy themselves. It also gave her a chance to unwind by doing some of the more tedious tasks that often got overlooked during the busier days of the week. This was what she had been doing when Ramiq had found her, and even as she told herself that Ramiq had her best interests in mind, she regretted leaving the peace and security of the tack room.

She knew by now that it would do her no good to ask again. When Ramiq decided to surprise her, nothing she could do would persuade him to reveal anything before he was ready. As he led her to the packed dirt road that led out of the Warriors' Compound, Tsuga could feel the gentle pressure from Bane's mind that was a wordless question.

?

I don't know.

Should I come along?

It couldn't hurt. There's no telling what he's got planned. I may need the support.

Laughter echoed in her thoughts, and presently the sound of hoofbeats announced the large horse's approach. Tsuga cast a sidelong glance at Ramiq as she reached up to lay a hand on Bane's muscular shoulder and found that he was grinning at her, eyebrows raised inquisitively.

"Calling in your backup?"

Tsuga laughed and gave Bane's shoulder an affectionate slap. "I have a sneaking suspicion I might need it."

In the four weeks since Trag had begun his preliminary studies at the Mages' Complex, Ramiq had come to think of the young boy fondly. He was mostly quiet and tended to keep to himself, but when he did voice a question or opinion, it was always well considered and thought-provoking. He had proven himself to be a hard worker and a fast learner, and the prolonged exposure to magic had, as Ramiq had hoped, helped to provide the spark Trag's magical development had needed to start growing. So far, the boy's progress was in keeping with the trend that most earth-based magicks followed: slow to start, but steadily gaining momentum – much like a boulder rolling downhill.

Over the course of the month, Trag had begun to master such skills as mage sight and basic shielding. He even had a nice start on becoming attuned to his element. He had been progressing so well that it was now coming on time for the boy to find his mage stone. It would be a perfect outing for mother and son to make together.

As they drew nearer to the Mages' Complex, Ramiq was surprised to find that he was jealous of the way Tsuga kept looking to Bane for comfort and support. The bond between a human and guardian was incomproble to anything else he had ever experienced, and no other person could even hope to rival the connection between man and beast. And yet, as he watched Tsuga grip the thick muscle at the top of Bane's stocky neck in an affectionate gesture, he found his stomach burning with envy.

"So?"

The sound of her voice startled him out of his dark thoughts, and he found that he had to unclench his jaw in order to speak.

"Think of it as a family outing."

Tsuga scowled at him, but he only smiled in response as he reached out with his mage sense and found Trag. As he had anticipated, he sensed the boy's magical signature in the student's room, and so steered Tsuga towards the small window he knew was Trag's. As they came into view of the boy's room, a canine head popped into view, hanging out of the small open window.

"Ramiq!"

The coyote's greeting came out as a yelp, and a moment later Trag's head appeared beside that of his guardian. Ramiq smiled and drew Tsuga to a halt beside him.

"Hello Temalon. Trag."

"Queen's Mage Ramiq. What's going on? There's no lesson today."

Ramiq smiled and reached out to scratch the child's guardian on the top of his head in the way that Lyra always liked. The coyote's mouth gaped open and his tongue lolled out as he leaned into Ramiq's touch.

"There's no lesson, but I thought you might like to spend the day with us at the market. I do believe it's about time to find your mage stone."

"Really?"

Before Ramiq had even finished nodding, Temalon had managed to launch himself out of the window and force the two adults to back out of the way.

"You know, you could use the –"

Tsuga stopped short of saying "door" when she realized that Trag was following his guardian's example and climbing out through his window. It would have been a tight fit for a larger person, but Trag easily maneuvered his lanky frame through the small opening.

"Oh I know, but this is faster. And I don't have to worry about talking to anyone else."

Ramiq and Tsuga exchanged a glance over Trag's head as the boy straightened his brown apprentice's robes (belted at the waist with a pale gray sash to denote his specific affinity), but neither of them commented on this oddly reclusive outlook.

"Have you given any thought to what stone appeals to you?"

Trag shrugged at Ramiq's question. "I don't know what the difference is from one to the next, really."

Ramiq caught Tsuga looking down at her own stone where the malachite pendant hung around her neck, separated from her skin by the rough fabric of the shirt she wore.

"I didn't either." Her voice was distant, and from the look on her face Ramiq gathered that she was reliving a powerful memory. "But when you find it, you just know. It calls to you, somehow." She reached down and took the stone in her hand to look at it consideringly.

"How did you find yours?"

Her gaze shifted to Trag when the boy voiced his question, and the look in her eyes was distracted.

"You know it's funny, I don't remember. I must have acquired it when I was in the army in Devali – I remember not having it one day, and then I remember having it. No idea what happened in between, though."

Trag's eyes had widened as she spoke, and he looked to Ramiq with a confused expression. "Is that normal?"

Ramiq shook his head with an apologetic smile and steered the little group out of the gate towards the town market.

"No. Your mother is a bit of a unique case."

At a look from Tsuga, Ramiq moved the conversation away from her memory loss; obviously she didn't want to go into a lengthy explanation at the moment. No doubt she felt the subject came a little too close to touching on her abandonment of the boy. She dropped her stone beneath the neckline of her shirt and tucked it into place against her skin as they set off.

"Now, most mages can use various kinds of stones, but one type will prove to be easier and stronger than the rest. So today we are going to visit a merchant friend of mine who specializes in gem stones and jewelry. You can try holding a few and see what happens."

As Tsuga walked along next to the two men, she mulled over the information she had just been given. She had always just assumed that mages found their stones instinctively, without really having to think about it. It had never occurred to her that it was such a process. She couldn't even remember how she had come to possess the malachite pendant around her neck, but it just seemed so natural that she found it hard to imagine having had to pick and choose from several options. So absorbed was she by this thought that she walked along without really experiencing the journey, and was only brought back to the present when Ramiq once again brought the little group to a halt.

When she turned her attention to her surroundings, Tsuga found that they had made it all the way to the center of the marketplace and now stood amongst a moving sea of people. The crowd flowed around them, keeping a respectable distance; the Queen's Mage and his companions were afforded a certain level of wary respect. Ramiq was making introductions to a middle-aged man with a mousy appearance and beady black eyes that held both cunning and merriment as he looked the three of them over.

"Good to see you again, Ramiq."

"And you, Louis. I trust you know our new Weaponsmistress, Tsuga. And this is her son, Trag."

"Well, of course I know all about you, ma'am, though I've not had the pleasure of meeting you. Didn't know you had a kid, though. And one in mage's robes, at that! How are you, son?"

Trag looked up from the display of gems and baubles and gave a small, polite smile that did nothing to warm his expression.

"I'm well, thank you, sir."

"So what brings you by today, Ramiq?"

"It is time for this young pupil to select his mage stone."

"Ah, of course, of course. Did you have any special one in mind, my boy?"

Trag shook his head, but Louis waved away his apologetic look.

"No matter, no matter. Let me see, you're wearing the colors of an earth mage."

The merchant continued to speak as he turned and moved a couple of small display cases around.

"The stones most attuned to that famly of magics are in this case here." He set down a small box and opened the lid to reveal several stones arranged carefully on a dust-colored cushion. Trag moved forward for a better look, and Tsuga moved so that she could look over his shoulder.

Many of the stones she recognized; there were emeralds, onyx, quartz . . .. Some, like the stone that appeared to be coated in gold that had begun to tarnish, she had never seen before. One in particular she recognized all too well. Her hand flew to the pendant that hung from her own neck, and the merchant's eyes followed the movement.

"Ah, malachite. An earth mage as well, then?" Tsuga shook her head, too confused to speak. She was grateful when Ramiq answered for her.

"Actually, Tsuga is a fire mage."

"Really? A fire mage with an affinity for an earth stone? Not unheard of, but highly unusual to be certain. Not as peculiar as, say, fire and water, mind you, but strange all the same."

Tsuga looked from Louis to Ramiq, still feeling a bit perplexed by all of this. Trag, meanwhile, seemed to not even be following the conversation; he was lifting one stone after another from the padded box and turning each one over and over in his hand, looking as though he was searching for something specific.

"Why is it so strange?" she finally asked. It was Ramiq who looked up from watching the boy's antics to answer her question.

"Typically, a mage is more prone to find themselves best matched with a stone that has a natural affinity for their particular element. Thus, fire mages tend to gravitate towards stones that are known to possess properties conducive to fire magic. But malachite is remarkably strong in earth, so it is highly unusual for anything other than an earth mage to be able to work with that particular stone."

Tsuga looked down to where the thumb-sized pendant rested between her small breasts and pulled it out to take the stone in hand.

"So why do I find it so easy to use?"

Ramiq shrugged. "One of life's mysteries."

Before Tsuga could voice another question, Trag caught their attention by holding a stone up to the light.

"What is this one?"

"Oh, peacock ore. When polished, it is almost impossible to tell it is not gold. But see, here, where it has started to tarnish?"

Trag turned the stone over in his hand, and Tsuga was able to see that the stone had taken on many different colors.

"Very strong in the earth element. There is a lot of metal ore in the stone."

Trag nodded absently, and after a few more moments of silence, Ramiq reached out to lay a hand on Trag's shoulder.

"What do you feel?"

The boy turned the stone over again and shook his head. "I don't know. It just seemed right. It kind of . . . fits."

"Do any of the other stones appeal to you?"

The boy took a moment to consider the other stones before he shook his head. "No, not really. They pretty much just feel like ordinary rocks."

Coins changed hands, and Trag tucked the stone into his pocket.

"What are the benefits a mage reaps from making use of a stone?"

The small group had returned to the Mages' Complex, and now the three humans were seated in the solar of Ramiq's suite. Trag and Ramiq both sat with their canine guardians by their feet, while Tsuga had positioned herself next to a window, her back to the wall. Her guardian's head poked through the opening, and she reached up to affectionately scratch Bane behind the ears as Ramiq started his lecture. Ramiq smiled as he watched them settle in.

"It acts as a buffer when dealing with wild magic. It prevents the mage from becoming overwhelmed and allows him to work longer and with greater amounts of power."

Trag was the first to offer an answer, using the sing-song voice of a student reciting from rote, without any true experience behind the parroting of knowledge.

"Good." Ramiq nodded, and then once again turned his attention to Tsuga. "What else?"

"It's a reservoir." She took her own stone in hand, looking down at it as she spoke. "Kind of like a water skin; you can fill it up and store power for later."

"Absolutely right. What else?"

When mother and son merely exchanged uncertain glances, Ramiq held up his own stone to emphasize his words as he spoke.

"Grounding. A mage's stone helps him to focus his efforts and center his spells. It gives him an anchor to the physical world while he is working magic, and prevents the power from simply using him up."

Ramiq had elected to conduct a joint lesson with Tsuga and Trag. It seemed a logical choice – the boy had just found his stone, and he wasn't sure how much of a background Tsuga had in this particular area.

"Now, the first step to being able to properly use your mage stone is to learn how to channel power into and through it. So, let's engage our mage sight, and we can begin."

Ramiq waited until he was sure that both of his pupils had done as instructed before he continued speaking.

"Now, Tsuga, you have been doing this almost by instinct, or as though acting from previous knowledge. But it is time that you learn the proper steps to ensure that your instincts do not fail you when you need them most. And Trag . . . up to this point, you have only done minor magicks and have not yet attempted anything which requires more than your own power. Learning to use your stone will open many doors for you, and is an essential skill if you wish to continue your training.

"By now, you are both familiar with how magic permeates the world around us. Everything in and around us, living or not, is made up of different kinds of magic – from the air we breathe to the food we eat, the water we drink, even the rock that shelters us from the weather. *All* things are made up of a certain inherent power. Without this magic, the world could not exist. Therefore, when a mage seeks to make use of this power, he must be careful not to disturb the delicate balance that exists between all things. Do not ever drain more magic than any one item or area is readily able to give. Doing so will destroy whatever item is drained – human or otherwise – and it will cease to exist. Not merely die – when things die, their energy reenters the world and is recycled back into the currents of power – but be utterly and completely gone."

Ramiq could see from the look on his students' faces that his words had hit home. Satisfied that they understood the responsibility that they held, he continued.

"Magic is most effectively used to manipulate the power that is already there, rather than taking it – though in order to charge your stone, you will have to siphon some of the energies into it to store for later.

"Now, magic can be unruly. It is best to clear your mind and remain calm but firm any time you seek to use magic, especially when dealing with vast amounts of raw power which has not yet been tamed. It is vital that you move cautiously but without timidity. I will demonstrate how to open yourself to your stone and how to draw power through and into it before giving each of you a chance to try for yourselves. Keep in mind that the more you work with your stone, the more compliant it will become and the better it will respond to you.

"Begin by establishing a physical connection: hold your pendant. Next, focus all of your attention on the stone and work to sink your consciousness into it until you feel the stone accept you. Eventually this process will become second nature and happen almost instantly, without conscious thought. For now, though, it is best to practice forming this connection each time.

"Once you have joined with the stone, expand your awareness through it and reach out to the world around you. Now, today you should restrain yourselves to reaching for smaller threads of magic. The next step up would be places where the power has created a little pool of power over time; these younger sources are tamer, in a sense, than the deeper or more established channels, and therefore easier for a beginner to handle without becoming overwhelmed. Establish a connection by dipping steadily into the flow of energy. You must be confident and unhesitating, without being forceful. It will take a few moments for the connection to settle into place – your first few times are likely to take longer, until you get used to the process."

As he spoke, Ramiq demonstrated the proper way to go through the steps he described. By now, this practice came as easily to him as breathing, but he forced himself to consciously go through each step, rather than simply doing it all without thought as he normally would.

"Once the connection has stabilized, you can begin to draw the power into yourself. Don't rush, or the magic may resist you. Instead, it is best to start by drawing in a very small amount of the energy at a time until you have a better handle on things. For mages who are just starting to learn this process, it is often easier to begin with a magic source that is attuned to your particular gifts – fire in your case, Tsuga, and metal in yours, Trag. Once you grow used to the way this works, you can draw power from anything.

"It is a large undertaking for a new mage to fill his stone all at once, so today we will only be taking small amounts at a time, until you grow more comfortable. When you are ready to sever the connection, you must first focus on slowing the flow of power into your stone, and then gently stopping it all together. Only when the flow has stopped is it possible to sever the connection without suffering a magical – and possibly physical – backlash. Now, who's ready to try?"

Tsuga allowed Trag to take his turn first, and though she had no right to do so, she felt herself swell with pride as she watched him ultimately complete the process of charging his stone. The boy beamed when Ramiq praised his success, and Tsuga caught herself smiling to see him feeling so accomplished. When Ramiq turned his attention to her, Tsuga found that she had to stifle her nerves before she could begin the procedure. She leaned forward and frowned slightly in concentration as she reached through the magical conduit that her stone provided and turned her attention to the thread of magic she had selected. The stone dangled from the leather thong about her neck, swinging in the air before her. As she began, a memory surfaced.

"How do you 'enter the stone?'" Affaila sighed and shook her head. Tsuga could tell that the healer was losing patience, too.

"I don't know how else to explain it. You feel the tingly sensation, right?"

Tsuga nodded.

"That means you should be able to use this particular stone with very little effort. You just focus on the malachite, and on making it a part of yourself. You do that, then you use the stone like a channel and pull the power through it."

Tsuga was shaking her head throughout this explanation; when Affaila finished, she spoke.

"But you said earlier it was like a bucket. That you fill it, then you draw from it. How can it be like a bucket and a channel?"

Affaila frowned. "If you were to make a fireball right now, you'd be using your own energy. Without the stone, you can't safely access the power that's flowing around you in the world. The stone can act like a container to hold some of that power and store what you're not using, but you haven't filled it yet. So right now, it's like an empty bucket. Now, if you were trying to reach through it and draw power to use immediately, you'd need to use it like a channel. Does that make any more sense?"

"Tsuga? Tsuga, it's time to withdraw. You need to pull back now."

She came back to herself slowly, and it was only when the concern in Ramiq's voice registered that she realized she had been pulling power for quite some time. Her mage stone was full to bursting, and as she began to slow the flow of magic, she realized she was shaking with the effort of containing the overflow. She remembered that first attempt so many years ago overwhelming her and rendering her unconscious, but now sweat dampened her hair and ran in little rivulets down her back. She swallowed reflexively as she realized the danger she was in.

"Ramiq, what do I do?"

His voice was steadier than hers when he spoke, but she could feel the fear rolling off of him as though it were a physical force.

"You've taken in too much power; you're going to have to dispel it, or it will lash out at you."

"How do I do that?"

"Keep the connection open, and reverse the flow of power out of yourself."

Her eyes burned from the sweat and the effort of extended concentration. "I can't. It's already slipping. What's plan B?"

Filled as she was with magical energy, her senses seemed magnified a hundredfold. She saw Ramiq swallow nervously, watched the muscles in his throat work reflexively as though time had slowed. It seemed the space of her next breath stretched on endlessly until at last Ramiq offered up an answer.

"Use it. Get rid of it any way you can."

She could hear her heart beating with frenzied speed as he conveyed the information. Tsuga nodded with great effort and licked her dry lips in an attempt to steady her nerves.

"Okay. Get out."

"Excuse me?"

"I will not be responsible for hurting Trag. Get him out of here. Now."

"But you –"

"Will be alright." *If only I believed that.* "I can't keep this up much longer, Ramiq. Now get my son out of danger."

Both men stood and left the room, walking quickly to the door.

"Tsuga –" Ramiq had paused, one hand on the doorknob, to face her again.

"Get out!"

She could no longer see through the tears in her eyes, but she heard the door close; the gentle click seemed to echo loudly. It was the last thing she heard before the world erupted and everything went black.

She flinched away from a stinging sensation on her cheek and struggled to open her eyes. The feeling came again, and a small whimper escaped her despite her every effort to hold it in.

Something chaffed against her raw, tender skin, and a painful pressure surrounded her so tightly that she found it hard to breathe. She struggled weakly against it until it lessened, and at last managed to open her eyes. They watered unbearably, but she kept them open and focused on Ramiq's face, which he held mere inches from hers.

It was his arms that had provided the suffocating pressure, and as she watched a tear drip from his chin and again felt the painful sting, she realized that it had been the burn of his tears against her tender and inflamed skin which had woken her.

"Ramiq?"

Her voice broke coming from her sore throat, and she tasted blood when she licked her cracked and blistered lips. He choked off a sob and covered her mouth with his. His breath was too hot and seemed to burn her, so that she had to pull away from his touch.

"Bless the Goddess for answering my prayers. You're alive."

Tsuga tried to shake her head, but the effort was too much. She settled for a grimace.

"Is that what you call it?"

Ramiq made an odd hiccoughing sound that she took to be a laugh and pulled back slightly.

"You nearly burned yourself to a crisp. I've healed the worst of it, but that's all I can do at this point. Your new skin will be tight and painful for a while. I was afraid it wasn't going to be enough . . .. Your lungs were badly burned. It's a blessing that your organs did not explode; there is no healing that. Oh Tsu, I was so afraid I'd lost you . . .."

He gathered her into his arms again so tightly that she had to once more struggle to loosen his grip.

"Can't breathe . . .."

He released her almost instantly, though she could tell it pained him to do so. She could still barely see, but somehow she didn't need to see him to know exactly how he felt.

"Gods, Tsu, I love you. Have I told you that? I love you. I love you. Don't you ever scare me like that again! I love you."

"I love you too, Ramiq. I'm thirsty."

Again, that odd gasping sound she took as a laugh. "Of course you are. Here."

The water was too cold; it hurt going down and sent her into a coughing fit. The frigid liquid hit her skin and made her cry out in pain. He moved the cup away quickly and held her until the spasms passed and she was able to lay back, gasping for air.

"You need to rest, and you won't be able to here. I'm going to have to pick you up for a bit so I can move you."

She gritted her teeth and managed a small nod. "Go on, then. No use delaying the inevitable."

When next she came to, Tsuga found that her pain was greatly diminished in the face of a nearly unbearable itching. Ramiq had been right: her skin felt as though it was intended for a person a good deal smaller than she was – like it was not quite meant to stretch to cover a frame like hers.

Stop scratching, Tsu. It won't do any good.

Tsuga startled and looked around the room – her room, she realized – but didn't see Ramiq.

Are you in my head? Do you have any idea how disconcerting that is?

The pressure in the room increased until she felt as though she would be pressed all the way through her mattress, and then released just as suddenly, leaving Ramiq standing over her and holding a tray filled with food.

"Sorry. I was worried about you."

Tsuga gave her head a little shake and struggled to sit up. Ramiq reached out to help her, and she watched his tray warily as it hovered midair.

"Do you have to do that?"

Ramiq sighed and sat on the bed next to her so that he could help her settle the tray comfortably. "I'm a mage, Tsu. It's a part of me; I can't change that."

"I know. It's just so unnerving." She looked to the tray's contents and grimaced. "Are you trying to make me sick?"

He had loaded her plate with sticky buns, cakes, pies, jams, and breads. She could see nuts in several of the pastries. There was a small portion of meat and cheese and fruit, but everything else seemed to be loaded with sugar. Ramiq smiled and shook his head.

"The body can be helped to heal. But your magical strength has to replenish naturally. The sugar will help with that. You don't have to eat it all."

Tsuga made a face and spread some jam and butter on a piece of bread. "Good to know."

Despite her words, it was not long before she realized just how much her body seemed to crave the sweets. Her first bite seemed to trigger a reaction, and she promptly cleaned her plate. She expected Ramiq to leave her once he had removed the tray, but instead he pulled aside her blankets and lifted her from the bed.

"What are you doing?"

"Would you just trust me?"

Tsuga sighed and leaned against his chest. At least her skin no longer burned, though the tightness and itching seemed likely to drive her mad. She wanted to protest that she was capable of walking, but fatigue was already setting in, making her limbs feel leaden and causing her eyelids to droop. Besides, she wasn't really sure she *wanted* him to let her go. For someone who did almost no physical labor, Ramiq was surprisingly strong; wrapped in his arms, she felt as though nothing could harm her. It was a comforting feeling. She must have drifted off for a moment, because the next thing she knew she was in her tub, up to her ears in perfectly warm, pleasantly-scented water.

"What is this?"

Ramiq smiled at the question, and when the humor lit his green eyes Tsuga found herself smiling in response as warmth spread through her body from more than just the water.

"This, Tsuga, is a bath. It's when civilized people use water and soap to wash off the dirt and stink they accumulate during the day."

She snorted and rolled her eyes. "Very nice, Ramiq. I meant all the smelly stuff. And the fact that you carried me to my bath? No one has done that for me since I was a child." *A very small child.*

"Well, then you've been missing out. And the 'smelly stuff,' as you so articulately phrased it, is to help you heal. Medicinals to speed healing, reduce stress, and boost energy. Oils to help soften the skin. And this," he finished as he held up a stocking filled with something she couldn't identify, "is a medicated scrub, partly composed of oatmeal, which will also help. Here."

As he spoke, he dipped the misshapen bundle into the warm bath water and then proceeded to gently wash her back. When he dribbled water over her head, she bit her lip and tentatively reached a hand up to touch her scalp.

She had never considered herself particularly vain; she chopped her hair boyishly short and cut it unevenly, wore men's clothing stained and torn from a hard life, and her hands were rough and calloused from her work with the weapons that were her livelihood. But all of these were choices she had always had the opportunity to make for herself. Now, as she ran her hand over the short, prickly stubble that was a couple of days' worth of growth on her otherwise bald head, she had to fight back tears.

Though Tsuga thought she had done a fair job of containing her reaction, Ramiq stopped his gentle ministrations and reached out grasp her chin so he could turn her head and force her to meet his eyes.

"The hair will grow back, Tsu. At any rate, it's not important. It doesn't change who you are, or how I feel about you. You're just as beautiful as always."

He leaned across the tub and pulled her in for a soft kiss that made her insides melt. She swallowed hard when he pulled away and opened her eyes slowly to smile up at him.

"You're out of your mind."

Ramiq laughed at her assessment and resumed carefully washing her new and tender skin. As he had promised, she could feel her body relaxing in the warm water; though it may have only been her imagination, Tsuga could almost swear she felt the tightness in her skin ease as he bathed her. When he moved from her back and began washing her arm, she began to sense that there was something he wanted to say.

"What is it?"

She could hear him swallow nervously, and just when the silence had stretched on so long that she thought she might have to ask him again, he answered.

"There's something we need to talk about, but I'm not sure this is the right time."

Her breathing deepened as he moved down to wash her breasts and her body began to respond to his gentle touch.

"You're probably right, but who's to say the time ever *will* be right? Just go ahead."

Ramiq exhaled loudly as he proceeded to move down to wash her stomach.

"Well, I realized it when I thought I'd lost you, but . . . are you familiar with soul bonds?"

"Mhm." Tsuga was finding it hard to concentrate as his hands moved to her legs, where he proceeded to gently wash and massage her feet and calves.

"And of course you recall all of the strange dreams we've both had. And lately, it's almost as though I know what you're feeling and thinking without even having to try."

He proved his point by moving further up her leg to massage her upper thigh. Warmth spread through her at his touch, and she turned her head slightly so that she could watch him.

"I've noticed that, too." In fact, that was probably contributing to the arousal she felt. "But what are you saying?"

He stopped what he was doing and sat back on his heels to look at her. Her stomach churned with nerves despite her relaxed state, and Tsuga knew that it was his confusing mix of emotions she felt – not her own.

"We're soul bonded, Tsu."

"Alright."

"Alright?!"

"What do you want me to say, Ramiq? Should I swoon? Squeal with girlish delight? It's hard news to take, but there's nothing to be done about it."

Ramiq frowned, and she could tell the comment had put his back up. "Hard news to take?"

She sighed and pulled away from him so that she could sit up straighter. "We're two very different people, Ramiq. I can feel you. I hear your thoughts. But the way I feel about this is not a reflection on you. I take care of *myself*. Always have. I've always been able to come and go as I please, do as I wish, just live my own life. Now, suddenly, there's this other person I care about, who I want to protect and be with all the time. Who I can't stand the thought of losing or being away from. It's a hard adjustment for me. Why are you smiling at me like that?"

"Just nice to know I'm so loved."

Tsuga laughed and attempted to pull herself up so that she could step out of the tub. She sighed when she realized that her limbs wouldn't support her weight and sank back into her bathwater.

"Alright, alright. You're loved. Now, can you help me out of here? I'm getting all wrinkled from the water."

Ramiq smiled and stood up to offer her a hand. Once she was out of the tub, he wrapped her in a towel and lifted her into his arms again. When he had lain her back in her bed and helped her settle against her pillows – he must have brought some extras in from somewhere; she only had one – and under a plush comforter that she had never seen before, he moved away and made to leave the same way he had come.

"Ramiq?"

"Yes?"

"Would it kill you to walk once in a while?"

He laughed and shook his head. "No, I suppose it wouldn't. Get some rest, Tsu. I'll be back to check on you later."

"I want to see Bane."

"I know you do. Your strength will start returning after a few days, and then you can go see her yourself. But if you'd like, I'll take you out to see her tonight."

"And my trainees?"

"Bane is taking care of things."

Tsuga sighed and sank down into the softness of her new mattress. It was obvious that Ramiq had taken some liberties with her furniture, but she couldn't find it within herself to be upset about it. The luxuries were actually quite nice.

"Watch it!" Tsuga let out a frustrated sigh and glared down at the tailor. "Goddess' tits, woman, if you stick me with that blasted needle one more time –"

"Sorry, Weaponsmistress."

"Calm down, Tsu." Ramiq laughed as she twisted around on the stool to glare at him.

"Easy for you to say. You're not a human pincussion! Remind me again why we have to jump through all of these blasted hoops? I mean, fancy clothes, a big party for people I either don't know or don't like . . .. What ever happened to skipping the formalities, not needing to conform to anyone else's standards?"

She could hear the smile in his voice when he answered. "What happened is that the queen found out, and you know how Sennorra *loves* a party."

Tsuga groaned. "But it's such a hassle!"

"I know. But if it's any consolation, you look beautiful in that dress."

She grimaced. "It's so frilly and girly. Can't I at least tone this down a little?"

"I'll see what we can work out. For now, let's just let the tailor finish getting your measurements."

After a great deal more poking and pinching, the woman declared herself satisfied. Tsuga hurried out of what seemed an ocean of lace and satin and back into her trousers and loose tunic. Ramiq had insisted that she leave her personal arsenal of weapons behind for the fitting; as a result even her own clothes didn't quite feel right.

A brief walk saw them back at the Warriors' Compound, and Tsuga hurried into her room and promptly began fastening on her various blades. Ramiq followed her iniside more slowly and closed the door behind himself. He sat on the bed to remove his shoes, and when she looked up from fastening her sword belt, she realized he was watching her with a little bemused smile.

"What?"

"You."

"What about me?"

He stood and crossed to her, and Tsuga couldn't help but smile as he took her into his arms.

"Can't a guy just enjoy looking at his betrothed?" She laughed and pulled him in for a playful kiss.

"I suppose I can let it slide this once."

"Oh, well thank you. That's quite a relief."

When she started to pull away, his grip tightened on her waist and his mouth covered hers again. The kiss built in intensity, and Tsuga's lips parted in response to his probing tongue.

Heat shot through her stomach, and she didn't have to feel Ramiq rising in response to know how aroused he was. Even as she felt her own body respond to his closeness, she could feel every sensation that her touch gave him.

Over the past several months, she had grown accustomed to the way their bond worked, and now relished the way each shared sensation built them both higher.

She gasped as his hands traveled up her arms to cup her face, then lifted her chin so that he could kiss under her ear and down to the nape of her neck. Her breathing grew ragged as her desire for him built.

Ramiq reached down to unbuckle her sword belt, and as it slid off of her slender hips she slipped her hands under his billowy tunic and helped him pull it off over his head. It seemed mere moments found their clothes on the floor and the pair of them entangled on her bed.

It seemed to take hours, yet at the same time did not seem long enough. When he moved to roll off of her, Tsuga tightened her legs around him and held him in place, shaking her head.

"Not yet. Stay." He smiled and relaxed back against her. She kissed him, enjoying the intimacy of the moment, and squeezed herself tighter around him. He let out a sigh and kissed her again, more tenderly this time.

"I love you."

"I love you too, Ramiq."

"Ramiq's with a prisoner now, and has asked not to be disturbed."

Never mind that he's completely blocked me out. For all I know, the bitch has slit his throat and even now is watching him die. *Her voice was cold when she spoke, level and calm despite her tempestuous thoughts.*

"I understand, General. But I have news from our agents in Devali which I think it best he hear immediately."

Tsuga drew herself up to her full six foot height and stared down her nose at the messanger.

"It may interest you to know, young man, that my husband is not the only person capable of receiving and acting upon such news. He may command our magical forces, but it is I who lead our 'ordinary' men and women in this campaign. You will convey this news to me, and then I will determine whether or not it warrants our mutual consideration. Now, out with it."

The man had paled at her reprimand, and now he swallowed nervously and ducked his head submissively.

"As you wish, ma'am."

Tsuga moaned and shifted in her sleep, one leg thrusting out from under the blankets as she turned her head on the pillow.

Ramiq! Blast you man, hear me!

Tsuga growled in frustration and set off across the campground to the tents where the prisoners were held.

Fine bloody time for you to close yourself off!

Never mind that he always shielded himself from her when interrogating the prisoners. Even when said prisoner was a beautiful and underhanded woman that filled his dreams at night.

Don't be ridiculous. We're soulbonded. If something were going on, I'd know. This is Ramiq, after all. He's never given me a reason to distrust him. It's just standard procedure.

"General!" Tsuga's eyes narrowed in annoyance at the worried tone in the guard's voice. "The Queen's Mage is with the prisoner –"

"Yes, I am aware. But this is urgent."

"But, General, I am under orders –"

"You are under orders from my husband, soldier. And just who do you think you are, to stand between a woman and the father of her child?"

She left the man – a good soldier, but at this moment merely an obstacle to be brushed aside – stammering his protests and swept past him into the tent.

As the flap fell behind her and she crossed the threshold of the spell Ramiq had set in place to stifle sound, it was the noise of slapping skin and rustling fabric that reached her first, even before her eyes adjusted to the dimmer light and she was able to take in the impossible sight of her husband's bare ass as he thrust into the half-dressed woman below him.

She sucked in a breath; he must have sensed her watching, because he looked up and caught sight of her standing with her mouth agape. She shook her head, unable to speak. Before he could move to stop her, she turned and fled.

Tsuga woke in a cold sweat and had to swallow against a wave of nausea. After nearly two years of close proximity to Ramiq, she had learned to recognize the difference between her own night terrors and when she inadvertently suffered one of his premonition-like dreams. The feelings, the smells, the emotions had all been far too raw to be anything else.

She turned her head to look at his sleeping form and did her best to stop shaking. The wedding was less than a month away. How could she marry the man, knowing he would one day betray her so completely? Even thinking about it made her heartsick to the point that she could no longer stand to have him so close to her. She rose and dressed quickly in the dark.

Outside, she found Bane waiting. Thankfully, her guardian did not speak as Tsuga saddled her and mounted up. She hadn't brought any money, and hadn't taken the time to pack her bags. She didn't know where she was going. She knew only that she had to get away.

Ramiq woke with the distinct feeling that something was wrong. Years spent mastering his empathic magicks meant that he was able to separate his own feelings from Tsuga's, but sorting through them all was another matter. He turned in the bed to reach for her only to find her gone, the half of the mattress which should have been filled by her sleeping form long cold and empty. He let out a sigh and sat up, rubbing the sleep from his eyes.

The sunlight streaming in through Tsuga's utilitarian curtains – he really should find her something more suitable – told him the morning was already well underway, and since the jumble of emotions would not allow for any further rest, Ramiq stood and retrieved his clothes from their heap on the floor. No doubt Tsuga was already torturing her poor students; there was no use trying to talk to her now.

With a sigh, Ramiq settled his pants about his hips and gathered the rest of his things without bothering to lace them. It was a matter of little consequence for him to teleport himself into his rooms at the Mages' Complex.

I can't wait until we're married.

Tsuga would not consent to move into his rooms until they had made their union official, and he was growing tired of sleeping on her uncomfortable bed every time he wished to share a night with her. He sighed as he looked around his room and crossed to throw open the doors of his wardrobe.

What took a tiring amount of time and effort each morning was the following assessment of his available clothes and eventual selection of the day's outfit. Luckily, his immense mahogany wardrobe had withstood the inferno caused by Tsuga's flash of memory those few months ago – he kept the thing carefully bespelled to protect it against such contingencies. He simply couldn't imagine losing his carefully assembled collection of clothing.

Little else had survived the fire, of course. While all of his important magical texts remained intact, most of his furniture and decorations were gone. Even after all of this time, the room smelled faintly of smoke. He had been staying with Tsuga while he had the suite restored. It was nearly finished now; he planned to reveal their new home to her after the queen's party celebrating their bond. Once he was dressed, Ramiq pushed the little bundle of emotions that was Tsuga to the back of his mind and set off to face his day.

This is not my day.

Ramiq sighed and pinched the bridge of his nose in an effort to alleviate the pressure that had built behind his eyes. The overflow of emotions from his bonded was pressing against the inside of his skull and demanding attention he did not have the time to give it. The effort of holding the feelings at bay was wearing on him, and blocking her out of his mind completely only made matters worse. It had grown increasingly hard to concentrate on his students, and it was with a feeling of immense relief that he dismissed his class of water mages for their lunch. When he turned to follow them to the dining hall, he was waved down by a young warrior trainee who had been watching for the last few minutes.

"Adept Nevarn?"

Ramiq dropped his hands to his sides and forced a benign smile. "Yes? What can I do for you?"

The young man ducked his head, and then drew himself back to his full height as though only just remembering that he was supposed to do so.

"The others sent me to ask you . . . if you had seen the Weaponsmistress today?"

Ramiq fought back a sinking feeling. "She was already gone when I left this morning."

"Gone where?"

His smile fell, and Ramiq shook his head. "She hasn't been with   her   trainees?"

"No, sir. We haven't seen her all morning. She usually arranges for another instructor if she knows she's going to be gone, but no one came today."

"I will look into the matter. Tell the rest of the trainees to go about their normal routines until this situation has been resolved."

"Yes, sir."

Ramiq waited until the boy was out of sight before he allowed himself a colorful string of curses. He had been so busy trying to push his awareness of her to the back of his mind that he had failed to realize she had been steadily moving further away from him all morning.

What is going on?

He shook his head and pulled out the crystal that served as his mage stone. One benefit of their bond was that as long as he could feel her, Ramiq knew exactly where she was. He had only to get himself to her.

Tsuga had a lifetime on horseback to thank that she wasn't lying flat on her back. She had clung to her guardian's saddle grimly as Bane swerved violently to avoid trampling the orange-robed figure that had materialized in the road, and as Bane skidded to a stop from the easy ground-eating lope at which she had been traveling, Tsuga leaned into the turn and gave the horse her head to avoid over-balancing the mare. When the dust had settled and Bane had found her footing, Tsuga drew her sword and seized her magic to gather it about herself in defense.

The figure turned, and Tsuga hissed out a breath as she recognized Ramiq, his usually-pristine appearance now marred by the road dust kicked up by their desperate manuevering. She tightened her grip on the reins and shifted her weight in the saddle.

Their bond spoke to her, telling her of his headache and how he worried that he didn't know what was going on. She felt his frantic heartbeat and the rush of terrified adrenaline that his near-trampling had elicited as though it were her own. She didn't bother speaking. There was no need for him to ask how she felt, any more than there was for her to tell him.

"Auriga's tits!"

The exclamation was lost in the confusion as Ramiq winced in anticipation of the impact of the immense horse thundering down on him. When nothing happened, he hesitantly opened his eyes to confirm that he was still in one piece. He swallowed his heart back down – for it felt as though it had leapt into his throat and lodged there – and then turned to face his assailant.

She glared down at him from her perch atop her guardian, sword in hand and blazing to his mage sight with the power she held at the ready. He could feel her scorn for his recklessness, along with her resentment that he was here. All of this was tinged with a concern for his wellbeing that she hid well behind her icy consideration. There seemed to be nothing to say about how they felt as they watched each other, so Ramiq settled for cutting to the heart of the matter.

"Where are you going?"

She neither resheathed her sword nor released the power she held, but he knew he was in no danger. Not from her.

"I don't know. Away."

He felt his eyebrows rise at this response; she must have read something in his reaction, because her eyes narrowed to slits.

"I see. And why the sudden urge to travel?"

She shifted her weight and looked away from him as though she were uncomfortable. He couldn't sort through the mix of emotions he was getting from her, so he didn't try. Instead he concentrated on trying to get to the bottom of the situation. She didn't answer him, so he took a moment to dust himself off before he approached her.

Devilsbane eyed him warily as he drew near, and when he placed one hand on the horse's shoulder and rested the other on Tsuga's knee, he could feel them both tense.

"Tsuga? What's going on?"

She sucked in a breath and turned at last to look him in the eye.

Tsuga looked down at the man she loved and felt herself torn apart by the knowledge that he would one day betray her so completely. How could she explain to him that she was afraid of something that had not yet happened; that had, in fact, been a dream? It would sound insane.

"I had to leave."

"Why?"

"I just . . . I had to. I couldn't stay."

"Why not? Tsu, what's wrong?"

She sighed and took the plunge.

"You're going to cheat on me."

"Tsuga, you know I would never – wait. Did you say 'going to?'" She nodded. "Are you telling me you're out here running because of things that might not ever happen?"

Tsuga sighed again and shook her head. "I know it sounds crazy. But Ramiq, I know the difference between a nightmare and a premonition. I couldn't stay, knowing what's going to happen."

Ramiq blew out a frustrated breath ramid shook his head. "Will you come down here and talk to me, please?"

She hesitated; she knew full well that if she relented, he would find a way to talk her out of her decision and convince her she was being ridiculous. The truth was, she wanted him to, despite her better judgement. She shook her head and deflated slightly as she sheathed her sword and released her hold on the power she'd held at the ready.

He moved back so that she could dismount, and once her feet were firmly on the ground he led her a little ways off of the side of the road and turned to face her.

"Now, let's start at the beginning. You say you dreamt that I'm going to betray you?" She shook her head.

"It wasn't a dream. It's not the first time one of your magicks has had a weird side effect on me. I know what I saw, Ramiq, and I know it was real. Just like those other dreams we shared before we came together. It was the same."

"Even if it *was* a vision of the furture, Tsu, it was only a glimpse of what *may* be, not what *will* be. A possible future, yes, but one of many that may come to pass. Our actions are what determine our futures, not the other way around. I can't see a future where I would ever do anything so stupid as to turn my back on you, but if it should happen, I promise that I will accept whatever consequences I deserve. But for now, please, come home, and let's not worry ourselves over things that may never occur."

He reached out to her and, as she had expected, she felt her resolve to leave him crumble like packed dirt when it was thrown. She stepped into his arms and let him embrace her. Goddess help her, even knowing what she did, she couldn't make herself stop loving him.

"Do you want me to take you home?"

She shook her head and pulled back slightly to kiss him, her eyes moist with tears she refused to shed.

"No. I was thinking I'd ride a while. I need a chance to clear my head."

Ramiq nodded and tucked a few stray strands of hair behind her ear. She hadn't worn her hair so long in years, but she could tell he liked it; she had to admit, she was growing increasingly fond of it herself.

"Alright. Be careful. Don't scare me like that again. I couldn't bear the thought of losing you."

"I'm sorry I distressed you. I love you, Ramiq. But I can't stand the idea that I'm not enough for you." He shook his head and pulled her against him for another kiss.

"You are more than I ever hoped for, and far more than I deserve." She flushed, but he only smiled at her again. "Enjoy your ride, Tsu. I'll see you tonight." He kissed her again, and then he was gone.

Over the past three years, many things had changed in Tsuga's life. She no longer had to wonder about the source of her next meal or the nuisance of finding a dry place to lay her head when she was tired. She had grown to, if not like magic, at least accept that it was a part of her – indeed, it was a necessary part of life. She had gained a title and had grown to like sharpening the skills of the young warriors who came to her for instruction. She had even, against all odds, found love.

Now, she stood in the middle of a packed dirt arena and stared at her husband as though he had just grown a second head.

"You want me to do *what*?"

"Walk through a fire. It's the test given to any fire mage who seeks to reach the level of Adept. You must be able to stand in an inferno and remain whole and untouched. When you are able to do this, you will have learned all that can be taught about your magic."

"I understand that part, and I still think it will kill me, but that is not what I was referring to. Why do I have to be *naked* to do it?"

"Because clothes provide fuel, and will make it more difficult for you to successfully complete this test. Your first time doing this will be challenging enough without your having to worry about keeping your clothes from bursting into flame, too."

She sighed and shook her head as she began to remove her sword belt. "I must be out of my mind for doing this."

Ramiq smiled and took her clothing from her as she handed it to him piece by piece. At last she stood before him, her bare skin glistening with a light sweat that was more the result of her nerves than the late summer's heat. He held out his hand to her again, and she turned a full circle.

"I have nothing else for you to take."

"Your stone, Tsu."

Her hand strayed to the rich green malachite pendant that dangled between her small breasts and closed around it defensively. "Won't I need it?"

"I'm afraid not. You must learn to master your element without its aid."

She looked down at the stone in her hand and gave her head a little shake.

"I can't remember the last time I took it off."

"It will be okay."

Tsuga took a deep breath and pulled the necklace off over her head. "I know it will," she said as she dropped it into his outstretched hand with a sigh.

"Alright, then. Are you ready to begin?"

Tsuga took a deep breath to steady her nerves and nodded. "Brace yourself; I'm going to have to shield your mind from distractions – including your guardian and myself."

She nodded again, unable to bring herself to speak in the face of the task before her. She felt the shield snap into place; all at

once, she was utterly and completely alone in her own head. There was a long minute where she had to fight back her panic before reason reasserted itself. She looked first to Ramiq, and then to Devilsbane.

Though her mind told her they were gone, her eyes served to reassure her enough that she was able to keep her panic contained. When Ramiq could see that she had a handle on her emotions he nodded. He made a casual gesture, and Tsuga found herself facing a corridor of flame at least five paces high and about ten long.

"Walk steadily and with confidence. You must remain calm and clear-headed, and always remember to keep moving forward, no matter what. That's all I can tell you; the rest, you will have to figure out for yourself."

She nodded as she looked at the towering inferno before her.

Well, no use just standing here looking at it. With a deep breath, she straightened her spine and stepped forward.

The heat hit her first, the impact like a physical blow. She continued to walk forward, taking one step at a time. Sweat broke out on her skin, and she could feel the moisture being sucked from her body.

I don't know how to do this.

She forced her doubts aside and focused on pushing the heat away from herself as she stepped into the flaming corridor. The fire fought her, almost as though it had a mind of its own, so as she took a second step forward, she pushed back even harder.

"Tsu, please! I can't –"

Affaila's last words were cut off in a fit of coughing, but Tsuga scarcely noticed. Without the steadying hand of her guardian, panic had quickly taken hold in this situation, and now she wanted nothing more than death – for what use was life, if she must endure it as only half a person? The temperature rose tangibly as the flames drew nearer, burning brighter in response to her decision.

Tsuga!

The familiar mindvoice jolted her to attention, stopping her just before she could make the suicidal reach into the currents of old magic.

"Bane! Where are you? Where were you? What happened?!"

Not now. Tsu, you have to stop this! Stop the flames!

"I . . . can't!"

Indeed, it was true. The magic had the bit in its teeth, so to speak. She had no choice but to let this fire run its course now. Her best bet would be to close her link to it, so that it could no longer draw on her for fuel.

Tsu, look at Affaila! She's not a fire mage; you're killing her!

The words sent a sharp stab of pain through her, and for the first time since waking, Tsuga actually saw her sister. Her skin was blistered from the heat, and she was weeping in pain and terror. She was on her hands and knees, too weak to move, coughing violently. Bane's words echoed again.

You're killing her.

Tsuga shook her head and found that she had to blink tears away. She had entirely forgotten about that incident. She smelled burning flesh – whether a remnant of a bad memory, or her own skin roasting, she couldn't quite be sure. As she took another step, she tried – and failed – to raise a shield around herself. The flames surged around her, and she found that it was growing harder to swallow down her panic.

Tsuga felt her blood run cold as she saw a line of fire lancing towards her, ripping through the air so quickly that it pierced the men in its way before the poor souls had even seen their deaths coming. Frantic, Tsuga bent her will to the flames hurtling towards her, giving a desperate mental push so that the thing swerved aside and missed her by less than the space of her hand. She tried not to hear the scream of agony that came immediately afterwards, and instead forced herself to focus on the snake of flames that was already circling around to launch an attack from behind.

Tsuga was surprised when the hissing tendril of fire simply puffed out, but she didn't allow herself the time to wonder why its use had been abandoned. She'd seen how it had been formed, what the other mage had done to wield it, and now she planned to use it against him. Devilsbane responded to the unspoken command to stand and braced her legs to provide a statue-still base for Tsuga's efforts. The girl drew on the power stored in her stone and let it build in her until she could hold no more, feeling the intense light and heat of it pierce her soul as though burning it clean. It was such an intensely euphoric pain that she merely stayed like this for a moment, reveling in it – she'd never tested her limits before, and she knew now that she held as much as she'd ever be able to. But she had a job to do. She tossed her head to regain her focus, and gave the power she held a shape and purpose. Then, she pushed.

Tsuga shook off her feelings of shock and tried to swallow, only to find that she had no spit. She was growing too weak to fight the flames any more. Somehow, she lifted her foot and took another step.

There was a gentle rustle of cloth behind her, and she spun quickly and cursed herself for letting her guard down. It was difficult to make out more than the black outline of the intruder. He sneered, his teeth a brief flash of white in the dark, and moved forward. Tsuga stepped back instinctively, but he reached out to grasp her wrists in a painful grip.

Why am I allowing this?

It would be so easy for her to free herself, but she couldn't seem to move. She struggled fiercely with the strange lethargy that gripped her mind, trying to scream at the top of her lungs and pull away, but her body leaned against his. Her voice remained still.

"You think you're something, don't you?"

He reeked of ale; she could smell it on his person, and when he spoke the stench of it on his breath made her retch. Or at least, it should have – even as her stomach clenched, she felt her lips twist into a smile, seemingly of their own accord.

"Soooo special."

His words were slurred, and he blinked a little too carefully in the dim light of the stars overhead.

"Everybody loves little Tsuga. A real prodigy. The best they've ever seen with a weapon. But you can't fight back now, can you? Can you?!"

Though she struggled against the invisible grip on her voice and muscles – on any freedom she could hope for – her body didn't even resist as he kissed her sloppily. For the sake of her sanity, her terrified mind retreated, hiding in a small corner and trying to ignore the proceedings. Somewhere in that small, frightened self, she realized that she was being controlled by magic. It scarcely mattered; there was nothing she could do about it.

She had to fight not to fall to her knees as she stumbled from fatigue. Tears streamed from her eyes, but were just as quickly vaporized by the intense heat of the fire through which she walked. She managed a step.

"Can't you make it shut its trap?"

Tau's jaw dropped in shock, anger igniting in her eyes. "He's hungry."

Tsuga just snorted. "So am I, but I'm not screaming. Feed it."

"He needs his mother's milk. Your milk. You feed him."

With that, she deposited the still-screaming baby into Tsuga's unwilling arms and left the room. Tsuga stared at the demon seed, lost as to what to do.

Finally, it occurred to her that there was nothing she could do to make the child stop its wailing. A mother should produce milk when she heard her babe's cries, but Tsuga's body remained unresponsive no matter how loudly the thing shrieked. After going so long without nursing the child while she was recovering, her body had assumed the boy to be dead. All motherly functions had, therefore, simply stopped.

Tsuga set the infant down on the bed and stared at him, head pounding painfully. She waited a while for Tau to return and take it away, but when the widow didn't come Tsuga at last gave up and lay back down, praying to the Goddess to grant her oblivion.

Her lungs burned. She felt as though she must burst from the inside. She no longer felt the will to fight her death. She stepped forward again.

The stench of the man threatened to overwhelm her, but she let him press his lips against hers and force his tongue into her mouth. She tolerated his clumsy, drunken ministrations as best she could and pretended to pleasure as he ripped his way into her. It scarcely mattered any more. She had done this so many times now that it didn't hurt now, and she could no longer make herself feel anything other than a dull resignation for what she was suffering. She had to make a living, after all. Better this than death. Barely.

Now that she was no longer fighting the fire, she found the pain easier to accept. Her next step was less of a struggle.

The air was dark and thick, making it hard for her to breathe. She started to pull herself to a sitting position, but found that she had no strength in her arms. She lay prone, and as she tried to remember what had happened, she took in the smell of smoke and the haziness of the air floating above her. She could recall getting out of her room, and a bit of walking down the hallway. After that, though, there was . . . nothing.

Her head throbbed as though she'd been kicked in it, and her mouth was as dry as could be. A light breeze lifted a few stray hairs, and she shivered as it cooled her feverish skin. It was only then that she realized she lay naked and exposed here in the midst of what was once her prison.

She grasped instinctively at her side, seeking the sword she'd taken, but found nothing. It was as though the inferno – for surely with her loss of control that was the only explanation for the state in which she now found herself – had burned away every vestige of her old self, leaving her as naked and vulnerable as the day she was torn screaming from her mother's womb.

The air stirred again, and once more she shivered at the chill it carried.

I can't stay like this, *she realized. Devali was still deep in the clutches of a harsh winter, and she would never survive lying exposed like this. She had to find some sort of shelter, and soon. Even if someone had come looking for her after she'd been kidnapped, she'd been gone too long; with the season being what it was, even she would have given herself up for dead by now.*

Unable to stand, Tsuga managed to pull herself up to her hands and knees, where she had to rest a moment while her stomach returned to its rightful place and the ground went back beneath her where it was supposed to be. Thus mobilized, she began to make her slow, painful way through the ashes and smoldering remains of the building and out into an unfamiliar and unforgiving wilderness.

The heat was becoming more bearable. As she learned not to fight the raw elemental force that enveloped her, she found it easier to accept the flames into herself. When she stopped struggling, she felt a change begin to take place. She took another step forward.

"How do you heal a memory?"

The brunette healer cocked her head to the side and smiled, her silver earrings making a soft clinking sound with the movement.

"I'm not sure. I found the book that talks about it, but all it says is 'an object close to you can hold your darkest secrets.' I'm not really sure what that means . . .."

"An object close to you, huh?" Tsuga reached up to the leather thong she wore around her neck and pulled out her small malachite pendant. Next to her weaponry, it was the thing that meant the most to her. Affaila had helped her pick it out, and many of the memories of her sister were attached to the item.

"Would this work?"

Breathing came easier. Her thoughts grew clearer. She stepped again.

"Fire is a combatitive element. Fight, and it fights you back. But it is not inherently evil or destructive. In the wrong hands, yes, it is deadly. But with a clear head and a firm hand, it can be a healing force. A farmer burns his fields in the winter to encourage spring growth. A healer may cauterize a wound or

*break a fever with heat. Cooking food, warming homes . . . fire
is as nurturing in the right hands as it is deadly in the wrong
ones."*

Tsuga could almost hear her sister's voice, as though Affaila
stood next to her now as she had then, trying to help her come to
terms with the cursed power she carried within her. She took
another step and found that the flames licking over her skin no
longer had any effect.

Fight, and it fights back.

She took a step. Fire was much like herself in that way. She
took another step and looked about herself as she realized that the
heat had lessened. She had come clear of the inferno in one piece.
Memories that she had thought long forgotten continued to wash
over her, but her sense of release was so great that she scarcely
registered them. She let out a sigh of relief as she saw the hall of
flame vanish behind her, and as though its disappearance had
given her permission to do so, she collapsed.

Ramiq remembered his own test all too well. He knew what
her body would be feeling, how her mind would try to fight
against certain death. From her perspective, the short walk would
seem to take hours, though it lasted at most a few minutes. As he
watched her vanish into the flames, he caught himself holding his
breath and had to let it out with a *woosh*.

He glanced down at the malachite pendant on top of her neatly
folded pile of clothes. He'd never really taken the time to
examine it before this. There was something slightly off about it,
but he couldn't quite put his finger on what it might be.

"Is she okay? Shouldn't she be out by now?"

Ramiq peered into the flames. "She's still standing. It's early
yet; have a little faith."

He had to admit he was worried, too, though his concern was
rooted more in the knowledge of the fear she still harbored. If
she let it get the best of her, this test could prove to be
troublesome. He was on the verge of calling it off when he saw
her emerge unscathed from the flames. He dropped the stack of
her things and hurried across the arena as he snuffed the fire with
a gesture.

Before he could reach her, she had collapsed to the ground.
Ramiq dropped to his knees beside her crumpled form and
opened the bond between them so that he could make sure she
was okay.

It no longer seemed strange to her when she woke in Ramiq's
arms with the feeling of cool air against her bare skin. What
struck her this time was the discomfort caused by the dirt under

her bare backside and the glare of the setting sun in her eyes. Ramiq was smiling down at her.

"What happened?"

"Well, you stepped out of the blaze, and then you collapsed. Not surprising; most people do. Let's try sitting up now. Nice and easy. There you go."

"Ramiq, I remembered something while I was in there. Well, a lot of things, actually."

"Of course you did. Lean on me; we're going to stand." She followed his instructions without thinking, not really noticing that he didn't seem to be listening. She needed to get this out.

"I remember everything. Why I've been so afraid of my magic. Why I shouldn't be. And, most importantly, I remember forgetting it all. Or...."

He was looking at her as though she were talking nonsense. "How can you remember forgetting?"

"Don't look at me like that; like you think I hit my head or something. I didn't just forget, Ramiq; a mind healer *helped* me forget. With that."

She gestured vaguely in the direction of her discarded things, still unable to believe that she had been so weak that she had been unable to deal with her past. What unnerved her more was the way that all of those insecurities had come back to her right along with all of those memories.

"With what? Your clothes?"

Her eyes narrowed, and Ramiq must have sensed that he had crossed a line, because he sobered.

"My mage stone. I don't know how she did it, but as long as I'm touching that, certain parts of my past are as though they never happened."

Ramiq turned his head to look at the innocuous little stone, lying where he'd left it tumbled amongst the discarded pile of her other things. She almost didn't catch his words when he spoke.

"So that's why . . .."

"That's why what?"

"Never mind. Walk with me, now. We're going to get you dressed. And don't worry about your stone. I'll make sure it is set right."

She nodded and let him help her into her shirt and pants. She had expected to be singed – burned to a crisp, really – but she felt no ill effects from her endeavor aside from her overwhelming fatigue. Bane came up beside them, and Tsuga shifted to lean on the mare for support while Ramiq gathered the rest of her things. She was shaking – partly from fatigue, to be sure, but more from shock than anything else. Long-buried memories continued to wash over her, hitting her like waves crashing against a rocky shoreline.

Ramiq was still speaking, but she could no longer focus enough to make out his words. Her breathing grew shallow, and had it not been for the stoic presence of her guardian, she would have collapsed to the ground again. The next thing she knew, Ramiq had dropped the armload of her weapons and gathered her into his arms and swept her off her feet. Her head spun from the sudden change in altitude.

"But my things –"

"Will be retrieved. You need rest. I'm taking you home."

Epilogue

Tsuga felt like a half-drowned cat: dripping wet, exhausted, and very much inclined to claw something. She had spent her day knee-deep in mud. A soldier had to be able to fight in all kinds of weather conditions, and though it was miserable, her students had handled themselves well today – as evidenced by their high spirits when she had dismissed them. She had only a short time to clean herself up before the festivities tonight. The young queen had seen to it that half of Sennor had been invited to the celebration, and that included the students from both the Mages' Complex and the Warriors' Compound.

She slammed the door to her room closed behind her and stood glaring about the space. Ramiq was nowhere to be found, so she began removing her small arsenal of weapons and peeling off her clothes. She was tempted to just burn them rather than try to clean the red clay mud out of the fabric, but instead she merely threw the offending garments into the hamper with unnecessary force, where they landed amidst the rest of her dirty laundry. She'd take care of it later.

When she walked around the screen that cordoned off her bathing area from the rest of the room, she found the tub already filled with clean – albeit tepid – water. At least there was that much she didn't have to do. The temperature was a simple enough fix thanks to her magic, and in moments she was sunk in steaming water up to her ears. She allowed herself a few moments to luxuriate in the warmth, but in the end practicality won out and she set to scrubbing off the muck that coated her skin and streaked her hair with a vehemence that many would have found startling.

Ramiq had made several changes to her room since she had destroyed his and he had begun sharing her living quarters. Tsuga now did something she had never in her life expected to do: she stood staring at herself in the full-length mirror he had purchased and placed in one corner. Thankfully, they had managed to talk the tailor down a bit from the woman's original version of the dress, and what Tsuga now wore was . . . well, tolerable.

She turned as she heard the door open, expecting to see a bedraggled Ramiq. Instead, she found that he was already fully dressed, not a hair out of place. She wasn't sure why she had thought he would be anything less than perfectly put together; perhaps she had simply hoped he would be half as frazzled as she was. He had, after all, been out there in the miserable weather with her today. The training session had been only one of many that the mage and warrior trainees shared; they would likely be fighting together one day, and so it only made sense that they train together as well.

"Oh Tsu, you look beautiful."

She had no reason to question him; the huskiness in his voice lent as much weight to his words as the rush of emotions that flowed to her through their bond.

"It's not as bad as I'd expected." She actually managed a small smile before she remembered her latest irritant. "But I have no idea what to do with my hair. It's never been this long before. I've always just chopped it off so I didn't have to deal with it."

Ramiq couldn't take his eyes off of her. The dress was form-fitting and accented her slender frame perfectly. It was composed mostly of a rich red-colored fabric, interposed here and there with flame-shaped slashes of the same shimmery golden, barely-opaque mesh material that made up her entire right sleeve.

The combination brought to mind the movement of dancing flames, especially when she turned to face him and the simple straight A-line of her skirt separated to reveal a length of tan, well-muscled calf through the slit that divided her skirt on the left up to the middle of her thigh.

She began fretting over her hair, and Ramiq had to smile. For someone who made it such a point to prove that she didn't care how she looked, she was thoroughly distraught now over her appearance.

As far as hair, she could shave it all off or wear it damp and stringy, as it was now, and he'd still find her more beautiful than anything he'd ever seen. He walked over to her and pulled her along with him.

"Come here. Sit down."

She sighed and let him lead her to the bed and pull her down to sit before him. Ramiq smiled to himself.

"Close your eyes."

"What? Why?"

"Would you trust me? Just do it."

She shook her head, but did as she was told.

Tsuga squirmed; she had been sitting this way for what seemed hours, while Ramiq meticulously fidgeted with her hair. Her skin tingled, though whether that was from his touch or a reaction to the magic that always surrounded him, she couldn't be sure.

"Hold still."

"How much longer?"

Ramiq didn't answer, but after a few more moments she felt him step back.

"There; all finished."

"What took so long?"

"I wanted to make sure I did a good job."

"And?"

"Come see for yourself."

He helped her stand, but stood back as she crossed to the mirror. She was almost afraid to look; she wasn't used to wearing such fitted clothing, and she was having a hard time adjusting to the sight of herself in such a clinging gown. When she finally did look up to take in her reflection, the sight took her breath away.

"Is that really me?"

Ramiq came up to stand behind her, and she could see his reflection smiling in the glass.

"Of course."

"I look . . .."

"Beautiful. As always."

"No; I look like a woman!"

Ramiq laughed aloud and placed his hands on her hips, just under the strip of opaque fabric that ran from just below her left breast to just above her right hip bone.

"Is that such a bad thing?"

"Well, no; I guess not. It's just so . . . different."

She turned her head to look at what he'd done with her hair. He had twisted it somehow to get it up out of her face, and it was studded with dozens of tiny gems that caught the light and made her seem to glow. She lifted a hand to touch the intricate yet deceptively simple-looking arrangement, and only then realized that much smaller versions of the same stone studded the thin orange-gold fabric that decorated her dress.

"These are —"

"Sunstones. I thought they would be a nice touch."

"They're beautiful," she breathed. Each one looked as though it held a tiny fire within it, which blazed more brightly when the gem caught the light.

"Here; I have one more little gift for you."

"Ramiq, you don't need to —"

"Hush. Let me dote on the woman I love."

She smiled over her shoulder at him as he reached into his pocket and pulled out a delicate-looking necklace of the same orange-red stones and settled it around her neck. As she stood there, staring at their reflection in the mirror, she felt herself tear up.

"Tsu? What's wrong?"

"Absolutely nothing. I just can't believe, after everything I've done and all that has happened, that I have been given so much happiness."

She turned in his arms and smiled up at him. "I love you."

"I love you, too."

She kissed him, and then stayed in his arms a moment longer to lean against him. "Do we have to go?"

She felt his chest shake with silent laughter, and she found herself smiling ruefully in response.

"Yes. It's *our* party. We kind of have to put in an appearance."

"I suppose you're right. We had better be on our way, then."

Tsuga stood a little apart from the rest of the crowd, watching the merriment progress before her. So far, she had managed to survive the banquet and the pretentious ceremony in which the queen declared the two of them forever joined in the eyes of the Goddess. Now, she had been granted a few blessed moments of solitude while Ramiq schmoozed with Sennor's nobility. She had never been very good at making idle conversation with people she didn't like, so she had politely excused herself from their company and now stood off in the shadows, reveling in her temporary anonymity.

This reprieve was short-lived, however; just when she was beginning to contemplate sneaking outside, she spotted Ramiq approaching. She smiled as he neared and stepped out from the shadows to meet him.

"That didn't take long."

"They started bickering about taxes and borders, so I excused myself to dance with my beautiful bride."

Tsuga flushed at the compliment but rolled her eyes and pushed him away playfully as though she hadn't heard it.

"You know I don't dance."

"Ah, but *I* do, remember? All you have to do is follow."

She sighed and allowed him to pull her out to the dance floor, where other couples had paired off and were waiting for the players on the stage to strike their first notes. They didn't have to wait long; the harp struck up a chord first, and then the lyre and other instruments joined in one by one until the entire ballroom seemed to fill with the strains of a simple three beat tempo. Ramiq took her into his arms with a smile.

"Now, just relax and let me guide you."

As they stepped out to the beat of the music, Tsuga mused that the casually graceful flow of their movements came much more naturally now than it had the last time they'd danced together.

Tonight was by far one of the best nights of his life. He had a beautiful woman in his arms, he was surrounded by friends, and his students had only caused one minor magical mishap so far. He had never seen Tsuga like this before; she usually gave him no small amount of grief about having to dress up and parade around for the stuck-up members of court, but not tonight. Though he knew she was uncomfortable without her sword on her hip, for once she hadn't spent the whole night complaining about how disomfitted she was or rolling her eyes every time he complimented her. She even proved to be a graceful dancer – no doubt years of honing her coordination and training her body to move with confidence and fluidity contributed a great deal to that.

He couldn't help but think, as he looked down at her, that she seemed happier and more alive tonight than he'd ever seen her. He smiled again and shook his head in wonder. She was almost glowing . . .. Something about that thought seemed to trigger an alarm in his head, and without really thinking he slipped into his mage sight and checked her over with his healer's senses. He knew her body almost better than he knew his own, and there was no question that something had changed.

"Tsu?"

"Hmm?"

"When were you going to tell me you're pregnant?"

Tsuga laughed and shook her head.

"What are you talking about? I'm not."

"Yes, you are."

She stumbled, and when she recovered, she stopped and pulled away from him slightly. He was only a beat behind her.

"No, I'm not. I can't be."

"Tsu, I'm a healer. I can *see* it."

Her heart stuck in her chest and she shook her head again, more emphatically this time. "But that's not possible. I don't bleed any more. I thought –"

She looked down at herself. Her stomach was flat and tight, just as it always was. She didn't *feel* any different, and certainly nothing about her appearance had changed.

"I'm pregnant?"

She hadn't thought it possible, after so long taking the drugs to prevent a pregnancy and the years of depredation she had put her body through.

Ramiq smiled and placed his hand on her midsection, as though he could feel the budding life there.

"You are."

She smiled and moved back into his arms when he opened them for her. "We're going to have a baby?"

Maybe – just maybe – this really was a perfect night.

Tsuga turned in her sleep and let out a sigh as she settled against her new husband's chest. Behind closed lids, her eyes moved as though taking in a scene.

The woman who stood before her could no longer be called a child, though Tsuga still remembered the small girl who had laughed and chased her about the yard. Always so bright and cheerful, her daughter had been the light of her life for the past sixteen years. But now the tall, slender creature stood covered in gore, her face streaked with tears. Her green eyes – like her father's – shone with tears and held a deep, haunted look as she met her mother's gaze.

"He's dead."

Tsuga nodded and looked down at the soldier – some anonymous face, another unnamed casualty of a senseless war. Though they had tried from the beginning to shelter her from the brutal truth of such a life, Tau had always been surrounded by death and misery. Tsuga still had not forgiven herself for putting her child through such a life. Now, seeing the pain that this death brought her daughter, Tsuga fought back a sigh.

"He is, though not for lack of effort on your part. Men die, Tau. Soldiers and mages alike. We're all flesh and blood."

Tau nodded sadly and pushed back from the cot occupied by the man's body. The battle had ended hours ago, but as one of only a handful of mages with any healing ability, Tau had been working over the wounded since the first arrow had landed. Though not possessed of any magical ability to mend flesh, Tsuga did know how to bind and doctor wounds, and so had been helping where she could.

She's only sixteen.

It pained her to see her daughter subjected to the sight of so much pain and death. With a look around, Tsuga determined that the remaining patients were not in dire need of help, and so could be tended by the remaining healers. She walked around the bloodied cot and took her daughter under her arm so that she could guide her away from the carnage.

"You need a break, Tau. You're about to drop where you stand. Why don't you go find Lilae and get some sleep?" Her daughter started to protest, but Tsuga shushed her. "Don't argue with your mother. Go. Rest. You've done more than your share. Killing yourself will help no one."

The girl slumped under this admonition and nodded silently as Tsuga steered her through the tidy rows of tents and around the campfires. Their camp was quiet, tonight. Too many had been lost in today's battle for the victory to be treated as such. Just another bloody encounter to add to the long list of incidents in this horrible war. They were so close to peace, but the rebels who sought to prolong the war held on bitterly to the only lifestyle they had ever known. The most recent attack had taken quite a toll on the numbers in the small contingent of loyalists.

In the center of their encampent sat a cluster of tents belonging to the various higher-ups in the army. Tsuga and Ramiq shared one. Tau had a smaller tent near theirs. At their approach, a head the size of a horse peeked out from behind it. After all these years, Tsuga still had to fight not to flinch away from the *enormous beast. Tau, however, had no such qualms; she never had. She broke from Tsuga's embrace and ran forward to the dragon to throw her arms around Lilae's muzzle – or as far around as they would reach, which was somewhat less than half. Satisfied that Tau was safe in the care of her guardian, Tsuga smiled tiredly to herself and turned towards her own tent. She could do with some rest, herself.*

End of Volume One

About the Author

Christina's love for story telling began at a young age, and has long been an integral part of her life. She currently lives in Cuero, Texas with her boyfriend Travis and their two dogs, Tau (pictured) and P.I.T.A. She enjoys working with her hands and spends a good deal of her time building and restoring wooden furniture. It has been observed that Tsuga's tendency to hoard weapons might have its roots in the author's penchant to do the same; her collection of decorative, historical, and functional weaponry is quite varied.

Family has always been one of the most important things in Christina's life, and she enjoys spending time with her numerous relatives. She also enjoys volunteering with the local Barlow Horse Kamp during the summers and horseback riding when she gets the chance.